Enlightenment

Also by Sarah Perry

The Essex Serpent
Melmoth
After Me Comes the Flood

Enlightenment

A Novel

SARAH PERRY

MARINER BOOKS

New York Boston

HarperCollins books may be purchased for educational, business, or sales promotional use. For information, please email the Special Markets Department at SPsales@harpercollins.com.

Originally published in the United Kingdom in 2024 by Jonathan Cape, an imprint of Penguin Random House UK.

FIRST U.S. EDITION

Designed by Jackie Alvarado

Illustrations by Neil Gower

Library of Congress Cataloging-in-Publication Data has been applied for.

ISBN 978-0-06-335261-2 (hardcover)
ISBN 978-0-06-338825-3 (international edition)

24 25 26 27 28 LBC 5 4 3 2 1

In memory of
David George Perry
A good Baptist
And a very good friend

There are two hungers, hunger for bread
And hunger of the uncouth soul
For the light's grace. I have seen both . . .

—R. S. Thomas, "The Dark Well"

PART ONE

1997

The Law of Ellipses

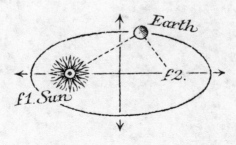

Fig. 1

Monday: late winter, bad weather. The River Alder, fattened by continuous rain, went in a spate through Aldleigh and beyond it, taking carp and pike and pages torn from pornographic magazines past war memorials and pubs and new industrial parks, down to the mouth of the Blackwater and on in due course to the sea. Toppled shopping trolleys glistened on the riverbank; so also did unwanted wedding rings, and beer cans, and coins struck by empires in the years of their decline. Herons paced like white-coated orderlies in the muddy reeds; and at half past four a fisherman caught a cup untouched since the ink was wet on *The Battle of Maldon*, spat twice, and threw it back.

Late winter, bad weather, the town oppressed by clouds as low as a coffin lid. A place spoken of in passing, if at all: neither Boudicca nor Wat Tyler had given it a second glance when they took their vengeances to London; and war had reached it only as an afterthought, when a solitary Junkers discharged the last of its ordnance and extinguished four souls without notice.

Thomas Hart was at his desk in the offices of the *Essex Chronicle*, surveying the town through a dissolving window. At that hour and from that vantage, lights appeared as fires set by travelers that crossed a soaking fen: strip lights in the shoe shops and newsagent's not yet shuttered for the night, and in the cinema and bowling alley opening for business two miles out of town; lamplight in the bar of the Jackdaw and Crow, and streetlights coming on down London Road.

A man of fifty, Thomas Hart, and a man of Essex, for his sins: tall, and retaining as much hair as he had at forty, which is to say more above the collar than the brow. Dressed, as has always been his habit, in clothes chosen to be admired by the observant—a jacket, single-breasted, in Harris Tweed; a white shirt cuffed with silver links; a tie of oatmeal knitted silk. A face he does not deceive himself is handsome, but understands to be memorable: the nose not symmetrical, but of a pleasing emphatic size; the eyes large, direct, and approaching green. An air altogether of occupying a time not his own—might he be more at ease in an Edwardian dining room, say, or on a pitching clipper's deck? Very likely.

Thomas was surveying an object on his desk. Two leather disks about the diameter of his own hand were fastened with a tarnished pin; the lower disk was painted blue and mottled with markings he couldn't have made out even if he'd been inclined to try. The blue showed through a large hole cut in the upper part, and gilded letters at the rim showed the months of the year, and the days of the month, and the hours of the day. Thomas touched it as if it carried a contagious disease. "What," he said, "do you imagine I should do with this?"

A younger man was sitting at the edge of the desk, swinging his foot. With the downcast gaze of the guilty he turned the upper disk with his finger. The hole moved. The blue persisted. "It belonged to my father," he said. "I thought you might make something of it." Nick Carleton, editor of the *Chronicle* and grieving son, looked with unconcealed amusement around the small office, which—despite the plastic venetian blinds and the computer's hard drive humming as it labored at its work; despite the twentieth century wearing itself out on the pavements three floors down—gave the impression that at any moment a gramophone might strike up a Schubert *lieder*.

"I was sorry," said Thomas gravely, "to hear of your loss. The death of a father," he said, frowning at the window, "is at the same time both quite proper in the order of things, and incomprehensibly stupid."

"I never saw him use it," said Carleton, containing tears, "and I don't know how it works. It is a planisphere. A map of the stars."

"I see. And what do you imagine I should do with it?"

The evening was coming doggedly in. Wind seeped over the concrete windowsill, and a bewildered pigeon struck the glass and slipped from view.

"You're our longest-serving contributor," said Carleton, flinching at the bang. "Our most admired. Indeed I should say our most popular." I'm beginning to speak like him, he thought: Thomas Hart is catching, that's the trouble. "I've often heard it said that it's a consolation—that's the general feeling, as I said to the board—to wake on Thursday morning, and find your thoughts on Essex ghosts and literature and so on, before turning to the matters of the day."

"Literature," said Thomas mildly to the planisphere, "is the matter of the day."

"Your work has an old-fashioned feel," Carleton pressed on. "You'll allow me that. I argue that's your charm. Other papers might seek out some young person to be the voice of their generation, but here at the *Essex Chronicle* we pride ourselves on our loyalty."

"I could hardly have asked to be the voice of a generation," said Thomas, "since there is only one of me."

Briefly Carleton considered the other man, of whom he'd made such a study he might have been appointed professor of

Thomas Studies at the University of Essex. He knew, for example, that Thomas was a confirmed bachelor, as they say, never seen in the company of a beautiful young person or a stately older one; that he had about him the melancholy religious air of a defrocked priest, and was known to attend a peculiar little chapel on the outskirts of town. He had a courtly manner considered an affectation by those who didn't like him, and irresistible by those who did; and if it couldn't be fairly said that he was strange, there was certainly the impression of his being the lone representative of his species. Of Thomas Hart's family, companions, politics, tastes in music, and weekend pursuits, Carleton knew nothing, wondered often, and would never ask. That Thomas had worked for the *Chronicle* since 1976 was easily established, as was the fact that he'd published three brief novels since that date. Out of a sense of delicacy Carleton never mentioned that he owned all three of these, and found them elegant and elliptical, couched in prose that had the cadence of the King James Bible, and concerned with deep feeling suppressed until the final pages (when some confusing event ensued, generally in bad weather). Were Carleton his literary agent, he might have pleaded with the other man to allow himself, in fiction at any rate, to say what he really felt, and not veil it all in atmosphere and metaphor; but he confined himself to glancing sometimes at the cheap green notebooks that attended Thomas like spoor and were now stacked three deep on his desk (*Monday*, he read surreptitiously, *late winter. Bad weather*—). It hadn't occurred to him that Thomas wouldn't know a planisphere when he had his hands on it, or that a tentative suggestion he look to the stars would be so unwelcome. Blinking, he recalibrated his idea of Thomas Hart, and became persuasive: "Loyalty," he said, "is a key concern of ours. But it is increasingly felt that you might benefit from new material, and it struck me you might like to write about astronomy. You see"—he reached for the planisphere, and moved it—"this is today's date, and so you'll find Orion in the south."

"Astronomy," said Thomas, with the look of a man tasting a bitter substance. He turned the disk. He extinguished the stars.

"In fact," said the editor, "it struck me that you could write about this new comet." He made a withdrawal from the store of knowledge inherited from his father: "It's a Great Comet, you know, with naked-eye visibility. People really go in for that sort of thing. Bird's Custard once put a comet on their adverts. Perhaps it's a bad omen, and there'll be a disaster, then we'll have something for our front page" (he brightened here at visions of catastrophic fires).

"What comet?"

"Thomas! Do you never look up? They call it Hale-Bopp. It's been on the news."

"Hale-Bopp," said Thomas. "I see. I never watch the news." He raised the planisphere toward the editor. "I have no interest in astronomy. This comet could crash through the window and land on the carpet and I'd have nothing to say about it."

Carleton refused the planisphere with a gesture. "Keep it. Give it a try. We have to think of something, Thomas: circulation is down. Do you want to write about this sheep they've cloned in Scotland, or about the general election? Celebrity gossip, perhaps, or the sexual intrigues of the Tory cabinet?" He received a look of admonition, as if he'd stained one of those pristine white cuffs.

"I am too old," said Thomas, "for new tricks."

"These days," said Carleton, hardening his heart, and further depleting the store of his inheritance, "a good pair of binoculars offers more or less the same magnitude as Galileo's telescope. Five hundred words, please. Why don't you start with the moon?"

"Is there a moon tonight?"

"How should I know?" Carleton was at the door; Carleton was almost free. "I've always found it unreliable. Five hundred words, please, and six if the night is clear."

"These days," said Thomas, "the nights are never clear." With bad grace he lifted the planisphere to the weak light seeping in and turned the upper part. The perforation slid over the painted leather, and half-familiar names appeared on the ground of blue: Aldebaran. Bellatrix. Hyades. Well, then. Five hundred words, and six if the night was clear; and meanwhile he was behind on his correspondence. A solitary letter in the steel tray, the flap lifting and the stamp not straight, the letter signed boldly in blue ink:

James Bower
Essex Museum Services
17 February 1997

Dear Mr. Hart,

I think I have some information that might interest you.

As I'm sure you know, we're doing renovation work at Lowlands House, and it has turned up some interesting documents. We think they may relate to a woman who lived at Lowlands in the nineteenth century, who disappeared and was never discovered. I've always enjoyed your column and remember especially your account of going in search of the Lowlands ghost—and it occurred to me the legend might even be connected with this disappearance! Could you be persuaded to come and visit me at the museum?

We are open daily from 10 a.m. to 4 p.m. I'm always at
my desk.

Yours sincerely,

James Bower

Thomas put down the letter. Was it possible the strip light
briefly dimmed, and summoned out of shadow the figure of a
vanished woman, now returned? It was not. Thomas smiled and
turned again toward the window. The stunned pigeon had left
its greasy imprint on the glass, and it rose like the Holy Ghost
behind the venetian blinds.

Late winter, thought Thomas, bad weather—he buttoned
himself into his coat; he left the offices of the *Chronicle*—that
was as good a beginning as any. The planisphere was in his
pocket, and pricked him with its bent brass pin. The adamant
cloud cover was burnished by streetlight, and somewhere behind it, he thought, Carleton's comet was concealed like a letter in an envelope, and no doubt bringing bad news.

   Gone five in the evening, and traffic pursuing itself out of
town; Aldleigh coming into view, and Thomas passing women
laboring with plastic shopping bags, and schoolboys who
bickered and swore. The rain eased into particles of mist
that swarmed about the streetlights like flies, and Thomas con-
versed with himself. What could account for his indifference
to the stars? The troubling thought occurred that perhaps he
was afraid the annihilating vastness of a comet's orbit would
end his tentative faith. Then again (Thomas was consoling
himself), Virginia Woolf had written about a solar eclipse,
and there was Gerard Manley Hopkins's slip of comet to consider: there were precedents. "Bellatrix," he said, feeling the

discomfort of the planisphere, but grudgingly delighted by the syllables. "Hyades." He stood now at a crossroads, where traffic went in haste to London or down to Aldleigh's shops and office blocks. Slipping between cars, Thomas crossed to the opposite pavement and stood there for a time. At his left, there was the broad road to town; at his right, the road that narrowed to a shallow bridge over the River Alder. Thomas looked neither left nor right, but rather surveyed a chapel behind iron railings on London Road. It was flanked by a mossy wall, and by a derelict patch of ground known to him as Potter's Field; its iron gate was fastened with a chain. Mutely the chapel looked back at him across a car park glossed by rain. Its door was closed, and newly painted green; beside the door a green bay tree flourished like the wicked in the Thirty-seventh Psalm. An east wind blowing up the Alder moved the cold illuminated air, and the bay tree danced in its small black bed. The chapel did not dance. Its bricks were pale, its proportions austere: it was a sealed container for God. No passerby would ever take it for a place of worship, and Aldleigh's children believed it to be a crematorium where old men were converted into ashes and smoke. No sacred carvings flanked the door, and no bells rang; its pitched slate roof shone blue when wet. Its seven tapered windows had the look of eyes half-closed against the sun, and on brighter days, light picked out a single disk of colored glass set in each window's apex. This was Bethesda Chapel, as fixed in time's flow as a boulder in a river: Aldleigh ran past it, and around it, and could never change it. Above the door a narrow plaque read 1888, and beyond the bristled threshold mat, 1888 persisted. All the dreadful business of the modern world—its exchange rates, tournaments, profanities, publications, elections, music, and changes of administration—washed up against the green door and fell back, dammed.

"Bethesda," said Thomas, leaning on the gate, speaking to himself and inclined to smile; then the iron chain, which ought to have been locked, unlatched and fell on his foot. Thomas, stifling surprise, peered in confusion through the haze. "What was that?" he said. "Did you see that?" Nobody heard, or could answer. He leaned farther in and doubted himself; it was shadows shifted by the passing traffic, nothing more. Still—"I wonder," he said. The chain moved over his shoe. Thomas felt the animal of his body respond: stiffened hairs at the nape of his neck and on his forearms, the chambers of his heart compressed—It's the Lowlands ghost, he said to himself, amused by his own fear, she's come vaulting over the wall!

The wet air parted, and briefly there was the impression of a shadow thickening and persisting against the green door, and slipping out of sight. Then, under brief headlight illumination, Thomas saw a mark painted by the chapel's iron knocker: something like a cross, if badly done, and blotted with a circle. The headlights went out. The mark returned to the shadows. Thomas, in whom disbelief equaled curiosity, went through the gate. Sound of bad-tempered traffic, of girls on the high street calling to each other from the pavements; sound also of some furtive motion by the green bay tree. Then abruptly a shadow there detached itself, became substantial, and crossed the car park toward Thomas. It came with such spiteful speed he called out, "Mind how you go!" with useless good manners, and stumbled as a creature with a white hood knocked him in passing. Briefly, three things: thin face; pale eyes; thin hand clutching a can of paint. Possibly also something said, but this consumed by the traffic and the muffling air—then Thomas, slowly turning, saw the intruder seep into the small crowd going up to town.

"Dear me," said Thomas. He approached the door. Paint ran between the boards; the circle surmounting the cross dribbled like an open mouth. Youths, he understood, were given to tagging railway arches in cheerful acts of defiance; but there was nothing cheerful in this inscrutable symbol already blurred by rain, which instead conveyed a kind of incompetent malice that left Thomas obscurely depressed. He took his notebook from his pocket, and one by one tore out pages that softened quickly in the wet air; and using these he cleaned the door as best he could. Then he turned his back and headed for the town, leaving the rest to the weather.

Bethesda receded. It kept the peace. Up ahead the newsagent's and grocer's were drawing down their shutters for the night, and a train leaving for Liverpool Street rattled the glasses in the Jackdaw and Crow. A man in a red velvet coat spread cardboard boxes at the foot of the war memorial, and made himself a pillow with the *News of the World*. "Evening," said Thomas, and received an imperious nod. He headed down a sloping alley and on to Upper Bridge Road, which passed in Essex for a hill, so that the redbrick terraces going over the hump had the look of a sleeping dragon's long articulated spine. So uphill, then down, and on into Lower Bridge Road, which ran under the dripping railway arch, and led neither into Aldleigh nor out of it—led nowhere, in fact. Here thirty-four Victorian terraces built for the engineers who had labored on the London line faced each other, withdrawn behind their cars, and gardens, and signs urging passersby to vote Labour, or Conservative, or to beware the dog. One house alone resisted the modern age. Here there was never any modern music heard, or exclamations from soap operas or films, and certainly no evidence of allegiance to any political party or social tribe. There was instead an insistent quiet, and the impression of a house set back behind a faint but impenetrable mist. Thomas Hart was home.

Nick Carleton, wondering how the other man lived, pictured with affectionate pity a solitary life in a fastidious apartment, and a narrow bed made each morning without fail. He was mistaken. Thomas lived where he'd been born, and where (so he often thought without rancor) he'd very likely die; and if he lived alone he was not lonely, that being a condition not of solitude but of longing, and Thomas was not a discontented man. The habits and tastes of his parents, which had been those of austere children of Bethesda's particular God, had been stripped with the wallpaper and carpets, and nothing remained of them now but Thomas himself. It was all exactly as he wanted it to be. The oak table by the window was burnished with decades of meals and work, and shone on fat turned legs. The sofa was deep, and blue, and partly concealed by a quilt his mother hadn't had time to finish. Edwardian and Victorian and art deco lamps which ought not to have agreed with each other nonetheless got on for the sake of Thomas, and shone from the sideboard and the floor. A broad bay window facing east allowed a single hour of rising sun before the room dimmed in the shadow of the railway bridge; and when a fire was lit in the grate, yellow marigolds bloomed on the surrounding tiles. The walls were obscured by books in arrangements that might have pleased a librarian, save that those by Thomas Hart were interposed here and there, since it pleased his vanity to imagine the phantoms of his imagination conversing all night with Emma Bovary in her vulgar gown, or Mrs. Dalloway fretting over shopping lists. Pictures were hung in curated disorder: a lithograph signed by Picasso in the plate, a skilled oil of a turbulent sea. Occupying a large space it did not deserve, a small photograph showed Bethesda Chapel on the day of its opening: 1888, and a godless sun scorching the lawn, while bearded

men stood somberly with women in their summer hats, and
beyond the chapel wall on Lowlands Park's unconsecrated
land, a bareheaded woman stood in the shade of an elm, only
ever looking up. Thomas, turning on the lamps, regarded her
a while. He'd feared her in childhood, since her face in
shadow had been featureless, but these days considered her a
lodger, her dress and her bent neck increasingly distinct behind the glass.

He prepared himself a meal: radishes in a saucer with Maldon salt and grassy olive oil; good rye bread; and red wine
poured with the pleasure of a man who's elected to sin. He
brought these to the table with the letter and the planisphere,
and surveyed these as he ate and drank. Perhaps there'll be a
disaster, Carleton had said; and Thomas felt again the blow
of the hooded creature fleeing Bethesda with paint on its
hands. But that had been no disaster, only something strange
and soon forgotten in the order and quiet of his home—so
Thomas, who had a gift for self-persuasion, placidly ate a
radish.

Late, now: the man in the red coat sleeping on the *News of
the World*, last orders at the Jackdaw and Crow, a baffled
robin singing on the streetlight, James Bower's letter stained
with wine. The table was heaped with cheap green notebooks
banked against a laptop computer that looked insolently
modern against the polished oak, and the empty gold-
rimmed glass. Sighing, Thomas raised the lid, and looked
with the writer's longing and reluctance at the blank document paining his eyes with its glare. He wanted nothing
more than to write, he would rather do anything but; it was
the purpose of his life, it was the bane of it. "All hopeless anyway," he said to the woman in the photograph, "nothing
wrecks a thing like trying to describe it. Besides, I've got

nothing to say." Sound of the robin singing—sound, perhaps, of the woman in the photograph speaking from behind the glass, from behind Bethesda's wall: *Get on with it, won't you? You're in your fifty-first year, and time is getting on.*

Well, then. Late winter, bad weather. As good a beginning as any. Get on with it, Thomas Hart.

THE LOWLANDS GHOST

THOMAS HART, *ESSEX CHRONICLE*,
31 OCTOBER 1996

Since it's Halloween, and the wall between the worlds of the living and the dead has got a hole in it, this night is as good as any to confess: I don't believe in ghosts, but I am afraid of them.

Humor me, my old friends! The fear arrived like this: when I was eleven, a friend of mine was absent from school for days, and it was said he'd gone mad because he'd seen the Lowlands ghost. I'd never heard of this ghost, and so listened with disbelief to stories of a gaunt and terrible lady who looked up at the sky with a neck that looked half-broken, and cursed those who saw her to be lonely and unloved, so that the workmen who'd seen her hanged themselves, and nobody cut them down; and children who saw her were thrown out by their parents to starve in the streets.

But there was a plan. My friends were going to break into Lowlands House on Halloween and wait for the ghost. Did I want to come, too, and meet on the steps at midnight? Here I was in a difficulty. My father was the pastor at Bethesda Chapel,

and our theology had no room for haunting. But since I believed in God I also believed in his adversary, and it struck me there was no ghost at Lowlands, but perhaps a demon. Here was a test of faith for which an early Christian martyr would give his right arm! All right, I said: I'll go.

So on the night of Halloween I crept out of the house and set off for Lowlands Park. There was no color in the world that night, only a kind of shining gray; and when I came to Lowlands House it seemed to me it was sinking in the grass, and that the boards on the windows were like the coins they put on the eyes of the dead. Then I waited and waited for the other boys, but nobody ever came.

I'd never been lonely before and have rarely been lonely since, but felt that night I was the only living thing in the world. When I called for my friends, nobody answered; when I tried to pray, I couldn't remember how. Then my heart turned and slammed, because I saw a light drifting back and forth in the upper rooms, as if someone was gliding on a kind of trolley past one window and then another, and passing through walls. Stupidly I began to walk toward the moving light without knowing why I did it, until my foot caught in a tree root, and I fell. The house disappeared from view as if it had finally sunk. Everything was quiet. The owls were gone. It occurred to me that every living thing in Essex, even the worms, was leaving me in disgust. An enormous tiredness came over me, and I turned my face into the mud and waited for the demon, or the ghost, or God—but there was only nothing after nothing.

At dawn a woman out walking her dog found me, and took me home with a cough that kept me from school for days, and prevented my parents from punishing me as they might have done. During my illness, I found that whenever I looked up I could see an old photo hanging at the head of the stairs. The photo showed a woman standing by the wall of Lowlands Park, and in certain lights it seemed that she turned and looked at me out of a featureless face in which there were no eyes.

As I say: I didn't believe in ghosts then, and I don't believe in them now; but I'd always call for my mother, and ask her to close the door.

The following Sunday, James Bower waited at the lights on London Road. The dissatisfaction that had dogged him all his life was amplified by the monotony of the day, and he was struck by the sensation that he'd always been waiting for events that never came. Then guilt arrived: he had a house mortgaged at a competitive rate of interest; a wife whose company he still enjoyed, and children of whom he was fond: what more could a man of fifty ask? But his watch ticked, and each tick portioned off an hour, and everything in view represented his failure to have lived the life he'd expected of himself. And would the lights never change—would he never be on his way? Sighing, he wound the window down, and music came over the lip of the glass: voices, an instrument of some kind—a melody he knew and couldn't place, departing the open doors of an austere gray building set behind iron railings, and flanked by the wall to Lowlands Park. James Bower regarded this building with surprise, as if it had been struck up at that moment with the instrument and singers. Its pale bricks had a pearly look, its narrow windows glistered; the music paused, and James saw a man come quickly through the gate. He was tall and wore a tweed coat with a collar raised against anticipated winds; he carried a leather satchel, and seemed an object set down in a place where it didn't belong. When he arrived at the chapel threshold, he paused and twice turned irresolutely toward the gate and back again. Then he stooped for a moment to examine the painted green door, patted it twice as if satisfied with it and with himself, and went in.

Then James Bower, startled by the changing lights and by impatient drivers at the rear, shook off the brief enchantment, departed Bethesda, and thought no more of it for days.

Thomas Hart, who'd come home that afternoon from London on the train, latched Bethesda's gate. The planisphere was in his pocket, and there were binoculars in his bag: five hundred words, he thought, resigned to the task, and six if the night is clear. He heard the congregation singing, "*It is well, it is well with my soul*," and the sound caused him to turn back twice to the gate, as if he'd left his own soul on the pavement. Then he went resolutely to the door and inspected it: a little stain between the painted boards perhaps, but no remnant of the meaningless symbol, no shadow unlatching from behind the green bay tree. He tapped the door twice. He went in.

Bethesda on the evening of the Lord's Day, and clouds receding over the roof: forty-seven members of the congregation on their feet with their souls in their mouths. The pews were hard and narrow, enclosed by high sides against which it was possible to lean when the sermon was long. Strips of brown carpet had been nailed down the aisles between the pews; the floorboards were pine. The walls were of a green so pale it couldn't be detected in certain lights, and in all seasons were cold to the touch: by the close of the service the worshippers' breath would run down like alcohol made in a still. Gas lamps fixed high on the wall could no longer be lit, since their pipes had been severed; their green glass shades had the look of tulips past their best. Light came instead from narrow tapered windows and opaque globes of milky glass hanging overhead like ten halted moons. The pulpit, raised against the chapel's farthest wall, also had the look of a tulip blooming on a broad oak stem, and directly beneath it, always under the eye of the preacher, the communion table rested on the carpeted stage and issued its instruction: THIS DO IN REMEMBRANCE OF ME. The preacher in the pulpit, gazing ahead, would see Bethesda's gallery, held up on the opposite wall by painted iron pillars; this gallery was painted white, and a clock like the clock in a railway station hung there. A woman with a feather nodding in her hat was playing the old harmonium, which had once been found floating in the chapel in 1952 at the time of the North Sea flood, when women on Canvey Island had draped their children over cottage doors to preserve them from the water (and so, said Thomas, the hymns puffed out on briny air).

Thomas, coming through the door, felt he'd walked into a dense illuminated cloud, through which the rest of the world was as faint and distant as a town across a valley. The congregation sat. Thomas sat with them, and looked not at the preacher, but at a black-haired girl seated beside a narrow window. She wore a drooping velvet hat, from which only a round chin protruded, and a shawl with tangled fringes falling over the raised back of her pew. Having heard the door admit the latecomer, she turned and acknowledged him, then looked scowling up at the railway clock and down again: You are late, Thomas Hart!

I am late, Grace Macaulay, it is true, he conveyed in a smiling nod, but I'm not sorry.

Grace Macaulay, then: seventeen, small and plump, with skin that went brown by the end of May. Her hair was black and oily, and had the hot consoling scent of an animal in summer. She disliked books, and was by nature a thief if she found a thing to be beautiful, but not hers. She didn't know she couldn't sing. She was inclined to be cross. She had the sudden wordless affection of a farmyard animal, and a habit of butting her small body like a lamb against Thomas, who loved and resented her as he imagined a father might love and resent a daughter. As the diligent congregation opened their Bibles and began the reading of the psalm, Thomas recalled first seeing her when she was six days old, with the petals of her skull not yet closed. That had been a cold fine day in 1980, and Thomas a man of thirty-three, unhappily seated in the pew where he was sometimes told his nature was an affront to God. That Sunday, he'd resolved, would be his last, and with gratitude he'd lock Bethesda's gates behind him and seal up what remained of his faith, and go to flourish in London, godless and at liberty. But a man had come in, carrying a baby in a wicker basket: Ronald Macaulay, of all men in Bethesda the most pious and most stern, whose wife Rachel had died in giving birth. He wore a stunned expression, as if shown something he'd puzzle over for the rest of his life, and there was milky vomit on his lapel. Instinctively, and with the faith he never could shake off, Thomas had commended the grieving man to God, and at the end of the service had gone to say with truth and good manners how sorry he was for such a loss. Then—without pleasure, without interest—he'd looked into the basket. There she was, Grace Macaulay, black-haired and ugly with fur at the tips of her ears. Her eyes with their newborn luster of oil on water had roved about the strangers' faces without interest, then lighted on Thomas and looked with sudden focus on him. "Oh!" he'd said—a man of thirty-three, he was, who liked children no more and no less than any other human being, which is to say according to their merits—"Oh!" he'd said, and "There you are!" She existed. She had not existed, and then she had, summoned out of whatever matter her consciousness had been made, and had stuck her small bare foot in his door. It was disastrous. There was a pain in his heart, as if it had acquired a new chamber to contain her, and so all his life he'd be carting her about. Then the infant had begun to howl with the indignant rage of a creature that had never asked to be born, and Thomas was fixed in place by duty toward a love he'd never sought and could not explain.

Now the congregation turned to their Bibles with the sound of wind passing over the pages, and there was the reading of a psalm. The planisphere pricked Thomas, and he took it out and put it with his Bible: *Andromeda*, it said. *Perseus*. The blue was remarkable against the Bible's thin black type. "*I will lift up mine eyes to the hills*," the pastor said, and Thomas lifted his own eyes to the vaulted ceiling, from which white flakes of paint sometimes drifted canting down. "Almighty God," the pastor said, "our heavenly Father"—Thomas turned and turned the planisphere, and the brass pin shone like the Pole Star.

Then the preacher said "Amen," and at that moment Bethesda's holy air was moved by the sound of broken glass. Something had come in from the world and struck the window where Grace Macaulay sat. Fragments of glass winked on the carpet. A golf ball rolled among them and butted up against a pew. Half the congregation, signaling devotion to their prayers, would not open their eyes; half looked at the girl in the velvet hat who now stood with her Bible in her left hand, exploring a cut on her neck with her right. Through the breach came noises: wind disturbing the bay tree, traffic going on to Aldleigh and all its worldly pursuits. Into this a single syllable arrived, and the effect was of a drop of ink spilled on a laundered tablecloth: "Shit!" The pastor grasped his lectern and repeated his amen. "Shit," came the voice again, with a despairing cadence; and Grace, standing with her thumb to a thin stream of blood, looked expectantly at the door, as if reminded of an appointment she'd failed to keep.

"*I was glad when they said unto me*," said the pastor with his rare dry wit, "*let us go to the house of the Lord.*" Then the inner door was thrown back and Thomas saw a boy come in. He wore a green coat, and his hair was cut to glinting stubble. Astounded by the faces of the congregation, he said, "Oh God"; and since that name had never been said aloud under Bethesda's roof with anything but reverence, the atmosphere broke as the window had broken. Attending to the change of air, the boy spoke quietly: "Sorry," he said, "lost my ball," and mimed the twisting, upward motion of a golfer's swing. Grace, inducing blood from her cut, said, "It's over there." Abruptly it struck her that despite her lesser sex she'd spoken aloud during a chapel service. Scowling, she sat.

The boy came up the aisle. He looked about with the peering, intent gaze of the shortsighted; his eyes were thickly fringed with remarkable dark lashes. Water ran down the sleeves of his coat and dripped on the carpet, and his trainers had green laces. The pastor looked helplessly down at his congregation. The boy quickly reached for the ball in the broken glass, and met Grace's eye as he stood. The brim of her hat made the upper part of her face dim; the weak chapel light struck her plump white chin and the bloody thumb at her neck. The trespasser gave her a kindly nod that struck off the pews, and the harmonium, and the wet green walls; then he tossed the ball from hand to hand, and left the chapel.

The door went quietly into the wall, and "Shall we sing?" the pastor said. The grateful congregation rose, and lifted Thomas with it. He sang; he saw Grace look back to the chapel doors with a watchful, hopeful frown, and was uneasy. It seemed to him that the earth had halted its ordinary turning, and began again tilted a little farther on its axis.

With the service ended, and the rain gone east to Aldwinter and Walton-on-the-Naze, the pastor and Ronald Macaulay surveyed the breached window. What a pity it was, they said, and what a sad thing to hear the name of God abused so casually; and would a square of cardboard make do for a mend, until a glazier could do his work? Grace Macaulay, hoping for a scar, showed Thomas the little cut. "Who was that boy," she said, "and why did he come in?"

"It was only an accident. He won't come back."

"But if God makes everything happen, then everything happens on purpose, and it wasn't an accident. So why did he come in?"

"If I knew the mind of God, I'd have better things to do than talk to children." He pulled at the fringe of her shawl; no harm meant, none done.

"What is that, Thomas?" she said, noting the planisphere as he put it in his pocket. "Is it a clock?"

"It's a way of finding the stars."

"The stars don't need finding. You go out and look up and there they always are."

"I suppose so," said Thomas. "But do you ever look up? I don't. Besides: there rivers always are, but you might still need a map to find them." He showed her the planisphere, and turned the leather disk. "Aldebaran," she said. "Pollux. Am I saying it right?"

"I don't know, but I doubt it. Now give it back: I'm off to Lowlands Park to find my way through stars," said Thomas, "and if the moon comes up, I suppose I'd better take a look." He clasped her shoulder and shook her a little roughly, as if she were a pet. "Sleep well," he said, "you wretched child. Now look. Your father's calling, and they're turning out the lights."

Behind the chapel was a steeply sloping lawn, where Grace as a child had played alone. This lawn was boundaried by a line of silver birches that screened the chapel from the world as a curtain screens a patient dying on a ward, and beyond the silver birches lay the five hundred acres of Lowlands Park. It was by that time gone halfway to ruin, and the careful planting of its oaks and limes gave the impression of an exhausted battalion marching on the house. The lawns were left largely untended, and stems of mullein and cow parsley dead since the end of summer rattled when the wind picked up. Immense formal beds had sunk and spread and become indistinguishable from the lawn, though occasionally a valiant plant seeding itself down through the generations bloomed in high summer. There was a lake left to silt up and become shallow; it was hedged by reeds and plagued all summer by midges dancing with terminal glee. Sometimes in good weather the lawns died back and the earth cracked, and it was possible to make out the remnants of a brick path going aimlessly down to the lake, the bricks marked here and there with stars.

Lowlands House, which listed on a shallow promontory at the end of the vanished path, was—at certain times, on certain days—a lovely place. The white facade responded to the Essex light, seeming sometimes pink as flesh, and in stormy weather gray as Bethesda's brick. Once it had been one of the great houses of Essex: not remarkable (sniffed Pevsner), but designed and constructed with all the terraces and Doric columns the fashion of the day could ask. When the family money had been dwindled down by venality and bad advice, and the sinking Essex clay had caused subsidence that cracked the plaster audibly at night, the last of the family line had staked the house he despised on a horse, and lost it to a man who never once crossed the threshold and soon forgot he owned it. So Lowlands quickly became disconsolate and damp, and was bought in due course by a wool merchant named John Bell. With his care and bright new money it had briefly flourished: it was Bell who'd laid the starry path and dug out the lake, and commissioned a statue of a woman to stand forever looking over the water (though some tragedy to which Thomas had never paid attention had put an end to all that, and quickly the rose garden choked on its own thorns, and the statue hurled herself into the lake).

A childish bad temper settled on Thomas. This was the effect of the chapel, and the broken window, and of Nick Carleton's impertinence: what business of his was a comet? What had the moon to do with him? It waxed and waned, and that was all he knew, and all he needed to know. His head ached. He walked on. It was getting dark. The dense stands of oak thinned into solitary sentinels as the lawn rose faintly to the house. Overhead, streaks of high clouds split and showed clear inky reaches not yet marked by stars. Somewhere, no doubt: the unreliable moon. He walked on, fetching the planisphere and notebook out of his pocket, and diligently recording the date and time. From this vantage, he could make out the pale house drifting down its shallow promontory, and steps descending to a wire fence that kept nobody out. Doric columns flanked oak doors surmounted by a shield of heraldry and secured by steel plates. The windows were blinded by boards that split and buckled in bad weather, so that trespassers beyond the boundary fence could sometimes make out the fireplace in the hall, and pale frescoes half-obscured by obscene and amatory graffiti. Meanwhile the ornamental lake was ceding to the Essex clay, and drowned the stone woman in silt.

Thomas walked on. The cloud thinned over a rising moon. Mist pooled in the hollows between the oaks. There was no wind. "Where are you," said Thomas, "where did you go?"— seeking out his old companion in the windows, inclined to persuade himself a light moved behind the splitting boards. Naturally: nothing. He shrugged; he turned to the sky. From east to west it was a featureless dark canopy, save for a pale place where the low cloud, startled by the rising moon, was dispersing into shining fragments. It seemed to Thomas he was looking up into a sea in which a silver shoal of herring swam; and after a time, when the cloud was gone, he raised his binoculars, and looked again.

FIRST LIGHT

THOMAS HART, *ESSEX CHRONICLE*,
24 FEBRUARY 1997

Dear reader, you have on your hands an altered man. This is the editor's fault, because he sent me to look at the moon.

But Thomas, you're thinking, have you never seen the moon before? Well, of course—I know its habit of pitching up at two in the afternoon, or tilting back like a rocking chair, but never found it any more interesting than any other thing. So I set off for Lowlands Park last Sunday without hope, and in a temper. There'd been rain that day, and there were no birds, no stars, and no moon: it was obviously all a waste of time, and my shoes were being ruined by the mud.

I was busily employed in cursing my editor when I realized that in fact the night had begun to clear, and that my temper was clearing with it. Stars had come out without my noticing, and there was an immense radiant place just above Lowlands where the moon was concealed by the last of the clouds. Then the wind took the clouds, and the moon came out; so for the first time in my life I gave the moon my full attention. First, I saw a melancholy face looking down at me, and was half-inclined to wave. But I was not, after all, a child, and really it looked to me like a greasy white plate, and I was tempted to shrug, and get back to my books. Then I remembered I had binoculars with me, and for a while fumbled with the focus wheel, at first seeing nothing but a shining blot. I swore. My feet were wet. I tried again; the blot dwindled down, and the moon came fully into view. The flat melancholy face had gone, and in its place was an astonishing and terrible thing bellying out of the sky. The more I looked, the larger it became. You mustn't think it came down to meet me—it was a question of flight! I saw nearby the lip of craters lit by the sun, and shadows falling behind them; I saw vast dark plains and places so bright you'd think they'd turned the lights on for my benefit. Toward the rim, where the hour hand on a clock stands at half past four, I saw a shining center out of which radiated lines too straight to have been made by chance—it is a city, I thought, and all roads lead to it!

A man in a red velvet coat was walking nearby and laughed at me, because I was saying, "Who are you? Who are you, up there?" I wanted to know who traveled on those roads, and in what vehicles—what was the name of the celestial city, and what were the laws and regulations of their principalities and powers? Were our sins their virtues, and their virtues our sins? What were the intervals of their music, and what did they eat in bad weather?

I put the binoculars down. I was bewildered and amazed: there was mud in the tread of my shoes, and lunar dust in the pockets of my coat. I saw the man in the red coat shaking his head and heading for town; I heard a woman calling in her dog, and music thudding from a car on London Road. But all that seemed as remote as foreign customs in foreign lands. What on earth did it have to do with me? I had become a citizen of the empire of the moon.

Nick Carleton, reading this dispatch from the shore of the Sea of Tranquility, looked up at Thomas Hart.

"Do you like it? Will it do?"

"I do," said the editor, truthfully, "but it's very strange."

"Ah, well," said Thomas, and left it at that.

"My father told me," said Carleton, "that when a telescope is used for the first time, whatever the astronomer sees that night is called the 'first light.' You're like a telescope yourself, Thomas: we took the lens cap off, and this is your first light. Well, then! We have a title." He was pleased with this; but when he looked for the other man's responding pleasure saw he was looking out between the slatted blinds. Half past three in the afternoon, but all the same: the moon.

Several cold days went by. Thomas roamed at night with the litter and drinkers and foxes, consulting the planisphere by streetlight. Overcast nights were a personal affront; his neck ached with all the looking. The scattered stars assembled themselves. He had the wonderlust. The moon waned: lights out in the great city, calm on the dry black seas. He consulted books on physics and astronomy, and when he understood Kepler's laws was brought almost to tears by such exacting beauty. I am superterrestrial, he thought, and passed untouched through crowds on Aldleigh High Street with the waters of his body drawn up by the moon with the tides.

From the last night of February, Comet Hale-Bopp could not be ignored. It came as a chalk smudge of light, and bright as a star of the second magnitude, so that men and women generally indifferent to the stars were compelled beyond the limit of their interest, and wondered what it was, and why it didn't move. In the Colchester barracks, bragging squaddies drunk on valor saw it, and argued over the cause; a girl coming out of the Jackdaw and Crow in tears over a broken shoe saw it, and tried to describe it, and couldn't. (The vagrant in the red coat saw it from the steps of the war memorial, but all day he'd been diligently drinking, so all the stars had tails.)

Ronald Macaulay saw it, and said to himself that the heavens declared the glory of God, but admitted that of that glory he felt nothing. Anne Macaulay saw it, standing at the kitchen sink. Grace Macaulay saw it, and shrugged. She was taking off her clothes. It was her habit to examine herself every evening by lamplight, as if her body were a bit of clay being worked on against her will. The hair between her legs was reddish; she thought this odd and beautiful. There was a spot on her shoulder she couldn't reach, and a splay of violet lines fading over hips that had broadened shockingly the year before. Her breasts and stomach were round, and she set her feet on the ground like an animal refusing to budge; muscles were visible in her arms and thighs. She hadn't grown an inch since she was twelve. There was a steep inward curve to the small of her back; there was a birthmark on her upper arm, and a quickly healing cut on her neck. She touched it, and wished it were worse. Her hands were small, and her nails bitten short. In this light she found herself erotic, and wondered if this was a form of desire that constituted a sin. Then she wondered if the boy who'd broken the chapel window would also find her erotic, and winced as her conscience pricked. She got into bed. In the front garden a silver birch stood between her window and the streetlight, and its shadow flinched against the wall. She prayed sincerely, and slept.

Thomas Hart, seeing the comet as he came home from work, felt he'd been waiting for it all his life: "Look," he said, grasping the sleeve of a stranger, "look at that! It is circumpolar," he said, "it will never set." (The stranger shook him off and went home with his hangover.) Later that evening it struck Thomas there was something he ought to have been doing, and remembered what it was, and did it:

Dear Mr. Bower,

I hope you're well. I'm sorry it has taken me this long to reply to your kind letter, which did indeed interest me. I am not so old that I'm unmoved by the prospect of solving the problem of the Lowlands ghost! If you can forgive my bad manners, and would still like to speak to the *Chronicle* about your research into Lowlands, I would be pleased to visit and see what you've found. I will come this Friday, if I may, at about eleven.

Yours sincerely,

THOMAS HART

SIGNS AND WONDERS

THOMAS HART, *ESSEX CHRONICLE*,
21 MARCH 1997

Well: have you seen it yet? We have a visitor. Look northwest after dusk in good weather, and you'll find it: Comet Hale-Bopp, tearing out of space and headed for the sun.

I imagine it brings trouble. In 1910, for example, people in the United States bought gas masks and sealed up their keyholes with lumps of soap and wax, believing Halley's Comet would release clouds of deadly cyanogen gas. In Haiti and Texas it was possible to buy anti-comet pills, and in Washington State a shepherd nailed himself hand and foot to a wooden cross and begged the authorities to leave him there. That same year in Essex, two wealthy sisters locked themselves in the attic and set themselves on fire, and were buried the following week in the same grave; and in London a pastor preached for twenty hours without pausing before collapsing in the street (his last words were said to have been "flee from the wrath to come"). In the end, Halley reached its perihelion without causing any greater harm than

terror (though some said it had been possible to smell something like burning vegetables, and marsh gas).

Comets have always caused a bit of a stir—in 1456, Pope Callixtus III excommunicated Halley as an "instrument of the devil," and in 1835 it was said to have caused a devastating fire in New York. Naturally ours is an age of reason, and that's a fine thing—but the arrival of Comet Hale-Bopp has shown our pleasure in fear isn't as diminished as we'd like to think. I've heard of a group in California who see in the comet's wake a "dark companion" they believe to be a spaceship; and this week alone the *Chronicle* has received three letters from people believing Hale-Bopp is the Star of Bethlehem, signaling the arrival of a new Messiah, or possibly the return of the old one.

And though it seems to me little more than a blurred star, I sometimes look up and remember a Bible phrase that frightened me when I was young: that in the last days there would be wars, and rumors of wars. You see how easily we're fooled by a new light! And in fact Hale-Bopp will reach its perihelion on April Fools' Day, which I suppose is fitting—but I think on the whole I'd rather be prone to being fooled than be too wise a man for wonder.

Friday, about eleven, and March going out like a lamb: Aldleigh lively under drifts of cherry blossom that blotted the steps of the old town hall and caused women in high heels to slip. Here Aldleigh Museum kept its stores of coins and mosaics retrieved from new roads and housing estates in the nick of time, together with its dancing bear stuffed and chained at the foot of the stairs, and its single mummified Egyptian cat which (so children claimed) could be smelled through panes of glass. Students from Colchester and Cambridge came now and then to examine its library and its manuscripts pertaining to witch trials, saffron, Blackwater serpents, and the growth and manufacture of thatch; and meanwhile a model of Boudicca, her hard breasts bare, drove her chariot forever across a carpet stained with gum.

James Bower's office was cold, and could never be lit beyond permanent dusk. The windows rattled when an east wind blew, and if on certain days he was charmed by the paneled walls, and by the Essex coat of arms above the door, now he sighed over the tedium of his work. I've been bored all my life, he thought, and now I am fifty: everything is behind me, and nothing is ahead. The clock ticked. He watched it. It was about eleven, and there were voices in the hall. This, he supposed, was Thomas Hart, whose letter and columns suggested a man who shed dust as he walked. James stood. He straightened the papers on his desk. Now there was a deep voice, accentless and precise. "Thank you," it said. "Should I wait here?"

"No need," said James, coming through the door. "Thomas Hart, I presume? In here, and we'll have tea, or coffee if you prefer." Dust drifted in the narrow hall, and briefly it seemed the morning guest, indistinct and featureless, was at that moment being formed out of a swirling mass of particles. Then he came into the clarifying light, and James was brought up hard against a memory. "Oh!" he said, fumbling his good manners, and frowning at the visitor with startled recognition. What was he, or what had he been? An old schoolfriend perhaps, but for the life of him—"Come in," he said, "and sit down."

With graceful deliberation Thomas Hart took off his coat, and James Bower understood it was not the features that were familiar, but the atmosphere attending the man. He wore a tie, and the line of a folded handkerchief showed above the breast pocket of his jacket: the effect was to give James the impression that his own shirt and jeans were in some way offensive. It would have been unkind and untrue to say he was a strange man; but all the same he conveyed the impression he belonged elsewhere.

"I hope you'll forgive my delay in replying, Mr. Bower," said Thomas Hart. "I've had the moon on my hands, you see."

"Please," said the other man, bewildered by the formality, "call me James."

"Ah yes: force of habit. James, then." He took out a notebook; he opened it on his knee. James began to hear a thin melody, as plainly as if coming through the broken window frame. "Oh!" he said again. That was it, he thought, that was it: the pearly gray brick, the solitary man—*It is well, it is well with my soul!*

"So then, James: you've found some documents relating to

Lowlands House? I love the old place," he said with charming sorrow, "and hate to see it sink so low." (James wouldn't have been surprised if he had said: I was there when it was built, and saw the last tile set on the roof.)

A silent woman brought tea in green cups on a green tin tray, and left.

"I could let you in," said James. "I have the keys." He was startled by a desire to interest this man. "I visit often of course, and never did believe in the ghost, but these days find myself listening for footsteps—you're making notes?"

"I write everything down," said Thomas, with the suggestion of an apology. "It is how I make sense of things." Then he became professional, brisk; if there were footsteps at Lowlands he was evidently resolved not to hear them. "Now," he said, leaning faintly forward, "about these documents?"

James willingly followed Thomas from the supernatural to the ordinary, and opened a file. "What do you know," he said, "about Maria Văduva?"

"Nothing," said Thomas. "In fact, I've never heard the name."

"She was the wife of John Bell, who owned Lowlands until his death in 1889, and we've never known anything more about her: it's as if she's been cut out of time. We have records of their marriage, but not of her death; we have no portraits of her anywhere, and when the house and contents were sold none of her possessions were listed in the inventory. We only know that in 1887 John Bell commissioned a statue of her to stand by the lake—look, we have a photo—but soon after this she disappeared, and now the statue has gone, too."

"I see." Thomas examined the image of a stone woman stuck on the verges of the lake. Black moss stained her skirts, and something was falling from her right hand. "I suppose she's in the water now," he said. "What is she holding?"

"I have always thought," said James, "it looked like a shotgun—don't you want your tea? I don't blame you."

Thomas looked at the cup he'd put down, and moved it farther away. "You've told me what you don't know," he said, "but I understood you wanted to show me something you do know?"

James, puzzled by his desire to impress and excite this visitor beyond the ordinary professional interest, reached again for his file. "We've been taking up the carpets," he said, "in the east wing. The floorboards are lifting up with damp, there's all kinds down there—a silver fork, a lens from a pair of glasses, bits of old clothing—and also, shoved down between the boards as if deliberately, we found these." He handed the other man a square of foxed and buckled paper, together with a larger document.

Thomas took the document and raised it to the window. Daylight seeped through seams where it was unfolded. It was a long letter, in a looping exuberant scrawl: ". . . *beloved inhabitant*," he read aloud. ". . . *Foolish Street . . .*" Briefly defeated by the ink, he frowned more deeply still. "*though truly it seems to me that I am a static object, changeless as the noble gases, condemned only to observe and never to move . . .* She goes on at length," said Thomas. "I see it was never sent."

"Not finished, and never sent. But dated, as you see, and the name is clear: Maria Văduva, writing at Lowlands on the twenty-second of May 1887."

Thomas put the letter down and considered it. "So then," he said, "certain facts can be deduced. Firstly, that her name was Maria Văduva, which is certainly not English. Secondly, that she was remarkable enough to have justified a statue, in which she may possibly have been holding a weapon. Thirdly, that she was alive and resident in Lowlands at this date. Fourthly, that she had at least one friend, to whom she sometimes wrote. It is very

strange," he said, with a direct assessing look at James, "that so little is left of her. This letter is long. I suppose there's more information here?"

"I've made copies," said James. "You can take one home and
read it."

"Thank you."

"Anything," said James, becoming magnanimous, "for the
Essex Chronicle. And then, you see, we have this." This: a
smaller sheet of paper, folded once, and showing an inked circle drawn with a schoolboy's exactitude. Within this circle,
there was a kind of scribbled blot. Thomas surveyed it. It was
without form, and void: no sense could be made of it. "You almost feel," he said, "that if you touch it your finger would sink
through the paper and be lost in it. But this is signed, too:
'Maria Văduva, M42, 1887.' M42." He shook his head. "As if
she means to indicate March, or May; only no month has
forty-two days."

"Perhaps," said James. "But really it might mean nothing at
all." Currents of air in the dim roof shifted and brought down
dust.

"Well, perhaps she was mad, and was shut away for it."

"Any of us might go mad at any time," said James.

"We might," said Thomas, "I suppose." And there was the
suggestion that he at any rate was a man beyond the reach of
insanity.

"One last thing," said James. "This had fallen behind a window seat. So now we have an image of her, and we are all
in love. She is not young, and no beauty"—here, gentle
disappointment—"but striking, you might say."

Thomas took the photo he was given, and saw a woman in a
black silk dress, the constricting high neck trimmed with lace.
Her face in profile showed straight black brows and a Roman
nose; her black hair was kept back from her temples with a

diamond pin. "How cross she looks," said Thomas, "but not, I think, insane." He frowned then, as if mocking the woman's concentrated severity. "Mr. Bower—James, I should say—I wonder if I've seen her before?"

"This image, you mean? This photo?"

"No." He put the woman down. "I have a photograph at home," he said, "from the day Bethesda opened." He hesitated then, and James was astonished to see color rise from beneath the other man's collar and stain his neck. "That is: the old chapel on London Road, that backs onto Lowlands Park. Perhaps you know it. At any rate, a photo was taken on the day it opened. It shows the chapel of course, and the first congregation; but what interests me most is that toward the edge of the picture, caught by mistake and almost out of sight, a black-haired woman stands the other side of the chapel wall, on Lowlands land. It is dated August 1888; so if it is her, it keeps her alive and in Lowlands for a further year. Perhaps I'll bring it and show you," he said; and it seemed to James that he leaned with shyness against the high back of his chair, and inspected his fingernails, as if to indicate that a refusal wouldn't trouble him at all.

"Yes," said James, "bring it, by all means." It would be quite natural then to say, And of course I know the chapel, Thomas, everybody does, and I saw you there—but this felt impossibly intimate. "I wonder," he said, smiling to demonstrate that he was aware of his own foolishness, "I wonder if we have named the Lowlands ghost? A strange woman, suddenly vanished—a statue drowned in the lake—what more could we ask. Is it worth writing about, do you think? Can you make something of it?"

"Certainly I can," said Thomas. He was returning his notebook to his pocket. "My readers are fond of Lowlands, and they're very fond of the ghost. They tell me she's come back, you know—that lights have been seen, where there should be no lights. But a real woman who has vanished interests me more than an imagined one who persists in showing up. We'll keep in touch"—he was standing; he was putting on his coat—"and you can tell me what more you find, and I'll tell you what I find. Like a mystery," he said (a smile then, passing quickly), "like schoolboys." He held out his hand.

There was a brief dry touch of palm on palm. The windows of the room turned with the earth and admitted the sun. A beam of light divided the room in two, and also divided the men.

"Well then," said James. "You have my number, and I have yours."

"Yes," said Thomas, "I think so," and with a peculiarly intimate smile headed for the door. Quite a strange man, thought James, watching him go—but what a relief to discover he still contained the capacity to be taken by surprise. He returned to his work, and with his old sense of tedium and futility put his name to a pink requisition slip, which concerned graves disinterred in the village of Aldwinter in 1954.

Maria Văduva Bell
Lowlands House
22 MAY 1887

To the only beloved inhabitant of Foolish Street!

Very well: since you ask, I will make a record of what is
happening—though truly it seems to me I am as changeless
as the noble gases—and by the time you reach my
signature, you'll cast poor dull Maria to the dogs—

So you see—I have left my homeland—I exchange both
warmth and cold for the nothingness of English weather!
John Bell conveyed me first by train and in due course by
means of a bone-rattling carriage to Lowlands, not a mile
distant from the village of Aldleigh, which I do not like
and cannot pronounce. I daresay I must call this my
home—though truly there never was so dank and drear a
place—though Essex being flat and featureless at least has
in its favor the kind of skies which all my life I have sought—

I confess to having been surprised by affection for my
husband—this dreadful emotion roused by discovering
that he has commissioned a rose garden, and an orchard,
and a lake, and beside this lake a statue of a woman holding
certain instruments of her trade—and this woman is
intended to be me. You would laugh to see it—she is as
fragile as women are intended to be, and as you and I are
not—and lifts her skirt above the water, but never above
her toes—but it caused me to soften against any man who
could conceive of me in this way! Then I regretted this
softness—and made a quick summation of his faults: that
he is without humor, without intelligence, and without

style; and furthermore—you will not deny this material fact—that he possesses a face like a boiled potato. (You must deploy this method for your own husband, since it is wise never to think too well of any man—or you will find, as I have found, they may become the rocks on which your ship is wrecked!)

How lax I have been in my task! I offer in mitigation that I have taken up my old nocturnal habits—since the weather has been good for hunting—

John Bell of course dislikes these habits and speaks to his land agent as if I were a madwoman. But I sharpen my wits to keener points, and speak to the land agent, and to the various housekeepers, groundskeepers, accountants, scullery maids &c. &c. (knowing you consort with socialists and radicals, I blush to confess that my husband is rich beyond virtue), with such precision and prolixity in their own language they appear first astonished—and in due course, when I apologize for the paucity of my vocabulary and the stupidity of my grammar, quite ashamed. So my sanity is not in question, and the instruments of my trade are preserved—

These are my days—I wake early, and rise late. My room adjoins that of my husband—the wallpaper is patterned with ducks that swim forever to the floor—my bed would require a ladder were I not the height of a man. Then I assemble myself in such grand array it is said of me that positively I clank as I walk (indeed I have in mind a gown to dazzle the admirer with whole galaxies of pearls and silver—one day you shall admire it on me). If there has

been a good night hunting, I pass an hour anatomizing
what I have caught, and the place I caught it, and labeling
its parts—then it is lunch with John Bell, and I attend to
his remarks on the stock exchange, and the growth or
diminution in the value of merino, Shetland, lambswool,
angora, and so on, until I feel I must sink under a soft hot
heap of his words—

25 MAY

I have entered sadness as one might enter a room—this
after weeks of my heart having for its habitation a place as
unyielding and flat as an Essex field in winter! John Bell
says: What ails you, wife? He produces gardenias, hair-
combs, lenses, bracelets in amber and jet, celestial
almanacs, a white hen—reminds me that the whole
exchequer of his affection and his accounts is at my
disposal—as if I were a capricious king, and he a
chancellor fearing for his neck—let me pluck and eat the
hen, I said—but relented for the sake of her fine eyes and
set her free to peck about on the terrace. What ails you,
he says!—as if he did not know, for I told him, that I love
a man who does not love me!

I lack the heart for hunting.

31 MAY

I walked this afternoon with John Bell in the gardens—and
my heart lifted (I gave it no permission) at the first flush of
roses—but I ought not to be happy! Isn't the value of my
love for M. set by the heap of my sorrow? This is my
calculation: to diminish my sorrow is to diminish my love
to an equal degree!

Three women were walking the grounds—as the people of Aldleigh are inclined to do, having no respect for the law— this being the Essex disposition. They were young, and of the type M. loved—for he confided in me often that he was no proof against beauty and youth—so I despised them, for the cheap coin of their good looks! And John Bell bowed deeply as M. would have done—only more deeply, and with more grace—so my lifting heart fell and resumed its proper position: at my feet, having been trampled.

Oh C.—if he had only liked my looks—if his tastes had not been so devoutly fixed on Veronica, who in her dreadful prettiness might have been his sister! Still I recall the words of the English queen: that she might well blush to show her face, but of her mind she would never be ashamed—

What have I told you of the man I love? You have seen his beauty in photographs—and it is remarkable—but you must not think that is the cause! It is that he stands on a high ledge, and I could not reach him—and you know what a weakness I have for what I cannot reach!

I learn that John Bell has sold a piece of land at the boundary of Lowlands, beside the new London Road. Astonishment and consternation above stairs and below it! Does my husband's exchequer falter? It does not: it grows fat on wool and the women that wear it. He confides in me that he was petitioned particularly by gentlemen of a dissident sect, which is called the Strict and Particular Baptists (I trust I shall never meet any man living under so pinched a faith), who have no place of worship and should like to build one. My husband has a fondness for any religion not overseen by the state—indeed at any mealtime he would speak at length on Wycliffe, the morning star of the Reformation, if I were to let him—so he has sold a half-acre at last year's prices, and the foundations are soon to be laid.

Now, my beloved: no cloud, no moon. I believe I see Lucifer at my window. Your friend must dress herself and go out . . .

———

I am on the floor—there is torn paper all about me—John Bell possesses a capacity for anger which I could not have imagined—indeed I like him for it! Why did I marry him, he asks—forgetting that I accepted him with these bare facts: that I love a man who does not love me—that I delivered my heart wholesale to M., who had no use for it—so that nothing remains now but to marry without feeling, only sense—and after all, John Bell is rich!

Then John in his envy commanded me to remain indoors, though the night was clear and fine—he is jealous of M., and of whatever else I love—though it would be better to instruct a priest not to pursue his God! So he tore my papers, and I liked him in his anger—and was faithful neither to M. nor to my sorrow—

How little you'll think of me now!

Thomas Hart, pleasantly if only slightly drunk, read this letter for the third time, and spoke to the woman who wrote it. He'd taken down the photo of Bethesda on the day of its opening, and propped it against the bottle of wine now empty on the table. "So was it you," he said, "that haunts Lowlands, and

haunted me?" (Maria Văduva, leaning on Bethesda's wall, refused to meet his eye.)

"It's no use," said Thomas. "I'm already coming to know
you, whether you like it or not. A little mad, I think; handsome and rich; bad-tempered and clever and miserably in love.
And I'm mad, too, I suppose, talking to a dead woman—what's
got into me?" He was laughing at himself and all the world,
and what had got into him was this—that superimposed on all
the world was James Bower's startled look of recognition: oh,
but it is you, Thomas, here you are at last! *He knew me*, he'd
said to himself, stumbling home past the war memorial and
the market square: *he knew me!* How to explain such surprised
and impossible knowledge—the unearned intimacy that had
made his mouth dry up, so that he couldn't even drink his tea?
Providence, thought Thomas, that was it: providence—God
had directed Thomas Hart, and had directed James Bower—
he'd set them in motion, and their orbits were fixed! Then
again (Thomas was an honest man) there was the fact of James
Bower's beauty, which in that dim closed room had made everything intimate and strange, which in the course of an hour
he had memorized, as he'd once memorized passages of scripture in Bethesda's Sunday School. "Everything about him," he
told Maria, indifferent behind the glass, "was gold—he radiated light—I could read in the dark by standing in his shadow!"
Now Thomas numbered off James Bower's virtues one by one:
his fair hair kept too long, out of vanity or neglect; his narrow
copper eyes, the whites of which had been remarkably clear; a
burnished look to forearms bared by a T-shirt he was really
too old to have worn, but which Thomas was prepared to forgive. The bones of his wrists had been too prominent, and the
glass on his watch had been cracked. His hands were large
and expressive, and he had moved easily in his chair, as if he
felt it a pleasure to inhabit a body of which he'd never been

ashamed—he'd smelled not of soap or fragrance but of clean
skin. His lips had looked as if they had ashes on them. "He
needs to drink more water," said Thomas tenderly, "or he'll get
headaches."

Never think too well of any man, said cautious Maria, leaning over Bethesda's wall and speaking urgently, *or you will find,
as I have found—*

"Yes, yes: they become the rocks on which your ship is
wrecked. So you said. But how can you understand? How can
you know?" He fetched more wine; he cut a pork pie and
smeared it with mustard. When he returned to the table Maria
vaulted the wall to join the congregation on Bethesda's lawn;
with her arm around the pastor's waist she looked unsmilingly
at Thomas and shook her head. "Let me explain," he said (if he
was going mad, he was inclined to let it happen). "I've read
your private letters; isn't it fair I tell you my secrets in return?
I have only ever wanted men. I have wanted them all my life. I
knew I wanted them before I knew all the words they have for
it, and long before I had heard them say from the pulpit that
men like me lived beyond God's grace—I knew when I was
thirteen, and went camping in the summer and watched boys
shave out of enamel bowls on the trestle table, and felt the pain
it caused me to see their throats move when they swallowed—
their bodies were so miraculous and strange to me you'd think
they were nothing like mine!" Maria, frowning and solemn,
looked once over her shoulder toward Bethesda and its narrow bricks. "Yes," said Thomas, spilling his wine, "yes, and
every week I sat in my pew between my parents, and after they
died I sat in my pew without them, and I tried to make sense
of it. Do you think you lose your faith, because your faith does
not want you? That would be easy! My life would have been a
happier one! But all these years there have been two fires in me
and neither puts the other out! So this is how I make sense of

it: in London I live that part of my life, and I never feel it to be a sin, and on the train between Liverpool Street and Aldleigh I set it aside, and come to Bethesda and I am another man. I've never had love," he said, frowning now, and looking at the letter on the table. "I've never expected it. It seemed to me that God would withhold it from me, for my sins. That has been the bargain, you understand? But if it was God's providence that sent me to James Bower—if this man has been looking for me, and found me—was it ever a sin, after all? Was I never a sinner, and never a saint, but only Thomas Hart?" There was pain in the sockets of his eyes, and at the base of his skull. I'm drunk and foolish, he thought, and I ask too much of life. The table was inviting and cool to the touch, and the robin was singing on the streetlight. I just need to sleep it off, thought Thomas, I just need forty winks—so he rested his head on his folded arms, and there was the scent of polish and mustard and paper. Easily, he slept; and as he slept, the woman in the photograph took her arm from the pastor's waist and crossed the parched lawn toward the camera. Her black skirts, thickly beaded at the hem, obscured the view of Bethesda; then her fine and muddied boots came over the frame, and were first set squarely on the table, then one by one on the floor: Maria Văduva Bell, assembled out of ink and speculation, and taking up residence on Lower Bridge Road.

ON THE MOTION OF BODIES IN ORBIT

THOMAS HART, *ESSEX CHRONICLE*,
28 MARCH 1997

Since I now divide my time between Essex and the moon, I go out whenever nights are clear to explore my second home, and give myself a constant headache what with all that looking up.

Keeping note of the moon's transit over Aldleigh, I've pictured it moving down the thread of its orbit like a bead on a length of string. Did you think an orbit formed a circle? So did I, but we are both mistaken. In 1609, Johannes Kepler published his laws regarding the motion of bodies in orbit, and in the first of these ruled that the shape of an orbit is not a circle, but rather the form of an ellipse (I'm as much a baffled student as any child, and have found it helpful to picture a drawing of a rugby ball).

As every child knows, a body must orbit something—so the earth orbits the sun, and the moon orbits the earth. The sun is the earth's focal point, and the earth is the moon's focal point.

This is quite straightforward—but I have discovered that the more I learn, the more I'm apt to be confused. In fact, there are two focal points inside the orbital ellipse: two dots drawn on the side of our rugby ball. The first is the primary focal point—the sun, for example, or the earth—and then there is another focus. There is no star or planet there: there is only space. You cannot see it, because there is nothing to see but maths. It is there, because it must be there.

Sometimes I think of my own body in motion. What moves me on? What moves you? I suppose I could tell you what kind of sun draws me down my orbit, but there must be other forces at work that I can't make out. It comforts me to think of us all in motion, helpless against the forces of time and fate. We are just like the earth, I think: "insignificantly small," as Kepler said once, "but borne through stars."

The following Sunday, Thomas Hart went out through Bethesda's gates when the evening service was done. Grace Macaulay was in his wake and the comet was overhead. "Look up," he said, "you wretched child—see it hanging over the roof?" Grace looked obediently at the pearly blur skimming the slates. Her soul was not moved. "Is that it?" she said. "Is that all?" She wore her Sunday best: a skirt sewn from a faded bedcover bought for a pound, and printed with a child's idea of birds; a silk blouse stolen from her aunt (it was too small, and its torn seams were concealed by a schoolboy's blazer). Her black curls, released from the loathed velvet hat, needed washing; they gleamed with oil from her scalp, and the rosemary and lavender oils she'd used as a perfume mixed unpleasantly on her skin. She carried her Bible. She walked with quick small steps as if always on the verge of tumbling over. "I think it's probably a sign," she said, "don't you? I think things are changing." (She looked at Potter's Field, and found nothing in it.) "And you're different, too. Something's going on. Why don't you tell me what it is? I bet it's all to do with that bloody comet," she said, and with this little profanity she smiled.

"It is not the comet exactly," said Thomas, declining either to applaud or chastise. "It's all of it. Look here, I've found a mystery."

"Thomas! Are you having an adventure?"

"I am," said Thomas. "They've found some papers at Low-lands House. Drawings nobody can make out, a letter from a woman called Maria, who was certainly a lunatic, and is possibly a ghost."

"The one you saw when you were a boy?"

"I imagine so, don't you? And sometimes I even see her these days, when I think to look—it seems her name was Maria Văduva. In 1888 she disappeared, and nobody knows what became of her. James Bower says—"

"Who's that?"

"A man at the museum. It's not important." Thomas was afraid he blushed, and that she'd see it.

"No: who's that?" said Grace. She stood rigid as a sight-hound in the slips, scowling into darkness punctuated at intervals by the streetlights on London Road. Look at her, thought Thomas. More animal than human, sniffing the air—he looked where she looked, and saw a figure moving ahead of them away from town. It leaped and weaved with happy devilry across the path, pausing whenever it found light, and basking briefly before dashing on.

"It's him," said Grace, with the wonder of astronomers. "It's him, it's that boy." She dashed forward, then turned to Thomas. "What should I do?" she said, with a curious sort of helplessness that was in no way childish. "I don't know what to do. Let's go back to Bethesda. They might not have locked the doors."

"But he's seen you."

"He has? Thomas, what should I do?" Hale-Bopp came out again. Nobody saw it. The boy, leaping into light, stood distantly surveying Grace. Cropped fair hair glinted on his scalp. He wore a denim jacket that was stuck all over with patches, which would certainly have been as inscrutable to the girl as they were to Thomas: a yellow circle marked with an idiot grin, a blue skull through which a serpent moved. The laces of his trainers were undone. He wore a splint on his wrist and had grazed his cheek; he peered myopically out of his extraordinarily deep-fringed eyes. He carried something. "Hello?" he said.

"He can't actually see who I am," said Grace, affronted. "Why doesn't he wear his glasses?" She went forward. "It's me," she said. "Can't you see it's me?"

"Oh." The boy blinked, waved, came nearer. "That's funny," he said. "I was coming to see you."

"You hurt me," said Grace. "You cut my neck. I'll have a scar. What do you mean, you were coming to see me—were you coming to tell me you were sorry?"

"It was an accident!" said the boy, in the way of a child to whom an injustice has been done. "How can I say I'm sorry, when I didn't mean to do it?"

Grace, seeming to examine this from a theological perspective, visibly relented. "All right," she said. "I'm Grace. But how could you come to see me, when you don't even know who I am?"

"Everyone knows"—he looked apologetic—"because, well: you know." A gesture with his splinted wrist took in her long skirt, under which filthy lace petticoats showed, and her boy's boots, and the Bible half-concealed under her hat. "But I like it," he said, with hasty kindness. "I'm Nathan."

"In the Book of Samuel," said Grace, "Nathan was a prophet who tricked a king."

"All right," said Nathan.

"What's that? Is it for me?" Grace Macaulay, inveterate thief, put her small hand on what he carried.

"I bought you chocolates. Not because I'm sorry, I just thought you'd like them. I ate some, to be honest. But there's lots left." He opened the box. Together they examined the contents, and placidly began to eat. Thomas watched, bewildered: here again was the sense that some significant thing was taking place, and perhaps had always been taking place—the comet had come out. "Hello," he said, intending a reproof.

"Hello," said the boy. He had the ease of a creature never told it was a sinner from the womb.

"This is Thomas," said Grace, without explanation. She stood close by the boy with the ease of long acquaintance, and seemed to Thomas they were in some way ranged against him—that it was possible to make out some connective tissue dissolving between himself and Grace, and re-forming between the other two.

"You busy?" said the boy to Grace. "Do you want to do something? What do you want to do?"

She looked astonished. What did she want to do? "I don't know," she said. The thought had rarely occurred to her. She knew what she ought to do, and what she ought not to do; the idea that she was allowed to want anything at all was appalling.

"Want to go in there?" said the boy, gesturing toward Potter's Field, a place of absolute darkness between Bethesda and the lights on London Road. "Someone's been lighting fires. Want to go and see?"

Grace looked at Thomas, who saw, superimposed on the child he loved, a woman arrived from further down her orbit, and exhausted by all her daily calculations of how to be good. She is seventeen, he thought, and eighteen soon—there's been so little liberty, and there may never be any more than this. The lights were out in Bethesda. The boy, despite the broadening shoulders and the scent of cigarettes sewn into his jacket with the colored patches, did not seem unsafe. "Go on, then," said Thomas, "just for a while. I'll go slowly, and you can catch me up." Grace made a wordless sound of delight, and squeezed his arm with bruising gratitude—then the children (surely, thought Thomas, that was what they were) had gone, talking of fires. Thomas waited. The comet ticked on.

Meanwhile: Anne Macaulay in the kitchen of the house on Beechwood Avenue stood frowning over her copy of the *Essex Chronicle*: *insignificantly small*, Thomas had written, *and borne through stars*. This troubled her. The people of Bethesda gave the stars very little thought: God had riveted them in place on the fourth day, and that was that. To think any further entailed reaches of time and distance at odds with Genesis, and so at odds with God—she put the paper down.

Thomas Hart, she felt, was becoming untethered from the pulpit. She'd pray for him, but this was no bother: she'd prayed for him nightly since they first met on the day they buried Rachel Macaulay. After the funeral Anne had sat against Bethesda's chilly wall with the infant Grace in her arms, feeling not an ounce of affection for the squalling child. That had been ten days since she was summoned by her brother out of a life she supposed nobody would have envied or admired, but which she'd remembered then with the baffled wonder of a dreamer: a flat overlooking a wind-scoured hill; a small cold classroom she kept in good order and pupils, likewise; psalms sung in the chapel where she'd been born and baptized and where she'd still thought she might marry; an unreliable yellow car she'd loved. Then her brother had phoned and said with dumb unemphatic syllables that Rachel had died, and was dead, and now there was a baby, and would she come down. So she did go down, on a one-way ticket to a county she despised, with its miserable fields of oil-seed rape and its new flatland towns. Her little life had ended for the sake of a scowling black-haired infant she didn't love, and at the funeral she'd mourned less for Rachel than for herself. This lack of goodness had compounded her grief with guilt, and she'd wept tearlessly as they brought out the silver tea urn and unhappy sandwiches, until Thomas Hart had quietly come to where she sat by the wall. "I'm sorry for your loss," he'd said, and the form of words was renewed when he said it, as if he grasped that Anne's loss was not that of the woman who'd labored into her own grave, but of the gorse and the hill and the classroom and the fifteen children in it. "I'm very sorry," he'd said, and reached for the baby's fist, and shaken it twice as if they were business associates who had a prior understanding. "We meet again," he'd said; and Grace Macaulay, ten days old, had vomited on his sleeve.

Then seventeen years passed without notice, and now came Grace's familiar impatient rap at the door. "It's late," said Anne to Thomas, "and the tea's gone cold in the pot. And whatever's happened?" she said, looking now at Grace, who it seemed had become disproportionately tired in the brief time she'd been gone. "Is someone hurt?"

"Nobody is hurt," said Thomas, "and nothing has happened. The comet came out, that's all."

"Auntie Anne," said Grace, seeming smaller even than her small stature, "can I go to bed?" Then without any apparent cause she began to cry in resigned quiet sobs; and Thomas, watching her wipe her nose on her sleeve as she went into the house, created fact by stating it: "You see," he said, "she is really just a child."

Midnight in Essex, and Hale-Bopp heading west in the company of Cassiopeia. Earlier that same day, in China and Mongolia and Siberia, a total eclipse of the sun had caused the comet to be visible shortly before noon. It turned counterclockwise every eleven and a quarter hours, and by the views and calculations of astronomers its tail gave the effect of ripples spreading from a stone thrown in a pond. Since perihelion wouldn't be attained until April Fools' Day, the comet had not yet reached its fullest magnitude; but it was bright enough, and it was new. So rats on the banks of the River Alder, conversing in a sunken shopping trolley, saw it, and paused, and took up their conversation; and pigeons on the roof of the Jackdaw and Crow saw it, and bloated themselves against the chill. In Lowlands House someone saw it, and in haste and terror spilled black paint on the steps. (Bethesda saw it and was untroubled, having its mind on higher matters.)

A fox in Potter's Field saw it, and began to caper and dash in the ruins, having no idea why. And what a reek there was hereabouts, the fox thought, kicking up cigarette butts and nosing at paper greased with scraps of food—what a reek, what a stench! It searched as it capered, and discovered a man sitting under a hazel tree, and leaning against the wall that divided Potter's Field from Bethesda's sanctified ground. He was occupied in unknotting rope. This was difficult, since all the knuckles of his hands were swollen, and his left thumb, seeming to have moved an inch or so down the wrist toward the elbow, was of no use. The watchful fox could not make out the size of the body inside the clothing, which consisted of several layers surmounted by a red velvet coat that must once have been a woman's. He wore torn jeans; he wore unmatched boots. The sun had stained his scalp through its thin pelt of white hair, and his eyes were blue. After a time he finished his business with the rope, raised himself with difficulty, and surveyed the hazel tree. It was young and pliant: it would do. He took a sheet of tarpaulin from a leather holdall, and with that same difficulty tied the tarpaulin to the hazel and made himself a shelter, then withdrew a piece of carpet, put it in the shade of the tarpaulin, and lay down to sleep. The fox, who was not by nature unkind, moved quietly on; there would be other larks elsewhere.

Thomas Hart on Lower Bridge Road, hearing the bark of foxes and the pain of rutting cats, sat by a dying fire. He averted his eyes from the corner of the room, since he was certain he'd see, if only he looked long enough, a black-browed woman cross-legged against the skirting board, scribbling on a square of paper: Maria Văduva Bell, going at her drawings like mad. Thomas thought of Grace with love and worry. She'd emerged from Potter's Field talking intently with the boy, who with exaggerated bows had left them by the lights on London Road and gone capering home on his own. "All right?" Thomas had said, understanding that she was both untouched, and altered absolutely.

"There'd been a fire," she'd said, "but it was out." She smelled of cigarettes; her cheeks were flushed. Furtively, and feeling despondently like a spy, Thomas had assessed her hair, and her clothing, and found nothing more untidy than it had ever been.

"All right?" he'd said again, and with more meaning; and crossly she said that of course she was. Did he think she'd never spoken to a boy before—did he think she couldn't look after herself? Thomas certainly did think these things, but pointed instead at Orion loping over the roof of the Jackdaw and Crow. "Be gone soon," he'd said, "and we won't see him again until it gets cold. Let's get you home."

Now Thomas turned his mind from Grace, and permitted himself to think of James Bower, and to imagine that Maria Văduva, crouching in the corner in her yards of black brocade, looked up from her lunatic scribbles and solemnly tipped him a wink. I've been moving toward this all my life, thought Thomas: a stranger who knew me, and a scowling ghost taking up residence in the sitting room. Then he resumed his new habit of reciting to himself everything James Bower had said, and all the looks and gestures that had signaled understanding, until he became ashamed of himself, and set aside his recollections, and began to write—

Thomas Hart
Lower Bridge Road
Aldleigh
30 March 1997

Dear James,

I was so pleased to meet you the other day. I hope you remember my saying I have a photograph that might interest you? I'm going away for a few days, so I enclose it for you here: you'll see it's dated August 1888. Surely this woman standing just out of sight is our lost Maria? I've always kept it near to hand, and was scared of it when I was a child, thinking it was the Lowlands ghost and she was so lonely she'd followed me home. But perhaps she is both?

I also enclose a newspaper clipping you might find interesting. It's from the *Essex Chronicle* the week following the opening of Bethesda Chapel. I'm not a member there myself—I have one foot in sea and one in shore, so to speak—but go often out of habit, and out of the kind of love one might have for a family member. It's a strange place, I suppose, and the people keep themselves separate from the world—though I'm quite often in the world, and never feel quite at home either in the pew or out of it!

Yours sincerely,

THOMAS HART

ALDLEIGH, ESSEX: CHAPEL OPENS FOR WORSHIP

ESSEX CHRONICLE, 25 AUGUST 1888

Religious affairs correspondent writes: The first service has taken place at the new Strict and Particular Baptist Chapel on London Road, Aldleigh. Members have until now met in the home of Pastor John Brandon, late of Wattisham, Suffolk. It is hoped the Chapel will attract those of the Nonconformist tradition in the town who currently lack a place of worship.

What's in a name?

Anglican readers puzzled by the term *Strict Baptist* should be advised the members are not themselves of a strict disposition; the point is a doctrinal and not a behavioral one, and refers to the question of *Particular Redemption*, and to the *Restriction of Communion* to those baptized by immersion. To this end, the Chapel is fitted with a baptistery capable of accommodating a fully grown adult.

"All welcome"

Services will take place at 11 a.m. and 6:30 p.m. on the Lord's Day, with Sunday School at 3 p.m., and Weekly Prayer Meetings on Wednesdays at 7 p.m. *All welcome.*

Lowlands House at dawn was unmoored on a pale sea. Mist drifting from the Alder had crossed the lawns, and now reached the steps and terrace as a soft tide coming in. A man in a yellow hat was on his knees, scrubbing at black paint spilled on the steps; as he worked the hat appeared repeatedly above the pale bank, and the effect was that of a signal transmitted and never received.

"I feel," said James Bower, who was unbuttoning his coat, "as if I were a boy again." He held a bunch of keys in his right hand, and these rattled in the stultifying silence of the queer wet light. "A boy," said James, "solving a mystery. What's this, and what does it mean? What does it have to do with Maria Văduva? Perhaps she stood here once. But where did she go, and what was she doing with her bits of paper? You probably think I'm being childish."

"Not at all," said Thomas Hart.

The men had entered through a vacant doorway from which brass hinges had been broken. Rags of mist entered at ankle height and dissipated quickly. A further door was set in the opposite wall, and this was padlocked shut. Boarded windows let in narrow shafts of light, revealing wallpaper that recoiled from the rotting plaster, and obscenities painted without much conviction. A long table on turned legs was pushed between the open door and the locked one; a pot of black paint was on it. At the table's farthest end, James Bower had made himself a place of work. A file marked VĂDUVA was propped against the wall beside the Bethesda photograph, and Maria looked hopelessly out toward the blinded windows. A gray marble mantelpiece with a deep shelf enclosed a vacant fireplace, and dead moths were ranged there like ornaments in the dust; a chandelier hung listing from its hook, and stripped of its glass drops made a grasping iron claw. Absent paintings had left their vacancies on wallpaper peeling like the bark of silver birch, and on the wall beside the window a black symbol, recently painted, dripped on floorboards that warped and gaped. The men regarded it.

"I've seen this before," said Thomas, with the note of an apology. He was conscious of the proximity of the other man, who still had about him the scent of his morning shower and the coffee he'd drunk after it. He'd nicked himself shaving, and Thomas looked with disproportionate solicitude at the bit of tissue sticking to the cut. "Someone was painting it on Bethesda's door. They seemed quite thin and frightened, and did a bad job. This one is better."

"There's another painted on the steps," said James. "We're having trouble getting rid of it. But of course it's only students, it's just pranks."

"I'm not sure," said Thomas, returning to the symbol on the wall: crossed lines surmounted with a teardrop, signifying nothing. "But I'm glad I came."

James took his phone out of a leather case clipped to his belt and looked at it, and sighed. "The men are late, as always—they'll leave early, as always." Dismally he began to speak of regulations concerning the preservation of listed buildings, and all this was incomprehensible to Thomas. "I'm sure it will be all right," he said, with optimism he knew to be both unhelpful and unfounded. Then the man on the terrace came in, removing his hat as if he stood on sanctified ground. He was young and tired. "The paint won't come off," he said. "You would think it had been there decades, not an hour or two."

"What about a pressure washer?" said James, drifting from Thomas in body and spirit, and peering between boards at the marred stone steps. "What about some kind of solvent?"

"Perhaps it has been there for decades," said Thomas, "only nobody noticed"; but James was too preoccupied for this whimsy. So Thomas left him to his business and paced about the room, conscious of a kind of pricking unease that seemed to have no cause. It was possible to think the dead moths were rousing in the dust and that the silence beyond the padlocked door was that of a creature holding its breath—Are you there, Maria, thought Thomas, have you followed me all the way from Lower Bridge Road? He turned to the window, where slips of light entered between the boards, and a paneled window seat retained rags of its upholstery. Where the floorboards bucked with the sinking of the house, the window seat had split. Thomas gazed at the fissure. Behind him, James Bower receded on his private orbit, speaking dully of what ought to be done, and when it ought to be done by. The splitting seat split wider as Thomas pressed the floorboards down.

Then a rat with a severed tail passed between his feet: with swiveling black eyes it made a study of the intruder, shrugged him off, and went about its business. Abruptly it slipped between two panels of the window seat, showing its little stump. There was silence. It was gone absolutely. A peculiar loneliness settled on Thomas. The other men had drifted from the room and were examining the steps; the pitch and rhythm of their voices traveled clearly through the mist, but their words were obscured. "Where did you go?" asked Thomas of the rat. No answer. He went down on his knees. "Where did you go?" Dust on the floorboards, thickly felting in the corners; moss where the wood was damp. The press of his knee caused the split to open farther. Thomas listened with longing to the rat's diligent clever feet, and detected also the impression of paper rustling, as if a reader had grown impatient with a book. He put his hand into the seat and patted blindly about in the chilly cavity, anticipating the rump of the rat, or possibly an iron nail. He held his nerve. He reached paper. He grasped it. Distantly the rat made noises. Thomas pulled his clenched fist quickly back, and the split wood rasped his wrist. The little pain was welcome. He looked at the paper he held. "Oh, James," he said. "James?" Carefully he stood and went to the table. The mist was clearing from the lawns—the light was less diffuse, and noises arrived from traffic on London Road.

James came in. He'd taken off his coat, and the scent of soap was fading from his body. "What have you been doing?" he said. "What's that?"

"There was a rat," said Thomas, concealing blood on his wrist with his cuff. He put the paper down.

"What is it?" said James with pleasant authority. "What have you found?" There were three sheets. Two of these were written in a familiar hand on fine blue notepaper, and in the poor light certain words asserted themselves—*Lucifer*, for example, and *goose-down pillows*. "Oh, Maria!" said James, as if exasperated with a friend. The third fragment was a smaller sheet of card, folded with precision; when Thomas opened it, the paper split on the fold and severed the square. "Oh," he said. Together they attended to it in silence. Here again was a circle drawn in black ink, enclosing a dark blot, and now divided into hemispheres; here again something inked at the rim, not possible to make out. The natural thing would be to bring the halves together, but Thomas was disinclined to touch the paper and participate in Maria Văduva's madness.

A rotting board, dislodged by ivy and time, fell from a window and broke on the terrace outside. The men flinched. "Maria!" said Thomas, feigning terror to conceal genuine fright. Wind entered, bringing voices. "There's somebody in there," a woman said. "Somebody's in there. Didn't I tell you? Didn't I say?"

It was certainly a woman's voice, and not a child's; but Thomas knew it. He said, as if the sin were his, "I know who this is." He put his face to the breach, and looked. The mist was clearing into shining particles that revealed wet lawns and solitary oaks, and revealed also the scarlet fabric of a red skirt held out from the body by stiff petticoats, and a pair of jeans torn over the knee. The skirt drifted over the jeans.

"A friend of mine," said Thomas to James, "and a friend of hers." He went out. James went with him.

Now: mild March weather, and nothing strange in it. Yellow aconites arriving at the foot of the oaks; the drooping wire fence plainly visible and broken in new places. Grace Macaulay in a flowered shawl stood on the steps, and Nathan stood with her. The smell of Silk Cut adhered to their clothes. "Oh," said Grace, seeing Thomas approaching, and it struck him with resentment that she'd never before greeted him with disappointment. Well, he thought, you've wrecked my morning and I've wrecked yours. Fair's fair. She looked at James. "Who's this, then?"

"James Bower," said Thomas. "Grace Macaulay. And this is Nathan." The boy hopped from foot to foot, animated by cold or by feeling, and grown broader in the days since Thomas had seen him last, so that the sleeves of his denim jacket were too short on his wrists.

"Yes," said Grace, examining James. "Yes, but who is he? What are you doing?"

"We are solving a mystery," said James, examining Grace with pleasure, and becoming extraordinarily handsome. "Would you like to see?"

"Is somebody dead?" This was Nathan, wandering to the window, looking in. "Did somebody die in there?"

Grace tugged with a possessive gesture at Nathan's sleeve. "Thomas thinks a woman went off her head," she said, "and vanished. He wants to find out all about it, so he can put it in his newspaper, which is the only reason he ever does anything."

"That is true," said Thomas mildly.

"Why don't you come on in," said James. "See what Thomas found." But no, thought Thomas, don't come in, leave us alone. The mist was gone. He could no longer smell the soap on James Bower's body.

"Come on," said James, "come in." And Thomas watched Grace run ahead, tripping on her skirt. She stood under the lightless chandelier. "I knew it would be like this," she said. "All my life I've wanted to be in here, and they wouldn't let me. Well I'm here now, aren't I?" She delighted in the ceiling, the shattered windows, the obscene graffiti on the plaster; she delighted in Nathan, who leaped backward onto the window seat, swaying as the wood cracked.

"Come and see what Thomas found," said James. He took them to the table where Maria looked over his files: "See here," he said, then silenced himself with an exclamation. Quickly Thomas came forward. "What is it?" he said.

"It was here," said James. "It was right here a moment ago— what have you done with it," he said, turning to Thomas, "what have you done with it?" The photograph of Maria Văduva had fallen face down on the table beside the file, but the severed square and the illegible letter were gone.

"What's happened?" said Grace. "What have you lost?"

"I found something under the window," said Thomas, showing her the wound on his wrist, "but now it isn't there."

"Did you take it?" said James, looking at the children one after the other. Abruptly he seemed remote and stern, and desirable because of this; so Thomas turned away in shame.

"I didn't take anything!" said Nathan. He leaped down from the window seat; he raised his arms: "I didn't see anything to take."

"He didn't," said Grace, "he isn't a thief!"

"Was it the wind?" said Thomas, stooping to look under the table. No paper down there, but a cracked glass disk. He left it.

"Listen," said James, "there isn't any wind." They listened. Sound only of traffic, of scrubbing on the steps.

"This house," said James Bower, "has taken against me. And what have you done to your hand—you're bleeding—why didn't you say?" His attention affected Thomas like tenderness. Briefly the whole morning struck him again as miraculous, and he was unable to speak.

Grace shook out her skirts and said, "What's through there, then?" She was looking at the second door. It had been unlocked and stood open. Through the aperture it was possible to see a pale wall diminishing into darkness, and dust moving in eddies. The padlock still hung on its chain.

"Christ!" said James Bower, and received from Grace and Thomas a double reproof. "What the hell is going on in here?" he said, laughing and shaking his head. "Did you hear that? Was that footsteps?"

Together the children and the men listened, and persuaded themselves there were footsteps in the adjoining room, and that every quarter of the house rang with the footsteps of all its residents and visitors.

"Wasn't it always open?" said Grace. "Wasn't it always like that?"

Nathan crossed to the door and examined the padlock. "Didn't actually lock it, you see, didn't turn the wheels. You have to actually turn it," he said, looking at James with kindly pity for the frailties of old men. "It doesn't work unless you lock it, shall I show you?"

Solemnly James said, "Thank you. But I think I understand."

"Then somebody is in here," said Grace. Her hands were on her hips. "Somebody is painting on the walls and stealing things." She stood beside Nathan in the shadow of the open door; and it seemed to Thomas that he saw them as children and adults simultaneously, their bodies flickering between time past, and time to come. It suits me to think them children, he thought with pain, but they are not: here is a man with cigarettes in his pocket and God knows what else, here is a woman defying me to defy her—"It won't be safe," said Thomas, "nothing will be safe through there."

"Things fall," said James, "and are lost. Men have been going in and out."

"Certainly," said Thomas, "things do fall," but the atmosphere in the room had altered, as if each were guilty, and conscious of being watched.

Then men came tramping adamantly into the hall, and a general consensus arose among them: bracing was required, certain reinforcements in certain places, it was a sodding wonder the chimney hadn't dropped into the hearth.

"Come on, then," said James, "let's go," and with a gesture impossible to refuse removed them all from the room.

Out on the Lowlands terrace Thomas fell into despondency. Something had been gained in that room, and quickly lost—"Besides," he said, turning to Grace, "shouldn't you be at school?"

"Yes," said Grace. "But I have sinned."

"Thomas," said James Bower, swinging a hard hat on a strap,

"I'd better get on. I'm glad you could come." He put on the hat, and this made him ridiculous. "Off you go," he said, taking them all in with his kindly dismissal. "Maria's bound to turn up soon. She always does." Thomas received a quick touch on the shoulder, and felt this was longer than it ought to have been, and concealed something in it; so his despondency lifted.

Now there was neither mist nor sunlight. All the world was uniformly dull, the brassy aconites tarnished, the palsied limbs of the oaks leafless and dry. A solitary point of color was coming across the park toward them, seeming at that distance to bob aimlessly like a plastic ball on the surface of a pond—a pink thing, unnaturally bright, resolving itself in due course into a long full-skirted coat fastened with buttons, everything that same flat, lifeless pink. It was a woman, speaking volubly in long unemphatic sentences, everything about her insistently artificial, her hair set like curls of butter back from a white forehead; and walking beside her, seeming to be formed as she walked out of the drab colors of the Essex soil, turning again and again to her companion as if enraptured by all that unbroken silly speech, was Anne Macaulay.

Dear child—now it is June, and you will think I have
forgotten you in your fine rooms at Foolish Street—and
indeed you think correctly! I forget what I ought to
remember, and remember most clearly what I most wish to
forget—so I have perhaps been mad, though I should like
to know what committees of men in their good wool coats
set about their taxonomies of sanity, and say this man is
sane, and this woman, but not this man, or that one!
Indeed I believe my body has lost its reason, and not my
mind—my intellect I assure you is entirely undiminished,
yet there is at all times a harsh note in my ears, like that of a
musician sounding a broken instrument, and the palms of
my hands become numb, or pricked all over with invisible
pins—I sleep and wake a dozen times and on waking my
heart is lodged throbbing in my throat—meanwhile
Lucifer at the window attends my mornings and beckons
me out and is fastened by the Belt of Venus and beneath
him the shadow we cast upon the universe is so dreadful
and so immense there is a dark place extending far beyond
the reach of my vision—

[All that was yesterday, and is done. I was induced to sleep,
and woke to find Lucifer departed. This has been a great
relief to me—I never could resist that light, for all that it
disturbs my rest—for that is the consensus: that there is no
ill in me that cannot be solved with three goose-down
pillows and what John Bell's doctor dispenses from his
bag—I am ashamed of my distress, and ashamed of the
cause, and ashamed of these pages—so I remove them and
hide them, and will not send them, that I may keep the
good opinion of my friend—nonetheless I do confess
myself to myself: MV]

"Do you think so," said Anne Macaulay, "do you really think so?" It is an ordinary Tuesday, she thought, and I'm going to have lunch with my friend. She flushed with childish pride: her own friend, acquired not in Bethesda but in the world. This was Lorna Greene, dazzlingly alive in pink satin, whose kitten-heeled shoes audibly struck the wet pavements with the noise of clacking teeth; who'd just then been saying how much she admired Anne's winter coat, with its black felt collar folded over rubbed gray wool, and how well it suited her.

Had Anne believed in chance, she might have said that chance was how they met: by virtue of having waited so often at the same bus stop that in the end not speaking would have been stranger than speaking. That Anne should notice Lorna against the granite of the nearby war memorial, the municipal bins, was not surprising. All winter she'd dressed in rustling layers of mauve and pink, and set her yellow hair in curls that resisted the weather; she wore a powdery scent that never faded from the folds of her clothes, and at all times looked about her with the bright assessing gaze of a blackbird. That Anne should herself be noticed she felt to be astounding, and she'd received Lorna's first attention with a confused shyness that looked aloof. But Lorna had pecked smilingly away, seeking her out in well-modulated tones from which the Essex accent had been excised: she was Scottish? How lovely. She lived on Beechwood Avenue? Such a lovely road, with its silver birches. How lovely to have a niece, to be gray haired, to have a brother named Ronald, to have once been a teacher, to attend chapel—quickly Anne became "dear Anne," and it had been impossible not to soften against the endearments, the praise, the unsought gift of a dragonfly pin with a crystal thorax and wing. They'd exchanged phone numbers; they'd taken walks. Now they were going to lunch at the Jackdaw and Crow ("my treat, dear Anne!"), because it had not been possible for Anne to explain that she'd never set foot inside a pub and had never intended to do so. Besides (she exculpated herself), nothing was ever chance, but only providence, and she might win a soul for Christ—"Do you really think it suits me?" she said, looking down at her sleeve, and thinking that perhaps after all neither her coat nor herself were as drab as she had feared.

Meanwhile Thomas Hart, in carriage D of the 10:42 from Liverpool Street, submitted dumbly to the affection of a red-haired young man with whom he'd spent the past three days. "You live in Aldleigh, too?" the boy had said that morning in New Cross, delighted by coincidence and the prospect of further proximity to Thomas Hart, whose age and diffident expert affection he liked. "Awful little place," he'd said, shuddering as he dressed, "we should move"; and Thomas had quickly concealed his disquiet. He survived, as he put it to himself, by dividing his nature from his soul; so he left his nature in London on the station platform, and picked up his soul in Aldleigh as if it were left luggage. How could he explain to this ardent boy that no, he didn't want to get coffee, and sit together on the train; that yes, he was aware of the various places in Essex they could visit and he disliked them all? So arm in arm they caught the train, and "Nobody cares, do they," the young man had said. "I got a black eye a few years back, but all a bit different from your day, I'm sure." Then with thoughtless touches, never having believed himself a sinner, he'd told Thomas of his ambitions and sorrows and revenges, all of which struck Thomas as petty, and only became pettier as the train passed Stratford, Shenfield, Chelmsford; as Aldleigh cast its shadow on the line. Now it was no longer possible to conceal his distaste for the boy's company—for his youth, his thin ideas, his clothing and speech, all of which marked him out in a way Thomas himself had never been marked out—and imperceptibly the red head had moved away from the tweed shoulder, and leaned now against the smeared window (and on the platform at Colchester a black-browed woman rapped fiercely on the glass: *You coward, Thomas Hart!*).

Then they were at Aldleigh, and there was Upper Bridge Road in view, there was the Jackdaw and Crow—there, if passengers cared to look, a farther view of a white house sinking into the lawns. Already the boy, resilient in youth, had recovered his brief petulance at a rare rejection, and was preoccupied with his prospects that night, and all the nights after—"Well, then," said Thomas, tearing up his ticket and instinctively looking for James Bower as they came out under the railway arch, "I'll leave you here," and he held out his hand in a rote gesture of good manners. The boy looked at it and laughed, and out of a kind of spiteful mischief kissed Thomas on the mouth, noisily and not without compassion; then with a last hard, admonitory embrace slipped into the incurious crowd.

"Thomas!" said Anne with delight, gesturing to the friend she saw standing with a curious distracted look on the pavement opposite the station. Lunch had been a pleasure, and the pub nothing like the den of iniquity she'd imagined, though the table had been sticky and it had all smelled unpleasantly of smoke. She'd steeled her courage to say a silent grace before she ate, and been glad to explain to watchful Lorna why she'd done so, and even gladder to find herself quizzed over fish and chips and tea about Bethesda. "How lovely," Lorna Greene had said, acquiring a kind of avid look, as if Anne had been showing her jewels on her fingers, "how lovely to have a faith, I do rather envy you, dear Anne: you remind me of my mother, who could recite whole psalms—and of course I'm really a terribly spiritual person, though I wouldn't say religious—you must let me come to church with you'—she'd yearned below the painted lids of her eyes—"I have always felt there is something missing from my life, and out there, you know"—she looked with distaste over Anne's shoulder, where the bowed window of the Jackdaw and Crow gave a view of men and women streaming off the London train—"out there"—she shuddered with a delicate motion of her blouse that let out puffs of scent, and suggested that briefly she had seen some tawdry thing.

So Anne had left the pub with gratitude, and the sensation that she'd pleased God and pleased herself: of course (she said) Lorna was welcome at Bethesda at any time, in fact there was to be a prayer meeting the following day. Then—upright among disconsolate crowds returning to serve out their sentences in offices and institutions—Anne had seen the unmistakable form of Thomas Hart in his suit of fawn linen, tearing up his platform ticket and frowning over some problem. He'll be thinking about the moon, thought Anne, he seems these days to have nothing else on his mind. "Thomas!" she said, waving with pleasure and a curious sense of relief. "Thomas!" But traffic intervened, and a fretful woman with a pram obscured the view, and when the way was clear again Anne had seen he'd gone. "That was a friend of mine," she explained, turning with apology to Lorna. "In fact he comes to chapel, and you will meet him."

"That man?" said Lorna, patting at her hair, fastening the plastic buttons on her coat. "That tall man, with his back to you?"

"His name is Thomas Hart," said Anne. "He writes for the *Essex Chronicle.*"

"And he goes to your church? Dear me—I should have thought"—Lorna gave a curious delighted titter, which Anne could not decipher, and which was quickly concealed—"but how terribly surprising! Well, we shall see"—she kissed the other woman with precision on the center of each cheek—"we shall see. God bless," she said, seeming to have already acquired Bethesda's habits of speech as if by osmosis, and went tripping back toward the town on kitten heels that surely could not have been comfortable. Anne had stood for a moment in the shade of the Jackdaw and Crow, patting her cheek. She felt that Lorna had left on her the imprint of her babyish scent and dry expert kisses, and left also a sensation of flattered pleasure, but equally one of unease.

Grace Macaulay, leaving school the following day, thought she might go home by way of Potter's Field. Five times she'd met Nathan here, because they'd planned to meet, or because (she thought) it was providence their paths should cross at certain times on certain days. That they'd become friends seemed to her both natural and miraculous. From the minute she'd seen him blinking behind the hard dark ranks of Bethesda's pews, she'd felt he belonged to her: evidently God had ordained the whole business. So it was natural that he'd come to seek her out with his box of chocolates and his cigarettes, and it was natural that if his journey home from school intersected with hers they'd walk together, and sit for half an hour in Potter's Field with their backs to Bethesda, and that he'd teach her how to use deodorant and chewing gum to conceal the effects of a shared Silk Cut. But equally he seemed to have arrived out of a world whose laws and habits and even clothing were inscrutable and sometimes frightening. When he spoke about Southend United or *Emmerdale* or the glorious tragedy of Euro 96, she was ashamed to admit she grasped the significance of these words only vaguely and with effort; *I bet he drinks Carling Black Label*, he sometimes said inscrutably, or *Hasta la vista, baby*, and Grace would feel her own strangeness and isolation so keenly all color would drain from the day. Often he had with him a Walkman and a pair of blue foam headphones he'd hold awkwardly to her ear and his, introducing her to music that unsettled and thrilled her, and set out to evoke sympathy for the devil from her Baptist soul. Occasionally she would seem to become the sole focus of his interest, and he'd interrogate her with the attention of a student making notes: why did she have to wear a hat on Sundays? Why did she never wear jeans? Why didn't she have a television? Was it true she'd never been to the cinema? When she answered, she said either it was because her father said so, or because God did; and as she answered it struck her that she was often unable to tell the difference.

Now she'd come to London Road: here was Bethesda, here was Potter's Field. She put herself between them on the pavement, where the chapel's iron railings terminated at a drooping wire fence. Two places of worship, she thought, turning from the chapel toward Potter's Field, looking with hope through the thicket of buddleia and nettle for Nathan's glinting head or the colored patches on his jacket; but he was as absent from her as the east was from the west. So this was all for nothing, she thought, looking down at the costume she'd assembled—the black skirt trimmed with ribbon at the hem, the belt that had once been a curtain tassel, and a pendant of dripping silver bees—everything amounted to more or less nothing, unless Nathan saw it. How abject this was! Did women really assemble themselves out of the parts they thought most likely to be wanted? Was that love's requirement? If so, she'd have none of it.

Nothing now in the weeds and litter to interest her, and her whole life consisting of her own disappointment: helpless against the arrival of her bad temper, she kicked a crushed Red Stripe can at her feet. It struck a broken breeze-block and startled a pair of jays that lifted off for Lowlands with their noise of a football rattle. It seemed also to startle some other

creature beyond the shrubs and bracken, back where a stripped
hazel grew against the wall. The air was bright and clear, but all
the same there arrived the sense that something dark and furtive had taken up residence in Potter's Field: it'll be the Lowlands ghost, she thought, nobody had loved her, either. She
shivered, and wished Thomas were at hand. But now she saw
that nearby a midden had accrued, of greasy paper packets and
bottles and filthy scraps of cloth. What use would a ghost have
for these? There was the movement again, and she saw it was a
blue tarpaulin tilting downward like the sail of a sinking ship,
with a leather satchel under it. Legs extended from the shelter,
and she became conscious of the scent of an unwashed body
that was peculiarly sweet. "Hello?" she said. Silence in Potter's
Field, and beyond the chapel wall. "All right in there?" It struck
her that perhaps she'd find some piteous vagrant, who'd look
with gratitude and love at his benevolent visitor, all marvelous
hair and kindness—"I won't hurt you," she said.

A man came out on hands and knees. He stood. He was ex-
tremely tall, and wore a scarlet coat, which he pulled about
himself. The effect was majestic, and Grace felt the balance of
power tilt in his favor; but feeling this was her land, she said,
"What are you doing here?"

The man said nothing. He shivered in his coat.

"Why are you shivering?" said Grace. "It's spring—look:
there are some daffodils—and it's not cold. Are you ill?" Was
he perhaps deaf? This was unfortunate. "Well? Are you ill?"
He shook his head, then bent to assemble hazel twigs on a
scorched pile of masonry. He tried to strike a flame. Grace
watched. The endeavor was hopeless. She saw the wrecked
thumb and the swollen knuckles over which the skin was
strained and white. Something disquieting, too, about the
fingertips—she looked again—they were curiously soft and
bulbous, their nails reduced to slivers: "For goodness' sake,"

she said, "give me that." She struck a quick flame. Pity made her impatient and cross. The fire took; the man, not seeming grateful, put a scorched trivet on it and set a tin cup of water to boil.

"Do you need anything to eat?" she said. She felt herself to be gracious and kind. "Shall I go to the shops?" The man looked at her with uncomprehending sadness, out of eyes as peculiarly vivid as Nathan's, then began to cry. This was appalling. "Stop that," she said, "it never helps." The water boiled. He made himself a thin black brew, and offered it to Grace with a gesture he evidently hoped would be refused. She did refuse. He drank.

"I'm Grace Macaulay." Lightly she thumped her chest. "I'm nearly eighteen. You?" Slowly the man shook his head. "All right," she said. "You don't need to tell me. See that building over there?" She nodded at Bethesda. He looked, and began to cry again. "It's called Bethesda," she said. She recalled her Sunday School lessons. "Bethesda was a pool in the New Testament. Sick people were taken to lie in the pool and wait for angels to come and disturb the water, and heal them. I live there, more or less. It's my chapel."

He looked quietly at Bethesda. "You live there?" he said.

The jays returned to the hazel and set about berating Grace for her sins. "Of course not," she said. The fire had gone out. "I live in an ordinary house." Then it struck her that Christ, if happening by Aldleigh that day, would certainly expect her to give up her bed; but she didn't want this man of sorrows with his rank-smelling velvet in her room. This thought was painful: how hard it was to be good, when goodness really wasn't in her nature—and at any moment God might punish her, for example by taking Nathan away!

It was getting dark. Low in the northwest a pale blur appeared: it might have been the comet, it might have been a scrap of cloud. "I think you should lie down. Are you safe here? No one can see you from the road." The man stood, and his magnificent dereliction reminded Grace of images she'd once seen of elephants ransacked for their ivory stumbling hopelessly about, disgraced and severed from their tribe—"I'm so sorry," she said, and found to her astonishment that now she was also in tears. "I really am ever so sorry." She hoped he wouldn't hold out his hand, because it was ugly and broken and she didn't want to touch it; but he only bowed, and this was so deep and courtly a motion, and the velvet coat was so sumptuous and bright, that quickly she was laughing then, and bowing, too: "All right," she said. "I'd better go. I expect I'll see you again." God, she felt, would approve of her kindness, but she ought not to have noticed the ugliness of the man's hands, still less recoiled from them. She held her goodness only lightly, and how easily she might drop and break it. The depth of her frown induced a headache. The comet was at her back. She went home.

That same evening the man in Potter's Field was woken by headlights from cars arriving beyond the wall. Watchful in his shelter, he saw Bethesda's door standing open, and heard music fading toward the traffic lights. Women and men solemnly progressed across the car park, and there was a kind of blood relation in their measured tread and grave smiles of greeting. He saw the girl who'd visited him go hastily in, looking from under the drooping brim of a velvet hat to the place where he was sitting, followed by a thin woman in a knitted cap, and a tall man with hair like a dandelion clock who looked about, as if at any moment some malefactor might steal his Bible. Then the last car came, and a woman stepped out, tottering because her pink skirt was too tight and her pink heels were too high.

Stooping to the mirror of the car, she adjusted her pink hat; then she headed for the chapel with a constrained and ingratiating gait.

When she was gone, and the man was certain of his solitude, he came out from his shelter, stumbling because he was drunk. He cursed in his own language, and fell against Bethesda's wall, which gave beneath him as if the mortar were wet, and the builder lately gone on his lunch. The man painfully righted himself and looked at the wall, which now bowed outward at the upper course of bricks. Compacted soil had shifted and broken open at the foundation, and cursing his own folly the man worked at it with his foot in hope of concealing his transgression. But as he worked, the soil seemed only more determined to make a breach and offer him a view. And there was a view, where the last course of bricks was disrupted by the hazel root—the man, exclaiming to himself, knelt with sounds less of curses than of invocations. He'd seen, animated by streetlight, a shining object, man-made and improbable, and insisting itself on him as if by an act of will. He brushed at the soil. This was difficult. He raised his hands, berated them, and began again. Soon it was possible to make out the corner of a metal box, buried by mistake or by design in the foundations of the wall, its shallow lid sealed with mud. He began to pull at it, but could find no purchase, and besides he was no match for the sullen Essex clay. Then one by one the lights on London Road went out, and the gleam in the soil receded. The man sighed and stood, and returned to the tarpaulin and the square of carpet. He'd try again tomorrow: he'd do better.

Thomas Hart stood in the dismal kitchen at the *Essex Chronicle* making tea, and thinking of James Bower. The daily papers were scattered about, but Thomas saw nothing of strikes threatened by the Fire Brigades Union, or the race-hate leaflets that had done the rounds in Harlow; and it made no difference to him that the current prime minister was likely totting up the cost of removing his furniture from Downing Street: he was still in Lowlands, cloistered in fog, attending to the scent of a clean body inside a cheap coat. Abruptly it struck him there was something abject in the circuitous devotion of his thoughts, and he shook himself as a dog shakes off rain, then saw just beyond the limit of his vision a movement in the kitchen. He pictured Maria Văduva picking at pearl buttons on her black silk cuff, having followed him doggedly from Lower Bridge Road: *I wonder if you have a weakness*, she said, *for what you cannot reach?*

"Evidently," said Thomas; then in another office someone turned the radio on, and idiot laughter did away with Maria and desire. Thomas gave himself an admonishing shake, and turning for the door was startled to find a silent girl standing at the kitchen entrance. The strip light lent a sulfurous cast to her loose white clothes, and to a complexion marred by spots extending from her left cheek to her neck. She looked frightened.

"Good morning," Thomas said. The kettle boiled. He poured it out. "Perhaps you'd like a cup of tea?"

Steadily and with a kind of insolent fear she looked at him. Her pupils were blown to the rim of a pale iris, and she had the sour smell of an untended body.

"Have you come to see anyone in particular?"

She made a minute adjustment to the set of her head. Thomas took this to mean that she had, and that she'd found him.

"All right," said Thomas. "Why don't you come to my office, and tell me why you're here?" He turned away, and with untroubled attention put the pot and two cups on a tray, and carried this across the narrow hall to his office. Here he sat and surveyed the visitor. "We'll give it a minute or two," he said. "Take any seat you like."

She was perhaps twenty. Her foot was braced against the carpet, and her leg vibrated violently; she had the quality of an animal that might either bolt in fear, or spring at him.

"Perhaps you have a story for me," he said, and pushed a cup toward her. A sluggish drop of blood was rising from the worst of her spots. "I'm a writer, you see. For the newspaper. I expect that's why you've come."

The girl scowled at the sharp note he'd struck, then took a notebook from the desk and tore out a sheet of paper. Silently she looked at him, then drew the symbol which had been painted on Bethesda's door, and on the wall and steps at Lowlands House.

"Ah," said Thomas. "I see. It was you. But what have you been doing at Lowlands?"

"I live there."

"You ought to live elsewhere. The roof is unsafe. The damp is shocking. You could dissolve in it."

"Nowhere is safe," she said. "You said so. I read it in the paper. I saw your name. Bad omens, you said. Dark companions."

"I see," said Thomas. The symbol disassembled and remade itself, and took on the form of a comet moving down its orbit and traversed by a cross. "Yes, I can see it now: this is all about Hale-Bopp." Understanding amplified his unease. The greasy bird-print on the window flinched.

"I never heard of it before," the girl said, trembling in her chair. "Never thought about things like that—plenty to be scared of down here, isn't there, plenty of ways to hurt yourself—but it's in all the papers now, we've only got a few days left."

"But there is nothing to be afraid of. It will come near us, that is all—it will pass between us and the sun at an immense distance—"

"Poisonous gases, you said, and pestilence—wars, and rumors of wars! Better to burn everything up now," she said, reaching for her pocket, "better to go before we all get sick and die."

"That's only ever superstition," said Thomas. "It is just the fears of children, and people who think like children." (But vaguely, as if it were a distant memory and not a newly arrived thought, it occurred to him that lately there'd been the sense of the world tilted a little further on its axis.)

With difficulty the girl pulled a handful of papers from her pocket, threw these on his desk, and rubbed her hands together with the motion of a fly. Thomas looked at the documents. They were foxed and buckled, and by the light of his desk lamp he made out familiar handwriting in familiar ink: *I do confess myself to myself*: *MV*.

"What's this? What are you doing with these? These are Maria Văduva's letters. You have stolen them."

"I saw you," she said. "I was watching, I saw you with that man. I don't think you know what's coming. I don't think you have any idea at all. I think it's better to burn it all up—"

Then she took a plastic lighter from her pocket, and set the paper on fire.

Thomas watched the ember and the thread of smoke with dumb surprise. "What are you doing?" he said. "What have you done?" Burning ash blew across the desk, and he patted at it; the fire had consumed itself, and the letter was gone to illegible air.

Now the girl's body was rigid and composed. "Better to burn," she said, looking at the muddy sky showing between the plastic slats of the blind. "Better than all this waiting." She stood, and the look she gave him then was frightening, because it was kind; and as she left he heard her making private incantations until her voice was consumed by the nearby radio.

Thomas sat for a long time watching the door. "What's happening lately," he said in a kind of exasperated despair, "what are they putting in the water these days? And what a farce!" he said, afraid that in fact it had all been farcical: Maria Văduva and her maddened letters, the arrival of James Bower, the intimacy of derelict rooms in a derelict house. Outside a wind was getting up. It crossed the windowsill, and reached the ashes on the desk; carefully it disturbed a bit of paper that had come like Daniel unmarked out of the fire. The paper shifted by inches toward Thomas: "Ah," he said, "thank you," and picked it up. It was the quartered segment of a formless blot, contained within a circle inked with childish precision, letters inked at the rim; a remaining fragment of the signature MARIA VĂDUVA truncated by the paper's torn edge. "Thank you," Thomas said again, smiling at his own foolishness; and as he examined it the letters at the rim became larger—seemed actually to display themselves to him.

Then understanding came. It surprised him like joy; his body responded and summoned up the blood. The wind died back. Thomas turned and turned the document, and saw there not the formless scribbles of an unhappy woman, but the birthplace of stars. He picked up the phone.

James Bower had never troubled to imagine how Thomas Hart lived, but it struck him as he came to Lower Bridge Road the following day that it was all he might have expected. He was conscious of an interest that was more or less anthropological, as if the other man were the citizen of a province of which nobody else had ever heard. And how strange it was to acquire a friend at fifty, when life was already portioned out! Fondly his wife had taken to calling Thomas "your ghost," saying after all she'd never seen him, and neither had their friends and acquaintances—in fact that she suspected her husband of roaming the grounds of Lowlands in the company of a specter in brogues. And it was an odd business, wasn't it, thought James: no other man wrote letters when a call or an email would do, or invited friends to lunch on weekday afternoons. But since everything Thomas wore and said and did seemed strange, all this was no stranger than that he existed at all.

Now James sat in a shadowy room on Lower Bridge Road, and was surprised by nothing. Lamps doubled their light on the polished surface of the sideboard and the table, and white tulips collapsed over the lip of a vase. Spring was strengthening in the streets, but the fire had been lit for the look of the thing, and the tiles that flanked the fire were embossed with yellow flowers that seemed on the verge of unfolding. There was no stereo or television visible, only books of every conceivable kind piled about, and on the farther corner of the table an expensive laptop computer that struck James as vaguely malevolent, because it was so unlikely. Now and then a train departed Aldleigh for London and rattled the knives and forks, and this would rouse James to a moment of troubling clarity; then quickly all the languid effects of the fragrant room and of Thomas's pleasant melodious voice would return. "Tell me again," he said. "Tell me what you think it means."

"It means Maria Văduva was not mad. Look," said Thomas, handing James the scorched scrap of paper with the black blot on it. "You see where she writes M42?"

"We've seen this before—a date, we thought, but written wrong—"

"She has done nothing wrong! I ought to have seen it sooner—it's all my fault: M42 refers to the Messier catalogue, which lists deep-sky objects discovered by the astronomer Charles Messier. Messier 42 is the Orion Nebula, which is visible even with binoculars in the middle of Orion's sword. Not demented scribbles by a woman disappointed in love: it is an image of a place where stars are being born!"

James looked again at the paper. "Yes," he said, "I see it," but this was a lie. The drawing in that bad light was as inscrutable as ever.

"You'll find it eventually," said Thomas. "Look—" With a gesture inconceivable in any other room, and from any other man, he lifted James's finger and described a pale curve in the center of the circle. "That is what they call Barnard's Loop," he said.

James took his finger quickly from the paper, and paused before he spoke. Then, reverting to professional seeking after fact: "So you think Maria Văduva was an astronomer—that this is what she meant, when she said she hunted by night?"

"An astronomer," said Thomas, as proud a man as if he'd at that moment coined the word and conceived of the profession. "Her drawings are of the stars, but we looked at them through cloud." He moved to the kitchen, and a train departed Aldleigh for Liverpool Street and rattled the knives. James wondered if he ought to return to the museum, and get on with other business; but Thomas came in with warm bread

and goat cheese softening in wax paper, and the languid effects
of the afternoon returned.

"Three times now," said James, eating what he was given,
"we've found lenses we thought must have come from specta-
cles. But perhaps she had a telescope?"

"Certainly," said Thomas. He was pouring wine. "She can't
have seen Messier 42 in such detail with anything less than a
six-inch objective lens." He put the bottle down, and looked at
James with one of his sudden apologetic smiles, as if caught
out in small sins. "You see," he said, "I am learning."

"Messier," said James. "Thomas, do you remember how often she wrote of an M., who seems to have broken her heart—
is this the man?"

Again, the apologetic smile. "I'm afraid not—Charles Messier was born in the eighteenth century, and gone to the worms
by Maria's day. He witnessed a Great Comet at the age of thirteen. This comet was visible by day to the naked eyes of the king
and his courtiers, and the farmers nearby and the beasts of the
field; and it's said that shortly after perihelion it developed six
tails that could be seen above the dawn horizon like an opening
fan." He was speaking happily in the same long well-punctuated
phrases in which he wrote, and the effect on James was the effect of the wine: he simply gave in. "Charles fell in love," said
Thomas, "and consecrated his life to the pursuit of comets. But
the skies are full of distant blurred objects that might be taken
for a comet, and like all astronomers he became prone to thinking he'd found what he loved, only to find he was mistaken. So
he set about making a catalogue of every galaxy and nebula it
was possible to view, and gave to airy nothing a local habitation
and a number. Have more bread while it's warm enough to melt
the butter."

"So this place here is not smudged," said James, examining
the paper again. "It is a cloud of light on a dark ground. But we

still have no idea who M. might have been, or what happened to Maria. Where is her body? Where is her telescope? I've seen the inventories. There's no mention of it. We ought to go back, and look."

"Yes," said Thomas. "We ought to go and look."

"And you say she wasn't mad," said James, considering historic charges against Maria Văduva in the light of fresh evidence. "But didn't she say she saw the devil at her window, and wanted to go out to meet him?"

"Not the devil," said Thomas, "but Lucifer. You notice she saw him in the morning? In the Latin, Lucifer means 'light bearer'; the equivalent in Greek would be Phosphoros, 'the bringer of the dawn.' So I think it is possible—are you sure you won't have more wine?—that what Maria saw was the planet Venus, which rises in the morning and is the dawn herald, and looks through even a decent telescope like an unfocused image of a pearl. And I wonder," he said, clasping his hands behind his head, and sighing—"I wonder if what her statue held was a telescope, and it's down there at the bottom of the lake."

James noticed the pale blue of the well-pressed shirt, and the narrow belt where it was tucked—suddenly the room was suffocatingly small and warm, its furniture creeping toward him across the carpet, the rank scent of the cheese and the exhausted tulips stirring his stomach. He felt his view of the day abruptly alter, as if he'd been hurled against the farther wall and forced to take a different view. He wanted to be in his office at the old town hall, he wanted to go home—his wife, he felt, would think fondly of them both: "You ought to take him out into the street," she'd say, "and stop a stranger and say, 'Do you see this man here, or is it only me?'"

Then Thomas returned to the table, and opened one of the green notebooks stacked there. "Let's examine our facts again. First, we know that Maria Văduva disappeared no earlier than

August 1888, when the photograph was taken at Bethesda. Second, that she had a telescope, and made a number of astronomical drawings, and that this telescope and most of her drawings are missing. Third, that she had a friend, C., who lived in London, to whom she sometimes wrote. Fourth, that her heart was broken, by this M., who perhaps loved a woman named Veronica, though we can't possibly hope to identify him. I suppose," said Thomas, frowning, "Maria's husband wouldn't have liked that."

James, laughing and relieved to be laughing, said, "I am sure he wouldn't! Husbands," he said self-mockingly, "can be very conventional where their wives are concerned." Here he received a look from Thomas so warmly complicit he was prompted to be brisk. "I'll take this," he said, putting the drawing in the file he'd brought, "it will be safe with me: I'll see it photographed, and catalogued, and treated as treasure. And there'll be more, there is bound to be more—perhaps even a diary. A body, if we are lucky."

"I almost hope," said Thomas (he was gathering plates; he was not looking at James), "we never come to the end of it, since that would be the end of the adventure—must you really go?"

"I must," said James, "or nothing will be done at Lowlands. I have to see to it we keep the house secure, before this woman burns it to the ground. Where is my coat? And is that the time, is it really?"

The fire in the grate ceded to ember. "This is the time. Let's walk together to town."

Thomas Hart, going down Lower Bridge Road with James at his side; Thomas lifting his face to the collapsing clouds. "It was good of you to come," he said. He did not say: please come back to me soon.

"My God," said James (they were approaching the old town hall, and dolorous music came from nearby), "is this your lot?" A group of men and women was standing by the war memorial. Last year's poppy wreath, wrecked by disrespectful weather, was rotting at the foot; the women and the men were singing. Thomas experienced that habitual longing for the sacred he never did shake off—there's the senior deacon (he thought this with love) and the pastor; there's Anne Macaulay in a new black hat. Then he saw, among the familiar faces with their familiar looks of patient piety, a woman in a full-skirted pink coat standing with her arm in Anne's. She was familiar with the queasy familiarity of something remembered from a dream. Her yellow hair resisted the wind that turned the pages of her hymn book, and as she sang she lowered her painted eyelids in pious sentiment. "I've seen her before," said Thomas, "walking with Anne through Lowlands Park, and I wondered—" He could not have explained to James how bizarre it was to see Anne Macaulay attach herself to a woman who might have been constructed like a mannequin to demonstrate every wicked thing Bethesda considered worldly. Her fine stockings strained over prominent ankle bones. The skirts of her coat blew open, and revealed the lower part of her thighs below a floral hem. "*There is a fountain filled with blood*," she sang, seeming on the verge of artificial tears, "*drawn from Immanuel's veins*"—and beside her Anne Macaulay, flushing with pride or humiliated courage, extended her hand to a careless passerby and gave him a gospel tract.

"Strange thing to be singing about," said James, "all that blood," but he was inclined to watch, and receded into the lobby of a shoe shop. Thomas, discovering with shame that he neither wanted to see or be seen, receded with him: "I suppose they are my lot. I suppose they will always be."

"*Behold, ye have sinned against the Lord*"—this was the

pastor cautioning the man coming out of the newsagent's rolling a cigarette, the schoolboys hassling each other by the burger van—meanwhile Anne and the senior deacon gave out their tracts imploring Aldleigh to flee from the wrath to come.

"Still," said James, looking at his watch, "nobody here seems to mind—I suppose they've seen it before. Now I must go"—but he frowned, and moved out from the awning to take a clearer view. "Did you see that? What's happening?"

Thomas saw the pastor flinch, feint left, and go on speaking; then there was the sound, distinct above the preacher and the crowd, of something striking the pavement. Looking in confusion for the source, Thomas saw—among the women with their shopping trolleys, and the girls swinging satchels from a single strap—a young woman standing some distance from the war memorial, holding a piece of cloth nailed to a length of wood pulled from a cargo pallet. This was a poorly made banner, already coming apart, and its message illegible. There was black paint on the wood and on the woman's clothes; her narrow body shivered with purpose.

"Is that her?" said James. "Is that the woman from Lowlands?"

"That's her," said Thomas. She held the banner in her left hand, and with her right took small stones from her pocket and threw them at the war memorial with a bad aim.

"Mad as a hatter, poor thing," said James, amused. "Now I really should go"—and meanwhile the woman in pink turned her back on Anne Macaulay and headed for the shelter of a phone box. Anne, valiant and uncertain, stood her ground. A stone landed by her shoe. She ignored it. Meanwhile people had begun to gather: "You tell them, love," said a man who nonetheless took a tract from the senior deacon with a nod of gratitude, "you tell them!"—but in fact the woman told nobody anything, only went on standing in the ecstasy of terror summoned out of the comet, and herself, and all the anxieties of a creature that had never asked to be born. "*From that time*," said the pastor, not looking up from his Bible, "*Jesus began to preach, and to say, 'Repent, for the Kingdom of Heaven is at hand.*'" He gestured to the cloud, which had taken on a greenish color. The woman shook her banner, but had no more stones to throw. The pastor said nothing, and did nothing, and there was the impression of an old religion and a new one ranged against each other, battling for all the souls of Essex. The greenish cloud darkened, and shrieking schoolgirls ran for shelter; again Thomas heard the crack of small stones on hard places, and saw it had begun to hail, pelting saints and sinners and raising glittering drifts on the steps of the war memorial. The altered air roused the woman with the banner: she bent her head and with the lowing noise of an agitated bull charged toward the place where the pastor stood. But he was now attending so closely to the word of God, and the noise of the hail hissing on the pavements was so great, that he failed to notice—"*They brought unto him all sick people*," he said, gravely intoning, "*and those which were possessed with devils, and those which were lunatic—*" Thomas, thinking he should avert an injury, stepped out of his hiding place toward the pastor, but at the last moment the woman altered her course and went running down the high street through the milling crowd, the banner showing overhead like a torn sail on a ship of fools. So relieved of his duty, and ashamed to be relieved, he returned to the shelter of the shoe shop: "It isn't really anything to do with me," he said, "these open-air meetings aren't something I've ever done"—but found he was alone. James Bower had gone, returned to the life of which Thomas knew nothing, and hadn't been able to guess.

Late March, late afternoon: the Great Comet hanging unseen somewhat north of the sun. The yellowish plume of its dust tail curved with the curve of its orbit, and a jet of bluish gas streamed out as straight as if it comprehended perfectly the laws of Euclid. Meanwhile Grace Macaulay, having turned eighteen in the small hours, surveyed her mirror with pleasure. She'd made her dress herself, and it was red as the rope the harlot Rahab had hung out of her window; but her face was bare, since no daughter of Bethesda would ever paint her mouth or eyelids like Jezebel (who ended up eaten by dogs, all save the palms of her hands and the soles of her feet). Grace, feeling at that moment she'd exchange an eternity of rest for a tube of lipstick, bit her lips to bring up the blood, and fell into desolation. It was her eighteenth birthday, and all she had at hand was a walk down by the Blackwater with her only two friends, and tea with her peculiar family. Other girls on days like these held parties to which they wore jeans, and scraps of fabric that showed their breasts and collarbones; where they drank until they were sick, and danced to wordless music; where everything was animated by sex, the sin that seemed to her a kind of necessity toward which she was helplessly moving. Some girls she knew danced at nightclubs in cages (nobody could explain to her why), and grew thin (it was said) on cocaine—others had terminated pregnancies they didn't want, or had tattooed moths or butterflies above their buttocks, and all this struck her as being both deplorable and glamorous, and the stuff of a life she'd never attain. But Grace had never danced, and always attended chapel with her head covered to make herself decent in the sight of God and men—I do want to be good, she thought, I do want to serve God, but what an effort it all is, and how tiring—though at least now it could be said she knew how to hold a cigarette and draw on it without choking, because God had made Nathan break Bethesda's window.

She heard her aunt calling from the foot of the stairs, as if detecting through floorboards the direction of her niece's thoughts; so flushing with shame Grace ran down, tripping on her hem, and hearing stitches tear in the seams.

Anne Macaulay smiled at the scarlet dress with shy affection. "They're here," she said. "They've come." Grace kissed her aunt out of duty, and saw Thomas upright on a dining chair, and Nathan beside him seeming almost to vibrate with the effort of remaining in his seat. "Hello," he said. He wore his glasses, and these obscured the color and clarity of his eyes and made him seem less remarkable, so that Grace felt the balance of power tip faintly in her favor. Laughing, she performed a curtsy, extending her small hand toward them.

"Happy birthday," said Thomas, "you wretched child." He was holding a leather box, and this was promising. "Is that for me?" she said.

"It is for you," said Thomas, watching her discover a gold ring, dented and thin, and set with small stones. Grace felt that if she'd ever seen another woman wear it, she'd have stolen it right off her finger. "That is the best thing I ever had," she said, giving Thomas one of her hard burrowing hugs; then having forgotten Nathan in her pleasure she sat cross-legged at her old friend's feet and leaned with thoughtless affection against his knee.

"It cost very little," said Thomas, fending off a troubled look from Anne, "but I happened to see it in London and the man had no idea of its worth. The stones spell out the word DEAREST—diamond, emerald, amethyst, and so on—because that is what you are." He delivered this tribute without embarrassment, then with diffident affection he patted Grace twice on the crown, as if she were a dog who'd pleased him.

"I didn't get you anything," said Nathan, with the good cheer of a sinner already absolved. "I forgot."

Then Ronald Macaulay came in with holiness in the pleats of his trousers. The atmosphere thinned, as if the room had been elevated nearer heaven. "Ah," he said, "Mr. Hart: you're taking these two to Aldwinter, I understand? Very kind." He didn't look at Nathan, whom he seemed to have accepted as he might have accepted a new piece of furniture he could tolerate but would never use. Then, "Journeying mercies," said Ronald, and with gratitude returned to his room.

"It isn't any trouble," said Thomas to Anne, who'd come in from the kitchen, "I've wanted to go for some time, and write about it."

"Have you told them?" said Anne. "Does she know what you're taking her to see?"

"I haven't got any idea," said Grace, turning and turning the ring. "Nobody tells me anything; I'm always, always in the dark."

"Come on, then," said Nathan, shrugging off the house like a coat, "let's go." He looked down at Grace and examined her dress as if he'd only just seen it. "You'll get mud all over that," he said. "You're really an idiot, you know."

They headed for the Essex coast, through industrial estates and shopping malls and plants for manufacturing farm machinery. In the passenger seat beside Thomas, Nathan searched for music never heard under Ronald Macaulay's roof, and behind him

Grace attended devoutly to the lyrics, and equally devoutly to the movement of Nathan's shoulders, and the tender place at the nape of his neck. I've fallen in love, she thought, that is what has happened. It is a disaster. It cannot end well—there's no way out of this that won't cause me pain—then there was a kestrel over the verge, and Thomas was delighting at it. "Look," he said, slowing the car, "the windhover." The kestrel stooped, and Grace's heart stooped with it; she was conscious of being hurled into feeling against her will. The silk cord she wore as a belt became abruptly too tight, and it was difficult to draw breath; she untied it, and tied it again. "Turn the radio off," she said, "turn it off, my head hurts."

"Not long now," said Thomas. Obedient Nathan turned the music off. They were passing through villages in which modern terraces were interposed between pink thatched cottages, and fields in which electricity pylons receded in ranks to a distant black point. Within minutes no more houses were in view, and it was bad weather on the Blackwater: slow brown river, marshes half-sunk. "Here we are," said Thomas. He'd brought them to a narrow road, terminating in fog that all day had been accruing in the ditches and hollows, and brought a muffling quiet. It's cold out here, thought Grace. Spring will never get this far.

"Anything could happen," said Nathan, grinning and untroubled. "A farmer might shoot us for frightening his pigs, and they'll have eaten our bodies by morning."

They came out of the car and stood under a dripping oak. "Thomas," said Grace, "did you get us lost?"

"Do you hear that?" said Thomas. "A curlew, I think, since they say it sounds like singing underwater—let's go. Don't you trust me?"

They began to walk. The thickening fog opened to admit them and closed in their wake. Grace discovered that in fact she didn't trust Thomas, and didn't trust Nathan, and certainly didn't trust the steep slick verges underfoot. She tried to draw a deep consoling breath, and found she couldn't, and a rootless panic set in. Nathan was walking into the dissipating mist ahead—look at him, she thought, the size of him: fear and delight ran through her like an alternating current, and the ring slipped on a finger made thin by cold.

"Now look," said Nathan, seeing nothing strange in all the world, "look," he said, "the sun's coming out." It was, and in the weak light he and Thomas were ordinary, and Grace was ashamed.

"Here we are," said Thomas. He spread his arms. "Here we are: Aldwinter, and the end of Essex."

Through receding fog Grace saw they'd arrived on a deserted village green, where long grass ceded to mud in wet black tracts. A handful of Victorian houses mutely regarded each other; behind these, new white bungalows huddled against the soil.

"Well, happy birthday," said Nathan. He pressed Grace with his shoulder. "Do you think there's a pub? I bet he drinks," he said, eyeing Thomas with his full eighteen years of worldly wisdom, "I bet he can handle it."

Grace surveyed the green. Mist disturbed the perspective: not possible to see how large the green was, or where it ended. Still—she stepped forward, and the obliging mist went with her—was it possible they were not after all alone? "Can you see that?" she said.

"It's just fog," said Nathan, "it's all just a lot of nothing"; and Thomas, some distance away, wrote something in his notebook.

"How can't you see it?" said Grace, feeling her temper slip. "How can you not see that?" She pointed to a place where the fog accumulated in the middle of the green, through which she made out a dark shape, high and irregular, with upper parts diminishing in mist, and a black mass spreading at the foot.

"Shit," said Nathan. "What's that?" He cupped his hands about his mouth and gave a kind of summoning yell.

"Stop that," said Grace, her temper now out of her hands. She walked toward the high black thing. It was the sole fixed point in a disintegrating world, and its stillness seemed that of a savage creature keeping itself in check—"Hello?" she said, thinking stupidly it was the man in Potter's Field, having taken off his scarlet coat and put a black one on, and grown incomprehensibly vast. "Grace?"—this was Nathan, or it was Thomas: they were one thing, quickly approaching. The sun came out, and drew the black object ahead out of the occluded air: a dark mass, with dark limbs extending either side and curving downward as if broken at the joints, and some pale hard protrusion pricking up out of it—so there's still giants in old Essex, Grace thought, doing away with deer to get horns for their crowns. "I told you there was something there," she said. The cord dropped from her waist into the mud, and she picked it up, and tied it again. "Didn't I tell you? Didn't I say?"

"I'd hardly have driven you all this way," said Thomas, "if there'd been nothing here."

"It's just a tree," said Nathan. "It's just some tree." No mist now. Late sun suspended in its decline; all things visible. "Just some tree," said Grace, standing now at the foot of an immense oak dying of time or some other malady. Its trunk was split open, and its upper limbs were bare as bones; here and there the lower branches looped into the soil and out of it, and were dying off or coming into bud. All this was quite ordinary, and hardly worth the journey's trouble; but "Look," said Thomas, pleased with himself, "do you see?"

Grace did see. Circling the trunk, in ranks two or three feet deep and lapped like the scales of a fish, were dozens of headstones removed from their graves. Some were wrecked by time and weather, their inscriptions overwritten by lichen and moss; others might have been propped there by the stonemason half an hour before. "*Called Home*," said Grace, circuiting the oak in a daze, and reading aloud where she could, "*Gone to Glory, Forever With the Lord*—get down from there, you'll break something."

Nathan, having jumped spring-heeled on to the shoulder of a broken angel, reached for a branch that cracked and complained. "What do you want on your grave, then?" he said. "What shall we write about you?"—the branch broke. He fell and righted himself, impervious to harm.

"You can bury me at sea," said Grace. "Oh look at this poor woman—*She Hath Done What She Could*. What a way to be remembered, that even your best was nothing much. But what is this, Thomas, why is it here—this dead tree, these dead forgotten people? What happened?" Her belt fell off again. She kicked it through mud, then tied it to a branch. It hung like a noose for a child.

"This is Traitor's Oak," said Thomas, "where Charles was said to have hidden from the law, though I doubt it, since Essex men and women were never really minded to kneel for the Crown." He chose a branch for a bench, and disposed himself and his coat on it. "This was a fishing village once, where they went down to the sea in ships and occupied their business in great waters, and what have you—past the green there was a quay, and in those days you'd see the oxblood sails of the old Thames barges going up the estuary with cargoes of oyster and grain, and a Saxon church with beasts carved on the pews."

"Beasts?" said Grace. "What kind?"

"I don't know. It's all gone now. The sea defences failed, back at the beginning of this century—so the tides came in too far, and they began to have trouble with the cemetery. The church warden would do his morning rounds and go picking seaweed from the headstones—"

"You're making this up. Nathan, truly, you can't believe a thing he says."

"—sea kelp and bladderwrack and once a flapping mackerel, which he took home and grilled for his breakfast. Then one winter, as the Great War began, and artillery was heard thumping over the Channel—"

"This is all lies—"

"—there was a high tide on a stormy night, and two graves flooded and their coffins burst, and the next morning the congregation had two new members, strange and thin, who never sang a word." Grace was laughing now, and she shoved Thomas with her animal affection. "This began to happen with such awful regularity," said Thomas placidly, "that in due course the bodies were disinterred and buried again near Colchester where it keeps decently dry, and the headstones were put here to remember them by. Look carefully and you'll find the last citizen of Aldwinter was buried here in 1921, with some interesting markings on the headstone."

"But why does nobody live here now?" said Nathan. "Where's the church? Where did they all go?"

"Some still live here," said Thomas, gesturing to houses and bungalows in which nothing and nobody moved, "because they can't bear to leave. But there's no work, and nobody wants to insure buildings on land so prone to flood. The church burned down and inch by inch the coast eroded, and now the whole thing's underwater, though they say at low tide it's possible to see the remains of the tower and the nave, and hear the old bell ringing."

"I don't believe you," said Grace, with a contradictory grin; and Nathan, never still, gleamed with possibility.

"I'm going," he said, "I want to look—come on, Grace,

don't you want to see if the tide's out? Don't you want to hear the bell?" He held out his hand. Grace looked at it, and her own hand lifted in response. Then she remembered her anger at the power he exerted over her happiness, and how unconsciously he exerted it; so she put her hands in her pockets, and shrugged, and delighted to see him flinch against this small refusal. "All right," she said.

Now the air was bright and clear, and the rim of Essex was nearer. Jackdaws were settling in Traitor's Oak, and down beyond the green there were curlews pacing in the shingle. "I'll follow you," said Grace. "You go on." So the woman and the man went down to the water, and Thomas Hart watched them go. Nobody spoke. Each was conscious of being absolutely solitary, and unsure of their destination.

Anne Macaulay was at home, wrapping gifts she'd bought for Grace. The first of these was a gift of duty: a volume of nineteenth-century sermons bound in oxblood leather, chosen with care by Ronald and inscribed "with love" in his neat inexpressive hand. The second had required diligent saving on Anne's part, and was a gold disk pendant engraved with XARIS, which was Grace's name in the common Greek and signified the undeserved favor of God. It was something beautiful and something good, leaving body and soul equally accounted for; so with a sense of a task done well Anne tied a narrow ribbon retrieved from a previous gift, and inscribed a single kiss on a card. She was surprised by the extent of her love for the girl, which had arrived late and often felt inadequate; all day the house had felt incomplete in her absence, its rooms too bare and too big. Lately her body had longed for that small, cross child, with a sense of physical need she'd always imagined was reserved for women who'd given birth; now the thought of one of those hard, burrowing hugs restored something to the day.

Downstairs the bell was ringing, and Anne was brought back to unease. This would be Lorna Greene, and not for the life of her could Anne remember how she'd come to invite the woman to her niece's party, only that perhaps it had struck her suddenly what a poor affair it would be otherwise—she took the gifts downstairs, and opened the door. "Darling!" said Lorna, lifting her cheek for a kiss. Her yellow hair was set in glossy curls, and her powdery scent was strangely like that of a baby; she was as small as Grace was small, but slight, so that in her presence Anne felt unformed and unwieldy. It was threatening rain. Anne quickly kissed her, and was kissed in return.

"Dear Anne," the visitor said, going unasked down the hall and into the dining room, "how pretty you've made it all." She took in the best white tablecloth, the primroses on the windowsill, the balloons already exhaling Ronald's breath and drifting on their garden twine—"And goodness," she said, blinking, "my word, look at that cake. I expect you did your best."

"Thank you," said Anne, who until that moment had indulged the sin of pride where the icing and the sugar roses were concerned.

"Not what you'd expect for an eighteenth birthday"—Lorna made adjustments to the cutlery, the folded napkins—"but I'm sure she'll be pleased. Mr. Macaulay," she greeted the man who'd come in silently, carrying a Bible with his thumb marking a passage, "your child has become a woman, and I am certain a virtuous one, with a price far above rubies."

The rain was holding off. Outside, the silver birch was motionless, and the sky deepened and cleared. Then Anne, whose spirits had sunk with the balloons, saw the birch leap in passing headlights: that was Grace, she thought, and Thomas Hart, and the boy that broke the window. "They're here," she said, going gratefully to the door, but already it was open and here was Grace hurling in. She'd lost her coat, and the absurd silk rope she'd been wearing as a belt; she was flushed and hectic-looking, as if she'd acquired a disease from the Blackwater.

"Aunt Anne," she said, "there you are—we've found a man, and brought him with us." Sound then of a slammed door, and familiar voices—"They're helping him now," she said, "they're coming." She saw her father gravely waiting in the narrow hall, and quickly became somber. "I hope I haven't done something wrong, but we couldn't have left him there."

"Gracious," said Lorna, arriving beside Ronald Macaulay. "Whatever have you been up to?" She moistened her lips with a delicate sharp tongue. Grace looked at her with something approaching contempt, which Lorna received with an unaltered smile, and another dart of her tongue.

Anne saw three men coming down the darkening drive. Here was Thomas Hart, upright and silent; here was Nathan, with his impatient onward gait. They had a stranger with them. He was a tall man, and thin, in a scarlet coat; and despite his drooping head he had a haughty look, like that of an emperor in the act of being deposed. He carried a satchel on his back. The other men drew him up the path.

"My goodness," said Lorna as the men came with difficulty to the door. "Do you think he is drunk?" She pressed a hand to her mouth, and her nails were hard and pink as shells.

Thomas looked placidly at her and with wary good manners said, "Hello."

"I found him," said Grace, as if to say: *he belongs to me.* "I found him living in Potter's Field. But we saw him walking on the verge miles out from Aldleigh and I recognized his coat, so we've brought him home." Possibly she'd expected praise for this show of goodness. None came. "Well," she said, looking about for evidence she'd sinned, "isn't it my birthday? Can't I do what I like?"

Anne said, "Bring him in." They did, and with difficulty sat him at the dining table. Roused by light, the man looked from face to face, and clutched the satchel. He spoke in long impassioned phrases that carried meaning through barriers of comprehension: he was grateful, they understood, but confused; he was tired, but neither sought nor required their pity.

Meanwhile the Great Comet, buffeted by solar winds, traversed the window trailing incandescent dust. Nobody saw it.

"He likes coffee," said Grace, patting the velvet shoulder, bringing up out of it the scent of an unwashed body, and of soil.

Lorna's mauve satin rustled. "There are institutions better suited to vagrants and drunks," she said. "Hostels, for example, and charitable causes."

Grace, with a level black look: "He isn't drunk. He's tired. Anyone would be tired who'd walked so far for so long." Again the cheap satin rustled. In a dark room, it would strike sparks.

Ronald Macaulay came forward with the look of a man incapable of an ungodly act. "No, he is not drunk," he said, "though I'm not sure that I'd throw him out if he were." He held out his hand. The stranger took it with astonishment; "Thank you," he said, and put his hands over his eyes. The satchel fell from his lap.

"He's probably going to cry," said Grace, bringing coffee to the table; then since it was her habit to sit on the floor she curled at the stranger's feet. "Look," she said, putting a hand on his knee with competent softness that astonished Anne, since it seemed to have been acquired in the hours she'd been away, "why don't you stay with us for a while. It's my birthday party, and I'm inviting you." She butted against his leg in easy thoughtless affection. "You can have something to eat, then we'll decide what to do." Her dress was red and so was the stranger's spreading coat, and Anne had the impression of a courtier at the foot of an ailing king.

"Yes," he said, "thank you." He fumbled with the coffee cup, and Anne saw with disquiet that his thumb seemed misplaced and loose, and his fingertips unfinished. She was transfixed by sympathy so intimate and direct it struck her as a variety of love, and because of this became brisk: "He should take his coat off or he won't feel the benefit."

With her satin rustle and powdery infant's scent, Lorna made herself known, and came to stand beside Anne with an expectant smile and pert sideways tilt of the head. "Oh, Mr. Hart," said Anne, "you haven't met Miss Greene. Miss Greene, this is our friend, Mr. Hart." Thomas and the woman looked at each other with the bankrupt politeness of politicians, and Anne, oblivious to Lorna's expression of secretive pleasure, said, "Ronald, perhaps you can give thanks, and we'll have something to eat?"

So Ronald, folding his hands, began to pray. Thomas Hart, not praying, now saw the diligent comet, and was the solitary witness. He saw, too, Anne frowning as she made her petitions to God; saw Lorna Greene raise and lower her pearly lids in a private assessment of the room and everyone in it. That acute attention reached Thomas, and remained there, and it seemed to him that she was making certain deductions that had never been made before in that room. There it was again, the perception of strangers—but this was not James Bower's smiling ease, it was a dreadful seeking-out, like the pricking of a witchfinder's pin. The man he was in London drew nearer and nearer, bringing other men in his wake: I'll be discovered, he thought, I will be known. He shivered, as if he stood under the shadow of the pulpit—now he saw Nathan in the corner, surveying Grace. Her badly made dress was slipping from her shoulder, her hands were folded in her lap; she frowned like her aunt as she followed the prayer. Nathan watched her with that same puzzled look that had come when she'd refused his hand in Aldwinter, and Thomas, understanding the boy had been inconvenienced by desire, both envied and pitied him.

"In Jesus name," said Ronald, "and for his sake: amen."

"Amen," said the stranger, and Ronald looked at him with solemn approval.

Grace and Anne together took the stranger's coat, and hung it in the hall, affecting not to notice the reek of the thing. Ronald directed him to a better chair: "You'd be more comfortable here, I think. Now," he said, "perhaps we might give Grace her gifts." But evidently this was the labor of women, and he receded from his daughter, and Anne came forward with the small present and the larger one, and said "Happy birthday" with a faint flush of shyness, as if afraid she might be contradicted.

"Charles Haddon Spurgeon," said Ronald as Grace opened the book. "Now: grow in the root of all grace, which is faith."

"Thank you," said Grace, "thank you." She stroked the book, and was moved by it. Then quickly she turned to the smaller gift, and having always been alert to beauty opened the gilded box with indecent haste, and dropped it, so that it took a moment to retrieve the gold chain from the carpet. "Oh," she said, examining the disk, and being a child of Bethesda knowing biblical Greek when she saw it. "Oh, is that my name? Thank you, thank you." She submitted to her aunt fastening the chain at the nape of her neck, and all the while beamed with uncontainable joy at everyone within view. "Isn't it beautiful? Don't you think it's the best thing you ever saw?"

"Very nice," said Lorna, flickering. "Such a lovely birthday. Still," she said, sighing and lowering her eyelids in sorrow, "there is a peculiar smell in here, most unfortunate. And dear Grace, I wonder if perhaps you ought to change your clothes. Did you make that dress? I thought perhaps you might have. How sweet. You've done ever so well. But you see: it's more or less falling off, and I am sure your father would like you to be decent. You won't mind my saying so. There's no side to me. I

speak as I find." She looked at Ronald with a pout of calculated prettiness, but discovered that he was attending to the
stranger. "Do we know his name?" he said. But they didn't,
and nobody liked to ask.

"Lovely little thing, isn't she?" said Lorna, taking her avid
blackbird's gaze to Nathan, and smoothing her satin skirt. "I'm
sure you've noticed." She put a white hand on his sleeve: "Men
do notice these things, don't they?"

Nathan looked ashamed of her, and of himself, and of
Grace, and of everyone in the small warm room. "Never
thought about it," he said.

"Not much of a party, either'—Lorna sighed and let out
gusts of her powdery scent—"does she have no friends at all?
Still, where two or three are gathered together, there is Christ,
in the midst."

Nathan glanced quickly at the door, as if the Redeemer might
have arrived in a taxi, delayed by the traffic, and ready to insist on
good behavior.

Time passed. "Happy birthday," they sang, in the full har-
mony every good Baptist learns in the chapel pew, and Grace
blew candles out, and the old foundling dined well on Anne
Macaulay's bread and butter. Now the comet was departing
the window, and Ronald, becoming playful, had turned the radio on, letting decorous music into the room. "Quite the young
lady now, isn't she, Mr. Macaulay," said Lorna to Ronald, cock-
ing her head, as familiar as if she'd been at Grace Macaulay's
cradle. "Grace, dear," she said, her well-modulated voice easily
penetrating the air, "now you are eighteen you must tell us
what you intend to do with the life ahead of you. Your aunt
tells me you're not an academic child; but perhaps you were
born to marry and have babies. That would be only natural,
really the most natural thing in the world." She rolled a giddy
hard eye at Nathan, who sank into the wallpaper. "Only

natural," she said again, and there was a pause, and every creature in that room understood themselves to be biped animals
enslaved by urges they could neither understand nor resist.
"Well," said Lorna—she sighed and smiled: it was all giving
her pleasure—"I'm sure your father only wants you to be
happy."

"Happy?" said Ronald, with the inflection of a man trying
out a foreign language. "I've never given any thought to happiness. I only pray she becomes a servant of her Heavenly
Father."

"I think I want to be like Thomas," said Grace. "I don't mean
writing, only that I want things to exist in the world because I
existed to make them. It would make me happy to know that I
left a mark."

"And we think Mr. Hart is happy, do we?" Lorna's voice was
sweet as a robin's. The whole room surveyed Thomas, and
doubted it.

"It's better to hope for contentment," said Anne, "than
happiness."

"Never emulate me, Grace," said Thomas, laughing. "I spend
my life doing the only thing I have ever felt was worth doing,
and because of this I wake each morning a failure, living in this
gap between what I want to achieve and my capacity to achieve
it. That's writing for you," he said, "nothing but spoiling things
by touching them."

"Then can't you stop trying?" said Nathan, looking at
Thomas with the same bewildered expression with which he'd
first entered Bethesda.

"I could," said Thomas. "Perhaps I will."

Lorna meanwhile had come close to Ronald, so that her
hard fair head was at his shoulder. "Oh Mr. Macaulay," she said,
sighing, as if perceiving some sorrow in the offing, "whatever

are you going to do with her?" She murmured and flickered her eyes; but Ronald's attention was still on the stranger.

"I was thinking what we ought to do with him," he said, taking in the vagrant's pleasure in the warm room, and the cake disintegrating on its plate. "Providentially, this afternoon I prepared a sermon on the words of Christ when he said: *for as much as you do it to the least of my brethren, ye do it to me.*"

"The very least," said Lorna. "I wonder what he has in that bag? Stolen goods, I shouldn't wonder." She came still nearer. Her satin skirt whispered as she moved. "Did you see the state of his hands? I've seen such injuries before in drunks, and fighting men."

Now Grace was showing the old man the ring on her finger—"*Dearest*, that's what it says, and that's me."

"Grace," said Ronald, in the admonitory voice he deployed in the pulpit; evidently he felt the evening should be brought to a close. But Thomas Hart was putting on his coat, and coming to speak to Ronald. "I'll take him home with me," he said. With deliberate bad manners he had his back to Lorna.

Grace looked quickly at him. "Yes," she said, "you take him, and put him in your lovely house. Isn't it good of Thomas," she said, and Ronald conceded that it was.

Lorna's face, which had altered as Thomas had supplanted her, reassembled itself into sweetness. She appeared now at Ronald's other side, and put her small hand in the crook of his elbow in a gesture that astonished him into silence. "Yes," she said, her gleaming eyelids lowering as she took in Thomas with her terrible assessing gaze—"yes, I should think that will be very nice for you, Mr. Hart," she said. Her voice reached them all—the comet attended closely at the window; she patted rolls of hair that had been unmoved all night. "You will like that, I expect"—she was smiling—"I should think you rather like the company of men. What a treat: another man about the house!"

Anne Macaulay looked down at her cake, and didn't want the broken roses with her thumbprints on them. The vagrant was sleeping. Ronald, for whom the world was paved with sin, saw no hazard at his feet. "Well," he said, "it's getting late."

"What do you mean?" said Grace. With difficulty, because her feet were tangled in her skirts, she rose from the floor, and looked at Thomas, who was having difficulty with his gloves.

"This isn't something you ought to trouble yourself with"— Lorna looked steadily up at Ronald—"but I would surely have thought—" The end of her sentence, not spoken, hung above the dining table. "There's no side to me," she said again, her small mauve body seeming to have grown smaller and more dense, and her greasy eyelids half-lowered. "When the right- eous give way to the wicked," she said, picking at something under her nail, "it is like polluting a well."

"Why are you even here?" said Grace, interposing herself between Thomas and the woman. "You don't belong here— you don't belong with us at all."

Lorna Greene shrugged, and the satin hissed in her armpits. "If you read your Bible," she said, "you'll know that evil com- munication corrupts good manners—"

"What are you talking about?" said Grace, bewilderment amplifying her anger. "If he is evil so am I, and so are you, and so are we all—just go away. Go away! None of us want you here."

Lorna placidly drew her cuffs over her wrists. "Such a pleas- ant evening," she said, "so delightful to take fellowship with you all. Dear Anne! It's getting late, and I rather think Grace has worn herself out and become overexcited, as children so often do."

But Anne saw painfully that the child she'd come to love

was gone, and that now she was required to learn to love this stranger who'd come back from the Blackwater and taken her place. "Must you go?" said Anne, doing nothing to forestall the woman moving to the door. "Must you really go?"

"I must," said Lorna, "but so look forward to seeing you all again." She kissed Anne, her lips rustling as her silk rustled, her yellow hair unmoved. "God bless you," she said, drifting through the open door, dispensing words meaningless in their repetition; and as she reached the doorstep she turned, and directed a last level look at the window, through which it was possible to see the vagrant standing in his scarlet coat, and raising his arms as if seeking an embrace.

"Tell me your name," said Thomas Hart, "since I have told you mine." He'd left the party with the stranger, and taken him from there to Potter's Field. Here they'd untied the tarpaulin from the hazel tree, and rolled up the carpet underneath it, and all the while the jays had been remarking on the lateness of the hour. Then Thomas had taken the stranger home, and finding him biddable and childlike had put him in the bath, and washed him without difficulty or embarrassment. He'd wiped filth from his back and buttocks, and from his starved armpits; he'd discovered old wounds ulcerating on ankles damaged by bad boots, and doused these in boiled water in which he dissolved a teaspoon of Maldon salt; he'd clipped the hair back to the sunburned scalp, and found things living in the clippings, and put them in the kitchen bin. All this had caused the man to weep into the bathwater.

"When I was young," said Thomas, pouring rose oil into a second change of water, "the boys and men I knew began to get sick, one after the other. Nobody knew where the sickness came from, or what to call it, only that it came to men like me. They became thin. There were black marks on their bodies, like the print on the fur of leopards, and a kind of white fungus grew in their mouths until it was difficult to eat—the newspapers called it the gay cancer, and preachers on street corners and in Bethesda's pulpit said we deserved it. Did we deserve it? I could tell you their names. I could tell you how they lived." Grief Thomas thought long accommodated struck him violently, and before him passed the dispensing chemist, horn player, failed architect, teacher of Romance languages, plasterer, bad cyclist, schoolboy, exhausted proprietor of a Wanstead café, all in the end wanting a pillow between the knees for comfort lying down, and a small view of birds. "A boy I knew died the week he should have taken his A levels, and his family hadn't wanted him saved—so it was left to his friends to do the work of his nurse and his mother, and I learned there really are such things as the death rattle, that death will eat a man like a pack of wolves in the night. After that I wasn't only ashamed of myself, I was afraid."

The man in the bath submitted dumbly to the story and the water, and Thomas, divining in his silence neither censure nor incomprehension, said, "Tell me, then—what do you think? Did he deserve to die at eighteen because he was homosexual? Do you think me evil—that I corrupt my friends by talking to them? Do you think God withholds destruction from the liar and the murderer but constructs a virus, in some celestial laboratory, to torment men like me—that my sin is greater than all the other sins that pass without notice? There is no sense in it, and they would have me think God a god of reason." Thomas heard that he'd become plaintive, and felt ashamed of himself.

The stranger in the bath shook his head with such sorrow it took in the whole world. Then Thomas, having lifted him easily enough out of the water, dried the old body, and put lotion on cracked and swollen hands; then having given him pyjamas

and put him in a chair beside the fire and the leaping marigolds he said, "Now tell me your name."

Pretending indifference to the stranger's refusal, Thomas
went out to the kitchen. He heated milk with vanilla sugar in a
copper pan, and brought it to the table in glasses. "Whatever it
is," he said, "and whoever you are, you needn't be ashamed. It
wouldn't take much to bring anyone to where you've been. A
bad landlord, say. A leg that broke and wouldn't set, too much
trust in bad advice, a mortgage unattainable by half a per cent,
and there we are: there I might be." (Thomas in fact did not
quite believe this, but wanted to be kind.)

The man reached for his glass of milk, then seeming to note
his own hands for the first time flinched, scowled, and withdrew. "I'm very tired," he said. "Can't you put me in a bed?" He
reached for the satchel, which all evening he'd kept nearby,
and his clumsy movements dislodged an empty bottle, followed by a packet wrapped in white cloth. Reaching after these
he knocked his useless thumb against the chair; then cursed at
length in his own language and reverted once again to tears.

"Let me," said Thomas. He put the bottle and the parcel on
the table. The parcel carried the sour sweetness of the vagrant's
body, together with a note of turned soil. Thomas examined it.
"But this is a book," he said.

"It is. You be careful." The man examined the bottle, and
when he found it empty swore again.

Thomas pulled at white cloth wrapping that came easily
apart, and found a dark book bound in leather, with a broken
spine. Lamplight picked out the title gilded on the cover, and
Thomas, leaning forward, read the word aloud: "*Amintiri*," he
said, "do I have it right?"; and in the corner of the room, certain shadows thickened in certain places, and took on the
form of black skirts being shaken out: Maria Văduva was clearing her throat.

The stranger laughed in delighted contempt, and said the word three times with a cadence Thomas could never have predicted. "This means memories, or perhaps you might say: recollections. It is Romanian, which is my own language. I found it by the place where I have slept, in a box which is broken up. It's been my company." Reverently he opened the cover and showed the title page that had resisted soil and time. He drew his finger down it: "*Jurnalul Stelelor al Maria Văduva*," he said. "You might translate this into English as: *The Star Diary of Maria Văduva*."

Thomas made a wordless exclamation and spilled the last of his milk.

The stranger frowned. "This is upsetting for you?"

"Forgive me," said Thomas. "It's just that these days it is all both absolutely surprising, and entirely to be expected." (Maria—frowning specter, companionable ghost—picked pearls from the hem of her skirt, and muttering, returned to the shadows.)

"You expected this book—you know this woman." Statement, not query.

"She's an old friend of mine."

"But she is certainly dead."

"She is certainly dead. But when, and why? It's a mystery." Thomas was conscious of the sensation of an igniting flame in his stomach—Just you wait, James Bower! Just you see what I've got for you now! He leafed through the book: inscrutable diary entries made in a familiar untidy hand, star fields sketched in circles of black ink. "Though perhaps now we've solved it, if you tell me what all this means."

"Perhaps I will. But first give me a drink that is not milk. I'm not a child."

"I'll give you whisky," said Thomas, "to help you sleep, but no more than this"—he poured a godly measure, and put the bottle back—"then I'll tell you my mystery if you will tell me yours. Fair's fair."

The stranger inclined his head, and Thomas felt he'd successfully petitioned a stubborn king. It was midnight. The comet had begun to rise again, and Maria Văduva in her chair by the window sat in pitying silence.

"Give me more to drink," the stranger said. "I ask not for pleasure, but for necessity. My name is Richard Dimitru Dines." He held out his glass. "I was a man of God once. More than that, Thomas. Too much will not be enough."

Thomas, listening as the stranger spoke, began at first to write with the acquisitive interest of the writer; but after a minute or two put down his pen. That had been a trespass. The only moral thing was to listen, and bear witness to these bare facts: that Richard Dimitru Dines, whose mother and sisters had called him Dimi, had been a pastor in a church in Bucharest when such a thing was deemed enmity against the state; that officials had stood each Sunday on the church steps and taken a register of every member of the congregation, down to the newborn babies; that in time he'd been taken from his apartment and accused of sedition and treachery, and kept sixty feet under the city of his birth, in a silent jail where guards wore felt slippers to conceal their arrival at the cell door.

"Then they take you to a room," said Dimi, whose body shook the chair he sat in, "and in that room you see what is being done, and feel it carefully and exactly—but you cannot believe it, because to believe it would make you insane, like the men who carried it out are insane. They took such great pains with my hands."

Thomas looked for the comet in the window, and couldn't find it.

"Now you are thinking," said Dimi, "that God abandoned me to the cell and the hammer, and so I abandoned him. But this is the truth, and it is not so easy to forgive: God was a very present help in trouble, and when trouble ended so also did the help. Eight years they dismantled me as a bad child dismantles a doll. Then the government fell and the West came East, and when I was brought up into daylight again I was blind for a week, because it was all brightness then, the cars too loud, the young people dancing to music in another language. I went back to the pulpit. Every week the congregation was smaller. You cannot serve God and Mammon, you see? I began to hate them. Also I did not sleep."

He could not sleep, said the stranger, and this had been maddening: in the small hours he'd walk the streets wringing his hands as best he could, and find he'd arrived at the prison gates as a dog might return to a violent home. When he read his Bible the print bled and he could make no sense of it. When he prayed he felt only the sensation of knocking his forehead against a pane of glass. His small congregation drifted elsewhere: now the church was possibly a café, or a library, or a shop, and what difference did it make? "Sometimes in a river you will see a branch," he said, "or thing thrown in that must go where the river goes. So I am washed up. So here I am."

"But don't you think this is the way for us all?" said Thomas, concealing his pity. "Though I never see a river—I see the motion of bodies in orbit, drawn by forces as bright as the sun, and other forces completely unseen. Perhaps you saw the chapel by Potter's Field and it drew you down your orbit—so perhaps you still feel the heat of the sun of God."

"Perhaps," said Dines. Then he looked at the other man as if he'd attained his pulpit again, and seen Thomas down in the pew. "How is it for you?" he said. "I think perhaps you are a man with his back to the sun."

"My trouble," said Thomas, "is that I have two suns, and

neither outshines the other. In Bethesda I'm the worst of sinners, and in London I'm the strangest of saints, and I am never
comfortable anywhere. Now go to bed, old man, I'll help you up:
there's time for my mystery tomorrow. Then I'll tell you about
James Bower, and the knowledge of strangers, and how we
hunt Maria Văduva down."

Morning. No sun, no stars: the 6:23 to Liverpool Street rattling the windows in their frames, dawn seeping over Lower
Bridge Road. Richard Dimitru Dines woke astonished to find
a glass of water within reach, and drank this by bending and
putting his mouth to the rim, because at such an early hour his
hands were bad. The mattress and sheets were astounding to
him, the sheepskin rug awaiting his feet was a miracle. Silence
in the house. The radiators ticked. The pain receded. Soon he
sat up against the pillow and sought out his companion in the
broken book. So Maria Văduva regarded him from the foot of
the bed, cleaning a lens with a soft pale cloth, and the hem of
her skirt was thick with silver thread: *All day a warm wind
blew*, she said, *so I went down to the place where the men were
building and found them all gone . . .*

Lowlands House
29 JULY 1888

Lucifer comes every morning at dawn—arrives like a lover at the window—so I go running out and can never get near—it seems to me nothing but a photograph of a pearl taken out of focus—then I think of M., and how also I could come no nearer him than if he were contained with the lens of the telescope—and I fall into my old habits of love—which are humiliating to me—

Bad weather by night. Essex enclosed in cloud as in a coffin—as I am enclosed in my petticoats of lawn, my silk and garnets, my casings of wallpaper, tapestry, plaster, and brick! Late in the evening I read the *Iliad*—I think I should have made as good a soldier as a sinner—I should have stood on the battlements like Hector and faced the spear of Achilles with a laugh behind my shield—let me first do some great thing before I die, that shall be told among men hereafter!

19 AUGUST

All day a warm wind blew. So I went down alone to the place where the men were building and found them gone, and the mortar drying on the bricks. What dour God might consent to dwell in such a place? It is all hard and gray and no beauty in it. As I stood men and women came and sang their hymns on the lawn—their voices were sweet, and I was moved against my conscience and my disposition!—I hid behind the garden wall and heard them pray for sinners. I think I would have been a sinner had I ever had the chance—

Then a rare black glittering night that had me reeling as if drunk—I turned my face to the sky and saw the Perseids had begun and were piercing Orion and Cassiopeia—filaments and spurs of light, and this light an absolute untainted white—few at first—then in due course such volleys I thought they might very well cut me where I stood, so that poor John Bell would come to the terrace at the appointed hour and find me in ribbons—and the moon in its last quarter, drifting through the field of view, like the sail of a ship bellied by strong winds—

C. asked me once why I put myself to such troubles—is it for the pleasure of knowledge, she says, so that my name will be known among men? I told her that it was, that men ought never to think the skies are in their possession for all that they parcel and barter the land—but I lied. What do I care for the commendations of men? What ought I to do with their respect? It is all done for one man—so that I might bring down the stars and hurl them at his door, so that he opens it for all the knocking!

Morning on Lower Bridge Road, the house taking in its solitary hour of sun: scent of good coffee, and of toast; scent of tulips sorrowing over the lip of their vase. Vagrant light passing over the diary with its broken spine, and arriving at the sheets of paper on which Dines was bringing Maria Văduva into English: *I would have been a sinner*, he'd written, *had I ever had the chance.*

"When I phoned to tell him," said Thomas, "I said he was welcome any time, and that the later he came, the more Maria he could read, since you were hard at work." Dimitru put a hand on a stomach that swelled under borrowed clothes: a day or so in the company of Thomas Hart would fatten any man to contentment.

"We should give him something good to eat," said the old man, having already acquired the comforts of a sitting tenant. Rising from his seat, he asked if by any chance there was yeast in the house, and flour, and fresh eggs; if Thomas could possibly find some jam. Thomas did have yeast. He had plum jam, and a dozen eggs; and so Dines, seated on a kitchen stool, directed Thomas to the manufacture of the pastries he'd liked best as a boy, which (he said) resembled the crown of the last Romanian king, who left his throne to wring the necks of chickens on a provincial farm. When all this was done, and the pastries were dredged in sugar and cooling on the rack, the men worked together in silence for a time among the books and papers and the planisphere; though Thomas found all his attention fixed on the pavement beyond the window, and his hopes resting on the sound of the garden gate.

Meanwhile James Bower, coming under the dripping railway bridge, stood at the corner of Lower Bridge Road and shivered. There was Thomas Hart, he thought, two hundred yards down there, concealed in that house arrested in time, with its curtains which were never drawn, and the purple acers coming into bud—there also was a further piece of Maria Văduva, disinterred from Potter's Field. He was conscious again of the two conflicting sensations that arose if he ever thought of Thomas. These ought to have canceled each other out, but never did: the man intrigued and puzzled him equally, with his elegant demonstrations of friendship and his occasionally complicit-seeming smiles. If ever he put himself to the trouble of thinking what distinguished Thomas from other friends of his, he struck a hard place that prevented his going any further, because this would be difficult and inconvenient and if nothing else (here was the house in view) Thomas Hart redeemed him from boredom, which was his old besetting sin. "We are pals," he assured himself cheerfully, "we are pals"—and there was Thomas coming to the door and seeming no more pleased than he ought to have been, if certainly no less.

"Now then, James," he said, bringing him to a chair, "I must introduce you to my good friend. This is Richard Dimitru Dines, though he says we should call him Dimi. Give me your coat and have one of these—Dimi says they're shaped like crowns, though I can't see it myself, can you? Then we'll show you what we've found." The room was warm. Apples circled an orange on the table. Hyacinths bloomed out of banks of moss in bowls on the windowsill, and their perfume was that of a woman who'd left in a hurry.

"Welcome," said the imperious vagrant, inclining his head, "I am pleased to meet the friend of Thomas." He wore a sweater of fine green wool, and slippers lined with sheepskin: he smelled of soap and whisky. With difficulty he lifted the plate of pastries, and James took one of these, and broke it. "Thomas tells me," he said, "that you found the book in Potter's Field?"

"Yes. I found it." (Impression here of pride: of having overseen the whole problem of Maria Văduva from the first.) "I saw it shining in the mud. The wall was badly made, and moved, and there underneath I saw a metal box. A casket," said Dimitru, selecting the word, and admiring it and himself, "a casket as you might use for bones."

"Yes," said Thomas. "We disturbed her grave. No wonder she haunts me now!" He nodded as if in greeting toward the corner of the room, where nobody sat, and certainly nobody raised a straight black brow.

James wiped sugar from his fingers. "Well, then," he said. "Why don't you show me?"

So the diary was opened on a shallow cushion to preserve its damaged spine, and Dines, touching with reverence the gilded title, said, "I have reached the summer of 1889. You see, I have made a translation. I make quick work of it. I understand she was not a happy woman: she did not have the trick of happiness, as some do not have the trick, for example, of folding up their tongue."

Carefully James Bower turned the pages of the diary, and unable to decipher the entries looked instead at the drawings interspersed throughout. "How obvious it is," he said, "and how stupid we were not to have guessed. See here, Thomas, the phases of the moon—here a galaxy, I suppose, like water going down a plug—"

"Andromeda," said Thomas: "Messier 31, and our nearest neighbor, which they once called the Little Cloud—"

"And this is Romanian, then. I've never seen it," said James, "never met a Romanian. I would have thought it was Italian." He attempted a word or two.

Dimitru laughed. He ate a pastry. "I implore you," he said, "as much as you pity an old man: leave my language alone. Have my people not endured enough? Now you will ask me what I know of this woman. I should tell you that she is clever, as you see. I have said she is unhappy. Well, clever women are always unhappy. When she is not unhappy, she is all a kind of stupid joy. She is rich. She complains of her broken heart, but keeps it like a pet and wouldn't mend it if she could. My mouth is quite dry." He rolled a bright eye at Thomas, who with a sigh, and indicating that here was a familiar transaction to which he submitted against his better judgment, reached for a bottle and poured the guest a measure. "Out with it," Thomas said.

"Look here," said Dimitru. "See how the writing on this day is hurried. Did her hand shake? You see the ink. Perhaps the pen broke here. Thomas, give me more. Now I can tell you. This is what she has written: *I believe the big thing*—no, I will perhaps make an amendment—*I believe the great thing that I have longed for has happened at last*—then she speaks of love, and so on." The glass was empty, the room was warm; he yawned immensely. "Now I want to sleep."

"A great thing she longed for," said Thomas, "and she speaks of love? This M. of hers, I suppose, come to Essex to tell her he was mistaken, that in fact he did love her, that he couldn't imagine what he'd been thinking—Dimi, are you tired of us already?"

James saw the old man's head drooping now, as if some essential mechanism had failed. "Shall we let him sleep?" said

Thomas, smiling with that curious complicit look, so that the warm room with its perfumed air became abruptly intimate. "Shake him," said James, "go on, wake him up." For a moment the men eyed the sleeping stranger, and the noises of the neighborhood came in. A woman desperate with domestic irritation was shouting just beyond the window—"Get back in here," she said, "just you get right back in here"—and this startled Dines awake. He looked bewildered around the room, seeming to make no sense of the men, the table with the notebooks on it, the woman shouting at the window. "What have you done with me?" he said. "What have you been doing?"

"Dimi," said Thomas, "it's all all right. Everything is all right, and has been for a long time."

"Don't do it," said the old man, "please don't, don't let them again." He huddled in the chair with his arms raised above his head, and Thomas came forward. "Dimi," he said. "Come on, now. See this table, these chairs? See the sun trying to come in? It is spring in Essex. It's half past one in the afternoon. Stand up, stand with me"—his arms were under the old man's arms, bearing the weight—"there's nothing to you, old man. There's nothing to you at all. I won't be long," he said, turning to James at the door. "I won't be long—will you wait for me?"

James Bower, waiting between empty chairs, felt uneasy in the absence of the other men. Every nearby object was too large and highly colored, the scent of the tulips stagnant as that of a pond. He turned the pages of the notebook—"*Let me first do some great thing before I die*," he read aloud; and oh yes, he thought, yes, me too! He looked about, expecting to find himself in company after all: Maria Văduva descending from the ceiling as if on ropes, deranged with all her unwanted love, pearl beads dropping from the hem of her skirt.

"Sorry about that," said Thomas, returning to the room.

"He is never entirely here; he is always in part down there, and sometimes so far down he can't be reached. Don't go yet, will you? Don't go. The coffee is still hot."

"He has worked hard on this," said James, looking again at the notebook, "and ought to be paid. But see how he stops just here, as if to taunt us!"

"He taunts us, and so does Maria. But all the same," said Thomas, pushing the notebook away, "more and more I understand what caused her to love the stars as much as she loved the man who didn't love her—see these apples, this orange? I try to teach myself interactions of the planetary orbits, and as soon as I grasp the mechanics it slips from my grasp. It is all so strange, so much more surprising than I knew—shall I tell you what I've learned about the moon?"

"Yes, please."

"They say it once turned much faster on its axis, but the relation of forces between the earth and the moon made it slow down, and in the end the time it took the moon to make one full turn was the time it took to circuit the earth, and a lunar day was the same as a lunar year. They call this tidal lock, which is the influence of the earth and the moon on each other. We might say the sun rules the earth, and the earth rules the moon—but the moon isn't helpless, it has power, too! So we have the tides, and even the ground rises up as the moon passes over: certainly one body is stronger, but the weaker one is not without effect. And I've been told the earth's rotation is also slowing down, so that eventually one side will eternally face the same side of the moon, and half the world will never see the moon at all—oh," he said (James glanced at his watch, and noted the hour with a frown), "I'm Scheherazade forestalling the executioner, and you have work to do."

"I notice the moon these days," said James Bower, "and

never did before. Yes, I should go; but we'll come back to this when Dimitru has finished his work, and we know what Maria found, and where she went. Then you'll get a book out of it, Thomas, you mark my words"—he was headed for the door—"you'll get a book out of it, and your best work, and you can dedicate the thing to me."

The following Sunday being Easter, every church in Essex prepared to celebrate the resurrection of the Son of God. In the cathedrals of Chelmsford and Brentwood, nervous choirs assembled in their stalls, and the clerestories made their hallelujahs ready; in the cold stone temple of St. Peter-on-the-Wall, white tulips were cut for white vases on white altar cloths, and half a mile around the headland the white reactors of the Magnox nuclear power station had the look of empty tombs where giants had been buried.

Bethesda Chapel, the old dissenter, had no use for Easter. It rejected the sacred calendar with the vigor of Martin Luther slapping a communion wafer from the hand of a priest, and gave to Easter all the attention it gave to Christmas, which is to say: none at all. But it happened that this was also the day of the pastor's anniversary, and since he'd stood in that pulpit for thirty years, it was not quite an ordinary sabbath. "There'll be a service of thanksgiving in the afternoon," said Thomas, cleaning the red velvet coat with mineral spirits, "and then we will have tea, and a service in the evening. You needn't come," he added, mindful of the old man's shame and doubt, "you can stay and keep Maria company."

Dimitru said, "I do not mind. But do you?"

Thomas attended to a button coming loose. "If you think I'll be kept from the pew by that woman's malice, you are

wrong. The more you send me away from the pew the more I
want to sit in it, and the more I'm told to forsake the world the
more worldly I become. So you see, I don't expect ever to be a
happy man—get up now, and put Maria down, or the sermon
will have already begun."

The two men found the chapel changed in the good spring
weather. The colored disks in the window were liquid and
bright, and wind from the west agitated the air. Seagulls blown
in from St. Osyth and Walton-on-the-Naze went screaming
over the roof; a fair was going on in Lowlands Park, and the
blithe cheer of the waltzers could be heard above the old
harmonium.

They were late. The milky chapel lights were shining on
their iron chains. The pews were full, the godly having come
from as far as Prittlewell and Aldwinter and Suffolk to be
grateful for the preservation of the saints in general, and of the
pastor in particular. As they entered some heads turned, and
took in the familiar man and the unfamiliar one with brief impassive smiles, then went back to the pulpit. Dines sat clasping
his satchel and surveying the chapel without apparent distress.
Beside him, opening with rote piety his Bible and his hymn
book, Thomas surveyed the women and girls with their heads
decently covered in straw hats or dark felt cloches, and the
dozen men and boys in their best black suits. There was Lorna
in a thin white blouse that showed the hard elaborate casing of
her underwear; there was the senior deacon going solemnly
into the pulpit: *"Be perfect,"* he read, squinting at the lectern,
"be of good comfort, be of one mind, live in peace." The women
had gone down early that morning to clean, raising dust that
still came streaming from the gallery, and Thomas imagined it
all to be astronomical, dispersed from the rings of Saturn and
settling in the leaves of his hymn book. Suddenly he was struck

by the obliterating knowledge of his smallness: but none of it matters one bit, he thought, leaning dazed against the back of his pew—how hard we try, and what are we but ants on a stone in a river going to the sea? Then they were on their feet, singing—"*Oh the deep deep love of Jesus, vast, unmeasured, boundless, free*"—and Thomas thought of other loves, which had been neither boundless nor free, but much nearer to hand than the love of God. He looked up to the gallery, and there was Grace Macaulay leaning on the ledge above the clock, in a dress of stiff pale blue fabric that buttoned to the neck and made her matronly. There too (Thomas was startled, and his exclamation was covered by the hymn) was Nathan, whose shirt and tie made him seem a boy lost in borrowed clothes. They were alone up there, in the box pews that could be fastened with a latch, where once when Thomas was young he'd found a note pushed between the seat and the arm of the pew—*Let him kiss me with the kisses of his mouth*, the note had read, and troubled him for weeks. Then the pastor was speaking, and everything under Bethesda's roof was pale, cool, serene— the walls that gave off the chill of brick and plaster, the vaulted ceiling and the moony lights, the cloth on the communion table, were all as still and white as if under a frost. Thomas saw the lights of the fair coming through the window behind the pulpit, and distantly he made out the bass of pop songs bizarre against the chapel quiet, and bells ringing as prizes were won and money was lost. "To the glory of God," said the pastor, "amen"; then the harmonium drew a difficult breath for the last of the hymns, and Thomas Hart stood with the congregation. He turned to look up at the gallery again: Grace had put down her hymn book. Neither she nor Nathan stood as they ought to have done or sang as they ought to have sung, but leaned on the balcony, facing each other and speaking quietly. Grace had taken off her hat. How could Thomas have explained to those going down to the fair, to the passengers in the cars idling at the traffic lights on London Road and the children peeling foil from their Easter eggs by the light of television screens, how indecent and defiant this was? She was a woman bareheaded in the house of God, and might as well have raised her skirt to her thighs—then with deliberate gestures he'd never seen before she piled up her hair and let it fall, and did it again. Ahead of him, three pews down, Lorna's white hat quivered. She turned, her nose moving like an animal scenting the air; she looked up and saw Grace. She lowered and raised her gleaming eyelids, then looked carefully at Thomas, smiling her knowledge and her satisfaction. Then the hymn was over, and the harmonium's last note faded among the hanging lights. "*Now unto him who is able to keep you from falling,*" said the pastor, leaning on the lectern, "*and present you faultless before the presence of his glory with exceeding joy*"—and Thomas thought: the difficulty is that some of us would prefer to fall.

"Amen," said the pastor.

"Amen," said the congregation.

Thomas said, "Amen."

The worshippers came out of chapel darkness into ordinary light, and greeted each other in holy friendship saying what an encouragement the sermon had been, and wasn't it a blessing that spring weather had come; then they retreated to the dim cold hall behind the chapel, and took their places at trestle tables covered with white cloths. On each of these a silver tea urn stood. There were cups and saucers of a pale institutional green, and sandwiches of banana and stewed dates between slices of thin brown bread; there were sausage rolls releasing grease, and a kind of sweet iced tart nobody ever saw elsewhere, and which was as particular to Bethesda as the hymns and the harmonium. The air was fragrant with sugar and tea, and the congregation sang a grace that battled the noise of the fair. Thomas dispensed tea, and was the only man in Bethesda who'd ever think of doing so.

Dimitru meanwhile concealed his hands in the folds of his red coat, and told whoever would listen that yes, he was the man who'd lived for a time in Potter's Field, with jays and foxes for his neighbors—that in fact he was Romanian, and missed the city where he was born (nobody but Thomas saw him take imploring nips from a bottle concealed in the satchel with Maria).

Nearby Grace and Nathan wrote by turns on a piece of paper, laughing and hiding what they'd written. The Ten Commandments in forbidding black calligraphy hung behind them in immense oak frames (the Essex damp had got behind the glass, and blurred the ink so that deceit and adultery had become matters of debate); and on the tuneless piano in the corner a pretty child in a pink straw hat worked slowly at "Abide With Me."

Thomas poured tea with the dazed content of a man submitting to sedation, briefly forgetting the thorn in his flesh. Then the air altered; there was a powdery scent like that of a spoiled baby, the rustle of satin so cheap it could strike sparks—the tea urn was cold, and rivulets of water ran down it and blackened the tablecloth. Lorna Greene, her white hat fixed and quivering over her brow, was coming slowly through the tables, drawing Anne behind her and murmuring in whispers designed to penetrate the sleepy air in which old men dozed over cake. "I'm only thinking of the child," she was saying, "I wouldn't for the world want you to worry, dear Anne, only you see"—she gestured to the empty places at their table—"you see: she's gone, and the boy has gone with her." Into these words she poured every conceivable wickedness. Anne's face was unhappy. Thomas saw that Grace had gone, and left her hat behind. "Mr. Macaulay," said Lorna, looking with ingratiating sorrow up at Ronald, "Mr. Macaulay, I am afraid dear Grace has gone off. Perhaps she's gone down to Vanity Fair, perhaps the boy tempted her to go. Really"—she flirted through painted eyelashes, rebuking the sin she invited— "really I did think to myself: I'm surprised Mr. Macaulay has such a worldly young man under his roof!"

"They've just gone for a walk," said Anne, "it's such a beautiful day." The girl at the piano fumbled the melody and slammed the lid, and in the absence of the hymn they heard the music from the waltzers.

"Perhaps we ought to look for her," Lorna said, patting Anne's arm with a gesture designed to arouse distress under the guise of allaying it, "perhaps Mr. Macaulay—" Thomas heard the screams of children and hawkers, and a volley of drum and bass that seemed ludicrous against the tea urns, the pristine tablecloths. "Oh," he said, "she'll be all right"—but as he said it something altered in the noise of the fair. A yell of voices merged in warning lifted over the music, and Thomas felt everything he'd eaten rise in his stomach: *peril*, he thought, *peril*, the word tolling with a pain in his head. He remembered these same people in this same hall, a baby among them, her mother dead, acquiring him with her newborn oil-on-water eyes: "I think she'll be all right," he said, and doubted it. There was the yell again, and Thomas experienced so sudden a contraction of worry in his heart that without thought or explanation he began to run, and heard behind him Anne's bewildered exclamation, and Dimitru grunting in his sleep. He came out into the light, and went stumbling up Bethesda's lawn to the line of silver birches; but now the yell receded under the music and the children laughing, and there was doubt again—it was just the noise of the crowd, and Lorna's whisper: no peril, no harm done.

Going through the silver birches he stood at the verge of
Lowlands Park, and from this vantage saw crowds that milled
between the fairground rides, and young men taking shots at
plastic horses captive on their plastic roads, and wanted desperately to be among them. Behind him in Bethesda the same
placid female faces were shaded by their sober hats, and the
same grave men smiled cautiously behind their beards—but
here was all the world, hectic and merry and heedless of their
souls, if in fact they had any souls to heed: girls released from
school uniform into constricting skirts or jeans, and prissy
mothers tending to their prams; shirtless boys taunting larger
men and running for shelter; women as old as his mother
would have been, half-cut on wine and yelling in censure or
delight.

Thomas walked on through air thick with candy floss, and
here was a helter-skelter painted like a barber's pole, and a skel-
eton hanging by a noose from the painted roof of a painted
house—here were children riding unicorns that bucked on the
brass poles that pierced them, and the grass was littered with
paper tickets. He felt unloosed—and was he really too old for
the carousel, too old to ride a blue mat down the helter-skelter?
Then again (he was recalled to himself by a noise nearby),
where was that wretched child Grace, and where was that
wretched boy? He stopped abruptly, as if at a signal, and heard
again that same gathering yell. Peril, he thought, peril after
all—two boys nearby halted, pointed upward, and laughed
without pleasure. He heard the noise of metal working against
an obstruction, and turned with the boys to find a ride like a
ship hanging inverted above the fair, its red steel sail an immense shovel poised above the grass. A dozen riders secured
by bars were suspended upside down above the mechanism,
which strained against itself with a shriek; a girl's hair fell
streaming down toward the greased teeth of the parts.

"Something's got caught," said one of the boys to Thomas, in the companionable way of strangers sharing disaster, "something broke off and got caught." Thomas found himself moving with the crowd toward the ride, until he could make out the sail's tip inches from the soil, and a man lying nearby. Here: quiet among the noise, and a man suffering in it, unzipped from thigh to knee. It was possible to see the astonishing brightness of the severed muscle, and the bone from which it had been separated as cleanly as if by a butcher preparing a joint; from time to time a hanging rider screamed for help, but in the reverent shock attending the man this seemed impertinent and nobody looked up.

The man was not quite conscious. His head was in the lap of a girl who sometimes patted his shoulder with useless affection. "There it is, look," said the boy to Thomas, with grave satisfaction, "it broke clean off." Thomas looked, and saw that a piece of the ship's sail had become somehow caught in the mechanism, and been flung out.

The crowd was intoxicated by disaster: a woman with arms full of plastic toys shouted, "Put a belt round his leg or he'll bleed out right here while we watch!"; and how pleased she is, thought Thomas, in time it will be the defining feature of her character that she was here—then there was the siren of an ambulance, cutting the air with its pendulum swing. The baffled crowd began to move from side to side, taking Thomas with it. There was a moment when he felt himself lifted so that the toes of his shoes skimmed the damaged lawn; then the siren stopped, and this left a hollow place in which Thomas could make out the injured man's sorrowing moan.

Something gave in the mechanism of the ride, and with a shriek the upturned ship swung down and came to rest. The violent movement raised drafts that blew paper tickets over the lawn, and the startled crowd dispersed. It threw Thomas out and caused him to stumble backward, grasping uselessly for purchase at the air. His heels slipped in the churned grass, and briefly it seemed he was airborne; then he stumbled again, and felt a blow to his hip. It came from behind, and was so direct and attentive a blow it occurred to him that he was being attacked, and had no means of defending himself. But there was no more violence, and the crowd was receding, and after a moment he discovered that he was sitting alone on the lawn, half-toppled against the steel generator that had wounded him with a surgeon's precise and disinterested assault. There was no pain yet; but with the clarity of prophecy he understood that some integral structure had been compromised and would never be right again.

Pop music came bumping from a nearby speaker, and Thomas fixed on the melody to quell the nausea setting in, trying to persuade himself it was a hymn. The yelling diminished. The injured man said nothing. Time passed, or seemed to. When eventually Thomas raised himself against the generator he found the crowd had thinned. The ambulance went quietly. A girl with blood on her dress ran briefly after it, realized her folly, and fell back. The sun was setting on the broken sail. Elsewhere rides still moved, and teenagers drifted aimlessly about: there was a furtive atmosphere, as if everyone was privately certain they were doing something wrong and afraid they'd be caught out.

Thomas went by inches through the fair. He was making for Bethesda, but it was difficult to order his steps. He'd forgotten Grace. He was certain something moved in his hip that was never intended to move, and it was this that made him vomit as he walked. Slowly he came to the edge of the fair, where lights were going on in caravans, and a folding chair had been put against an oak. Here Thomas sat among a litter of spent cigarettes, and was surprised by his own cry of pain. He judged the time by the declining sun: soon they'd start singing in Bethesda again—soon it would be dark, and he'd see the comet rise. Dazed contentment settled on him, and this was frightening—how easy it would be to succumb to this sinking sensation, and be taken for a discarded prop in a haunted house. "Up you get, Thomas," he said fondly to himself, and didn't.

Now: twilight. Pale things visible in the dim air; movements nearby in the oaks that fringed the park, as if cloth had been left hanging from a branch. Thomas went forward, raising pain almost ecstatic in its effects, so that minutes passed when the world consisted of nothing but sensation. When this receded the evening light was altered again, and the pale cloth was more plainly visible. "Oh," he said. "Yes, I see." Grace Macaulay in her ugly dress was leaning on an oak, pulling and releasing her skirt with odd thoughtless gestures while Nathan unbuttoned her from neck to waist. The buttons gave him trouble. He had an angry look. Grace laughed, then the dress opened like the case of a beetle: "Come here," she said. "Come here." Nathan had her by the shoulder, and swayed as if half-drunk; then his hand was inside the bodice and he made a sound like that of a man in pain. Grace laughed with a kind of tender mocking, and Thomas saw with astonishment that the boy didn't know what he was doing. He pulled at the dress and there was Grace's shoulder and her breast, and Thomas saw the extraordinary pallor of her skin, on which coursed the single tributary of a vein. Then she was offering herself to the boy and her breast was in his mouth, and she bent and kissed him on the crown of his head, as if she pitied him this shock his flesh was heir to.

Thomas stood in a confusion of envy and unspent desire— it was never like that for me, he thought, and now I am old.

With an animal instinct for refuge, he headed for Bethesda. After a time it occurred to him it might be easier to crawl than walk, and so he lowered himself to the ground, and encountered the sensation of his scalp lifting from his skull, and with it an immense release of pressure. In pain's delirium, Thomas saw that suddenly it was the hard light of noon. The last of the crowd, falling silent, was parting one by one to clear a path and let a man come dancing through: James Bower, his upturned face good to look at in the strange perpendicular light, and behind him Richard Dimitru Dines in his scarlet coat, pushing a shopping trolley that had rusted in the river. Maria Văduva was riding in it, grasping her shabby chariot and looking for the moon: "The thing I longed for," she was saying, "has happened at last."

"Wait for me," said Thomas, "I'm coming"; but they didn't wait, and he couldn't go. The noon light went out. Darkness came in like a blot from the edge of his view. James Bower dwindled to a pinprick, and so did the scarlet coat and the tilted shopping trolley. Thomas fell back. The Essex soil was soft and took him in.

Night, now. No clouds: first stars out. Then there it was, there it was: Hale-Bopp, the Great Comet of the age—radiant above the Lowlands pediment, and falling through Perseus like the last of the rebel angels.

In the meantime, and before the fall: Grace Macaulay went back to the chapel with Nathan, and found the congregation gone and all the windows shut. Ronald was waiting with her aunt by the doors, moving the heavy chapel keys from hand to hand, and clasping his Bible under his arm. Grace made hasty apologies: they'd taken a walk, she said, and time had run away with them. Then there was the sound of the gate, and of Lorna Greene going through it with her white hat on, having done what she'd set out to do. She paused to take them all in with a level look, before lowering her pearly eyelids and receding through the evening toward the town. "Oh," said Grace, understanding with perfect clarity: Lorna must have followed them to the fair and seen their sin, and run to tell her father, whose white hair now more than ever had the look of a halo designating his virtuous state. Grace felt neither ashamed nor afraid, still having with her the scent of the loam under the oaks, and nature's indifference to sin. "Go home," she said to Nathan, feeling older than him by years, "it's time we all went home."

"Yes," he said, blinking, "all right," and did as he was told. Grace watched him go, and this disrupted her calm with a flare of anger as intimate and particular as love. There he went, careless and at ease, and meanwhile her father was coming toward her, when after all it was Nathan that broke the window, not her! So she discovered that after all she was afraid, and that she was sore and felt a little sick. "I'm sorry," she said to her aunt, who wouldn't meet her eye—but it struck her that she was not sorry. She was afraid, it was true, and now there was the beginning of shame; but she was afraid of her father, and ashamed of having wounded her aunt. There it ended. She was not sorry, because she hadn't sinned.

Ronald, putting the chapel keys in his pocket, walked past his daughter. "Get in the car, please," he said, and obedient Grace sat behind her aunt, whose shoulders shook with the effort of retaining her tears. Nobody spoke as they drove home to the house on Beechwood Avenue, where new leaves were arriving on the silver birch, and Anne had already set out the breakfast things.

Ronald Macaulay, putting down his Bible and taking off his coat, spoke to Grace without looking at her: she was to go to the room where he slept alone in the bed he'd shared with his wife. Silently, and unable to summon the memory of Nathan's face, she obeyed her father. This room faced north. It was cold with a penetrating damp drawn up from the Essex clay, and Grace began to shiver. What remained of her calm dissipated. She'd wounded her aunt, she'd wounded her father, she had probably wounded God. Once in the pulpit a man had told her that no sin was a small sin, and every sin was a blow of the hammer on a nail in Christ's palm; so now she saw against the painted wall a good man's hand convulse against a length of wood. She thought of how quickly Nathan had left her, and the intimate anger returned, and this was shocking: nobody told her it was possible to love and be angry. There were two white pillows on the bed, and on one of these the impression of her father's head was full of shadows. Grace looked for a time at the second pillow and tried to imagine the color of her mother's hair in the morning, and couldn't.

Ronald came into the room and sat on the bed and began to unlace his shoes. This took a very long time. His hair in the lamplight had a sickly yellowish look. He asked Grace if she knew that what she'd done was wrong, and again she lied and said she did. And did she understand, said Ronald, that she ought to be punished, since it was a father's duty to punish his children, and in so doing protect them from their wretched natures, and direct them to salvation? "Go over there," said Ronald. He looks frightened, thought Grace. "Go over there," said her father, who loved her: "choose a belt." There was a white cupboard in the room, where hung fastidiously ordered ranks of shirts and trousers, and several belts. "You take one of those," he said, "you choose one," and left the room. He crossed the hall to the bathroom, and locked the door, and Grace wondered what he was doing in there. The room was turning toward the moon. There were no cars on the street. She looked at the belts. She loved her father and she wanted to be good. She wondered if she ought to choose the heaviest of the belts, which would hurt the most severely, since she supposed she deserved it. But it hadn't felt like sinning, she wasn't sorry and she wouldn't lie—then she heard the slip of the bathroom lock. She looked at the belt she held. Its leather was cracked, its buckle was tarnished, it ought to be thrown away. She began to laugh: what the hell does he expect me to do? she thought. Do I hold out my hand—do I bend over like I did when I was a child, and he caught me out in a lie? Lights were on in the neighbors' houses, and she imagined someone looking in and seeing a white-haired man solemnly beating a stooping woman, then returning the belt to the cupboard and going down to put the kettle on. It's ridiculous, she thought (she went on laughing), I won't do it, and how could he make me? Suddenly the faith of her childhood struck her as comical: the idea that hell boiled away under the tarmac and pavements of Beechwood Avenue, that if she put her ear to the carpet she'd hear the ringing of pitchforks forged on devils' anvils, the hissing of embers on penitent flesh—how ridiculous it was, how evidently only nightmares to frighten children!

So Ronald Macaulay, when he came in, had on his hands not a pliable reckless child to be drawn back from the brink of the pit, but a woman laughing beyond speech. Grace looked at her father, expecting to see all the old sorrow and censure, and here was the day's last shock: he was smiling. It was brief—it went—but she saw it. "Never mind," said Ronald. "Never mind." He put his hand on her shoulder, and it was there for a long time, and she wondered if he were praying. Then, "Go to bed, Grace," he said. "Lights out."

Lights out in Aldleigh. Lights out in the bedrooms on Beechwood Avenue, where Grace Macaulay touches herself, and finds she's sore; where Anne Macaulay grieves to her worn chintz pillowcase. Lights out in Ronald Macaulay's study, where he sleeps with his forehead on his open Bible, absorbing the book of the prophet Isaiah through the frontal bone: *though your sins be as scarlet, they shall be white as snow.* Lights out on Ward H of Aldleigh General Hospital, where Thomas Hart is told he's a lucky man. Damage has certainly been done, but he'll escape the blade and stitches, if not a month or so of pain (in opiate dreams he encounters Maria Văduva standing in Bethesda's balcony and filling the open baptistery with astronomical dust). Lights out in Potter's Field, the nesting jays mourning their solitary egg lost to a magpie that same afternoon, the buddleia cultivating cabbage whites, the hazel coming into bud so fast you'd almost hear it squeak.

On the verges of a slip road on the outskirts of town, Richard Dimitru Dines lights out for another territory. He's got a shopping cart with him, and put Maria Văduva in it. Lights out in Vanity Fair, the false ship's sail cordoned and preserved for scrutiny, rats fat in the litter bins, the moon on the wane. Lights out in Lowlands House, the candle pinched out at the wick, no light but moonlight. Boards prised from a window, the small panes polished, Hale-Bopp making a transit, blown by the winds of the sun. Here a solitary figure sits with her thumb on the wheel of a plastic lighter making occasional flames, all the while repeating private incantations, of which a passing rat can make out not a single word.

"Thomas, who are you looking for?" Impatient Grace was repeating herself, since rain raised volleys against the window, and Thomas, dazed on pain and pain relief, seemed not to have heard. "You keep looking over there in the corner but there's nobody here but me. Do the drugs they gave you make you see things?" She'd brought cheap roses secured with an elastic band, and their smooth green buds were splitting and showing pink frills in the slit.

Thomas had been home for days, and now sat bolstered by cushions, and tilting like a vessel holed below the waterline. Grace saw he'd been trying to work, since there were green notebooks near to hand; but the open screen of his computer was dark and showed only his reflection distorted by a fingerprint. The house, thought Grace, was wounded with him. Flowers sagged in stagnant vases, and dust was accruing on the sideboard and lamps. Thomas himself was thinned out, as if he'd undertaken a forced march on hard ground, and not passed four days in bed. His shirt was untucked, and there was a stain on the collar that was curiously painful to Grace. How had it come about that she must now care for Thomas, when she had on her hands the question of her mortal body and immortal soul, and had no idea what to do with either?

"I'm sorry," Thomas said, "what did you say?" He looked

with a puzzled frown about the room as if something had been mislaid, but he couldn't think what.

"Never mind," said Grace. "Look: you ought to eat." A sandwich curled uneaten on the table. The rain persisted. "Tell me how you are. How long it will last?" She meant: how long before you come back to me?

"My hip isn't quite broken," said Thomas, "but something's gone wrong with the ligaments there and it hurts like hell. They had me on a ward with old men, and now I'm old, too, I've caught time like a virus—did you see that?" He peered through to the kitchen in a fuddled way she disliked. "Did you see that? Is anyone there?"

"He's gone, Thomas," said Grace, thinking she'd like to shake Thomas back into the form of his old self. "I told you: Dimitru has gone."

"Yes," said Thomas, sighing, "and so has Maria. Tell me again what happened that day."

"I wasn't there," said Grace, "because Nathan and I had gone for a walk." She paused. Together they looked at the opening roses. "My aunt told me that after you left the chapel, Dimitru woke up and looked for you. But you were gone, and he was frightened and angry, and a bottle fell out of his satchel and broke, and one of the children from Prittlewell cut her foot. Then Lorna interfered. She spoke to him, and only made it worse—he knocked the table over and all the cups and saucers broke, and Lorna said she was afraid he'd hurt her—that his hands were broken because he used them to fight." She looked at Thomas. "I hate her. I've never hated anyone before, and I like it—it feels like power, and I've never had any of that! My father said Dimi really ought to go, that it would be best. And he went. Nobody has seen him. I've looked for him in Potter's Field, I promise I looked, but he isn't there."

"And he took Maria's diary with him."

"Thomas, you're white. Haven't they given you what you need for the pain—don't those tablets work?"

"Did they look for it? Did anybody see it?"

"He left nothing behind. Does it matter so much?" But Thomas turned away and rubbed his face with his sleeve; and Grace was appalled to find him reverting to tears. She felt the weight of all the years already lived, and the weight of the years she'd not lived yet, and taken together they tired her out. "Thomas," she said, "why do you go to Bethesda? Why do you stay?"

This startled him. Briefly the rain held off: blackbirds in the street, water on the windows in blots that shone like mercury. "I stay," he said, "because I want to."

"That isn't enough," she said. "Wanting something can't be a good enough reason to do it."

"It can," said Thomas. "It is. You'll see." A cushion slipped and caused him to tilt further; he grimaced, and his pallor spread. "It aches," he said, "I doubt I'll ever be free of it. And I daresay it's over now," he said. "Dimi has gone, and taken Maria: so that's the end of the affair. No reason to haunt Lowlands now—no reason anyone might haunt me!" His despondency seemed to her so entirely out of proportion to the loss of some inscrutable documents retrieved from ruins that her pity ceded to irritation. "Come on now, Thomas," she said, brisk as her aunt sometimes was, "come on. You'll find more letters, you'll work things out—or there'll be another mystery, there'll be another ghost."

"No," he said. "There was nothing like that before—there'll be nothing like it again."

"Oh," said Grace. "Yes, I see." It struck her there were things she'd known for some time, but never looked at directly, and now they drifted into view. "Thomas," she said, "is it Maria you think you've lost, or is it James?"

"You see, he hasn't phoned me," said Thomas. "He hasn't called. He only comes when I ask, and I only ask when there's news of Maria—so if Maria is gone, how can I ask him to come? I lost my faith," said Thomas, "I don't know where I've put it, and now my house is empty and I live alone." Then the understanding that had been drifting into view arrived with such clarity Grace blinked at the brilliance: he is in love, she thought, he is actually in love with James Bower; and abruptly her native instinct to console poor Thomas Hart chilled in the shadow of Bethesda's pulpit. It is a man he loves, she thought: Thomas is a homosexual. She discovered that she'd shifted away from him, as if her body had been trained into distaste—he was a queer, a sodomite: the Bible (she'd been told) numbered men like him among the thieves and liars that would never see the kingdom of God. And this was her first and only friend, whose home she loved, whose food she ate, whose wisdom she prized—she found herself reverting to anger at Thomas, because he had inverted their natural order, and now she was required to understand and console him, when he had always been her comforter. "Come on," she said, "you're being stupid. It's just an old diary. It's just a man."

"Yes," said Thomas, "yes: just a man." He was laughing, and for the life of her she couldn't understand what was funny. "Yes," he said, "you're right, you wretched child! Put the kettle on, would you, I'm parched."

How was it possible to accommodate the idea of his desperate sinful state against his old endearments, the familiar galley kitchen, the teacup she liked best that was chipped where she'd dropped it? Grace discovered that her distaste and her love existed simultaneously and to an equal degree, and that neither could cancel the other out. I'll make sense of it, she thought, and they say no sin is past redemption, but I don't know how to think of him now—and she glanced back at him, sitting a

little more upright in his chair, with the familiar scent of san-
dalwood in the folds of his clothes.

Thomas reached for the pills that made it possible to pre-
tend the pain was happening in another room. Perhaps it was
also the drugs, he thought, looking hopelessly about, that
caused the sensation of loneliness which was the first of his
adult life: where had Maria gone, who looked over his shoulder as
he wrote, and never gave him a moment's peace? Where was
Richard Dimitru Dines, and what had James been doing while
Thomas dozed with the old men in Ward H? But then here
was Grace with the tray, frowning as if something in the
kitchen had made her cross. Silently she poured the tea, and
for a moment Thomas had the impression of looking at every
version of Grace eventually to be seen in time—that she was
eighteen, and twenty-eight, and a woman almost forty, and
that one by one all these women were already lost. He drank
the tea she'd poured, and then with effort set aside the loss of
Maria and of James. "Well then," he said. "What have you been
up to? What were you doing, while I was laid up in bed?
What's it been like, life as a documented adult? Do your knees
ache? Is your hair going gray?"

"I've had three gray hairs since I was thirteen," she said, with
a frowning refusal to meet his eye, so that Thomas thought he
must have wronged her, but couldn't think how. Then abruptly
the frown cleared. "Is that a blackbird, Thomas? Do they always sing like that, only I never noticed before?"

"They've always sounded just like that. So you see: you are
changed."

"Perhaps I am," she said, looking at him with a kind of an-
guish. "Thomas, I try and try to be good, but I don't know
how. I want to be free to think my own thoughts about what is
good, and what is bad—sometimes I wonder what it would be
like to wake up on a Sunday morning and have it be just

another day—to wear makeup, and jeans, and go to parties, and not think every minute that I've made God angry, or been ashamed of the Gospel of Christ. Then I'm afraid that if I fail to be as good as I ought to be, or love God as I ought to have done, then He'll take something away from me, and in the end I'll be unhappy, because I was never saved."

Then I've failed you, thought Thomas: I have failed. He recalled again the day of her arrival at Bethesda, and the peculiar claim on him arriving out of the wicker basket. He'd resolved that day to keep a foot in the chapel door, and let a little of her spirit out and a little of the world in. And certainly he'd tried: at the age of seven, for example, she'd burned her hand on steam from the kettle, and wailed as Anne held her hand under the running tap and Thomas stood watchful nearby. Ronald Macaulay, coming distractedly in, had inspected the scalded palm. "Does it hurt?" he'd said, and there'd been a moment when Thomas had been certain that stern sorrowing man would bend to kiss it better. But he'd become sterner and more sorrowing, and said to the child: "You must remember that although this burning will end, there is a place where the fire is never quenched, and there is nobody to bring even a drop of water, and that is the wages of sin." And Grace had received this dreadful sermon without surprise, because already her world contained the wormwood and the gall, boiling away below the Aldleigh pavements. But: "Look what I found," Thomas had said, coming forward as if for all the world he'd seen nothing odder than an ordinary father with an ordinary child, "look what I found in my pocket!" And he'd brought out a silver acorn charm and given it to her, and Grace had forgotten hell. So he did try, and he had gone on trying, but here she was: as fastened to Bethesda as the pulpit and the pews. He had failed.

"Grace, you aren't a child. You can leave Bethesda, if you like."

"Can I? If I can, why can't you?"

"I leave it sometimes, and return sometimes—I think of myself as two men, and that suits me well enough, though it's tiring."

"But why do you come back—do you believe in God? Do you believe in everything they tell you there?" She paused then, seeming to examine a thought and discard it. "And besides," she said, evidently unable to speak frankly, "how will I know how to be good, if there is nobody to tell me?"

"Oh, goodness, what is it? Nobody can agree," said Thomas, in whom pain relief had raised a nauseated giddy sensation. "I scarcely agree with myself from one day to the next— sometimes I think goodness is something fixed and certain that we move toward as best we can, sometimes I think the nature of goodness shifts, which only makes it harder to obtain. But always I think it exists somehow alongside sin—that the two things never cancel each other out. Do you want to know the worst thing I ever heard?"

"No," said Grace.

"It wasn't murder or adultery or deceit. I have always felt it's possible to do any one of those things, and perhaps be motivated by love—so then the sin is tempered by a kind of goodness. Surely the worst we can do is sin because it is sinful, and only because of that. Did you ever hear," he said, "about the ortolan?" Grace shook her head with its three gray hairs. "It's a small brown bird," said Thomas, "and the only thing it's known for is suffering. Every year, as they migrate for winter, they're caught in great nets. Then they're caged in the dark, and in their despair and confusion gorge themselves on grain, until they go blind and are too heavy to fly, and are thrown in vats of Armagnac to marinade and slowly drown. Then they're taken out dripping and roasted for seven and a half minutes exactly, and given to the diner, who holds the bird by the foot and tips back his head and puts the whole body in and eats it, spitting out the beak and bones. And the diner does all this with a white cloth draped over his head, because he is full of shame and must hide himself even from God. And the thing is," said Thomas, deriving delight from the horror he caused, "that there's no pleasure in it—no flavor that couldn't be obtained without such a parade of cruelty, just a mouth cut by shards of bone. It's the worst sin I ever heard," he said, fancying himself for a moment in the pulpit, "I think there must be other sins like this: that no matter how you examine it, and by what light, you'll find no goodness there. Keep it in mind," he said, "perhaps that's the best any of us can do: to never be so ashamed we must hide our faces not only from each other, but from God. How, I have no idea. You must work that out for yourself, either in the pew or out of it!"

"Thomas, what would I do without you?"

"Without me? I'm injured, not dying. Now leave me alone. I'm either going to sleep or be sick, and those are best done privately."

Later that same day, Thomas pulled his body up the narrow stairs, and having slept for an hour or so woke to find the adamant blackbird singing. He listened. No footsteps in the kitchen, no sound of an old man surprising himself with laughter and putting the bottle down. But was there a rustle in the shelves, down among the poetry perhaps—was Maria Văduva coming up the stairs to slip letters under the door? A passing train shook him out of his self-pity: what was lost but his capacity to walk without aching, and a diary that was rotting away, in a language he couldn't read? Somewhere in

Aldleigh James Bower was taking off his tie, and pouring himself a glass of wine—in fact (Thomas smiled at his own foolishness) there was Maria, look, there she was, having clambered out of the shopping trolley and abandoned Dimi on the Lowlands lawn, and wandered down Lower Bridge Road. She leaned against the doorframe admiring the rings on her fingers, and said: *For God's sake, Thomas Hart, for God's sake: isn't it all a question of orbits? Things go, things come. Something's bound to happen soon.*

The sun was going down.

ON COMING AND GOING

THOMAS HART, *ESSEX CHRONICLE*,
20 APRIL 1997

I'm afraid I write this lying in bed. You see, I am injured, and as I recover I've got nothing to do but write and watch Hale-Bopp make its transit past my bedroom window. I've been timing it. It seems to me to go at more or less an inch an hour.

The night I was injured it was just the other side of the window in Ward H, and seemed so nearby I thought I could touch it, if only I could break the glass without bringing the nurses to tell their most difficult patient to behave. Of course, this was just a trick of the light, together with the things they gave me for the pain. Really it was always quite a distant comet, never any closer than 0.9 astronomical units, which is to say nine-tenths of the distance from the earth to the sun. Other comets come much closer to the earth—Comet Hyakutake, for example, came as close as 0.1 astronomical units—but they're often a fleeting presence, passing more or less without notice in bad weather. I suppose that's just like us: so dazzled by beauty we convince ourselves it's within reach.

Soon Hale-Bopp will cross into the southern hemisphere, and we'll never see it again. It passed the perihelion on April Fools' Day, and now it is coming to the end of the third week of a journey that will take 2,533 years. Already I suppose it's slowing down, and will only get slower until it begins its return to the sun—then picture it running with relief and joy, like a dog in sight of home.

I'll mourn Hale-Bopp, but be glad I ever saw it at all. Don't things go, and new things come? Lately I've been reading the diaries of a woman called Maria Văduva, who lived in Aldleigh's Lowlands House, and was always hoping to see something remarkable in the Essex skies (one day soon, I'll tell you all about her). She quotes from Homer's *Iliad*—"Let me first do some great thing before I die, that shall be told among men hereafter"—and reminds me that every night, someone scans the sky over Maldon or New Mexico or Kiev, patient and hopeful and cold, waiting for some great thing.

Nathan, running full tilt through a monastery under scarlet banners, misjudged a flight of stairs and fell for the fourth time—"God's sake," he said, and threw away the controls that took him to imagined islands whenever he chose. Sometimes he found himself looking at his ordinary life with Grace Macaulay's eyes—what would she make of the television, the PlayStation, the three beer cans he'd emptied and crushed and left on the floor where he sat cross-legged all afternoon? Her house was so quiet the ticking clocks sounded like dripping taps, and subject to a thousand laws nobody ever explained—here there was laughter and argument and music forever spilling out of bedroom doors. His father rode bikes in bad weather, and could pick an egg out of boiling water without burning his hands—Grace's father had an undertaker's face. His own mother danced often, if badly—Grace had no mother, and her aunt certainly could never have danced. They lived with God, he thought, as if they had a lodger upstairs who'd bang on the floor with a broom if they ever made a noise.

Nathan found more beer, and drank it. He'd kept Grace secret from his friends, certain they'd find her ridiculous, or (this was worse) that they wouldn't. It occurred to him that she arrived as if from 1887: bewildered by his music; indifferent to the general election in which she was eligible to vote; and appalled by the thought she might exchange her petticoats for jeans. She ought to have been priggish, but her stern morality was applied after a haphazard logic he couldn't fathom. She asked to be taught how to smoke, saying she couldn't for the life of her think of a Bible verse strictly forbidding it, but would never share his beer. She swore sometimes with pleasure, but said that blasphemy was a different matter, and that she'd never take the Lord's name in vain. When he thought of that half hour under the Lowlands oaks he was ashamed. There'd been other girls, of course there had—he was nineteen in November—but that had always been easy and sometimes funny and afterward things had gone on more or less as before. With Grace it had all felt bewildering, every placement of his mouth and hand significant and doubtful and slow—there'd been the strangest sense that she was immense, that she'd had command of things.

He was confused by how she compelled him, that was half the trouble: she was too short, and he disliked the smell of the oils she used on her hair and skin. Her legs were sturdy and her hands were like a boy's, with unpainted nails bitten short, and she had no idea how to dress—but he was so acutely attuned to these deficiencies he had her memorized. She was the most alive person he'd ever met. The sight of her coming toward him roused a kind of animal alertness in his body, but he could never be certain whether that was the instinct of predator or prey.

He finished his drink. It was getting dark. Somewhere in his room, he thought, there was bound to be some weed. He found it. The curtains were closed, and the moonlight in the slit was cold, as if there'd been late snow. Inexpertly he rolled a joint, and thought with loving contempt of Grace's attempts to share his cigarettes, and refusal to admit they sickened her—then there was a noise at the door, and his sister was yelling for him; and oh, he said, that'll be Grace, that will be her. He ran down, mis-judged the stairs, and fell for the fifth time.

Nick Carleton surveyed Thomas Hart. Should he remark on his gaunt, pale looks? Should he say: Thomas, it's gone half past seven, go home? He should not. Carleton was never cer-tain of his authority's reach where Thomas was concerned. He looked instead at the documents spread on the desk and said, "I'm afraid I'm not sure this is enough." Lightly he touched the photograph of Maria Văduva standing by Bethesda's wall, and the green notebook with Dimitru's translation. "I like these drawings," he said, looking for stars in a smudged black blot, "but nobody would be able to make them out. The whole story is unfinished. It lacks resolution. If only you hadn't lost the diary."

"Well," said Thomas, "I am sorry." He rubbed his hip with a distracted motion that had already become characteristic.

"What about your friend at the museum?" Carleton was leafing through the notebook. "I like this," he said. "*Let me first do some great thing before I die!*"

"In fact we spoke this morning on the phone," said Thomas, with eagerness Carleton thought childish. "He said there's bound to be more—between the floorboards, say, and in other rooms. Look, Carleton, where the translation ends—you see Maria met somebody, or saw her great thing. If we knew what—"

"But we don't know, and the diary is gone." The editor aimed for a finality of tone, and achieved only rudeness. He flushed, tempering his voice. "All the same," he said.

"All the same." Thomas reached for the drawings, and the motion disturbed something in his hip. Carleton saw him whiten and submit to passing pain. "Go home," he said, rising from his seat. "You ought to take time off. Oh!" He crossed quickly to the window, and moved aside the open slats of the blind. "Thomas," he said. "Do you see that?"

"I'm a writer, young Nick: there's no time off. What are you looking at?"

"Don't you see it?" Carleton opened the blinds. "What's happened to the moon? I think I must be going mad."

Anne Macaulay, kept from Bethesda's weekly prayers by a bad cold in the head, went to bed early, and thought the light that night was strange, but closed the curtains all the same.

Ronald Macaulay, locking the chapel door when the prayer meeting was done, found himself in tears. He wiped his eyes and looked about, and located the moon. "Do you see that?" he said, forgetting his solitude. "Do you see that?" He held his Bible tightly.

James Bower came out of the Jackdaw and Crow, pleasantly a little drunk. He stumbled as he went, and this caused him to think of injury, and then of Thomas Hart. Really (he thought) he ought to visit. It would be fair to say he'd missed the other man. Now he was coming to London Road, and what a strange dark evening it was, given the spring—then he understood that in fact he was walking through smoke streaming down-wind. Fragments of ash appeared on his sleeve and shoulders; an ember extinguished itself on his hand. He walked more quickly, and arrived at Bethesda where a man was standing by the iron gate. His stiff white hair showed like a nimbus in the gloom, and he had a displaced unworldly look that called Thomas Hart (again!) to mind. "What's happening?" said James. "There must be a fire"—but the man seemed untroubled by the smoke and embers, and was looking up past Bethesda's roof. "What's up there," said James, "what are you looking at?" and instinctively looked with him. "Oh," he said, "my God. My God." The hair on his neck and forearms lifted as if in response to a static charge. Was this fear? He supposed so. But if he was afraid, why did he long to look, and go on looking?

"All right," said Nathan, "you don't have to stand there, you can come in." Grace wore a white dress she'd evidently sewn from washed-thin linen sheets, gone gray at the uneven hem and pulled taut at the waist with a black scarf. A new pair of trainers showed absurdly when she walked. Nathan stepped aside, incited and embarrassed as he always was by this peculiar girl, who looked crosser than ever: "I have to talk to you," she said, trailing him up the stairs. "So this is your room." She looked with disapproving awe at the television, and the posters of famous women she could never have named—"Where shall I sit?"

"Anywhere," said Nathan. So here was the body that preoccupied him against his will, concealed somewhere in the folds of grubby cloth—here again the bewildering sense of attraction and repulsion she roused. And why had she come? Desperately he cast about for a defense against accusations he'd caused her to sin, with the outraged misery of an innocent man who sees the knotted rope.

She chose the floor at his feet, cross-legged and small; and with a nauseating shift of perspective the motion of her hair against her neck persuaded him there was never any girl as desirable as her. "What's that smell?" she said.

"I've been smoking weed," said Nathan, hoping to invite her playful censure; but she only nodded, and abruptly folded over herself, clasping her stomach with a groan. "What's the matter? What have you done?"

"Just cramps," she said, with defiant shame, "my period has

started"; and together they considered the implications of this, and were relieved. "So that's all right," she said, "but I didn't come to tell you that. I want to talk about Thomas." The pain had passed for now. She resumed her bemused assessment of his room.

"Ah! Why?" (The hangman stowed the noose.)

"I found out something, and don't know what to do, or how to feel."

"What have you found out?"

"Why he won't be baptized. Why he goes away from Bethesda, why he lives alone. Why he goes to London, and what he does. Oh, and my stomach hurts."

"Why don't you try this," he said, lighting again the joint that had burned out in a saucer. "My sister says it helps with cramp. But not so much," he said, dreadfully moved by how obediently she took it, and with what concentration she drew in the smoke; "just a bit more, then give it back. That's right. So what's the old man been up to?"

"Remember when we found him at Lowlands, that day the mist was everywhere and I didn't go to school?" She coughed three times; her eyes watered. "Remember we found him with that other man?"

"Of course," said Nathan, laughing with the mechanical levity arriving with the smoke.

"Thomas loves him," said Grace, with enormous solemnity. Then, "I think I feel sick," she said, and her wounding smile came without warning—"I feel sick," she said, "isn't that funny?"

"It is funny," said Nathan. "Everything is, if you think about it. So Thomas is a poof," he said cheerfully, and was startled by Grace reverting to her temper.

"Don't say that," she said. "Don't use the kind of words they say. Do you really think it's so bad of him? When I realized, I moved away as if I'd seen a spider on the wall—give me some more." Again the concentrated attention on the joint, the choking cough, the quick helpless smile. "First I was angry with myself for thinking badly of my friend, then angry with Bethesda for making me think badly at all, but in the end I was angry with him. He should have told me. People should be what they seem to be. If they're not, they're liars, even if they never lie!"

"It isn't bad exactly," said Nathan. He saw how peculiar the light outside was, and turned away from the window. "It isn't bad. It's just weird. I think they can do what they like as long as I don't have to see it."

"They told me men like that were wicked. And I try and try to think Thomas is wicked, but I can't, it's like trying to write with my left hand. Do you think I should ask God to make me disgusted? I can't. I won't. Look at me. Nathan, look at me! How funny. I can't really see your face—can you see mine? Can you smell burning? Is it us? Have we burned down your house?" The thought delighted her.

"Only you," said Nathan. "And don't you ever brush your hair?"

"I can smell me, too. I put rose oil on but I think I smell of blood—look: something strange is happening, something is happening out there—" She came quickly to her feet, stumbling inside her skirts and laughing, and reaching easily for his shoulder to steady herself. "Look," she said, "stupid boy. Look at that. Look at the moon."

In the offices of the *Essex Chronicle*, Thomas Hart came to the window with Carleton and saw the waxing moon rising in the east. "Ah," he said, with the inflection of a cry of pain. He put his hand on his editor's shoulder. "*Let not your heart be troubled,*" he said, "*neither let it be afraid*"; but his own heart briefly failed him, because this was what caused James Bower and Ronald Macaulay to stand dumbfounded in Bethesda's car park, and what caused Grace to reach in appalled wonder for the boy beside her at the window: the moon's toppled crescent was a radiant, maddening blue. Thomas, casting about for how best to describe it, thought of the blue of gas flames and speed-well; of copper sulfate, broken Wedgwood plates, the old man's tarpaulin in Potter's Field. It was no good. No other blue would ever do. The moon was only as blue as itself.

"There'll be some explanation," he said, looking instinctively for Maria Văduva (and yes, yes: there she was, assembled out of the thick evening air, perched on the windowsill three floors up and delivering the consolations of natural philosophy—*You must remember, Thomas, that light is altered by whatever stands in its path, and we are a part of all that we have met*).

Carleton said, "It might be the end of the world."

"It might," said Thomas, "but will not we fear, though the mountains be cast into the midst of the sea, and so on"—then cautiously, because his bad hip ached, he opened the window to its furthest extent and leaned out. "There, don't you smell it? Bonfires, blowing over the town."

Carleton's phone rang. He took it, listened, put on his coat. "It isn't as bad as all that," he said. "But Lowlands House is burning down."

Grace ran. The fire, not visible from Nathan's window, was burning all the same on the television, and they'd been summoned downstairs to see it. "Is that Lowlands?" they'd all exclaimed in delight and sadness. "Is that the old house on fire?"

"Let's go," Grace had said, "let's go and watch"; and without thought or anxiety they'd run, laughing, half a mile to the Lowlands gates. Now they were crossing lawns still bruised by the

Easter fair, and the weed's first giddy pleasure was gone, leaving a curious drowsy sense that everything was amplified: the clutching in her womb, the iron reek of her own blood, the transfigured moon. Increasingly the air had the warmth of summer. Nathan ran ahead, perpetually just beyond her reach. Then he halted, and she butted up hard against him and saw the old white house enclosed by old black beeches. The east wing was burning from basement to eaves. "Oh no," said Grace—a dreadful twist occurred in her abdomen, and at that moment the fire convulsed, causing the boards to split from their windows. Smoke plumed through shattered glass and formed a pall that rode the mild wind out to the fringes of the park.

"Is anybody in there?" said Nathan, blinking rapidly against the light. "Is everybody safe?" Threads of people drifted in from every entrance to the park, looking about with troubled awe; the air was full of birds.

"Nothing but ghosts in there," said Grace, "and they'll survive"—then she saw a rim of white hair made coral by firelight, and knew this was her father. She began to burrow through the crowd with animal determination, and when she reached him was startled to discover she wanted to hold his hand—"It's all right," she said, having no idea who was consoling whom, "it's going to be all right." His cold grip tightened, and released her.

"Where are they," a man beside her father said, "why has nobody come?"; and Grace saw this was Thomas Hart's friend, who in that peculiar light had the adamant beauty of a dead stone king. "Hello," he said, with a frowning smile at Grace and Nathan, "are you two always here?"

By unspoken consent they all drifted with the quiet crowd to the wire fence that kept the house from trespassers: "They can't do anything," said Nathan, "they can't stop it." There was a rending noise, as if the house were a garment tearing at the seams, and this went on for some time, concluding in a thud that shook panicked birds out from nearby oaks. The smoke took on the look of morning mist igniting with first light. There were no sirens yet.

"Look how the flames make the shadows move," said Grace, but her father's eyes were closed.

"Yes," said James Bower, "look"—there was the impression of worry joined with an ecstatic kind of interest, as if seeing something he'd longed for all his life—"you'd think there was a party going on, and everyone was dancing." The house was full of noises. Panes of glass burst on the terrace, and roof beams split and dropped; occasionally there was an almost-human cry of metal against metal.

"I can't believe it," said Grace, "I can't believe my eyes." The pain in her stomach returned, with the sensation that something had actually become detached, and was turning and turning in there. "Why won't it stop?" she said.

"In His name and for His sake we pray," said Ronald, opening his eyes. "Amen." He looked at his daughter, he looked at the fire. "Yes," he said, "you'd almost think somebody was running around inside." The maddened moon was going down. Deer bolted for the forest from the copper beeches. Now: sirens.

"There's the sirens," said Thomas, leaning on the stick he needed and despised, watching men at the Lowlands gate beckoning to fire engines turning in from London Road. He ought to have been in pain, but his interest in the moon decreased his capacity to suffer, and so he walked quickly with Nick Carleton toward the fire. Was that gas flame color fading, he thought, or was it that already it seemed the moon had always been blue?

"Hear that?" said Carleton, who'd thought to bring a Dictaphone for the sake of the front page, and held it at arm's length. "Sounds like screaming."

"That's just the fire," said Thomas, "now slow down"—a gathering crowd kept them from the house. Bellowing importantly and without meaning, Carleton cut through, sometimes bringing his Dictaphone near a watching man or woman to record their distress; then Thomas saw white hair kindling above a solemnly bent head. "There you are," he said, "there he is"—as if it were inevitable that Ronald Macaulay should be praying at the burning threshold, and that Grace in a curious white shroud should be standing with hands pressed to her abdomen and saying to Nathan, "I think the hairs are burning on my cheeks."

"Keep back," said Thomas, with his old instinct for the preservation of Grace. "You should keep back"—then he saw James Bower coming through smoke. "Hello, James," he said, taking in with pleasure the unshaved cheek, the hair which surely was a good inch longer than it had been before the fall.

"I just happened to be passing the church," said James, "and saw the fire. But how are you, Thomas, and should you be out?" He looked with compassion at the stick.

"I hardly feel a thing," said Thomas, as if he could impose strength on himself by an act of will, and for the sake of James.

"We should go closer," said Carleton, "we ought to go and look"—but in fact it was James Bower who first walked toward the fire. "Is it the metal beams," he said, "that hiss and sing like that?"

Now the engines had come nearby, and men made cumbersome by heavy yellow garments were drawing out a fire hose that bucked against the lawn and unleashed a bow of water. "They'll put a stop to it," said Thomas, "they'll get it under control." A wind was getting up, causing smoke to form in thick blots that obscured and revealed James in turn as he moved nearer to the house.

"Do you hear that?" said Grace. "Do you hear something singing?"

"Just air escaping," said Thomas, "or an animal is hurt"; but he was helpless with ignorance. Beside the fire engines two men were bending now against unnatural drafts, and headed for steps down which tumbled blackened bits of brick. The door was gone, and in its place a sheet of fire made do for a curtain.

"They can't go in," said James, calling back through smoke. "If they go in, they won't come out."

"Look," said Grace, "I didn't think a house could scream like that—somebody's in there, I told you so!" The men, bent double, entered the burning house through a breach in the wall, and the crowd produced a low harmonic moan of anticipated sorrow.

"Shit," said Nathan, "fucking hell," and Ronald Macaulay nodded as if these profanities were prayers. Unguessable minutes passed, then the men came back through the breach with a drooping figure. "I told you," said Grace, "didn't I say?" They laid the figure on the grass. It did not move. Thomas was grateful he could make out no more than the white fabric of its clothes. Briefly it seemed all Essex held its breath in reverent silence; then the wet white bundle began to move, like animated cloth under an enchantment. It convulsed and lengthened, then was abruptly upright, showing weak haphazard limbs. The men, kneeling in their heavy suits, reeled in surprise, and the watching crowd moaned. The white figure, liberated for a moment, let out an eerie melodious shriek; then it bolted back into the fire. Briefly it was visible in the vacant doorway; then there was another rending noise, and the door's stone lintel broke in pieces on the threshold.

"Incredible," said Carleton, leaving them to range among

the crowd clasping the Dictaphone like a sacred icon, "there's never been anything like this before."

"*The Lord shall preserve thy going out,*" said Ronald, wringing his hands, "*and thy coming in—*"

"I think we're going to see somebody die," said Nathan.

"Oh no, no," said Thomas, seeing James Bower moving closer to the fire with the dogged slow step of a man in a trance. "James. Don't. What can you do?"

The watching firemen, cautious and impassive, drew back and made adjustments to their clothing. A woman came forward, upright with authority, evidently saying they ought to be doing this, and doing that; meanwhile the men listened, and did nothing. The shadows were dancing in the house again, and grew substantial: it was possible to make out something dashing back and forth behind the bursting windows. "Look," said James, "there they are." The light struck his hair and the fibers of his clothes—he was rimmed with borrowed splendor: he is just like Maria, thought Thomas, always waiting for some great thing, and here it is. "Here they are," said James, and ran. Instinctively Thomas began to move, forgetting for a moment he was leaning on a stick, and stumbling hard against the uneven lawn now soaked with water running from the house. The pain he felt then was the pain of a new wound, and his shocked howl was concealed by the howl of the crowd.

"What's he doing?" said Grace. "Why didn't you stop him? Why isn't anybody doing anything?"

The firemen on the steps, sealed now behind their visors, reached the broken lintel; but James had arrived at a window briefly free of flame, and scrambled over the cracked sill.

"Idiot," said Nathan, with a kind of untroubled excitement, as if watching a fellow player make a bad move in a game.

"Do something," said Grace, clasping her arms across her stomach.

"I can't move," said Thomas, uncertain if it was pain that fixed him where he stood, or a kind of calm that was like the beginning of death.

"I can," said Nathan, "I can go"; and this was said carelessly: he might have been sitting cross-legged on the bedroom floor in the light of the television screen, with several lives in hand—"Yes, all right then," he said, and began running with the easy power of his youth. Arcs of illuminated water ranged across the house, causing vents of steam that first obscured the view, then split to reveal the dying fire.

Thomas closed his eyes in resignation: it is preordained, he thought, it is the order of time—the rain falls on the just and the unjust, and God would have mercy on whom he would have mercy. Sirens again, and raised voices; Thomas opened his eyes. Grace Macaulay, on her knees beside him, clutched a bloodstained length of skirt in her fists, and prayed inaudibly with a child's passion. She is bargaining with God, thought Thomas, and no good ever comes of that—then there was an insistent pressure on his shoulder, and this was Ronald's hand. "Shall we pray?" said Ronald, and with dumb obedience Thomas clasped his hands together. A murmur set up, and for a moment Thomas thought the crowd was praying with them—but "There he is," a nearby woman said, triumphant, "there he is." The blue moon had set. The roving arcs of water stripped dead leaves from the copper beeches. "Look!" said the woman, now beside Thomas, pulling at his sleeve, and Thomas looked. Nathan was coming out from behind the house, slowed by shock and soaked clothing. His face was blurred by soot, and he held up his hands with the defeated gesture of a man under arrest. The firemen followed, and

quickly all three were obscured by waiting officials and para-
medics that moved with the purpose of a single machine. The
pain in Thomas's hip was only the memory of pain. No other
man came out. Grace watched with an expression of triumph
modified by fear. "Amen," she said. "Amen."

Dawn. Thin and early rain. The birds returning to the park,
dismayed in the ruins; rats in the bracken doubled in number,
every species of tenant now evicted from the house. Lowlands
holding fast on the Essex clay: the west wing damaged, the east
wing wrecked, the house confined by yellow plastic barriers
that toppled on the lawns.

Mist in the fireplace, trespass in the ruins—Thomas Hart,
sleepless with mourning and confusion, stood enclosed by the
east wing's outer walls, from which the remnants of the upper
floors dripped filthy water. Elsewhere men and women went
about their business past the cordon, not seeing Thomas put his
hand against wet walls retaining the night's warmth, or choosing
not to see him out of pity. Was it here James took his last breath,
thought Thomas—did he rest against this beam when his lungs
failed, or that one? Where had his body gone, and what had they
done with him? Thomas was struck by how peripheral he was,
how much an afterthought: nobody would think to tell him
that James Bower had died, and one day he'd limp through town
and see a hearse and have no idea what it contained—I ought to
have stayed to the end, he thought, recalling with shame how
readily he'd succumbed to Ronald Macaulay's solemn insistence
that it was all over and best left to those in charge.

The house began to speak: he listened. He heard in the crack-
ing plaster the voice of Maria Văduva at midnight, exclaiming
over the sky; of John Bell alone in some other room lamenting
over his wife. He heard the striking of the match that set the fire,
and heard James Bower speaking in the hissing of water against

brick. Then he heard himself crying readily and without shame, and discovered that sorrow was as ecstatic as pain sometimes was, and as much a proof of life. Other proofs presented themselves, vivid in early light—a thin-tailed fox going untroubled to the lake, the Potter's Field jays breaking their fast on St. Mark's flies swarming fat over the grass. The house was speaking again. Plaster had split from the brick in the heat and revealed a flaw in the wall. Between the vacant fireplace and the door the mortar was more pale and the bricks more red: it had the look of a poorly matched patch sewn on a coat. The fire had caused this patch to unstitch itself, and gaps had appeared in the seam between the new brick and the old. *Look*, said the house, shifting on the soaking lawns: *look, I've got something to show you*.

"I didn't think it would still be standing," said James Bower, speaking with Maria Văduva, with John Bell, with the groaning house: "I didn't think it would still be here." Something dropped on Thomas Hart's shoulder—irritably he shook it off—the pressure increased, became a clasp. "Thomas," said the voice, "what are you doing? And what have you done to the wall?"

Slowly, because his bad hip ached, Thomas turned, and discovered James Bower holding his left arm in a sling against his breast, as if he'd been given something fragile he didn't particularly want. The remarkable face was made more remarkable by scorch marks treated with a clear substance that ran like sluggish tears on to his collar. Thomas was astounded by a need for violence; how dare he, he thought, how dare he subject me to shock after shock, while all the while he wears that unaltered easy smile—"I made it out," said James (the easy smile in fact a little altered by the burn), "I found a way out and brought the woman with me. I brought her out myself. 'I did it,' she kept saying, 'it was me.' They think she'll be all right, but she says she did it, and police are waiting in the hospital—don't look at me like that,

Thomas, I'm all right. Though they tell me burns get worse as
the shock wears off, and my knees were full of glass. So perhaps I
am still in shock"—he looked about with interest, and took his
hand from Thomas's shoulder—"perhaps I should be at home,
but I kept thinking of Maria Văduva and what she left behind."

"I thought you were dead," said Thomas. "Why did you do
it? Such a risk, and for a stranger?"

"I don't know—I can't explain it—only I thought: I can
choose now not to be an ordinary man. But you'll never understand," he said, shaking his head, wincing over his burns.
"You're content with your life. Why should I have to be content with mine?"

Impossible to explain, even to himself, what a peculiar kind
of cruelty this was. "I understand," said Thomas, who understood only that his bad hip ached, and that the distance between them was impassable. Then there was a violent shearing
sound that caused a woman on the terrace to exclaim in fright,
and sent flies swarming in the fireplace—"Look out!" said
James, and the mismatched portion of the wall peeled back in
a single piece, and dismantled into reddish bricks that lay distributed on the ruined wet floor. Thomas, silenced by surprise,
experienced a tightening cold sensation on his scalp: the damage had revealed a shallow cavity, and the rising sun struck
steel and glass. "Oh!" said Thomas. "There you are!" The need
for violence of some kind had departed, and James Bower was
at his side, smelling of soot and antiseptic. "There it is," said
Thomas. He raised his hand in greeting, and laughed. "Her
telescope," said James, so reverently that Thomas thought perhaps he too saw a tall black-browed woman in embellished
clothes bending to the eyepiece and exclaiming in delight. Together the men looked into the lens. The lens looked back.
Hadn't it always been in the habit of seeking out light? It went
on doing so.

Grace Macaulay stood alone in her father's shed. The faithless swifts had gone: it was the restless period between summer and autumn, when it was never possible to guess the weather, or dress correctly for it. All day and all night the sky was dull and uniform, and it seemed absurd to think there'd been a comet once, and a blue moon setting through stars.

The shed was warm, and fragrant with creosote; moss grew in soft green curds beside cracked panes of glass that rattled in the wind. Grace leaned against the workbench and looked down the garden to the illuminated house. She felt dislocated, as if it all had nothing to do with her, and it was impertinent to watch her father stooped over his Bible in the study, or her aunt coming to the bathroom in a thin towel dressing gown. Then she returned to the task of sorting through the pile of nuts and bolts ranged on the bench. Carefully she selected the heaviest of these, discarding washers dulled with rust that would stain her clothes. How many would she need? She had no idea. She'd never done this before; certainly she'd never do it again.

Low clouds brought an early dusk and caused the house to shine more vividly at the garden's end: there was her aunt, moving to her own narrow room, where she'd put on the smartest of her blouses and her chapel hat; there was her father standing to relieve the scholar's ache in his back. And there also was a man, coming down the garden path with the step of someone acquainted with pain: "Thomas!" she said, going quickly to the door. "It's been a month. Where have you been? You abandoned me!" She withheld her embrace by way of punishment, and took frowning account of his long coat in pale wool, his shining shoes, the wicker basket he carried and the white cloth that covered it. The coat and the basket embarrassed her: could he not dress like other men, she thought, could he not use a plastic bag?

"What are you doing here so early?" she said, absently turning her ring. "It isn't for another hour."

"I've been in London," said Thomas. He put the basket down. "I have been about my business."

"All you think about," said Grace reprovingly, "is that stupid telescope." That Thomas and James Bower had discovered Maria Văduva's telescope in the aftermath of the Lowlands fire had pleased her at first, feeling Thomas's happiness was almost her own. Then she suspected she'd been supplanted first by a person and then by an object: now she'd gladly have seen the thing pushed into the lake, and the man after it. She understood that her irritation and envy was somehow also to do with Thomas being a homosexual, a word she found bizarre for its suggestion of a diagnosis. Sometimes out of a sense of duty she attempted to disapprove of Thomas; but she never could, and what was most confusing was that she never thought she should.

"That is true," he said, "I dream about it. Sometimes I think the lens still contains every star it ever saw. Now what are you doing?" He hung his coat on a nail.

"Aunt Anne made me a baptismal dress. She said if I do it, I'll make mistakes and it would come apart in the water. But I have to sew weights into the hem of the skirt, or it will billow up in the water and show my legs."

"I'll help you," said Thomas, who seemed livelier than she'd ever known him, despite the loss of Maria's diary and the pain in his hip. "If you'll tell me how you are."

A blackened seedpod of some kind had got in with the nuts and bolts, and Grace examined it. "I'm all right," she said.

"Then tell me how Nathan is."

Grace felt herself color with unhappiness and pride. "He's got a job, and a car. Nothing about the fire hurt him—nothing ever does. Sometimes he's always calling me, sometimes he forgets me. He keeps saying I'm his friend, as if he's forgotten what we did—as if he doesn't know that I remember everything! But he's coming today," she said. "I told him weeks ago, and yesterday I phoned, and he said he'd come."

"So you are to be baptized like John in the River Jordan, and Christ after him. Perhaps a dove will descend, or at least there'll be pigeons on Bethesda's roof! But you have more courage than I ever did, and certainly more faith." Thomas found a washer furred with rust, and set it aside.

"I have to do it," said Grace. She rolled the seedpod in her hands and crushed it. "I promised I would."

"Two more here." Thomas handed her a pair of heavy steel screws. "Promised whom?"

Grace, leaning on the workbench, smelled again smoke drifting from the Lowlands fire, the blood seeping from her body, the weed that had made the night's events both amplified and muted. In that haze, the faith that all her life had been an exhausting obligation had been brought down to a single lucid certainty: that the God of Abraham and Isaac, at whose name every knee shall bow, happened also to be present in a small Essex town on a Wednesday evening, and out of the unfathomable sway of his power would attend to the prayers of a girl on her knees in the mud. "Will you laugh at me?" she asked.

"I might," said Thomas, and this caused Grace to smile, and

buffet him with her shoulder in her old way, and say, "I promised God. That's the thing. I said: Bring him out of there, and I'll be good. Bring him safely out and then I'll be baptized, and I'll serve God all my days. Then there he was, walking out with his hands up, and not even his clothes were burned. I was so happy it was like being mad. Then I was afraid because I understood I was in debt to God and one day I'd have to clear my debt. And I should be baptized, because I do have faith, I do! And didn't God say that if you honor him, he will honor you, and doesn't he always keep his promises?"

Thomas was silent for a time. "More bargaining," he said. "You look like a little witch, casting her spells with old iron. And I'm a poor backslider, Grace, but even I know this is pretty poor theology."

"Perhaps I am a witch!" Then it struck her that this was blasphemous. "But it isn't a spell," she said, "it's a prayer."

"Grace," said Thomas, speaking gently, "do you really believe in all this?"

"I don't know! All these rules, Thomas, all the things I can't do—the hats I have to wear, the music I can't listen to—I've never been to the cinema. I've never danced and nobody will ever tell me how! But all the time"—lightly she thumped her breast—"there's this thing in me that won't let me go. And doesn't it mean more, isn't it more amazing, to have faith against your better judgment?"

"It might be faith. But it might be fear, or love, or all those things, or none of them. You said to me once"—Thomas was looking with interest into a garden with nothing interesting in it—"that you felt you ought to be good, or God would take away the things you loved."

"So what?" said Grace, almost submitting to a childish desire to stamp her foot in her temper. "So what? You think I'm doing this so God gives me Nathan?"

"I do think that. And haven't I known you all your life?" Now she had twenty pieces of steel to weigh her down in the baptistery. They were lined on the workbench, and began to shine: the sun was coming out.

"I haven't seen him in so long," she said, "and when I don't see him everything is dull and flat. But I asked him to come, and he said he would. He will, I trust he will." She closed her eyes against Thomas; and when she opened them again, her aunt was coming quickly up the garden, carrying a white dress.

Shortly before four in the afternoon, as Bethesda's harmonium began to play for Grace, a violent wind dispersed the oppressive clouds that had enclosed Aldleigh all day. Thomas walked alone up London Road with the basket containing soft white rolls and apple cake made because Grace had asked him to do it. After her baptism, when her soaked clothes were exchanged for dry ones, they'd go together to the cold hall behind the chapel and have tea, where once an old man in a lavish coat had drunk himself into confusion. As Thomas walked, the beeches blazed where the low sun struck them, and the effect was of walking alone and unharmed through a forest fire.

Thomas thought of Anne coming to the shed with the baptismal dress, and of her cautious greeting: "Oh," she'd said, "you're here," conveying her sorrow that since the fire he'd been absent from the house of God. How could he explain that he'd exchanged the substance of things hoped for and the evidence of things not seen for James Bower, and a ten-inch reflecting telescope interred behind a wall?

It struck him that he'd never been so happy, but was wise enough to understand that his happiness consisted largely of hope. Their meeting in the ruin had been intimate and strange, and had sustained his spirit for days; but quickly they'd reverted to their easy pretense of being boys with a mystery on their hands. So they spoke only of where Maria Văduva had gone, and whether another casket of papers had been buried in the park; but all the while, Thomas attended minutely to every phrase and gesture, and worked at decoding them.

Meanwhile James Bower walked in fine weather with his wife, thinking with gratitude that he was briefly content with his lot. All day they'd been occupied with the administration of a shared life, and now accepted the beauty of the evening as an annual grace. The children would be all right in the end (she'd said, taking his hand), and if the oldest was quite a silent child it was not (he said, kissing the hand that held his) their fault, and likely wouldn't last. There was trouble with a bill or two, but that would resolve itself; and James was always tired (now she was laughing at him), but then he wasn't as young as he'd once been, and after all quite battle-scarred and not such a beauty these days.

They rounded a corner, and there was Bethesda on London Road, where James had once heard the harmonium, and seen Thomas Hart going quickly across the car park. Was it possible he heard that same melody again? Wind released beech leaves from their branches and raised eddies that made James think a devil was on the move; then "Look!" his wife said. "Look: isn't that your ghost?" The leaves abruptly dropped. "It is," she said.

It wasn't necessary for James to look up in order to see quite plainly the long coat of fine pale wool and highly polished shoes; the curious poise arising partly out of pain, and the old way of seeming to occupy an atmosphere that bemused and charmed his friends. But he did look: behold the man, behold the coat. He carried a basket, which gave him a strange feminine aspect, and he was standing very still. James felt oddly ashamed. It wasn't that he thought Thomas too strange a man to be introduced to his wife—wasn't he at all times courteous, and clever, and kind?—it was that they'd existed together on the margins, chaperoned by a woman who was dead.

"I think he looks wonderful," she was saying, laughing as Thomas came nearer, and it struck James unpleasantly that he'd like to cross the road to avoid him. Now Thomas was shifting the basket from hand to hand as if it were heavy, and he was coming nearer. "Introduce him to me," said his wife, smoothing her hair, "though perhaps he'll vanish and you'll see he really was a ghost after all—oh James, poor man. Don't look." Thomas Hart was on his knees. The basket was in the gutter, and white things were scattered on the pavement and rolling under cars. Thomas fumbled with the dropped cloth; he gave a small frustrated cry audible above the traffic and harmonium. Then he stood with the care of an injured man, and came toward them, his coat blackened at the hem, the wicker basket frayed. He's embarrassed, thought James, that's why he looks so odd.

His wife, going forward with the unfailing kindness he loved, held out her hand. "I promise," she said, "I didn't see a thing."

Thomas showed her his palms, which were wet with mud from the gutter. "I'm filthy," he said, "I'm afraid. James, good afternoon: you look well—you must have been to Lowlands without me. And this is—?" He gave James a look of inquiry, reserved and polite.

"This is Emily," said James, "this is my wife. Emily, this is Thomas."

"Emily." Thomas spoke as if he'd never heard the name before, and the syllables were giving him trouble. "Your wife," he said, and inclined his head in understanding. The harmonium struck up again.

"He often talks about you," said James Bower's wife. "In fact I've sometimes been jealous of what you two have been getting up to with your mysteries and your ghosts. So I'm glad to meet you," she said, "I'm glad to have met my rival. But listen, aren't you late?" They stood by Potter's Field, and heard the congregation singing: "*When sorrows like sea billows roll—*"

"I expect I got the time wrong," said Thomas, "I'm always making mistakes." He moved away with a gesture of farewell, and a look not possible to decipher behind the hard glaze of his eyes. James took his wife's hand. He almost felt he was doing so for consolation. "Goodbye," he said; but already Thomas Hart was headed for Bethesda as if for a shore. "I think I've heard that song before," said James. *It is well, it is well with my soul.*

Thomas found the chapel altered. The communion table had been put by the harmonium, and the baptistery was open. The small deep cavity was tiled blue like a municipal swimming pool, and filled to the brim with water that had poured all day from copper taps. The water had been warmed by an iron heater clamped to the rim beside the steps, and this caused threads of steam to dissipate in the cool chapel air.

He found the pew that had been his since birth, and sat under the ten stilled moons bewildered by humiliation and loss. Emily, he thought, childishly despising the name, and the kindly smile, and the easy acceptance of her husband's hand; despising her hair, her clothes, the pavement where she'd stood. But what was lost, after all? Hope, that was it—the sensation of the world opening out with each encounter, of every word foretelling the next word, and the next, until—now that was all gone. Worse, everything that had been done and said was now absurd, and Thomas himself ridiculous. It has all been false pretenses, thought Thomas, relieved to find anger arriving alongside loss: he knew what he was doing—wasn't he there, too? Now the congregation bent their heads in prayer, and how could Thomas join them? What prayer or praise could he rustle up now, with bruises coming up on his knees? The world consisted of nothing but the hard familiar pew. He looked at Grace, seated between her father and her aunt. She had a new hat on, and it drooped at the brim; there was defiance in the set of her shoulders under the loose white dress. This is all because of that boy, he thought, but he won't come, not if I know men, and I do. It would be better if he went away, because how can she stand it, when she's only a child?

The pastor came down from the pulpit. He put fisherman's waders on to protect his chapel suit from the water, and called Grace Macaulay to the lectern to give an account of her salvation. The atmosphere in the chapel was merry as she spoke of the helplessness of her eternal soul and surety of her salvation: a sheep was being gathered safely into the fold. But Thomas knew loss when he saw it, and that she cried less for her soul than for her body. Nothing but trouble, he thought, pouring anger on a careless boy: you've been nothing but trouble all along.

The pastor walked down into the water and held out his hand to Grace, who stood barefoot at the brim. I object, thought Thomas, I have a thousand just impediments! The pastor began to pray. Grace sighed, and frowned, and as she came forward caught her hem with her heel. There was the sound of tearing cloth, and of a handful of shining weights rattling down. With a humiliated exclamation of distress, Grace bent to pick up what she could, and Thomas heard the chapel door quietly open. He turned. Nathan was on the threshold. His colored clothes were violent against the cold pale walls; music came faintly through headphones clasped about his neck. He sought out Grace and couldn't find her. He took his glasses from his pocket, and looked again. There she was, in her absurd dress, kneeling at the rim of the water. You are late, thought Thomas, look, you've already caused her pain, and she'll just keep bearing it over and over again. Then the young man's gaze found his, and his expression altered: There you are, Thomas Hart! He smiled and came forward. Thomas shook his head with the slow deliberate motion of a threat: You aren't welcome, you're not wanted, you never were. The boy flinched as if struck, and briefly Thomas pitied his bewildered look, which was almost one of pain. Nathan saw Grace reach for the pastor's hand, and enter into the water with her back turned to the door. His bewilderment deepened, and possibly there was also a look of resignation. He nodded once at Thomas, and turned his back, and left.

The pastor spoke to Grace. She nodded: yes, she said. Yes. She smiled. Someone began to sing. One by one that solitary voice was joined until the pale vault of Bethesda's roof threw back the song. The water reached the child's waist and blackened her dress; then easily, as if they'd practiced the steps of a holy dance, the pastor passed an arm around her back, and grasped her wrists where they were crossed at her breast. "In the name of the Father," he said (the chapel door banged shut), "and of the Son, and of the Holy Ghost." Then the roving sunlight struck the disks of yellow glass fixed in the windows by the pulpit, and refracting down at the ordained degree lit the surface of the water in the baptistery. So Grace Macaulay, turning with unmet hope toward the closing door, entered the shining pool not with the look of falling but of something headed for the sun, and the body of the sinner was lost to unmerited light.

PART TWO

2008

The Law of Equal Areas
in Equal Time

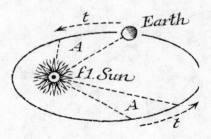

Fig. 2

It was October. The earth and all her passengers, listing to starboard, sailed through the wake of Halley's Comet, causing a meteor shower that was brighter and more lovely than Halley's last transit had been, the memory being better than the event.

October, then; and stars fell over the wet black verges of the A12, and the wet green lawns of the Colchester barracks; they fell over the Aldwinter tomb tree, and the housing estates in Chelmsford going up where poorhouses and leper colonies had been. Being fair-minded, they also fell on Aldleigh, and on a tall man coming down the high street with a satchel on his back. He wore the vestments of a Catholic priest, which suited him so well he might have grown them out of his own marrow: a white chasuble thrown up by his hasty, long-legged gait, and a fringed stole dripping underneath; a cincture signaling continence and chastity, and a green amice embroidered with a cross from which gold thread came unstitched. Those who saw him noted the impression of power he gave, for all that he couldn't have been a day under seventy; they noted also the scent that followed him, which was of incense and whisky. Essex being a place of dissent, he received none of the deference that might have come his way in Norfolk, and certainly in Dublin or Nice; but a man leaving the Jackdaw and Crow was visited with ancestral memories of the confessional, and crossed himself without noticing he did it.

All change, thought this man in sorrow, passing the Aldleigh war memorial, which had lately been polished and regilded; all change, he thought, wondering where the butcher's had gone, with its sawdust floor and its chains in the door to keep bluebottles out. Where was the shoe shop with its striped awning, and why was it all so clean? Faintly he recalled potholes in the high street, and newsagents advertising cigarettes, and a café where once he'd been given bacon and eggs by a woman who certainly knew he was in no position to pay. A star fell on the roof of the old town hall, where two gray-haired men wearing green carnations kissed without shame on the steps and ducked under confetti—where had the museum gone, and the man who'd sat in its offices? Now he came to the Alder, and it was all change there: the water cleansed according to certain municipal decrees, the drunken shopping trolleys absent from the bank. He watched the tidy river running and drank from a bottle he kept in his pocket, then struck out for London Road. No change yet in Potter's Field, and no use found for the land: brambles dotted with unpicked berries blasted by weather, and a single censorious jay.

When he came to Bethesda he found it unaltered as the Northern Star. The chain was off the gate. It was the evening of the Lord's Day and the harmonium was playing. Against the austere chapel brick the old man's garments had the splendor of kings. He took a hymn book from the lobby table and went quickly in, and saw with gratitude the ten lights with their look of moons stalled in their orbit, the narrow windows with their meager disks of colored glass. But all the same, change in Bethesda, too—where was Anne Macaulay? Where was her brother, with his look of having seen a sorrow that had passed the whole world by? And where was that child Grace, with her petticoats edged with lace; where was his friend? It was a congregation of strangers.

A man came down from the pulpit and stood beside the communion table, which had a white cloth on it. His beard was silver and square as a shovel, and the visitor recognized him with gratitude and relief: this was the deacon, not much changed, who'd once welcomed him in with a hand on his sleeve. "*For I have received of the Lord,*" said the deacon, "*that which also I delivered unto you, that the Lord Jesus the same night in which he was betrayed took bread.*" There were silver platters on the table, and cubes of cheap white bread on them; beyond the narrow windows squabbling cars blared their horns, and only the visitor heard it. Solemnly the deacon came down to the pews, and the silver plate was passed from hand to hand. "*This do,*" said the deacon, "*in remembrance of me.*" The bread was chewed in silence, and the body of Christ was broken again in Essex.

The visitor stood. He raised his arms in the moony light. "Please," he said, "I must take bread with you also." The congregation turned, and took in the Catholic vestments, the scent of whisky. "Please," the old man said. The deacon paused. He surveyed the visitor. Impossible to judge what calculations of manners and theology went concealed behind that beard; but after a time he went down the narrow aisle and offered the old man the plate. The visitor took bread, and ate it, and crossed himself; and this act, having as much to do with Bethesda's Protestant God as the slaughter of three black hens, caused a watchful child to gasp. "*After the same manner also,*" said the deacon placidly, "*he took the cup, saying, 'This cup is the new testament in my blood.'*" He poured thick liquid from a silver jug into a silver beaker, and was smiling privately. "*This do ye,*" he said, "*as oft as ye drink it, in remembrance of me.*" The cup was passed from hand to hand, and wiped at the rim between each supplicant; then the deacon put the tilted rim to the old man's mouth, so that he could drink without use of his

hands. "*For as often as ye eat this bread,*" said the deacon, returning to the shadow of the pulpit, "*and drink this cup, ye do
shew the Lord's death till he come.*"

The harmonium drew a breath and brought the matter to
an end. The stranger spread his vestments out, and watched
the chapel empty of men and women who passed his pew with
wary courteous nods. The senior deacon, last to leave, took
keys from his pocket and said, "I know you. I'm certain I do. I
trust you found the service a blessing."

The visitor inclined his remarkable head.

"Ought I to call you Father?" said the deacon, who gestured
at the gold cross unwinding on the stole (it was clear that under no circumstances would he call any man Father, no matter
the length and whiteness of his robes).

"No need for that." The visitor stood and with difficulty put
his satchel on his back. "I came looking for my friend," he said,
"but he isn't here." The deacon put the ten moons out. The
stranger pursued him to the door. "Please," he said, "could you
tell me where he is?"

They came out to the car park, and a falling star briefly
stitched a thread of light above the town. Solemnly the deacon
locked the chapel doors; solemnly he put away the key. "He's
rather a man of the world, these days," he said. "You'll find him
where he has always been: at home, on Lower Bridge Road."

At home, on Lower Bridge Road: Thomas Hart, upright and
contented at his dining table. Little change here; though the
keen observer might think the painting over the mantelpiece
has the look, does it not, of an Augustus John; that the sideboard sports no fewer than fifteen bits of gilded Moser glass.
There is altogether a look of richness about the place, and
about Thomas himself, who was buffeted by the winds of

acclaim at the age of fifty-eight on the publication of his novel *The Horse and Rider* (dedicated *for J. B.: His Book*). Carleton, reading the novel as he walked home from work and late in the evening by lamplight, was pleased and startled to find the ambiguity he'd deplored in the early works of Thomas Hart replaced with a candor he admired, but which he could never reconcile with the nicely composed gentleman at his desk. Now and then, in Aldleigh or on Bishopsgate or in dentists' waiting rooms, Thomas encounters strangers part avid and part shy, and sometimes the brisk inquiry: "Didn't you write that book—and didn't you win that prize?" Yes, he confesses: and nobody (he assures them) could be more surprised than he, for who wants the work of a dusty old Baptist, whose sentences run on for a page? Readers attend the readings he gives and queue beyond the door—often his hand is mutely squeezed, he's sometimes embraced and embraces in return. In some quarters he's believed too sentimental to be taken seriously, and fatally flawed by a tendency to think too kindly of his characters—but Thomas believes that any writer who thinks himself better than the products of his own imagination should seek out some more appropriate profession (such as dentistry, for example, or the construction of dry-stone walls).

He keeps up his column in the *Essex Chronicle*, to the bemusement of its younger staff. He remains a citizen of the empire of the moon, and has devoted the past ten years to acquiring a schoolboy's understanding of astronomy and physics: ask him about the easiest means to observe storms on the surface of the sun, for example, or how the spectrometer splits the white light of a star and reveals the fingerprints of God, and he becomes a talkative man. He has not dispensed with God, for all that this would be simple and convenient:

sometimes on a Sunday morning his feet take him to Bethesda, and he doesn't object. He's rarely in London these days, and prefers his own company to that of other men (none of whom, after all, are James Bower). He is happy, except when he isn't; and the old wounds in his hip and heart still sometimes give him trouble.

Maria Văduva, made more or less incarnate, has become a sitting tenant. He does nothing to evict her. Often as he writes she reaches over his shoulder and puts her finger to the screen: *Come now, Thomas Hart*, she'll say, polishing a lens on the sleeve of her gown, *come on, you old deceiver, it wasn't like that at all*. She is the organizing principle. Did Thomas love a man who did not love him? Well: so did she. Does his neck ache, what with all the looking at the moon? Hers will one day break. Can he think of Lowlands without sorrow? She hands him a handkerchief and it's already wet. "One day," he tells her, watching Orion walk over the railway bridge, "I'll get to the bottom of this, you mark my words." She doubts it.

So Thomas, upright at his dining table, emailed Grace Macaulay. A year had passed since last they met; but since she changed not at all in the first twenty-nine years of her life, he imagined this last one hadn't dislodged her black curls, her costumes of brocade and lace, her adamant affection and deplorable temper. *Come home, you wretched child*, he wrote, *it won't be long now—*

— it can't be long. Last week they brought in the hospital bed, and we put it where the dining table was, where every Sunday we ate tea at five o'clock and your father read from his Bible. Now I can hardly remember the room without it: the present comes in like a tide over the past.

Your father is a fine nurse. Did you ever see him boil an
egg? Now he scrambles and poaches them to tempt her,
and never burns the toast.

Every day she asks after you, and I'm running out of
ways to lie. She is busy, I say. Or: she is in Paris. But
you've never been to Paris and have no excuse for not
being here. Come home, you wretched child! Do you
think yourself no longer welcome, because you've
dispensed with God? Do you think you will need to
make a pretense of faith, for her sake? She will accept
you as you are, and so will I—your father, I suspect, will
not. But he always said you were a sinner, so what did
he expect?

A train leaves Liverpool Street tomorrow at 5:03. I'll be
waiting at the station. I'll take you home.

"Wretched child," he said with a prick of anger he imagined
must be like that of a father: amplified by love (his household
ghost solidified against the window, obscuring a solitary
star—*Nonetheless*, she said, speaking out of his own memory
and guilt, *might you say you played your part in this, Thomas
Hart?*).

"Leave me in peace, Maria"—but he smelled the water in
Bethesda's baptistery and saw Nathan turned away at the door,
and time had not passed as it ought to have done: there was
Grace pulled out of the shining water, her face all hope and
wanting. *All my love*, he wrote. Evening ceded gratefully to
night. Stars fell on the railway bridge. Somebody was at the
door.

*

Richard Dimitru Dines said, "Hello," and with difficulty put down his bag.

"Hello," said Thomas. Ought he to say what a surprise it was, to see the old man on his doorstep dressed like a priest with a communion wafer in his pocket? Perhaps, but this would not be true. Things pass, and they return—"Hello," he said; and then (what use are manners, when you've washed a man in the bathtub and picked lice from his hair?): "I see you're drunk. You'd better come in. I'll put the kettle on."

"It is true," said Dines equably. "I am drunk. I am also hungry, and would like to sit down, if you please."

Thomas did please. He dislodged Maria from the armchair (she shook her black skirts and seeped sulkily into the wall) and put Dines in it. "It suits you," he said, "this ludicrous getup, though I don't believe for a minute that you ought to be wearing it."

"Ought I not?" Dines raised his arms, and lifted the wings of his chasuble: he looked angelic, if angels ever grew weary of their duties and consoled themselves with drink. "No," he said, "I am not ordained exactly, but a man might be ordained by the Almighty as much as by a seminary. It is quite surprising to me that you doubt it."

"Then tell me: are you a Catholic now?" said Thomas, not troubling to conceal his Baptist distaste.

"Why not!" said Dines. He raised his hands again, and Thomas saw that here time had been kind: the pitiful nubs at the nail beds were almost what they ought to be; the knuckles, if swollen, did not look as if the bone might at any moment erupt through the skin. The loose thumb, neither use nor ornament, had been removed, and a new scar marked the absence. "Why not?" said Dines again. "And I like to have these things on me, so that people look and say: There goes a man of God."

Thomas, speaking from the kitchen, said, "You've found your faith, I see, no doubt in the last place you looked." He ground coffee; he unwrapped parkin cakes from brown paper. "You shouldn't drink so late," he said, seeing Dines pull ecstatically at a bottle. "Alcohol produces poor-quality sleep, and you look tired."

"It is empty," said Dines, and threw the bottle at the wall. Thomas, seeing the old man was not so blithe as he seemed, put buttered parkin on a gilded saucer and gave it to him.

"I haven't found my faith," said Dines between bites. "I wonder where I put it?"

"But isn't this faith?" said Thomas, tugging at the fringed stole, noting that it could do with a clean. "Doesn't an attempt at faith constitute faith itself? It's a dreadful thing to confuse faith with certainty."

"You were yourself absent from the house of God today, were you not? And what is wrong with you—does something hurt you in your hip?"

"I had a fall," said Thomas, "and nothing has been right since. And these days I seek out my faith in other doctrines"— he gestured at a spectrograph nearby and a four-inch reflecting telescope fitted with filters to aid in observations of the sun. "I supplement God with physics, and understand each as well as the other. Which is to say: not in the least! But I find it magnificent, knowledge piled on knowledge, and the matter never closed—it's all no less strange and marvelous to me than the Resurrection, and it takes as much faith for me to believe it."

In companionable silence they ate and drank; and Dines took off his stole and with it his priestly look. "Where's that black-haired girl," he said, "who might have come from my country? Her pew was empty."

"She lives in London. In Hackney, which she tells me these

days is quite fashionable, above a pizza shop. I wrote to her to-day and told her to come home. Her aunt is dying from a tu-mor in the stomach that was in her brain and bones before she knew she was ill."

"And what then of your friend," said Dimi, growing astute. "What of your man, whose name was James?"

"Gone, I'm afraid. Gone from Aldleigh, from Essex, from me—gone in fact without saying he was going until after he was gone. Now, I'm no fool, old man"—Thomas, smiling, heard on the stairs the movement of black skirts shedding pearl beads—"is it possible that you didn't come here alone?"

The old man regarded him in silent mischief, then put his satchel on the table. "The mystery is solved," he said. With dif-ficulty he brought out a file, and a black book that still re-tained, in its stitches and binding, fragments of the earth in Potter's Field.

"You still have her diary," said Thomas, not with surprise, but satisfaction.

"I always have it with me, and the translation is complete: it has been the last work of my life to raise Maria like Lazarus from her grave. So I shall tell you again: the mystery is solved."

"All solved?" said Thomas (and James, he thought: where are you now?). "You know what she did, and where she went?"

"Not, I confess, solved entirely," said Dines, "but much is clear. For example"—he examined the diary and found its last written page—"you see that her final entry was on the seven-teenth of June 1889. After that: nothing. I daresay this date means nothing to you, being English."

"Nothing whatever." Thomas bent to see words blotted by a woman in distress. He touched the page, and was surprised to find his hand unstained by ink.

Dines, speaking importantly as if from the pulpit, said, "Maria Văduva Bell, on the seventeenth of June 1889, the same night on which we might think she disappeared, believed she discovered a comet. Let me read to you, Thomas, from the translation I have made. It was *a pearly smear*, she wrote, *extending fully two degrees from a nucleus—seeming to thicken and brighten as I watched*—she grows excited. *A comet— neither sought, nor expected*—now: you see she has a tendency to sentimentality, which we may forgive—*seen first by me*, she writes, *a woman now of Essex, whose heart was broken, but whose mind never was!*"

Thomas said, "A comet."

"A comet," said Dines.

"Have I always been blind to everything? Did I never see what was in front of my eyes?"

"It does surprise me," said the old man in haughty reproof, "that you did not think of it."

"But where is it in the records? Is it a periodic comet— when is the return?" (Silently he pleaded with the celestial mechanic: God, let me see it—let me have that, at least!)

"That is not really the sort of thing I know," said Dines, "but certainly she made her observations and noted its position—"

"The right ascension and declination, yes," said Thomas, "that is the location of any point in the sky at any point in time, just as latitude and longitude—"

"But the document is gone. It is not there. Look." Dines displayed the empty pages of the book.

"I must be clear on this." It was midnight. Thomas was alert down to the last filament of his body. "Maria Văduva Bell, having discovered a comet from the grounds of Lowlands House, disappeared that night or soon after, and did nothing whatever about it?"

Immense, triumphant, as if he himself had set the comet rolling down its orbit: "Yes," said Dines. "Shall I tell you more?"

"Not yet," said Thomas. He turned to the computer. "First, we should establish whether she did see a comet, or whether it was only her wanting that did it—you know it is possible to love in such a way that you command reality, that your sight cannot be trusted! If there was a comet, it would have been observed in this hemisphere, and there'll be a record. Nothing on the seventeenth of June 1889," he said, frowning over the astronomical catalogues, "but the following day in France, the astronomer Vincent du Lac identified a comet in Cassiopeia, which was first designated 1889 III (du Lac) and then, because I suppose nothing about comets can ever be straightforward, 330P/1889 L1 (du Lac)—might it be possible that in fact Văduva was the primary observer?"

"It might," said Dimitru.

"I wish you wouldn't keep interrupting," said Thomas. "And—yes—it is a short-period comet—an estimated period of a hundred and seventeen to a hundred and eighteen years— so it is coming back to us: we need only wait ten years!" Thomas Hart, seated in his dining room with his deerskin slippers on, closed his eyes, and felt the charge of the comet's tail and its streams of astronomical dust; he was untethered again from the earth, a dutiful citizen of celestial empires, and riding the solar winds. "Well," he said. "Fuck me."

"But ten years," lamented the old man. "We'll be dead by then, Thomas, we shall have obtained our reward. Now I've come a long way, and you must listen. Maria wrote often of a man she loved, who did not love her. Perhaps you remember."

"I remember."

"This man was indicated by the letter M. We may call this a clue. In due course I came across another. You recall how she speaks of Lucifer arriving at her window as if he were a lover?"

"That's no mystery. That is merely a reference to Venus, the morning and the evening star."

"You are quite mistaken, Thomas, having no facility with the poets of any languages which are not your own. I, on the other hand, was in an instant transported to the classroom, and to the studies of Romanian literature, and in particular of Mihai Eminescu, the greatest of our poets, who conceived of Venus as Lucifer the Morning Star, who arrived at a woman's window and caused her to love him. Mihai. M. A great man, whom she loved, as I understand it, without hope and without return. You will also I am sure recall her envy of pretty Veronica. That is certainly Veronica Micle, who was the poet's lover. So"—he spread his hands; he was magnificent—"you see the matter is solved."

"Say his name again," said Thomas, "spell it for me"; he turned again to his computer, and there in a moment the poet was, drawn down through time and seated with them at the table. "Yes," said Thomas, "yes, I see," and looked with envy and admiration at the poet's full mouth and soft down-turned eyes, which seemed only softer against the firmness of his jaw. "Poor Maria—it isn't fair," he said, surprised by grief. "It isn't fair that beauty secures love so easily, and often without meaning to."

"I should tell you," said Dines, "that his face was better than his work. Still: do you see the date of his death? The fifteenth of June 1889—two days before the comet came. He died in the sanatorium where doctors tormented him with mercury for his syphilis, and his dying hope was for a glass of milk. So Maria had the news—she did the great thing she hoped would bring her love—but already the source of love was gone."

"But if Maria saw the comet on that date, it is hers: after all she did one great thing that should be told among men. It is hers, and not du Lac's—we owe a debt," said Thomas, "to truth. Perhaps she buried her observations back in Potter's Field— perhaps in the walls of Lowlands House—something must come right. Am I to give my readers nothing but longing and loss?"

"If I were her I should go home and take my papers with me. What is Essex, when there is Bucharest? Even now, with all that was done to it by ignorance and power, it is our Little Paris. So this is what we are going to do, Thomas. I will take Maria back to my country, and speak there with the librarians and the Eminescu scholars, who'll be kind to an old priest. And I will leave my translation with you, and you will look for her in Essex. Now my hands hurt. You should have put me to bed by now."

Thomas returned the old man to his old room. He knelt at his feet and took off his boots with the quiet untroubled attention with which he'd once washed him in the bath, and dressed him in pyjamas that were too small. The tall broad body smelled as if it were failing, as all bodies fail in the end. "Thank you," said Dimitru. "Please leave on the lights."

Then sleepless Thomas sat up late in the company of Maria, and no stars fell.

17 JUNE 1889
Lowlands House

Astounding night—my heart beats in my fingertips and
disturbs the pen!—still I must make my account—the great
thing I longed for has come to me at last!

These past days I have been sick—my head has ached—
indeed I vomited three times, which caused John Bell joy,
imagining we were to have a child, though thank God we
are not. So being sick I slept last night as a child might
sleep, having no thought of the hands of the clock—and
woke before dawn to a sky with no cloud in it, and no pain
or trouble in my mind or body. What then could I do,
being awake and strong as a boy, but go to my telescope?
John petitioned me with tears to remain indoors, but it was
good Essex weather, the sky having the look of a black pool
on which sunlight sometimes played—so I made some
observations of Jupiter, my heart tender at the circling
moons, and perfectly comprehending their stupid loyalty—

Since the moon waxed bright above the southwest horizon,
I turned toward the darker portion of the sky, and passed
an hour slewing back and forth, released for a time from
the sorrow attending me on earth—then all at once my
heart and mind halted, as a loose dog might halt at a high
gate! It was a stop upon my soul! My eyes did not stop—
for they had seen a blur in Cassiopeia, faint as a bird's
breath might be in winter—and having also a bluish look! I
discovered that I was weeping, and could no longer see, and
could hardly have told the moon from Jupiter for the heat
and thickness of my tears—I wiped my eyes on my sleeve
and looked again, in terror that I had knocked the eyepiece,

and so lost my treasure as if I were on board ship and had
thrown it overboard—but there, again: a pearly smear
extending fully two degrees from a nucleus, this nucleus
also having a blurred look, only seeming to thicken and
brighten as I watched—a comet, beyond doubt or
confusion!—undiscovered, unexpected, arriving in Essex
out of the chilly vastness—seen first by me, a woman whose
heart was broken, but whose mind could never be! I felt
myself divide, as a cell divides in its dogged pursuit of life—
so that in part I was dancing in Cassiopeia, and standing on
its points with the comet in my palm; and in part I was
with M. in some street in Bucharest, bringing him what I'd
found as a dog going to her master—

I will repeat my observations tomorrow—I will be sure of
what I've done—and have made meanwhile a document,
which I shall take to the Royal Astronomical Society
in London, that the matter may be examined and
corroborated. The injustice done to Maria Mitchell was
quickly restored—but who'd count on a woman's luck!

Dear James,

When I took all these shameful letters out from where I
hide them, I saw a year had passed since I last wrote your
name. But all the same: I've had you in mind. Do you
remember me—do you ever have me in mind?

And do you ever think of our old friend Maria? Well, I've
got something to tell you: her diary has come back to me,
and I have it with me here. Again and again I read the final
page, and still I can hardly believe my eyes. All that time,
here at my table and in Lowlands House with the mist
coming in, we wondered who she was and what she
saw—all that time, and now we know. James: it was a
comet, and the comet's coming back. Shouldn't we have
known? Shouldn't we have guessed?

So now I have a new task on my hands: I'll see to it Maria
gets her name in the books of stars. I won't have her
forgotten. There is a comet they call Miss Mitchell's after
the woman who found it, but it would have been wrongly
named for an Italian man had she not argued her case.
Well, since our Maria cannot argue hers, I will argue for her.

(I paused just then to look up Miss Mitchell's Comet, and
found it has a hyperbolic orbit. Do you know what that
means? It means it has escaped the draw of the sun, and
will never return. I want to say: how are you, James Bower,
moving down that orbit of yours? Will I ever see you again?)

((But I will never post this letter. I'm no fool.))

THOMAS HART

ON FRAUNHOFER LINES

THOMAS HART, *ESSEX CHRONICLE*,
12 NOVEMBER 2008

Imagine you wake from uneasy dreams to find light beaming from the soles of your feet and the palms of your hands. If you woke in a temper, I suppose the light might be red, and if you slept well, perhaps a peaceable green. Now I hear all my readers say: What strange notions you have, Thomas Hart! But bear with me: this isn't quite as absurd as it sounds. In fact, all your life you've been radiating electromagnetic waves, but since you never radiate the part of the spectrum that can be seen, we can tell nothing about you just by looking.

The stars are another matter. Look carefully, and you'll see their ancestry. Starlight and sunlight, split by a diffraction grating, display their own distinctive patterns of color. I have always wanted to see this for myself, and recently bought an old spectrograph. It resembles two miniature telescopes mounted on a dais marked with numbers, and has been testing my poor skills and my patience for weeks. Then yesterday, just past noon, I finally saw the full spectrum of the sun projected on a sheet of paper pinned to the dining-room wall: a vivid rainbow flattened to a bar, the colors interrupted at intervals by narrow black bands, where there was no light or color at all.

These absences of light are known as the Fraunhofer lines, and show where light has been absorbed by the matter it was passing through—and their placement allows us to determine the nature and composition of the matter present in the moment of its birth, in the nebula of formation: the fingerprints of God.

The strange thing is that when I first saw these lines I was almost afraid. Even a child knows the shape and color of a rainbow, and I hated to see the rainbow broken on the wall like a shattered window. It was as if I'd been speaking to a friend I'd known all my life, who by a single word or action showed that in fact I knew nothing about them at all.

Imagine you are radiating light, I said. Well: perhaps you are—but I suspect you withhold it, too.

Grace Macaulay—in whose veins ran Essex rivers and Bible ink; in whose philosophy the devils of hell and the saints of Bethesda did battle with her reason and her nature—sat with her phone on the bare floor of a Hackney room and thought of Thomas Hart. *Come home*, he'd written, *you wretched child*, and I am wretched, she thought, and I think I'd like to go home.

She was twenty-nine, and ten years gone from the pew. That is to say: she was gone from her pew no more than Thomas was gone from his. It was true that she was no longer fastened there by guilt and love and obligation, but sometimes found herself back in the shadow of Bethesda's pulpit more or less out of habit, head covered by a borrowed hat and submitting to the consolation of the hymns. But the lucid certainty of her faith in the Lowlands fire now struck her as the last act of a child. Had she really believed that God—setting aside Albania and Afghanistan and continents of children dying under torn mosquito nets—would attend to a shortsighted reckless boy in Aldleigh? She had believed it, and had been willing to submit to baptism in her gratitude, but God after all had not been faithful and just (steam rose forever from the baptistery; the narrow door to the wide world never opened for Nathan).

She thought of the boy she'd loved with anger and

sorrow accommodated in the bare facts of her life, along-side the date of her birth and the size of her feet. That he hadn't come had betrayed her faith in God, and love, and the rewards of reaching after goodness. That afterward Na-than had never thought to seek her out had aroused an im-placable fury nothing like her childlike bursts of temper that so often ended in an embrace. All the same, in those past ten years she'd looked for him on the upper deck of buses and on station platforms and in the dreary offices where she worked, and never found him. Every year or so, with a painful opening in the chamber of her heart where he was kept, she opened social media profiles and con-structed an idea of herself that seemed to her lovable; but she never found him, and he never found her.

The room was cold; it contained nothing of what Grace Macaulay loved. No absurd petticoats of lace and silk—no pendants, bangles, hair-combs, and boots with laces replaced by ribbon. She had severed herself from herself. No scent of frankincense or lavender oil rising out of her hair and arms, only the penetrating smell of greasy dough rising perpetually up from the pizza place downstairs, diminishing her appe-tite. A pack of Silk Cut and a lighter were set beside a saucer on the windowsill where often she leaned out to shudder at the smoke, and watch the overground trains head for Croy-don and Dalston. Her few clothes hung austerely on a rail, and a television overlooked the foot of the bed; she watched it indiscriminately and with confusion, trying to make Bethesda's child into an ordinary woman. And indeed she was ordinary, where certain essential matters were concerned—had not believed in hell since the day she'd laughed at the belt in her father's hand, devoutly hoped to one day see Thomas Hart with a man he loved on the steps of the registry office in the old town hall, was untroubled by the idea her ancestors had been stooped, and naked save for their own pelts. Each day she sent this ordinary woman out into the world, and passed more or less without notice, acquiring friends and lovers and colleagues; and what had at first been an anguished sense of her own strangeness had dwindled down to the discomfort of rough clothes worn over sunburn.

But *come home*, said Thomas; and now she heard—above the crowds headed for the station, the hungry customers converging on the pavements—the old harmonium and the sound of her aunt singing, and saw Bethesda's lights like moons against the rented wall. It suited her few friends to imagine she'd been subject to a thousand physical and spiritual abuses, and been thrown out of chapel doors that then were bolted against her. It was difficult to explain that her father and her aunt received her absence with sorrow tempered by their trust in the will of God. She would return to Bethesda, or she wouldn't, and really Grace herself had little to do with it: it all came down to predestination. Distance permitted her to view them clearly—her father's grief, and his sincere determination to serve his God; her aunt's shy diligent affection—and to love them better, and wish she could please them.

She looked again at her phone, which was busying itself with inconsequential messages: was she free tomorrow? Had she seen the news? What time on Friday? And there in the London noise was Thomas Hart, writing as if seated with sheets of ivory paper at his table on Lower Bridge Road: *come home*. She smiled, and smoothed her jeans as if they were yards of scarlet cotton over a rotting satin petticoat, and wrote:

Dear Thomas—all right. I'll come home tomorrow. Will you really meet me? Does she know I'm coming? And does she know I kept away because I can't believe this is happening and I don't want to see it?

I read your column online. I think you're the only person in
the world who knows all my colors and I'm the only person
who knows all yours! I still always want to tell you
everything. Like this: last night I think I saw eternity.
I often used to try and see it when I was little, because
I knew that to die is to enter eternity, but I never could.
I'd imagine a trapdoor opening under my grave, and
something waiting underneath, but I could never picture
time without end.

Then last night as I was almost sleeping I felt the strangest
thing. Something was lifting up my bed, and it was tilting
up at the foot, and I was sliding against the mattress
toward the wall. I went on sliding and the wall was
opening up to let me in and the bed was tilting and I was
falling—but I understood that I was falling upward, and
because of that I'd never stop, it would just go on and on.

What do you make of that?

See you soon—

G

I'll be there, of course. I'll take you to her. We'll surprise
her with you.

It sounds to me like you are having visions—you are Julian
of Aldleigh, you should sit all day in a white stone cell and
weep with joy at the wounds of Christ. This is what I make
of it: I'm quite an old man now, and will die before you. In
that case my eternity will begin before yours—but if
eternity has a beginning, how can it be infinite?

I think this is eternity, Grace Macaulay—I don't think it
begins, I think it has begun. So this is eternity, we are
taking part in it right now—I send this email in eternity,
and I'll see you in eternity on platform 2.

THOMAS HART

Anne Macaulay, sick and tired, woke early after dreamless and unrestful sleep, and watched dawn illuminate the thin blue blanket on her knees, the paper kidney dish into which she'd vomited, the furred leaves of the African violets ranged in their saucers on the windowsill. The light also struck an orchid upright in a fluted white vessel, but could find no life in the plastic stem and petals. Dust settled on it. It would never die, thought Anne, and that was a loss. Briefly she inhaled the powdery scent deposited in the air the night before, when Lorna Greene had come in weeping, and kissed Anne with lips wet with tears, and said if only she'd heard sooner, if only she'd been told! Anne had received her embraces quietly, having no choice, and tried to be grateful for them. "How long has it been, dear Anne," Lorna had said, pushing violets aside to set her plastic orchid where it would best be seen from the street. "How many years?" She spoke as if her absence had been forced on her by circumstance, when in fact she'd grown quickly tired of Bethesda, and in the intervening years been a Methodist, and a Unitarian, and briefly a spiritualist, and presently (so Anne wearily inferred from the new gold crucifix on its new gold chain) a Catholic. But Anne was too tired to bear a grudge, for all that there was so little distance left to bear them; so she'd succumbed to Lorna's scented presence, and her quick pats that had sometimes felt like smacks of reproach:

"Now whyever didn't you let me know sooner, whyever didn't you call? Silly dear Anne! Silly girl!"

Gratefully the light left the deathless orchid, and arrived at the table where every Sunday at 5 p.m. Anne had poured her pots of tea and buttered the bread she made; so her memory populated the room, and there was Ronald bent over his Bible, and the old vagrant in his red velvet coat, and Lorna in her whispering cheap satin—there was Nathan with his arm in a sling, and there most vividly was Thomas Hart, unchanging and unchanged; "Good morning," she said, raising a hand to nobody, smiling at her own whimsy. Then the smile faltered: where was Grace, the child she loved because she'd been required to love her? She tried to account for time's transit, and could not—the girl might have gone just now into the kitchen, or might have been absent the whole span of her life. Bleakly Anne discovered that the only memory available to her was that of a toddler, bustling and plump and given to tempers, whose body had smelled of oats and oil; and the noise she made then was like the one she made in pain.

Ronald Macaulay came down the hall, holding the notebook in which he kept a record of the drugs he dispensed, and the intervals at which he dispensed them: she is in pain, he thought, and berated himself. He knocked on the door, and entered without waiting.

"Anne," he said, "is it happening again?"

"Where is she?" said Anne.

"Did you sleep?" He saw the thin green vomit in the dish; he saw the sweat that blotted the hospital pillow. The skin peeled from her fingernails, her palm was dry: what a disease this is, he thought, it grinds her bones to make its bread. Her coarse gray hair, thinned out to the down of a dandelion clock, was sticky on her neck. He poured water from a plastic jug into a plastic cup. How unfair it was that everything became ugly toward the end of life: the walker she'd used when the disease had not yet done its worst; the hospital bed with its rails and rubber; even the blanket, pitifully thin, the depthless institutional blue of every ward he'd ever visited.

"Where is she?" said Anne. "Why doesn't she come? Doesn't she know how things stand with me?"

Ronald in his later years had discovered that Bethesda's demands weren't always equal to life as he lived it. He ought to say: She may never come, and that will be all very well, if God wills it. But by this brute logic God had willed every malign thing that had ever occurred, and would ever occur, and so he set the virtue of kindness above that of truth, and sinned. "She's coming," he said. "She isn't sure when—there's dreadful trouble with the trains, I heard that on the radio—but she'll be here soon. You must decide what to wear; she notices these things." The blanket moved, and he saw the skin sloughed from her feet in little rags—she's slipping out of herself, he thought, she's going. He found among the litter of bottles and packets the lavender lotion Grace had sent with a hasty affectionate note. He rubbed this into Anne's feet, and the brittle tendons in the softening skin put him in mind of Rachel who had also died, and the balls of wool she'd held in her lap and pierced with knitting needles.

"Thank you. Have you always been this kind?"

"I don't think so," said Ronald, "but I can't remember." This was true: life seemed always to have consisted of days meted out in portions of sleep, pain, sleep, the nurses' arrivals and departures, sleep, pain, sleep.

"I should have spoken up for that homeless man, Ronald," Anne said. "Do you remember him, and his red velvet coat? We shouldn't have sent him away. Did it matter that he was drunk, when he was made in the image of God? I've carried it all this time. I wish I could see him again, and ask him to forgive me. I'd like to put it down."

"Even if you'd meant to cause harm," said Ronald, pouring morphine into a plastic cup, "it would all be washed away. Even if it had been like scarlet, it would now be white as snow." She drank the sweet thick liquid, and licked the rim like a child wanting the last of her ice cream. "Read to me," she said. "Read the bit I like best." So he fetched the copy of *Pilgrim's Progress* in which ANNE MARGARET MACAULAY: HER BOOK was written on the title page in green and yellow pencil, and recalled having sat with her once in Sunday School, their feet in buckled shoes not able to reach the floor, awestruck by a magic lantern show in which Bunyan's Pilgrim did battle with the Giant Despair. "I suppose I'll meet John Bunyan soon," said Anne. "Do you think he was as ugly as his picture?"

"I doubt anyone is ugly in heaven, or if they are we'll be unable to see it. Now you remember that Mr. Valiant was called to cross the river, and he said to his friends, *I am going to my Father's—*"

"*I am going to my Father's,*" said Anne, who could not these days recall what day of the week it was, "*and though with great difficulty I am got hither, yet now I do not repent me of all the trouble I have been at to arrive where I am.*" She leaned across the high rail of her bed and tried to be sick, and could not.

"I'll leave you," said Ronald. He kissed her on the cheek; he took away her book. Gratefully Anne felt drowsiness lop at her consciousness and relieve the weight of guilt and sorrow. What remained had the persistence of a root, and this was the belief that she was not alone—that in fact she'd never been alone, because she was a child of God, and loved by him particularly, in all the particulars of her nature and her faults. She pulled the blanket to her breast. She was tired. Darkness came in from the periphery until the blanket was the whole of her view—and how marvelous it is, she thought, how remarkable, and it has simply been there on my lap all this time! Look how deep the blue is in the folds, look how the sun strikes it and makes the fibers burn—she lifted it to her cheek, and there'd never, not in all her life, been a sensation like it. She breathed it in, and there was scent of lavender and laundry powder and her own body wasting in the ugly bed; then beyond this, like a field seen through a gate, the smell of the lanolin that oiled the sheep's wool and the sweat of the farmer that sheared it—then last of all, in a base note of wet iron, the blood of the ewe that nursed the lamb in the hours it could hardly stand. This is a miracle, she thought, it is a miracle: if this were the last thing I ever saw, I'd go to my long home glad, I would take it with me to glory. It is well, it is well with my soul!

A change of weather. Rain blew up the Blackwater with companies of shrieking gulls; it came to Bethesda, and turned the slate roof blue. It came to Lowlands, and caused the lake to seep across the lawns—it came to Lower Bridge Road, where it rapped on the windows, wanting to be let in.

Richard Dimitru Dines had defrocked himself and descended to the ranks of the sinners; he wore a borrowed dressing gown. He spoke with the scent of toothpaste and whisky: "So then. Your small friend is coming home."

Thomas was in the kitchen, cooking eggs. "She is coming home. It's a year since I saw her last, but really I find that nobody ever changes—that we all contain ourselves from the day we are born. I was up all night with Maria." He cut butter from the dish. "You have done good work, old man. It ought to be published. Perhaps I can see to that." Careful to retain the softness of the eggs, he whisked the butter in. "I feel more than ever that her papers cannot be lost; it can't have been her lot to love and not be loved, and then to be forgotten. Don't look at me like that, old man. This is not my story." He distributed eggs on buttered toast.

"Soon this rain will blow itself out," said Dines, as if he'd arranged the matter with meteorologists both mortal and divine, "and you will take me to Lowlands House. I saw it once only from a distance, and it seemed to me it was haunted, as such places are. Once in the days of my degradation I saw a man walking there, looking at the moon. A man of sorrows, it seemed to me, and acquainted with grief—"

"I am not at all sorrowful. I never was. It was all just a trick of the light."

"—and I could not have known that I would one day haunt his house, turning up like a bad coin!"

"You'll find Lowlands House as changed as I am unchanged. They've driven the ghosts out with a broom—they've washed the steps—I'm told there's to be a new glass case for Maria's telescope. I must say, Dimi: it would be mad to think we'll find a flagstone come loose, and her comet underneath it, melting into the mud."

"But we are mad," said Dines.

Meanwhile two men named Peter stood at the brink of Lowlands lake. Barriers behind them; also diggers, and articulated arms for dredging mud; sacks of concrete, and the means to mix it. Work could begin the following day, said the men, though it was in some ways a pity. "Swam here once upon a time," said Peter the elder, in whom sadness arrived like weather. "Fished in it. Pike size of a cow, couldn't land it." He stirred the water with his boot. The rain-swelled lake inched diligently over the lawns.

"Did you ever see the ghost?" Peter the younger was prepared to believe whatever he was told.

"No. But I saw the graffiti, saw the fire. Was here that night—everyone was, you'd think it was the Easter fair. Didn't know anyone was in the house, of course. Wouldn't have watched if I did." Together they turned to survey the house, which now had the uneven look of a man walking with a limp. The facade of the east wing, hollowed by fire, was buttressed with concrete and plate glass. Its roof was flat. It was accessible, air conditioned, spacious: no ghost would dare. The west wing and the center portion, marvelously undamaged, had been restored. The ivy was gone from the plaster. The unblinded windows looked at the oaks. The oaks looked back. "Funny thing," said Peter the elder, "could've sworn the moon was blue." Then "God's sake," he said, "who's this?" A priest was coming over the lawns with a rushing onward gait. A companion came in his wake, and this man had the careful tread of a man acquainted with pain. "What have you been up to," said Peter, "got anything to confess?"—and the odd thing was, the younger man did begin to feel he was in need of absolution, but couldn't think what he'd done.

The priest arrived. The rain had cleared. The sun struck Lowlands white as bones.

"What," said the priest, "is going on?" He raised his stole as he spoke, and it seemed to the workmen that it was indeed all a moral matter: the waiting diggers, the sacks of concrete, the barriers tipping in the reeds.

"Dredging," confessed Peter the younger, wringing his hands. "Improvements. It really isn't safe," he said, "it hasn't been for years. Last year someone got drunk and lay all night in the mud. He could have got Weil's disease!"

The man who was not a priest rubbed absently at his hip, and showed a courteous interest. "Well," he said. "Did he?"

"Not that I know of. But it was possible."

The man considered this with interest, and at length. "It was among the probabilities, certainly," he said. The cloud cover slipped.

"Tell me," said the priest, "did you find anything in the water deep down? Such as, for example, a sealed box of Romanian make, very fine? Perhaps in fact you discovered it in the foundations, when the work was done?"

"No," said the men together, "not a thing." Then Peter the younger, responding to the atmosphere of holiness settling on the lake, said, "They keep saying someone's down there, mind you. Nobody's seen anything. Nobody's heard anything. But someone quit last week: said he remembered the blue moon, didn't fancy being here when the dredgers went in." The visitors were silent for a time, then spoke incomprehensibly between themselves. The priest was thirsty. He drank. He offered the bottle to his companion, who refused it, and thanked the men for their time with a fine hand pressed to the fine tweed of his suit. The men, vaguely enchanted, inclined their heads and watched them go.

"What was all that about?" said Peter the elder to Peter the younger. Jackdaws had gathered on the margins of the lake, and also sought an answer. The rain set in.

Five o'clock: Thomas sheltering from the solemn weather on platform 2. From this vantage it ought to have been possible to see Upper Bridge Road with its look of a dragon's spine, but rain obscured the view. It was rush hour. The arriving train pursued its own lights up the track. Thomas heard the ticking of the lines, and bags and bodies jostled through the doors—saw girls dressed for the city praising each other while men watched with indiscriminating eyes. Thomas also watched: he waited. A boy came last off the train, hurling down the platform and dropping a paper cup. Abruptly he slowed, as if remembering something unwelcome, and looked back with longing. How delightful he is, thought Thomas, with the old reflex of desire. He noted with pleasure the beautiful head revealed by black hair clipped to the scalp, and the hollow where the neck entered the skull; then the boy encountered rain, and pulled up the hood of his coat. His white face receded from admiration, and Thomas watched the boy come closer, and felt vaguely he'd been in some way tricked. Then there was a sudden reversal of perception that tilted the ground under his feet, and faintly repelled by himself and by the lovely head concealed in the hood, he said: "You!"

"You did say," said Grace Macaulay, putting back her hood in the station shelter. "You did tell me I should come!"

Yes: I told you to come, but where have you gone? thought Thomas. She was altered beyond recognition. Where were her ribbons and skirts—where the soft brown arms, the cheap bracelets and rings, the silver bees dripping silver honey? She was thin. Tendons showed in the backs of her hands. She wore jeans, and boots that were too large and impeded her walk; her eyes retained something of their newborn oil-on-water shine. She had evidently shaved her head herself: a black tuft remained behind her ear. Did she have no friend to help?

"I did," said Thomas, and discovered that at least her scent remained familiar: neither pleasant nor unpleasant, a little feral and rising out of her scalp.

"Have you been very cross with me?"—and there was his bad-tempered affectionate child, and Thomas with a relieved laugh said that yes, he had, but that that was all right: she was his dearest. So she hurled herself against him, and in her brief embrace he felt her shoulder blades flaring under her clothes, and the thought arrived, as if Maria had tapped him three times on the shoulder: she is unhappy, and it's all my fault.

"Let's go," he said, holding his umbrella above them both.

"We have company. Richard Dimitru Dines has returned to Essex and is sitting in my car."

He discovered she still possessed the suddenly arriving smile: "Dimi!" she said. "Remember I found him, Thomas? I saw him first!"

They went under the bridge, and there was the car in view. "It's been a year," said Grace, "and it might have been ten—when did they paint the Jackdaw and Crow? Was the traffic always like this? Everything changes, and don't you think all change is loss? But you're not changed, despite your clothes," she said, reaching for the old man in the back seat and conferring on him her acquisitive affection. "Look at this"—she shook the stole with its goldwork cross—"look at the work on this, and what have you done with your red velvet coat?"

"Where also is your shawl," said Dines, "and what have you done with your curls—change and decay in all around, I see!"

"Shall we go?" said Grace. "I want to see her, and I'm afraid to see her, and how can both be true?"

"You can't expect only to feel one thing at a time," said Thomas, "though certainly it would be convenient. You can want to see her, and want not to see her, and neither cancels the other out: you are a woman, not an algebraic equation."

"I can't bear it."

"Well," said Thomas, "you will have to learn how." Rain boiled on the pavements, and smeared the windows with the lights of stationary cars that confined each other on the roads. We are all thinking about Anne, thought Thomas—much to say, no time to say it. Impatient drivers leaned on their horns, and went nowhere. "We'll go as soon as we can," said Thomas.

Dear James,

It's midnight. There's no moon, and Anne Macaulay is dead.

It was difficult to write that. Let me try again, and bear it better: Anne Macaulay is dead.

I'd planned to see her this afternoon. I'd planned to take Grace, who has been absent for so long, and old Dimitru who's come back to Aldleigh again. I'd imagined the surprise, and the pleasure I'd give—"How good of you, Thomas," my friend would say, "how kind you are!" I wonder if we ever do kind things without thinking of the kind light we'll be standing in?

So we drove there through the vengeful rain; but as we came to Beechwood Avenue it seemed to wear itself out. There was that kind of brilliant sunshine that only comes after a storm, and already the road and pavements were dry. It was six o'clock: birds losing their minds in the silver birch, children coming out of doors. When Grace saw her father on the doorstep she ran to meet him, and when she put her head on his shoulder I saw him pat her like a dog.

Then we all went together into the room where Anne has lived these past three months. I saw the sun suspended in the window, and how the light made everything wonderful, everything—even the horrible bed, the rubber mattress, the pill packets, tissues, incontinence pads, antiseptic wipes, teaspoons stained with tea. Anne wore a white cotton nightgown with plastic buttons that looked nothing like pearls, and stroked a thin blue blanket as if she'd never held anything so soft.

Grace looks these days like a half-starved boy, but Anne knew her without any trouble. "Come here," she said, "come here," and you'd think the wretched child had only been gone a few hours. So Grace climbed onto the bed and curled there and said nothing, and was never more like a little farmyard animal, and all the while Anne patted her and patted the blanket and looked at us all as if all the things she'd ever hoped for had been given substance. Her old shy smile was unchanged by pain—it came drifting up like something shining underwater: "Thank you," she said. "Thank you." That was the last thing she said to me, and I'm glad.

Dimi went forward then, and my memory dressed him in the old red velvet coat, and put birthday cake on the table and the Great Comet in the window. He held out his hands, and you'd think they'd healed overnight, you couldn't see the scars—"Anne," he said, "Miss Macaulay." I was afraid she wouldn't know him, but she did. She said only that she was sorry, and he said it was all right, and the river had gone under the bridge.

Then Anne looked at Ronald and there was her drifting smile again and she said, "It was so heavy, and I've put it down." Then there was an hour when she said nothing, and her hands were still on the blanket and sometimes she breathed quickly and sometimes not at all. Every now and then Ronald dipped cotton wool in water and used this to wet her lips, and I put my hand on hers and wondered what was passing through her mind—if she was thinking of her brother and her niece, who were bone of her bone and flesh of her flesh but each in their way so solitary—if she was thinking of her earlier life in the hills, and the life that waited on the other side of Jordan.

Then the angle of the sunlight altered, and suddenly every
shadow was long and slanting on the wall. Anne roused
herself as if she'd slept well, and looked at us one after the
other with her old clear shy look; then she moved the
blanket into the light and showed us the blue, and said,
"Isn't it all a miracle? Do you think there was ever any
other life like this?" Then I suppose something essential
somewhere failed, and Grace—

Thomas, whose bad hip ached, looked up from the letter that
wouldn't be sent, and saw Maria Văduva in the empty armchair. Skirts three inches deep in Lowlands mud, eyes looking
sternly out of the shadows: *Thomas Hart*, she said, *do you think
I wasn't there—didn't you see me at the window? You old deceiver, you father of lies, it wasn't like that at all!*

"I wish you would leave me alone," said Thomas, who'd persuaded himself absolutely, as he'd always been able to do, "I
wish you'd let me have a moment's peace. No," he conceded, "it
wasn't like that. But all the world is composed of probabilities,
and of all things this was the most probable, and the most
right!"

Then black-browed Maria, righteous in death, spoke with
the indignation of his conscience: *You never could bear to see
things clearly, Thomas Hart. Look again.*

Look then, Thomas Hart: the car not ten yards from the
station, windscreen smeared with the distorting rain; impatient Grace becoming bad-tempered and raising her
phone—"Why aren't they moving, Thomas, for God's sake,
we've been here half an hour, and my phone's out of charge,
and why don't you ever have yours with you?" Above them on
the railway arch another train departed, and farther down
the road a maddened driver got out and uselessly berated

whatever was unfolding half a mile toward the town. Now the rain was coming in fat drops that rattled on the roof with a noise like shot, and Dines in the back seat had reached the last of his drink—"Why are you keeping me down here," he said, "why are you doing this to me?" So Thomas turned and saw the old terror surfacing—"Wait a little longer, Dimi," he said; then in a car close by a passenger gave up hope, and throwing back the door struck the car where Dines sat, causing him to flinch and cry out. He fumbled with his seat belt, speaking rapidly to himself in Romanian, and clutching the satchel more or less fell out onto the pavement. "I will not I think go with you," he said; "you will not make an old man sit so long. Let me go, Thomas, let me go, I'll find you in good time." He slapped the car as if it were the flank of a horse: "Now things are moving, and Anne is waiting, and you must go." And the traffic was moving, and Anne was waiting, and there was so little time. "We can find him again," said Grace, "we always find him somehow."

Look again, Thomas: Grace Macaulay on the doorstep of her father's house. Lights out, bad weather. Grace, uncertain of herself and all the world, not knocking yet. Something altered in the look of the place, in the gone-over garden, the silver birch: something departed. Ronald coming out. Quick embraces, nothing said. Grace taken to the dining room. Ugly bed with nothing in it. Scent of lavender. Scent of vomit. Antiseptic. Tea. John Bunyan open on the table: *I am going to my Father's, and do not repent me of all the trouble I have been at to arrive at where I am.* Thin blue blanket on the floor. Ronald saying, "It was only three hours ago, and they came for her so fast—did nobody else die today? Did they have nothing else to do?" Ronald bringing in a plastic bag: "Let's clear up, let's get rid of it all, she doesn't need it now." Thomas at the door, knocking once. Grace picking up the blanket, thinking:

doesn't look very warm, does it, I hope it was soft enough, she always did have trouble with her skin.

Later that same day, at the bell of last orders, two women left the Jackdaw and Crow, pausing at intervals to talk and kiss on soaked roads glossed by streetlight. They reached the shadow of the railway arch, and were there for a time against the wet brick—then "Oh," said one to the other, sobering abruptly, "something isn't right." In a long fuddled moment they sorted through what they saw: parked car, bollard, ticket booth, bin, all these in their proper places, unremarkable—then, between a van and the parking meter, a spread of white cloth, as if ready for plates, knives, glasses. Closer then, hands gripped now for courage: a booted foot turned out, and white cloth falling from a crooked knee—a fringed scarf with a gold cross unravelling, and at last a face propped against the curb, a streetlight halo on the bald and marvelous head. It wasn't necessary to say that he was dead: because the eyes were open, sightless and wondering, fixed on the moonless sky.

How curious that none of this was frightening—that it was easy to hold his hand and remark that some damage had been done to him a long time ago. But it was all right now, they said to him—it was all right, it was all over now, and wasn't he a priest, wasn't he a man of God? They'd probably be waiting up there, probably put bunting on the pearly gates. Sirens then, and lights, and no efforts made to retrieve what was already gone; and nobody seeing in the gutter a black book with a broken spine dismantled by bad weather, the pages going one by one down the storm drain, and coming in time to the Alder and the Blackwater, so that by the morning of the following day, by the hour of Lucifer rising, Maria Văduva Bell was renewing over and over in the matter of the sea.

THE CLOUD OF UNKNOWING

THOMAS HART, *ESSEX CHRONICLE*,
20 NOVEMBER 2008

I hope you'll forgive my recent absence. The fact is I've suffered a loss, and have been consoling myself not with religion, but with physics, reading about quantum mechanics and discovering it has all the strangeness of theology. It doesn't call laboratories to mind, but a mystical work on the nature of God they call *The Cloud of Unknowing*.

Let me try and explain. When I was taught about the atom, I drew in my exercise book a nucleus, and an electron orbiting it as the moon orbits the earth. As it turns out, my teachers were mistaken: we ought not to think of electrons orbiting the nucleus. This is because we don't know exactly where an electron is, only where it's most likely to be.

This has been demonstrated in an experiment that makes my head ache. First, I want you to imagine you drop two pebbles in a lake, causing two sets of waves to intersect. Where a peak meets peak, the peak is higher; where a trough meets trough, the trough is deeper. Where a peak meets a trough, the waves negate each other, and the water is flat. This is called wave interference, and it also happens to light: when light is shone through two slits, that same interference pattern appears in bands of light and shade against the opposite wall.

Now imagine that instead of shining light at a barrier perforated by two slits, you are firing electrons. You might imagine the electrons would pass through, making two patches like two pools of water under a leaky roof. Instead, something remarkable happens: a pattern begins to form that looks like the bands of wave interference: the electrons have behaved like a wave.

What is more astounding is this: if you fire the electrons one at a time, the wave interference pattern still happens. It is as if, while the electron has chosen to pass through the slit on the left, it has also passed through the slit on the right, interfering with itself. It seems to have taken into account all the possible outcomes of its own movement. This is why it's said that nobody can be certain where an electron is, until it is measured: it exists in a kind of cloud of probability.

Physicists bicker like sisters over the implications of the double-slit experiment. The simplest explanation, I suppose, is that we are mistaken in our understanding of it, and that quantum mechanics as it's proposed today may well be modified tomorrow. There is also a more astonishing explanation, though I daresay it's the most unlikely: that while we can only observe one outcome of all those probabilities, we cannot say that all the other outcomes are either real or unreal—that in fact there are infinite numbers of universes, constantly generated, taking into account the fulfillment of every probability, at any time. And since there is no means to disprove this preposterous-seeming theory, it has the lingering substance of a dream.

I'd thought the study of physics would be for me the study of certainties, but my hope has not been met: because of my wonder and the limits of my understanding, the study of matter is for me a question of faith—though it comforts me to think that where quantum at least is concerned, certainty isn't necessary for the world to function. So I'm baffled, but grateful for my wonder. In the fourteenth century, the author of *The Cloud of Unknowing* wrote this: "Whatever you do not know is dark to you, because you do not see it with your spiritual eyes."

Dear Mr. Hart,

I'm writing to invite you to the formal opening of the New
East Wing at Lowlands in December: please see attached.
We've been so grateful for your help with the Văduva
papers, and I hope you'll be pleased to see her telescope
on permanent display.

Regards,
Anna Fonseka
Essex Museum Services

Thank you for your invitation. I'd like very much to attend,
and in fact recently came across some interesting new
information regarding Maria Văduva. Would it be possible
to bring a guest?

Best,
T. Hart

How exciting. Delighted you can come. Do bring a
guest. Best, A.

Dear James—I wonder if this email is still yours?

I'm writing to ask you to come back with me to Lowlands
House. More than ten years since the fire, and at last
they're putting Maria Văduva's telescope on display.
I've attached an invitation to the opening. Won't you come
with me, and be my guest? I have so much to tell you.

My regards to your wife and family.

Yours sincerely,
T. Hart

Please note I have retired, and this account will not be
monitored. I can be contacted on my personal address.
J. Bower.

Ah—I always hoped I'd see you again! But since hope
depends on doubt, I must have doubted it too. You won't
see this. I suppose I can say what I please. But I never did,
and wouldn't know where to begin.
T. H.

Please note I have retired, and this account will not be
monitored. I can be contacted on my personal address.
J. Bower.

Every day I think of things I want to tell you, and things I
want to ask. Did your life become what you wanted it to
be? Did anybody ever tell you why the moon was blue?
And did you ever go to a bookshop and find a novel called
The Horse and Rider, and see your initials there—did you
understand it is your book?
T. H.

Please note I have retired, and this account will not be monitored. I can be contacted on my personal address.
J. Bower

ON THE NATURE OF BINARY STARS

THOMAS HART, *ESSEX CHRONICLE*, 27 NOVEMBER 2008

It's taken me all my life to learn not to trust the sight of my own eyes, and it was the stars that taught me. They ask me to look, and look again, and be certain of what I've seen: I often think what trouble I could have saved myself if I'd learned this when I was young!

I was out the other night with my binoculars, taking a look at the Great Bear, and realized that what I'd taken to be a single star located in the "handle" was in fact a pair. I can't say why this delighted me, only that I went home and passed the night learning what I could about the nature of binary stars.

In 1617—the same year in which our old friend Kepler set out his laws on the motion of bodies in orbit—Galileo Galilei began to examine the pair of stars I saw. The larger star is Mizar, which comes from the Arabic meaning apron, or wrapping, and the second is Alcor. Together, they're known as "the horse and his rider." But Galileo, looking more closely than I ever

did, discovered that Mizar itself consists of two stars fifteen arcseconds apart, and locked together in orbit around a common center of mass.

Stars, like comets, are travelers. Sometimes a pair is formed as one star compels another toward it as they make their way through the galaxy; but it's more common to find binary pairs that were born like twins when immense clouds of gas and matter collapse in the act of creation.

Most stars, I'm told, are binary stars, and these pairs affect each other profoundly. One star might waylay another in space, but find in due course it suffers from this new proximity: it is possible for one star to draw matter from another in what they call mass transfer, growing larger and more bright at a dreadful cost to its companion. In this way the bodies of the stars are formed by the forces of attraction between them, and the closer the relation, the higher the risk.

If there cannot be equity, I wonder

if it's better to receive the greater proportion of love, or give it? I wish I knew. W. H. Auden, whose poem "The More Loving One" considers the stars' indifference to the love of men, wrote this:

If equal affection cannot be
Let the more loving one be me.

Five days after Anne Macaulay died, the moon passed between the earth and the sun; and since by an absurd coincidence of celestial geometry the moon's disk slotted perfectly over that of the sun, it sealed in the light. At the time of total eclipse, animals and men in Novosibirsk and Kazakhstan and northern Canada stood in the lunar shadow and saw starlight before noon, and in due course a corona surrounding the absent sun with the look of iron filings compelled by a round black magnet.

"They tell me the moon is slowly drifting away," said Thomas. "I wonder if there'll come a time when it will seem too small to cover the sun? In that case what a stroke of luck, that the age of humanity happens to be the age of eclipses." He was walking with Grace in Lowlands Park. These were the early days of grief, when the death of Anne Macaulay was sometimes so improbable as to be forgotten, and sometimes the whole business of the day. Grace had woken that morning to find her old room so unaltered she'd thought she must be unaltered, too, and it had been distressing to discover that in fact she had no hair, and that every tendon was visible on the back of her hand. For a time she'd watched the light traverse the wall and highlight her possessions: the Romanian shawl she'd worn until the fringe was filthy, the books awarded each year at Sunday School (*To Grace Macaulay, for Attendance*), the Bible with its pages folded and underlined—all as unchanged as Bethesda, and almost as persuasive. But she wasn't fooled. The alterations were absolute. The absence of her aunt did not exist only in the places where she ought to have been—in the empty bed, the tapestry armchair, the places on the kitchen floor where she'd worn the linoleum thin—it existed down to the last corner of the house. She was gone from the bathroom pipes, she was gone from the doormat, she was gone from the bone-handled knives she'd set out for Sunday tea. She was gone from the cushions, bookshelves, and bathroom light-switch; from the African violets that were dying on the windowsill because nobody watered them. Only her father, in mourning all those years, went unchanged by loss.

"It will do you good to get out," Thomas had said, arriving at Beechwood Avenue with flowers. "Come with me to Lowlands—there's a partial eclipse in an hour, and no cloud"; and she'd felt her affection for him increase by the quantity of love her aunt no longer needed.

She said she wanted to go into Lowlands the old way, as if she were a disobedient child again. So they'd walked past Potter's Field, where with a kind of stupid instinct she looked for Nathan; then down through Bethesda's car park and the line of silver birches that kept the chapel from the world. "At least nothing here has changed," she'd said, arriving at the margins of the park and deceiving herself—the altered wing of Lowlands House showed hard-edged against the copper beeches.

Now they stood some distance from the lake, where the dredging had paused, and the men were passing eclipse glasses and sheets of dark film from hand to hand. Beyond the lake, schoolchildren were lying on their backs, holding silver filters overhead. It was the last days of autumn, and the light was defiant on the lawns. All day the insolent moon had chased the sun, and had at last attained it. "There'll be no totality here," said Thomas, handing Grace a flimsy cardboard pair of glasses with lenses of black film, "it will reach sixty-two per cent, and in ninety-six minutes it will be over—Look"—the schoolchildren gasped and cheered—"it's begun."

Seen through the solar filter, the earth's near star was reduced to a coral disk clipped at the rim. This clipping never seemed to move, but each time Grace looked, the absence was larger.

"If you were to return to this spot in about fifty-four years," said Thomas, "you'd see this same eclipse, at this same time. And this is because of something called the Saros cycle, which repeats an eclipse every six and a half thousand days or so." But the devastating sight of a damaged sun was invisible to the naked eye, and not yet affecting the daylight. The men by the lake lost faith, and returned to their tasks. The sound of diggers began again, and the children fought and rolled down a shallow incline.

But Grace, grateful to have been lifted out of Aldleigh, went on watching. "I think I understand," she said, "how you fell in love with the moon. Is it nearly done?" She saw the sun half-gone, and briefly wondered if permanent damage had been done, and it could never regain its proper light.

"This is almost the end of the beginning," said Thomas, "hold on." His bad hip ached: he rubbed it. Now perceptibly the late-autumn light was diminishing. Jackdaws lifted from a stand of oaks, interrogated the air, and settled. It was as if the entire afternoon had been excised from time, and abruptly it was six o'clock. "It takes eight minutes for the light to reach us from the sun," said Thomas. "If it ever went out, darkness would spread out from it like a stain. And since no form of communication exceeds the speed of light, for those eight minutes we'd have no idea all life was coming to an end."

Nearby a bewildered deer, drifting out from denser stands of oak on the margins of the park, looked mistrustfully at Thomas, and bolted. The children were clustered around a solitary adult, who made hopeless entreaties that went unheeded.

Grace, moved unbearably to remember Anne, felt the new shock of loss. "It gives me the feeling," she said, "that nothing I ever do will matter. But at the same time, to be alive at all—to be with you in this park, at this moment—it's so strange and so unlikely!" She looked at Thomas—at the fair hair, neatly brushed, and gone grayer in her absence; at the well-cut coat and well-chosen shoes she recognized, surely, from back when she was young. "You've been almost everything to me," she said, with furious affection, "because without you nobody would ever have told me what was on the other side of the chapel door. And I used to be angry because you were all I had—but wouldn't it have been more likely that I never had you at all? Give me the glasses," she said, "let me have my turn." The shadow was diminishing on the sun. The untimely evening receded.

"Have you been happy, Grace?"

"Of course I'm not happy! I'm not even sure I exist! I bargained with God, and I lost. What's left of me now? I don't know how to dress, or how to speak—I drink and smoke and sometimes go out dancing, but I remember every hymn I ever sang, and cry when I remember them. And I still pray, Thomas, I still look for the face of God, and think every day about how to be good. But what does that mean when there's no one to tell me how to do it—and besides, no one is watching?"

"Was it such a bad thing to lose Nathan?" said Thomas, examining the mending sun. "You were just children—did it matter so much?"

"Don't you see what it taught me? It taught me how alone I am!" They'd drifted nearer the lake. The children had gone, full light was restored; the air was briny with the scent of water disrupted by the dredgers, and of black silt being drawn up. "You must think me mad," she said, "to still love a boy I last saw ten years ago. But it doesn't make any difference, not to me."

"No," said Thomas. "Distance separates you from him, and if the units of distance were miles and not years, nobody would think it strange—but would your life really have been so different, if he'd come that day?" On the lake's farther shore an older man in a yellow jacket raised his hand in greeting: "You, again?" he shouted. "Where's that old priest of yours?" A wind was getting up, and bringing clouds.

"How does that man know you?—Oh, it would have made all the difference in the world." Grace couldn't suppress the smile that came at the thought of Nathan at the chapel door. "It would have kept God alive, and kept love alive—I'd have been content to stay in my pew if Nathan had sat with me! You don't believe me," she said, seeing misery in Thomas, who for the first time in her life wouldn't meet her gaze. "Not even you can understand! Are you all right, Thomas—does your bad hip hurt?"

"Stand there a minute, Grace, stop walking." He was pale, and it occurred to her that perhaps he too was gravely and secretly ill, and she was about to sustain another loss. This brought the relief of her old temper: "For God's sake what is it, Thomas, what's wrong with you?" Then he spoke, and it was difficult to hear above the sound of the dredgers and the man in the yellow coat who was summoning other men from farther round the lake. "I can't hear you," she said. "Say it again."

"He did come," said Thomas. "I think I should tell you that. It might help."

"You're always trying to make things better for me," she said, shaking her head. "You just think it would all be easier for me. But I'm not a child now, Thomas, you can't always make things better."

"He was five minutes late," said Thomas, as if reciting lines committed to memory a long time ago. "He wore that denim jacket that had got too small. He had his headphones on, and I could hear the music. He came in and saw you kneeling down, because your dress was torn, and he watched you, and he wanted to come in. But you'd already been so unhappy, Grace. You were just a child and already you were learning what it is to love and not be equal! So I sent him away."

Grace was laughing. Was she really expected to believe that the sun had diminished and regained itself, that her aunt was dead, that Thomas on a whim had altered the course of her life? It was absurd—it defied all the natural laws. "No," she said, "you couldn't. How could you do that?" She heard the old man in the yellow jacket shouting, and saw the arm of the dredger leaning over the lake as if yearning for the water. "Why would you do it, when you were always my friend?" She shook her head, refuting the evidence of Thomas's pallor. "Why? Why would you be so cruel?" She began with difficulty to move away from him through the sodden lawn at the spreading rim of the lake.

"I don't know," he said—"I didn't think it would matter. You were just a child, and children heal quickly, don't they? Come back from there," he said, "the water's dirty and deep."

But her muddled disbelief was clearing, and in its place her old temper mercifully flared. "Don't tell me what to do," she said. "Haven't you already destroyed my life? Look at me— look what you did—you killed God!" Thomas spoke again, but other men were shouting and the wind was painful in her ears—she thought of her room in London, with its bare walls that blackened with mold in winter, and the light of the television illuminating the narrow bed; that's my home, she thought, I will have to go back to that nothingness, and look for my own life. She was aware that she was shivering violently, and thought she must be cold, but her body seemed something she was tethered to and it was difficult to manipulate her feet against the mud. The thinning clouds allowed a pewter gloss to settle on the surface of the water; and where the dredger breached the lake, the light broke and mended. Thomas came toward her, and she was afraid that if she looked at him she'd find him as altered as Lowlands was altered—"Leave me alone," she said, and turned away too quickly. Her feet were slipping in the black silt, and the water was shining at her knees. "Oh," she said, "I think someone needs to help me," but couldn't think who that might be. The men were shouting, the silt sucked at her; there was a moment when she felt she could resist the water if she chose, but was too tired. Now there was an absurd slow fall which would go on forever, and her hands were full of a silken rotting substance and the hard stems of grasses, and something living that eluded her. Then a hand met hers, down in the enclosing water, and distinctly she felt the rocking motion of its greeting and rough grasp of its palm—so after all, she thought, wondering why it had become difficult to breathe, after all I am not entirely alone.

Peter the elder, for whom the sun held no interest, had been watching the man he recognized talking with the black-haired girl across the lake. Where was the old priest, he thought, and why did the girl insist on stumbling back toward the water: they ought to have put more barriers up, there would be hell to pay—but the men were calling him, and there was Peter the younger with his worrying look: "Something's down there, it's got caught," he said, gesturing to the toppled dredger straining audibly against the mud.

"There's all sorts down there, I shouldn't doubt," said the older man, untroubled; then the dredging arm's reach exceeded its grasp, and the digger was impelled toward the water. A confused flurry of bodies eluded the arm, and gave out incomprehensible warnings and instructions; then "Watch out!" he said, looking not toward the digger but yards distant on the far bank, where the black-haired girl was sinking as if she meant to do it. The dredging arm swung back and forth and raised a reek of rotting vegetation; then the girl was gone, and the man in the tweed coat was reaching for the place where she'd been.

"Stop!" said Peter the elder. "This is an emergency! This is an emergency!" He left the toppled digger and ran toward the man, slipping as he skirted the lake and gathering others as he went. Someone cut the digger's engine, and in the ensuing silence he heard the man in the good tweed coat say, "Is it all really my fault?"

"Step back, for God's sake, this is an emergency!" Peter pulled him from the rim of the water: "Let them go in," he said, "best to let them do it."

Other men went shouting and plunging through the reeds—"Got her," said Peter the younger, rearing up and coughing, "got hold of her down here, got hold of something."

"Is it my fault?" said the watching man, wringing his hands.

"Sometimes things just happen," said Peter, "sometimes it's all just mud and bad weather."

"There we go," the men were saying, in the soothing way of a mother comforting a child, "there we go, we're all right now"; and together they pulled against the mud and reeds, seeming to strain against an immense weight. The watching man rubbed his hip. "But she's only a little thing," he said, "she was always so small."

Then there was a triumphant cry, and the men reeled back in the mud. "Got her," they were saying, "got her safe and sound"; but Peter in fact saw two women lying speechless in the broken reeds. One surveyed the sky with unsighted eyes, and raised a stone skirt with a stone hand; the other clasped her with a choking grip, and rested her wet black head on an unyielding white shoulder. Her lower lip was split, her open palm was raw; jackdaws came and looked, and asked whatever was going on, and why. The mended sun came out.

"There you are, you see?" said Peter, but he was not able to say if the movements he saw were those of the black-haired girl stirring, or nothing but baffled creatures drawn up with the silt and leaving the folds of her clothes.

"Maria!" said the man at his side. "There you are! There she is," he said, turning to Peter and smiling with a curious relieved radiance, "things pass, but don't they always return? Didn't I say?"

Later—when the girl had been taken home, and the stone woman given a tarpaulin shroud; when the men had exchanged their soaked clothes for dry ones and were talking it over in the Jackdaw and Crow—they all said how strange it was to see that radiant smile dissipate, and the man begin to cry with the adamant sorrow of a child. And it was equally impossible (they said, forgetting him soon after) to tell whether he cried with relief, or with loss.

Anne Macaulay was twelve days dead. They'd taken away the communion table and put her small coffin in its place. This done in remembrance of her: a small spray of flowers on the bolted-down lid, a photograph propped beside it; the old harmonium exhaling its scent of the North Sea tides, the congregation packed in the pews. All the same: few tears, scant mourning. She'd gone to glory, she'd obtained her reward—and wasn't there peace in that valley where the lion lay down with the lamb? The congregation, biding time until they joined her there, raised the rafters with their hymn: "*Forever with the Lord! Amen: so let it be!*"

But Thomas Hart, who still feared death's sting, was grieving in his pew under the halted moons. Weak light shone on the brass plaque bolted to the coffin: ANNE MARGARET MACAULAY. So that varnished pine contained her flushed cheeks, walking shoes, prudence, preference for Yorkshire tea, shyness, cuttings of African violet, habit of testing the heat of the iron with spit, facility with mental arithmetic, dutiful affection, diligent faith. No other woman ever had her qualities, and none ever would again, and all that was particular about her was returning to the general matter of the earth. Thomas felt himself depleted by loss. James Bower, Anne, Grace—he numbered them off. Grace was three pews down, grazes on the stem of her neck visible under the brim of a borrowed hat, and was as lost to him as if she'd never been dredged with Maria out of the Lowlands lake. The thought occurred to Thomas that it might have been preferable to lose her to water than to anger: then he might have mourned the girl who'd loved him, and not been subject to withdrawal of that love. Then God forgive me, he thought, and it would have to make do for a prayer.

Brief noises in the lobby, where the undertakers in their high black hats were waiting; then the senior deacon stood in the pulpit. "*Behold*," he said, "*I show you a mystery: we shall not all sleep, but we shall all be changed*"—and such change, thought Thomas, and wasn't it all his fault? Sometimes things just happen, the man by the lake had said, sometimes it's all just mud and bad weather; but it wasn't just that, Thomas had thought, I had a hand in the mud. In those years since Grace was baptized he'd persuaded himself that he'd disrupted the course of her life out of wisdom and love—that he'd sent Nathan away to preserve his small friend from the humiliation of inequitable desire. Noble Thomas Hart, with the judgement of Solomon, with the compassion of Christ, and so on! Now this self-deceit was no longer possible—it had been his own envy and sorrow that did it, he'd still been on his knees in the gutter, and James Bower had still been holding his wife's hand. And when Grace had come to her senses in the mud and reeds, Maria Văduva Bell submitting to her frantic embrace, it seemed she'd simply not seen him. She'd taken the hands and coats of strangers, and accepted their chastisement and care, and meanwhile Thomas had stood close by saying how sorry he was, and what a wretched child she'd always been, and her eyes had passed over him without interest or recognition.

"Push you, did he?" a young man had said, and there was a moment when Thomas had felt them all ranged against him, instinctively suspicious; but his evident shock had pleaded his innocence. "No," the older man had said, "don't be daft. Just mud, just bad weather. I'll take her, shall I? Why don't I take her home?" So he'd taken Grace, who hadn't looked back when Thomas called. And meanwhile Maria Văduva Bell had raised an empty hand to her right eye, holding nothing, seeing nothing—"She must have been looking for something," said Peter the younger, "and now she'll look forever."

"That's all right," said Thomas, "she'd have wanted it that way."

Now the senior deacon, speaking with the voice of the apostles, returned Thomas Hart to Bethesda: "*For the trumpet shall sound,*" he was saying, "*and the dead shall be raised incorruptible*"— and look, thought Thomas, there's the incorruptible dead, followed me down from Lower Bridge Road: Maria in her yards of funeral silk, seed pearls and Lowlands mud dripping from her hem, taking her seat beside him in the pew and putting a fond arm through his: *It is right to be unhappy*, she said. *Isn't the value of your love set by the heap of your sorrow? Now tell me, Thomas: who is that, sorrowing so noisily over there?*

Thomas heard weeping from the front, then a high wavering exhalation that penetrated the gospel descending from the pulpit, coming from a shining satin hat trembling with the performance of sorrow. Now and then the woman raised a useless scrap of handkerchief to her eyes, and withdrew it stained with mascara, and no tears: Lorna Greene, thought Thomas, discovering that his dislike and distrust were undiminished since he'd seen her last. She'd returned to Bethesda to display her piety and grief, and wouldn't wait until the closing hymn to do it—now she gave a gulping sob that caused the congregation to examine their open Bibles more closely in embarrassment. "*Though he were dead,*" said the deacon, admonishing such faithless grief, "*yet shall he live.*"

Soon the undertakers came up the aisle with their rehearsed solemnity to retrieve their possession, and Thomas looked up at the moony lights, refusing the evidence of the brass plaque: that Anne Macaulay would never again go briskly across the car park and greet him. He heard again that ludicrous choking sob, and saw Lorna Greene contrive to follow Ronald Macaulay, who followed the coffin out—then came Grace, shockingly slight, passing so close the scent in the creases of her clothes and skin reached him, and she had the blank uncomprehending look of a woman who hadn't even seen a stranger, had seen nothing at all. Thomas, whose consciousness refused the loss of Anne even as she was carried out on the shoulders of strangers, comprehended the loss of Grace absolutely: she'd left him as decisively as she'd claimed him under this same vaulted roof.

He was the last of the mourners, and encountered Ronald at the chapel door, who said what a lovely morning it was, as if briefly he'd forgotten that this wasn't an ordinary Sunday, with Anne already halfway home to put potatoes on for dinner.

"That went well," said Thomas, "didn't it?" and wondered what the years of his profession had ever taught him, if he couldn't locate one word of consolation. So he took Ronald by the elbow, and said how kind the undertakers had been, hadn't they, how professional. The two men walked together to the safety of the hall behind Bethesda, where time never passed, and never tried to: the white cloths on the trestle tables, the steel tea urns, the Ten Commandments bleeding ink behind their mottled glass, all resisted the ticking of the gallery clock.

Ronald paused for a moment on the threshold, and seemed inclined simply to turn and leave; but the congregation parted for him, and so he drifted half-smiling through, clasping and releasing the hands he was offered, and arriving in due course at a chair behind which stood Lorna Greene, her hat pierced by a pearl-headed pin. "Sit down, dear Mr. Macaulay," she said, "sit down," and began to fuss over him in a penetrating

whisper that affirmed to everyone present that of all who
mourned Anne, she mourned most, and most generously.
"You will be hungry, I should think," she said, with sugared solicitude, "let me bring you something to eat"—then she saw
Thomas, and arrested herself, pressing a hand to her satin
breast and saying, "Dear me," blinking rapidly, and shedding
flakes of mascara on her gleaming cheek. "Dear me," she said
with an embarrassed laugh, as if Thomas had transgressed
every social and theological rule merely by coming forward
with a cup of tea in his hand. "You think it appropriate—even
now, under these circumstances!—really I would have felt—"
Then she amended her tone to something more solemn, and
attended again to Ronald: "I'm sure nobody could be more
sorry than I am for your loss—though heaven has gained another saint"—here she concealed her crucifix in her palm, for
consolation or to forestall Ronald's Calvinist distaste for the
cross. Watchful Thomas was inclined to think it all false—but
her cheek was gleaming, he thought, it was wet: after all she'd
wept for Anne as sincerely as anyone had wept. Abruptly, and
with unwelcome compassion for a woman he'd despised so
cheerfully and for so long, he understood what loneliness had
compelled Lorna to Bethesda's door, and to all the church
doors after it—recognized, in fact, her capacity to modify herself to please her company. Wasn't he a different man to different men? It was among the least of her sins. "Mr. Hart," she
said, tears drying on collar and cheek, "you won't remember
me"—but I remember you, she conveyed with her blackbird's
gaze.

"I do remember," he said, "of course I do"; and the warmth
with which this assurance came out startled them both, so that
briefly behind Lorna's hard glazed hair and lips and breasts it
was possible to see a frightened and uncertain girl who all her
life had tried only to make herself wanted. Then the girl was

gone, and in her place a scented construction that put a hand on Ronald's shoulder and stooped to his ear and said: "I'd rather understood from dear Anne that Mr. Hart had left the chapel, and found somewhere better suited to his nature . . . still"—airily she looked at the trestle tables, the discreetly mournful sandwiches, the men and women now attending to her as if to the change in weather—"still, your dear sister would hardly turn a sinner from the door! I hope I'm not rude. I speak as I find."

"Sinner?" said Ronald, unable to pick any malefactor in particular out of the general mass; then he saw his daughter: "Ah yes, Grace, there she is."

Grace crossed the hall, her small body altered and seeming a tall gaunt thing rubbed down by life; her clothes were dark and ordinary, the neglected tuft of hair curling behind her ear, her swollen lip recalling her old babyish petulance. But she was not babyish, she was not petulant—lightly she touched her father's shoulder, and "Yes," she said, smiling at Lorna, holding out her hand, "yes, I was surprised to see Mr. Hart here"—she was horribly composed, her quick temper and pained joy gone—"he never really belonged, did he?" She stood beside Lorna and patted her satin sleeve. "Good afternoon," she said smilingly to the senior deacon, the elderly sisters down from Colchester in their knitted hats, the restless children eating funeral cake, "thank you for coming, my aunt would have been so pleased to see you here."

Where have you gone, thought Thomas, where are you, unable to find his wretched child in these brittle social graces; then the gaze that had avoided him so painfully took him in with a bright contemptuous assessment. "You never belonged here," she said, with Lorna's trick of speaking with sibilant quietness that reached the back of the hall.

"You aunt," said Lorna mournfully, "would have been so

dreadfully shocked"; and gradually Thomas became aware that all the men and women were attending to her, listening frankly or affecting to speak among themselves.

"Shocked?" said Ronald, shaking his head, and frowning over the problem of Thomas.

"Didn't you see?" said Lorna. "Didn't you wonder?"

"Grace," said Thomas, "do I deserve this?"

"I wish somebody would explain," said Ronald, dwindling in his seat, his white hair thin as an infant's, "I really don't have any idea"—but Lorna clasped his shoulder and stooped to his ear, and explained, and explained again, with distasteful precision it was not necessary for Thomas to hear, because he'd heard it so often elsewhere.

"Grace," said Thomas, "not now—not here"; and it seemed to him that out of some common understanding the men and women and children were receding from him, that he was alone on the thin brown carpet under the Ten Commandments bleeding ink—"Grace!" he said, and could barely see her for the distance between them.

"All this time?" said Ronald.

"All this time!"—and this might have been Lorna, and it might have been Grace, so closely were the two women pressed together, so similar their voices; now Ronald was shaking his head in censure or confusion or both, and very lucidly, making her declaration, Grace Macaulay said, "So you see, he never really did belong," and turned away shrugging, as if she'd done nothing more than note the bad weather in the window.

I never did belong, thought Thomas, I never belonged anywhere, and was certain he saw comprehension arrive in one face after the other, and expressions alter from kindly grief into disquiet and distaste.

"But does it matter," said Ronald, "should we cast the first stone?"—and with astonishment Thomas saw that of all the mourners present it was Ronald who understood most, and was least troubled—"Mr. Hart," he said, "why don't you sit down?"

It does matter, thought Thomas, on whose tongue there was now the taste of a copper penny, whose bad hip ached—he saw his last link to Bethesda severed, and one by one every Grace he'd ever loved coming up to sever it. "It's all right," he said, feeling again the jealous clasp of a newborn fist around his finger, "it's all right. It's true, I never did belong."

"Look at that rain," said Ronald, "I hope they drive carefully"; and behind him the hearse moved slowly past the window.

"This is so pretty," said Grace deceitfully, fiddling with a gilt bangle on Lorna's wrist, "where did you get it?"; and it seemed to Thomas that he'd been erased from that moment and all the moments that preceded it, and that no pew or hymn book would retain the imprint of his hand. "Well, then," he said, "I'll be going," and encountered the untroubled nods of strangers; so the last he heard of Bethesda for some years after was not for example a hymn, or the apostle Paul rebuking him down through the centuries, but a false affectionate laugh from a child he'd loved: "I couldn't possibly take it—well that's very kind of you! That's very kind!"

The small hours. Dawn slow coming, rain gone, Aldleigh at uneasy rest. Silence in Lower Bridge Road, where Thomas Hart looked vainly behind closed curtains, under empty armchairs, for a black-haired frowning woman at hand to castigate and console, and found not one dropped pearl or inscrutable sketch. Thomas who was never lonely, who was once content—who balanced Christ and Eros so neatly on the points of his intellect—had become a man of sorrows and acquainted with grief. He was alone, he'd always been alone, the worms were fleeing from him through the soil—no old man at his table, no red velvet coat hanging in the hall; no cross affectionate child, no somber congregation, no loving stranger's look of recognition, no household ghost: he was born in sin and shaped in iniquity and the lights had gone out on the moon. It struck him that there were no practical, ethical or religious reasons why he should be obliged to endure a life that might soon become intolerable. A sensible man could achieve that final thing easily enough, he thought—then rested his head on the table and submitted to such penetrating weariness of his body and spirit that he thought a fatal harm had been sustained—so he need only wait, and the end would find him.

Then something shifted under his cheek: a cheap green notebook, the stitches coming undone at the spine. Thomas raised his head, and looked at it. He looked at the dozens of these heaped on the table, astonished there were so many; looked at the silver laptop with the print of his own hand smearing the lid. Sighing, sitting up straighter, he looked at a handsome white hand loaded with rings, frilled with a black silk cuff; heard a familiar voice, half-admonitory and half-amused: *Get up, Thomas Hart*, said Maria Văduva, assembling herself at the table. *Get up. Haven't you got work to do?* And it was true, thought Thomas with despair, looking at the notebook. He'd tried out titles on the cover, then crossed out their decisive capitals as the writer's doubt set in—ON THE MOTION OF BODIES IN ORBIT. ENLIGHTENMENT. THE BAPTISTS????

Thomas opened the notebook up. *Monday*, he'd written: *late winter, bad weather.* Ten years or more, and he'd never finished the task he'd set himself, dissuaded and distracted by love and circumstance—what, would he go now, and leave his sentences unfinished and unrefined, his thoughts muddled and self-pitying? *Poor Thomas Hart*, they'd say, shaking their heads, *to think his last work was to have been his worst, and what kind of title was that!* The thought was more dreadful than the thought of his body discovered dirty and disarrayed—"My God," he said, not irreverent, "my God— will I have to go on a little longer for the sake of a fucking book?"

Dawn broke. Light slipped under the railway bridge, and over the lip of the windowsill: it arrived at the carpet, the notebooks, the uneaten toast; it lit the opposite wall with Pentecostal fire. Thomas felt the matter of his body respond, helpless against the ordinary wonder of the world turning again and again to the nearest star—*Come on then*, said Maria, tapping the table, dissipating with the shadows. *Get on with it, Thomas Hart.*

Look here, James. Just one more thing: Maria Văduva's comet will return in the winter of 2017. Look up, won't you? Don't forget. T.H.

Please note I have retired, and this account will not be monitored. I can be contacted on my personal address. J. Bower.

And did I ever tell you about the laws of Kepler? The first describes how heavenly bodies orbit the sun, and that is the law of ellipses. The second law I've memorized as I used to memorize Bible verses when I was young: the semimajor axis sweeps out equal areas in equal time. This means that bodies in orbit move faster and faster as they near the heat of the sun, rushing like a man into his lover's arms. Then they move past their perihelion, the embrace is done, and they become listless and slow in the dark.

Lately it's seemed to me that you became a kind of sun—that since you've been gone I've moved through a world with no warmth in it. But my orbit is closed, and everything that passes will in its time return—so I imagine myself moving again toward some heat and light I can't make out—T.H.

I came to the office to collect some correspondence and found your messages. It would be good to see Lowlands again. I'll meet you there on December the tenth, if still convenient?

J. B.

Thomas walked to Lowlands in December, accompanied by all the probabilities: James Bower mocking, James Bower pitying, James Bower chastising—James offering his hand, and James withholding it; James the man Thomas had known, James a man he'd never known at all. Ahead on the illuminated path Maria Văduva fastened the lace at the neck of her gown: *Didn't I warn you, Thomas, didn't I say? Never think too well of any man, or you'll wreck your ship on their rocks!*

"You did," said Thomas, "and I have, but I'm not sure I mind." Aldleigh in winter mimicked Bethesda's gray austerity. The pavements were pale with tracts of grit laid down before the frosts, and the parks stripped back to vacant beds; color arrived only in litter blown up against garden fences and the undecided traffic lights on London Road. I'm sixty-one years old, thought Thomas, and my bad hip aches, and my hands are like my father's hands, if I remember them correctly; but I polished my shoes and spent the morning in the barber's chair, as if I were thirty again and all London made available to me—and what do I hope for? *A clear night*, said Maria, *a good night for hunting*, and receded toward the lake. Thomas was alone. The house in the distance gleamed between the copper beeches, and moonlight struck the glass panels on the renovated wing.

Music arrived, and Thomas so disliked its thin tuneless

complaint that his mood altered, and he began also to dislike each last square foot of Lowlands Park, James Bower in all his iterations, and last and most of all himself—then, "Thomas Hart?" A woman of calculated beauty dressed in pleated silk and amber beads came down the steps with hands outstretched, grimacing at the music and tipping her head as if to indicate she too disliked all this unholy racket—"Thomas Hart? Anna Fonseka. Thank you for coming. Are you warm enough? It's a lazy wind, as my mother would say, going clean through you to save itself time."

"It looks wonderful," said deceitful Thomas, surveying the new steps of York stone, the obstinate glass panels blotted with white marks to dissuade birds from harming themselves in flight. Beyond the glass were Christmas decorations, and ranks of cheap wine on trestle tables, and unremarkable people in unremarkable clothes moving aimlessly across the floor. Thomas longed for the splitting window seats, the obscenities and symbols painted on the peeling walls; and for James Bower, desirable beyond endurance under the lightless chandelier. He took a notebook from his pocket. "Remind me," he said, "of the cost of the renovation, and the name of the funding bodies, and the date of opening again to the public." Anna Fonseka gave her answers, then touching his shoulder with practiced deferential gestures conducted him across the threshold. "This is Thomas Hart," she said, adroitly smiling to this person and that one, left hand in bondage to her amber beads, "who was there when they pulled the statue from the lake—who found the telescope himself! I'll leave you here," she said, having identified across the room some person of more importance; and becoming perceptibly still taller and more adroit left him in the company of Maria Văduva, rinsed of reeds and silt, and standing on a wooden plinth.

"Hello," said Thomas, "you look well." His old friend's feet were bare, and her small high breasts were those of a girl; her head was a little larger than it ought to have been, and had a remote untroubled beauty in which it was not possible to discern her indignant sorrow. The right hand raised to the right eye looked absurd with nothing in it, and her stone skirts gave out the briny scent of the lake. Beside her, and just out of reach, her telescope was sealed in an immense vitrine of toughened glass that had a greenish cast. It reflected the oblivious men and women passing back and forth, so that it was difficult to see beyond these shining phantoms to the telescope itself. Coming closer, and leaving a handprint on the glass in a deliberate act of trespass, Thomas saw the renovations made to the optical tube and eyepiece, and engravings on brass fixtures from which the Essex mildew had been cleaned; but the objective lens had been left in place out of reverence for the passage of time, and was cracked across with a fissure that would break the moon like a plate.

Thomas turned his back and examined the room in which he'd once stood under a vacant chandelier while fog rolled in across the park. He felt himself enfolded in persistent time that had only ever seemed to pass—that everything that happened in Lowlands was still happening, and would always be happening: if I peel that new wallpaper back, I'll see a symbol with the paint still wet—if I look down I'll see a rat running with a severed tail. Here's Grace, and she smells of rose oil and borrowed cigarettes; here's Nathan leaping down the steps—the men are coming in to measure the hole in the roof, and I can smell James Bower's body in his winter coat. I'm Canute, he thought, amused, I'm holding off the tide of time. So he saw the unremarkable people in their evening clothes begin to ebb, and the Christmas lights grow dim with distance against receding walls. He could no longer make out the aimless conversation or the music: he was alone in Lowlands, and his bad hip ached. Then: he was not alone. A man was crossing the vacant floor toward him. The distance between them was so great this took an hour or two, and in that time Thomas felt no anxiety and no surprise: "James," he said, smiling with an uncompromised happiness he knew would be brief, and taking account of the ways in which the man was altered. The gilded hair had tarnished and thinned, and been expertly cut to conceal its thinness; the body was narrower at the shoulder and hip, or had always been so narrow. His coat was gray and fit him well; his shoes were cheap. He came nearer. Now it was possible to see how the skin drooped at the ears as if an essential stitch there had come undone, and that the old burns had healed in shining patches on his forehead. But these did nothing to conceal the careful sculpture of his skull, and if those copper eyes had tarnished it was with the green of verdigris; so Thomas was struck again by beauty. "Hello," he said again, and wondered if he ought to hold out his hand.

"Hello, Thomas!" They embraced efficiently. Then James folded his arms, and surveyed the statue and the vitrine with professional interest. "They've done a good job," he said, "that can't have come cheap"; and for a time the men talked about the difficulties of securing sufficient funding for regional historical projects, and the inadequacy of the new parking arrangements; and all the while Maria Văduva stood at the window solemnly shaking her head, and Thomas noted that James had changed his aftershave, that his socks didn't quite match, that he'd grazed the back of his hand. Then, "A comet," said James, with a more serious and more intimate look at Thomas, as if coming at last to the matter at hand, "a comet, you said!"

"A comet, I said"—Thomas looked at the telescope as if he might find, drifting behind the broken lens, particles of astronomical dust—"a short-period comet, returning in the year

2017 or thereabouts. When Maria saw it they say it was distinctively blue, with a tail extending ten degrees at its highest magnitude—though perhaps this time we'll hardly pick it out of the sky. That would be my luck. But a comet, James—who would have thought it? Though in some ways I wonder if we ought to have done."

"But what are you going to do about it," said James, "who are you going to tell?" He spoke with such serious attention that Thomas responded with equal seriousness, as if they'd been introduced moments before over cheap wine in cheap glasses: "I'm told I must contact some official institution, but I have nothing to show but the diary of a woman who vanished and was driven mad by love, and a broken telescope."

"What a pity," said James, his seriousness deepening still further, "how disappointing for you." How funny this all is, Thomas thought: there was a time I'd rather have seen your face again than every comet in orbit together; and now you're here and I asked how the traffic was on the A12—"Are you laughing at me?" said James Bower. "Have I misunderstood?"

Thomas felt laughter cede to an awful tenderness. "Look," he said, reaching for the other man's sleeve, "let's go. I can't talk to you here."

The room pressed in. Women danced with movements that made nonsense of music. The Christmas lights went out, and were coaxed on again. Nobody looked at Maria. "Come on," said Thomas, conscious of sounding imperious and perhaps angry.

"Ah," said Anna Fonseka, arriving as if out of the vitrine, "I've been looking for you"—but already Thomas was slipping out with James in his wake. He went more quickly than he ought to have done, and the other man found him biting his tongue to quell a complaint, and rubbing at his aching hip;

"Are you all right? I am sorry," said James, "I expect this is painful for you—" He flushed. It resembled shame.

"It isn't that," said Thomas, "it's an old pain. And in fact I should say sorry," he said, "writing to you the way I did. It was childish and ungracious—I find each year that I grow no older, no more wise: only that I cart the same old Thomas Hart about in a body showing signs of wear."

"You didn't know I'd see your messages," said James.

"It was improbable, but possible!"

"But I am sorry. I had no idea. I didn't understand how it was for you. I didn't know."

"You see"—Thomas was gentle—"I think you did know." A full moon was rising. It was horribly large, and as yellow as streetlights.

"I am sorry. But I never meant you any harm—Thomas, why does the moon seem so big, and so low?"

"That is a perigee moon, moving through the nearer part of its orbit, and seeming larger because so near the horizon—but that's also a trick: it's just the same old moon. And I don't think you should be sorry," said Thomas. "Don't say you are, don't feel it. It's true you caused me pain. I think more pain than I ever knew before or since, and perhaps that means I'm a man who's led a happy life. But now I think the pain was a tax on riches. I'm grateful for it, I'm glad—how could I have written what I did without it? But it's strange, it seems to me almost a humiliation: after all this time I want to touch you, because I never did."

"You never did," said James. He was looking with fear at the lamenting moon. "You never did. But do you want to, even now? You can"—he seemed to be leaning out of himself—"I'm just here." He breathed as if the air were thin. His lips were red. The buttons on his coat had come undone, and he looked at

Thomas with an elated will that had no desire in it. I know that look, thought Thomas, I've seen it before, when Lowlands was on fire. He always did want some kind of disaster to lift him out of his own life: I could have been a schoolgirl, I could have been a gambling debt.

"You think I pity you," said James, "but I don't, I never did."

"I might have taken pity—I might have preferred that. But I am not a disaster. I'm a man." I have refused him, thought Thomas, amazed at himself, I have refused him. The appalling moon was rising and pulling up the Essex earth, and Thomas rose with it. I did love you, he thought. I have loved you, I would have loved you, I do.

"Someone is coming," said James. He was far below, inaudible, he was buttoning up his coat. "I wonder if we'll see each other again?"

"Thomas Hart?" Anna Fonseka, her amber beads lost or removed, held out her hands. "I was hoping you would say a word or two."

"It isn't convenient," said James, "leave us alone"; and it was possibly the authority of his beauty, which time had made austere, that caused her to blink in surprise and recede obediently over the lawn. "I don't suppose we'll meet again," said James. "There'll be no reason."

"I suppose we won't," said Thomas, and for now it was possible to think of this without pain. The music had finished in the house. Men and women were heading for their cars, stumbling sometimes against each other; a wind was getting up. "Goodbye," said Thomas Hart.

"Goodbye," said James. "It has been good to see you." No handshake then, and no embrace; only a curious boyish salute as James walked away, and the brake lights of departing cars ignited the fabric of his coat. Possibly he spoke again, but somewhere a woman was noisily indulging her tears. "Yes," said

Thomas, "goodbye." Distantly he felt a pain like that of the ache in his hip. It would recede; it would return. He turned his back to the house, and thought he could make out the silver birches, and Bethesda's sloping roof. The dreadful moon was on his left, the Pole Star pinned the night in place; Nick Carleton was in his office, and Grace Macaulay was on the London train—James Bower in the driver's seat was calling his wife, and over in Beechwood Avenue Ronald Macaulay was falling asleep. How astonishing, thought Thomas, and how terrible—how it all just goes on regardless! Darkness visible! Heaven in ordinary! The lights were going out in Lowlands House.

Dear James,

You see I am back to my old habits now, of writing paper
letters I won't send, because I don't need to send them.
All the same I want to tell you what I've learned—what
came to my full consciousness as slowly and with as much
wonder and difficulty as the laws of physics. I have learned
it was love that arrived with that first look of yours, and
that first look of mine—it was love that caused the world
to alter because it had you in it!

And this is also true, by virtue of predestination or fate or
the mischief of time: I had already loved you all my life, as
a condition of my immortal soul—and so in your way, you
altered God.

But I won't have you think my heart was broken because it
was a man I loved. My heart was broken because I am
alive.

THOMAS HART

PART THREE

2017

The Law of Harmonies

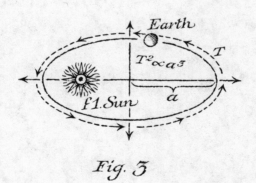

Fig. 3

A woman was leaving the asylum on midsummer morning. She went warily down steps leading to a gravel drive, observing her own feet with interest and care, as she might have watched children inclined to run into the road. The drive traversed a clipped and dying lawn between box hedges tended to by orderlies and patients; at the farther end a taxi waited with an open door. The distance to the taxi seemed to this woman an unjust punishment. Her back ached, as did her hips; the early sun coaxed out spiteful insects to suck at the backs of her knees. Occasionally she paused to scrutinize the sky, as if expecting something up there besides the obstinate sun; then with a shrug either despondent or relieved she'd move slowly on.

She reached the taxi. It was difficult to get in. The manipulation of her body required care and strength: she gave it. The driver was untroubled by her appearance, or by her tongue's habit of slipping out: "Lovely morning," he said, and mutely she agreed that it was. He departed the hospital. The hospital departed her. He'd had a cousin in there once, he said, five years, that sort of thing ran in the family but had never come his way, touch wood. "Came out a different man," he said, "but then who doesn't change in five years?" He was not unkind; but when she discovered him watching her in the rearview mirror she was ashamed of her appearance and her unbiddable tongue.

"Been long, has it?" The driver wound the window down. "Been a while since you were out?"

"I don't know," she said, "but I think so." She examined the sky. She was afraid of nothing, and this was astounding: she'd been more or less afraid for twenty years. Aldleigh was approaching, and not much changed. These surely were the gates of Lowlands House—how could the old terror keep at bay, under such provocation? Schoolchildren waited at the gates in yellow vests; the lawns beyond the gate were striped and wet. Then very faintly—rising from the taxi footwell, the steering wheel, the driver's seat—she could smell smoke and water, and the tick of her heart halted. But that passed soon enough, and ordinary time took up its tick behind her ribs. "Do you think," she said, emboldened by courage, "that you could take me to the town?"

"We can go where you please, love, no skin off my nose. Where d'you have in mind?"

The woman looked at her bag, which contained all that remained of her life. Toothbrush, sandals, two folded shirts that didn't fit; a paper bag containing medication she required and despised. A cheap book with a broken spine (*The Virago Book of Women's Life Writing*); and, making do for a bookmark, a new envelope containing an old one. "Would it be all right," she said, "if you took me to the office of the *Essex Chronicle*?"

Thomas Hart had attained at last his threescore years and ten, and was sitting at his desk. Doubting, diligent, unchanging Thomas; clever old Thomas, the noted Thomas Hart. He went no more a-roving on the Strand and Bishopsgate, but there was no celestial border he didn't seek to cross, and he owned a telescope that would make Maria Văduva weep and break a lens. You mustn't think that doubting Thomas lacked in those days for sacraments: wasn't he a citizen of the empire of the moon, and a supplicant of its religions? So the sky at night offered him a liturgy, and he attended devoutly to the inscrutable beauty of its syllables and propositions: redshift, blueshift, and the proper motion of the stars; Ophiuchus, Andromeda, and Perseus; zodiacal light and solar wind and the movement of bodies in orbit. Now and then he attempted the study of an A-level textbook on physics, which drove him almost to tears: what a stupid man it transpired he was, and had always been, to so fatally lack a facility with numbers and calculations, and never to have understood the nature of the electromagnetic spectrum! Occasionally it struck him that his love for the stars was no less a matter of faith than his remaining love for God; so his two faiths weren't opposed, but took up equal residence.

He'd lost perhaps half an inch in height, and gained perhaps an inch in breadth; but generally speaking the years had glanced off him without damage, and he was as unaltered as Bethesda's pews. His office had more than ever the look of an Edwardian gentleman's salon, and nobody ever thought to dislodge him from it—besides, Nick Carleton had acquired a temper alongside an OBE for services to the regional press, having secured the future of the *Essex Chronicle* online against a year-on-year decline in print sales, and who'd risk the violence of his outrage by suggesting that Thomas Hart ought surely to retire? So Thomas remained known for his curious columns on the stars, his curious Romanian pastries that tasted of Turkish delight, his curious habit of rubbing at an aching hip. That he was a man of seventy surprised him every morning in the mirror, and he'd removed the clock from his bedside table, disliking the slicing tick that pared down the time remaining to a little stub.

Not much was going on in Aldleigh, those days. Essex, it seemed to him, would do well to recall its heritage of martyrs burned to the glory of God over logs of green wood, and sea serpents plaguing the estuary, of gangsters shot in Land Rovers on icy country lanes and peasants revolting in the streets. Not much going on: so he occupied himself with the cheap green notebooks heaped high as ever on his desk, and the manuscript taken up and abandoned over twenty years that was now spread disconsolately among them. *Praise and Blame*, the title read, and suddenly this struck him as absurdly pompous— who do you think you are, Thomas Hart—Lev Nikolayevich Tolstoy, who died in a railway station on account of his bad chest, and could never sit comfortably on his heap of laurels? He crossed the title out, then heard with relief a single authoritative knock, followed by the arrival of Nick Carleton at the door.

"Thomas," said the editor, "you have a visitor again." He

looked displeased, with the frank displeasure only safely afforded a friend.

"I can't help that," said Thomas. "I'm very famous, these days."

"She tells me you've met before. Go in," said Carleton, now speaking to somebody out of sight, "go in, sit down." He stood back to let a woman pass, and looked at the other man as if to say: what trouble are you causing now, Thomas Hart? He closed the door; he washed his hands of the matter.

The visitor came in with the self-possession of a person who understands they cannot pass without notice, and judges nobody for noticing. She was tall, and fat after a fashion that had caused her skin to take on the puffed and shining look of satin. Her face was broad at the cheekbones, and soft at the chin and neck, and here the skin was very white, and unmarked by any pore or blemish. She had a jackdaw's cautious, watchful, blue-eyed gaze, and her tongue roved over her lower lip as if there were something sweet on it. Thomas was startled to note that her clothes were shabby and cheap, since she had such a majestic look about her, and such a stately slow gait, that ermine and ribbons would have suited her better. He felt compelled by her, as if she possessed a gravitational field to which all lesser bodies would be subject, and came forward with hands outstretched to bring her to a seat.

"Thank you," she said, and for a moment recovered her breath; then looked at him and, "Yes," she said. "Yes. It's me."

Ought he to know her? He looked again at her hair, which had been badly cut, and had a pretty reddish look; he looked again at her worried, silken face. No bells rang. "You see I meet so many people," he said, "and have no memory for faces." He returned to his own seat, and was grateful for the expanse of desk between them: it was not that she caused him unease, only he was conscious of something very like a sustained note ringing out above the ordinary register. A jug of water was near at hand; he poured it.

"I've never been much good with time," the woman said. She smoothed her cheap gray leggings as if they were silk. "I suppose ten years, at least?"

"Ten years?" said Thomas. He examined them, and couldn't find her.

"I sat just here," she said. "I sat just where I am now, and burned a piece of paper. Look: I left a mark." Thomas looked, and saw a dark blot on the desk.

"Oh!" said Thomas. "No—not ten years. Twenty." There, superimposed on his startling visitor, was the silent girl who'd sought him out, and burned Maria's letter to ashes; there too was the Lowlands fire, and the slumped and boneless figure on the terrace rising out of sodden clothes. He shifted in his chair, and put between them an additional inch of space.

"I'm sorry," the woman said, her voice rising quickly to childish misery, as if he'd begun to berate her. She put her face in her hands and shook with the effort of her sorrow: "I shouldn't have done it. I don't know why I did, only I'd been waiting all my life for something to happen that would change me, and it never did. I think that man was hurt, I think he was burned—maybe even he died. I asked and asked, and nobody would tell me."

"He did die," said Thomas, "but not for a long time, and not of his burns." There was the sensation of a taut string behind his ribs being plucked once, and this was grief, and would pass.

"Ah," she said, as if the news were painful. "I am sorry. He was such a good-looking man. I remember that. And he seemed so young—what was it? What happened to him?"

I don't know, thought Thomas. I don't know, I don't know, I don't know. "I think possibly cardiac arrest," he said, taken over by a peculiar exhaustion caused not by events but by himself, "or some inherited weakness that finally gave out. They say it was a quiet quick death while he was sleeping. I found out two years after. Nobody told me. Nobody knew they should."

The sorrow he'd learned to contain overspilled in this stranger, who gave a single sharp sob as if the loss had been hers. "I'm sorry," she said. "I'm very sorry."

Thomas disliked and pitied her. "Take my handkerchief," he said. "No: keep it. And have a glass of water."

She drank. The remarkable skin was mottled, as if sorrow were a communicable disease. She put the water down. "I expect you think I'm mad," she said.

"Yes," said Thomas, "I do begin to think that. Though the nature of madness," he said, "depends really on the habits and conditions of the world we find ourselves in. They used to set madmen adrift on ships, which they called the ships of fools, and since there was no law or constitution on board to regulate the mind, how could any of the passengers be mad?"

The woman considered this—seemed briefly to thrill to it—then said, "They told me I was not mad, only unwell. Poorly, they sometimes said, like I was a child being sick—they gave me names for it, and the names changed every few years. What they really meant was that I was mad, but it never seemed like madness to me. Didn't you put it in the paper, and didn't I read it? The comet was coming, and there was a dark companion, and a comet was always a bad omen!"

"But I meant nothing by it—I write all kinds of things. It wasn't important, I thought nothing of it at all."

"Don't you think it matters, what you do and say? It always matters. Everything touches everything else. So I knew the comet was coming, and the dark companion, and I thought it wanted me. Every night I watched, and waited, and then there it was, but it was just a light. It brought nothing with it. It changed nothing. Everything was always going to be just the same. So I will make the change, I thought, I'll change everything, and I started the fire. You don't understand what it's like," she said, "to want something so much, and never have it, which is faith. Nobody ever does."

"I understand," he said. "I do."

Scornfully, eyes obtaining the facets of a gem: "Go on then. Tell me what you believe, if you believe anything at all!" Her splendid body refused the confines of the chair, and the note struck in the room, seeming to emanate from her, rang in the high corners and against the window.

Could Thomas raise Bethesda on his desk and take it down again, to show her the tides of his faith? He could not. "I believe," he said with great care, "that we move toward the good. That we're like ships who make their navigations, and drift toward a pilot light." She was dubious. "That is," he said, "I am not sure that we can help it—as if it really is the vessel that tends toward the light, whether the captain wants to or not. Now," he said, becoming brisk, certain she'd sink this formless morality, "don't you think you ought to tell me why you've come?"

The glint receded. She took on the look of a rightly chastised child. Slowly she opened her bag, and sourness rose from the contents. Thomas, with a pluck of recognition, saw a paperback as familiar to him as one of his own. "I have that book," he said. He felt peculiarly dazed. "The diaries and letters of women who should never have been forgotten—an old man I once knew translated a diary, and I gave it to an editor, who published it." (Now came the rustle of silk skirts behind him, and he refused to turn his head. Can't you leave me alone for five minutes, Maria Văduva Bell?) "Have you read it? The translator died. He died without my knowing, alone under the railway arch, and in the rain."

"You can't know he was alone," said the woman, "unless you were there; in which case of course he wouldn't have been alone." She looked at him with faint benevolent contempt. "But yes," she said, "you are right, this book contains Maria Văduva's diary, and she lived at Lowlands House, and so did I." She took an envelope from between the pages and reached into it. Her smooth upholstered fingers were dexterous and quick. The room was resolutely quiet. "Did you know I'd been in Lowlands for weeks before the comet came? Nobody saw me. Nobody knew or cared and nobody ever hurt me. There was a rat I loved, that had no tail—I saw the swifts come back in May and the white heads of their chicks up there in a row. And I was always finding things: broken glass and hairpins and torn-up bits of paper. The people who lived there hid things from each other. This was put between a mirror and a wall and I kept it with me, though I don't know who wrote it, or why." Now she was holding a pale blue envelope, surveying it with a kind of wary attention, as if it were the drawing of a face she no longer loved. She put it on the table. "Why don't you take the letter out?" she said, "Why don't you look?"

Thomas took the letter out. He looked. He saw a folded sheet of paper, damaged by fire and water, the ink blooming in places. "A letter sent from London," he said to himself, to the various ghosts now drifting in and reading over his shoulder, "and sent three days after Maria Văduva's diary ended."

"Read it to me," she said. "I like to hear it."

Obedient Thomas lifted the paper to the light. "*My beloved friend*," he read:

"My beloved friend, you cannot ask this of me. It is not a fair test of my affection! Do you think I (of all women!)

shall consign you to darkness for the sake of a man (of all things!)? Have you not told me that a woman ought to live by a brighter light than that dim and solitary candle!—how angry I am—I will leave Foolish Street on foot and walk to Essex and box your ears myself! Write at once and assure me that you have regained your reason. Meanwhile I absolutely rain pearls—and I am as ever your devoted—C."

"I never had a friend like that," she said, "did you?"

"I did once," said Thomas. But what should he do with this? It raised Maria, it raised James, and on they went as they always had—vital, unterminated, coming at him over the Lowlands lawns (it raised Grace Macaulay, in fact: he turned his back). Abruptly he was tired. "This is no use to me. It is no further information. There is no address. The postmark is hopelessly smudged. There is not even a name!"

His visitor shrugged, and this was a slow languorous raise of her shoulders. "Do with it as you like," she said. "Burn it, for all I care." With deliberate heavy grace she rose from the chair. "If I were you, I'd wonder what it was Maria asked this woman to do, and whether she did it. But"—again, the luxuriant shrug—"perhaps you are too old to trouble yourself." She was putting away the book, she was moving to the door.

Thomas went in her wake: "It was good of you to come," he said, bringing out his old civilities, quelling the desire to look back and see if she'd left scorch marks on her seat. "I am glad to see that you are well, and grateful you brought Maria back to my desk!" But he was not grateful, he was not glad—a lancing pain went through his hip, and this caused him to stumble, and rest on the slope of her shoulder, and the comfort of this sensation was appalling to him. He righted himself, and received a final quick blue look.

"Well," she said, "I am done, and it is finished. Goodbye, Thomas."

Thomas said, "Goodbye."

Carefully now the woman walked through Aldleigh town. Tarmac softened on the heatstruck roads, and a steely haze was settling in potholes, and on the threshold of distant shops. How altered Aldleigh was. She'd never seen this bank before, or that café—had no recollection of the library, for example, or the war memorial; but possibly that was only the effect of the heat. Now and then she put her hand in her bag to feel for the envelope and was puzzled by its absence. But that was all right—the last link was severed—the fear was gone.

She came to the Jackdaw and Crow: a woman came out of it. This woman was short as a boy, and plump, with a narrow back scooped deeply in above broad hips; her arms were bare to the sun, and the skin on them was radiant and dark. She wore a red dress seeming to disintegrate about her as she walked, or to be formed out of scraps with every step: it had a corseted bodice embroidered with stars, and a full skirt knotted to show white petticoats. Her sandals were cheap, and she was dirty between her toes. She'd contrived a little additional height out of black hair bundled above her brow and fastened with a pencil, and there was a white streak in it. It was not possible to make out her face, since she was bent to her phone, and intently considering what she saw—but it would be a marvelous face, no doubt about it: how I despise her, she thought, pinching the thin white skin of her forearm. What did women like her know of wanting change, and never finding it—of obtaining faith, and losing it—of carting about a body that ached in all weathers?

Now she was coming to the station, and the London train

was due; she was pressed on all sides by departing passengers. The shallow steps at her feet reeked of chicken bones taken by foxes, and of urine and spilled sweet drinks; she went up them with difficulty, and without fear. Up on the platform, the sun beat back from shining tracks and set up a pain in her head like the tolling of a bell. Lowlands drew her, as the north draws the compass needle—she drifted across the platform and saw it shining in the copper beeches, under the railway lines that sagged and ticked. No comet visible above the sloping roof, trailing its dark companion; no smoke unwinding from the window. A kind of weary ease settled on her. The white house between the copper beeches was impossibly near—it was nothing but an inch or so below the painted lip of the platform edge: look, the boards were down from the windows, the door between the white pillars was open, she could reach it if only she tried. She heard distant voices in the lower rooms, and these were calling her by name, they were calling her in; then there were trumpets sounding a welcome, and white banners hurled from the upper windows—so I am wanted after all, she thought, I am wanted! It was remarkable; it was what she had always expected. She ran forward.

Let's say the jays in Potter's Field, now in their seventh generation, were shaken from the branches of the hazel by a thud; let's say the rats in Lowlands Park paused briefly in their scavenging, and shrugged, and went on with vital business, as did the men in yellow jackets tending to the potholes on Station Road. Let's say Grace Macaulay, coming out of the pound shop into white perpendicular light, heard the bloodless mechanical wail that followed the thud, and thought perhaps a train had hit the buffers, or struck a deer wandered in from Lowlands Park. But she had no time to spare on imagined disasters, and went briskly over the road to the Jackdaw and Crow

where a woman watering hanging baskets agreed with Grace
that certainly it was much hotter than she would have liked,
and that yes: she'd certainly heard that bang, but this was Aldleigh, and did anything ever happen here? No, said Grace, no,
it never did; she walked under dripping baskets and delighted
in the water, then went up an iron staircase fastened to the
pub's external wall in case of fire. As she went up the world
went down, and dwindled to something inconsequential at
her feet: she had no stake whatever in the thud, the potholes in
the street, the customers converging on the threshold of the
pound shop. She covered her ears against sirens coming now
down Station Road, and was home.

Grace had returned again to the town where she'd been
born, and where she thought she'd likely die and then be
burned or buried. The slow tide on which she'd drifted to London had simply turned and brought her back to Essex: it had
all felt inevitable—it had all felt irresistible; she'd neither chosen nor refused her own life, only inhabited it as she inhabited
her body. She'd liked London well enough, for its capacity to
diminish her down to an anonymous working part in an immense machine, and because it was there she'd been tutored in
the ordinary sins she might otherwise have practiced and per-
fected in her teens. But relative poverty had driven her out,
and it had never occurred to her to go any farther than Essex
and the clay where she'd cultivated her soul. Now she lived in
the attic of the Jackdaw and Crow, the pub she'd been raised to
view with fear and suspicion as a den of alcohol-soaked iniqui-
ties. This attic had been abandoned the year Victoria died, and
left to become a damp cavity certain (so drinkers said at last
orders, looking up in pleasant terror) to be haunted. But since
the present landlady was a woman who knew good business, it
had been turned into a small home in the eaves, rented out to
tenants in no position to mind that in winter their breath was

visible even when the radiators trickled all night like digesting animals, and that in summer its several sloping windows gave the effect of a greenhouse. So Grace Macaulay, who all her life had barely had twopence to rub together, lived here alone in exchange for rent she often couldn't find, and one shift a week at the bar, where she poured her measures with the hectic cheer of a woman delighting in sin.

She came over the threshold with the gratitude of an animal returning to its burrow, and threw open windows tinted with the grime of passing trains and traffic. A weariness not in the least unwelcome overcame her, and demanded the submission of her spirit in her body. She undressed, and lay on the floor in the heat with her limbs arranged to prevent skin touching skin. Dimly she was conscious of flies at the window, and evidence of mice on the rug; of the scent of her cheap jasmine perfume that came in a tin, of butter going bad in the dish, of herself. Then: sleep.

Must we imagine Grace Macaulay happy? Regarding evidence for the prosecution, the court should be advised that she is only thirty-eight and made of stern stuff as regards bone, musculature, immune system, and so on; is rarely seen to sneeze, or to complain of a bad head; that she has the kind of beauty undiminished by time, predicated not on youth but symmetry of bone, together with self-possession and color and vitality. All children want to be ordinary, and she never was, and that had been difficult—but all adults want to be extraordinary, and now she amplifies her strangeness, delighting in her ignorance of worldly matters and her tendency to speak sometimes in a biblical cadence, telling men she meets that she was born in 1887 (this being the year they dug Bethesda's foundations) and meanwhile allowing her dress to slip from her shoulders. As to that: she has never loved a woman or a man as she loved

Nathan, nor does she expect to; but is fluent in various love languages, if always with the accent of a stranger. Her father is not dead yet. In his dotage he has become childlike, affectionate and easily teased: it's hardly possible to believe she feared him once, and smelled fire and brimstone in the seams of his clothes. She rises early in summer, and late in winter, and breakfasts on bad coffee from the pound shop and soft white rolls she bakes herself (and Anne Macaulay at her shoulder cautions her neither to under-prove the dough, nor over-bake it). She is servant to no master. She occupies her days with clothing—in the mending and embellishment of it for purposes theatrical and ecclesiastical, in ironing and starching it; even sometimes in constructing new garments out of old ones, and wearing them through Aldleigh in the knowledge that she is seen and admired and enviously mocked. Sometimes she is asked how she came to be doing such a thing, and did they teach her in London; but the truth is she has always done it, and she taught herself—her hands simply knew how to do it, it was as native as original sin. That it became her profession had really been a question of one garment after another—of favors extended and sought, of exasperated theatres in pantomime season desperate for another pair of hands. And her work these days is fine: she binds her seams in silk, her goldwork and embroidery would shame a bishop's cope. Her curls have come back, with their consoling animal scent; she eats and sings as she sews, and her softened body refuses jeans and insists on petticoats and silk. Her fellow women she views with affectionate suspicion, with an anthropological interest: their willingness to suborn themselves to men and to the mechanics of reproduction strikes her as peculiar, but she generally wishes them well. She mourns Nathan when she remembers to mourn him, and wonders what she might have been if she hadn't lost him; but she knows who to blame for this loss. It is not herself, it isn't that she was incapable of securing Nathan's love: it was all the fault of Thomas Hart. She nurses her anger with intimate attention; when she sees him sometimes on Aldleigh High Street or on the station platform a prick of rage goes through her like a current, and she lives off this vital spark. Speaking of anger: Lorna Greene has gone to the genteel west, to Cheltenham possibly or Bath, and consequently is as good as dead. She loses her faith much as she sometimes loses a pair of dressmaking scissors, for example, or the lipstick she favors most; it turns up behind a sofa cushion, in the pocket of her winter coat. She attends Bethesda now and then, and there are even mornings when she comes near the mercy seat and prays with the sincerity of her childhood: *Thou art my hope, O Lord God, thou art my trust from my youth*. She is not certain of the condition of her immortal soul, but navigates as best she can toward the pilot light, the nature of which she hardly needs to know, only that it shines.

Might the court be persuaded to find her guilty of happiness, on such compelling evidence? Perhaps; but nonetheless steps forward, adjusting his horsehair wig, counsel for the defense. Grace Macaulay is poor, and only a rich fool thinks money can't buy happiness. In due course she imagines she'll inherit her father's house, but gives this little thought and scrapes by cash-in-hand. There have been winters she bathed out of water from the kettle poured into the plastic bowl in which she also washes dishes; there have been days when sometimes even bitter pound-shop coffee is beyond her means. Wherever she goes, she is alone. At the bar in the Jackdaw and Crow she is Bethesda's child, and deplores all their profanities; in her chapel pew she is a woman of the world, and deplores her sinful state. Often she tries to turn her *dearest* ring, forgetting it slipped off one afternoon and out of spite she refused to pick it up; often she thinks *I must tell Thomas*, forgetting that she can't and won't. That her body is aging is a matter of horror: what (for example) has become of the skin on her breasts and her neck, and did she always bleed like this? She sleeps badly, in little fits and starts. She's prone to blisters, and to an infection in the finger that's pricked most often as she works. She can never find her needle when she wants one, though her rooms are full of needles. She has never been to Venice. She loved Nathan, and he did not love her; so at night on her bed she seeks him whom her soul loveth, she seeks him and she finds him not, and what have you. Does she try to be good? Certainly—but how exhausting and uncertain that is, when there is nobody to show her how—*O Lord God of my salvation, I have cried day and night before thee, my soul is full of troubles!* Case rests.

The judicious reader might well think neither prosecution nor defense have brought sufficient evidence before the court. Well, then. Grace Macaulay on the charge of happiness: case dismissed.

"Hear that?" said Nick Carleton, returning to Thomas that same afternoon with the avid look of an editor who scents a headline. "Hear that? Man under a train, doubt there's much left: they'll be out there for hours with buckets and shovels. I've sent someone to take a look—but Thomas, you seem unwell: whatever did that woman say to you? Go on home, go on. The sun's out."

The sun was out: light passed between the plastic slats of the venetian blinds, refracted through a glass of water, and arrived at the scorch mark on the desk. Thomas passed his upturned hand between the scorch and the sun: "Look at this," he said, as if showing Carleton bright water cupped in his palm. "Look—all those photons, born in the heart of the sun one hundred and seventy thousand years ago, and traveled eight and a half minutes for no task more serious than warming me up at my desk. Did I tell you there's a storm up there these days, and bad weather on the sun? In fact," he said, spilling the sunlight and rising to his feet, "perhaps I'll go and take a look."

"Take a look, and write about it. Five hundred words," said Carleton. "Six, if the skies are clear."

On clear nights, or nights when hope spoke louder than the weather forecast, Thomas these days would set up his telescope in the bare garden behind the house on Lower Bridge Road. Maria Văduva, baffled by its technologies, refused to learn the nature and utility of satellites and GPS, but admired the ten-inch objective lens, and directed him to Delphinus and Andromeda. Its shining barrel was surmounted by a camera, which scanned the stars to determine its position under the celestial sphere. Then Thomas—always with a boyish feeling that he was possibly doing something wrong—would take the control resembling an old-fashioned telephone on a spiral cord, and ask the telescope to find binary stars and galaxies and shining cities on the moon. There'd be a pause, and then a seeking whine as if the telescope yearned with Thomas to leave the earth; slowly it would turn and lift and fix its gaze on the desired object. There were nights it was all hopeless, the stars soon consumed by clouds; there were nights the seeing was good, and he resisted the cold that thudded in his aching hip, and sat for hours in the company of Maria: *Look, Thomas, see how the sky seems a black pool on which the sunlight plays?*

Now: the sun was out, and the telescope capped with silvered film to preserve the eyes. It was noon at midsummer, and the optical tube was almost perpendicular to the earth; so it was necessary for Thomas to crouch to the eyepiece to meet the near star. There they were, he thought, marveling at the sight of solar storms: three sunspots drifting toward the eastern limb of the sun, with the look of drops of black ink dispersing in a pool of orange paint. "Every eleven years," he said to a disbelieving sparrow on the garden wall, "the magnetic poles of the sun swap, and then a new cycle of activity and solar storms begins—" The sparrow departed with a dismissive shrug of its wing, and the sun slipped past the field of view, and Thomas was lonely: how he'd have liked Grace Macaulay to come quickly down the garden, willing to be amazed.

He abandoned the sun, and sat for a time in the shade, seeing the garden populated by the girl he'd loved in all her iterations—the bad-tempered infant prone to sudden bouts of joy, the black-haired bustling girl who brought him her troubles, the vengeful creature in a borrowed hat refusing to meet his gaze. There, too, was the unmistakable stranger he saw now and then coming out of the Jackdaw and Crow, or going with her old determined gait down the station platform: a small dark woman approaching forty in shabby opulent clothes with a white streak in her hair. How obdurate her anger was, and what a wretched waste it had all been. I gave up the freedom of my soul to stay in my pew and keep my foot in the door, he thought, and she betrayed me! A father's love for his own child is all very well, but essentially selfish. I loved her even though it was never my duty—oh I could knock her onto the railway track, I could chuck her in the river! But Maria was stooping to the telescope: *Then why are you crying, Thomas Hart?*

"Sometimes," said Thomas, wiping his eyes, "I have the strangest feeling that things happen not one after the other, but all at once. I felt it years ago, in Lowlands House, and here it is again. I can't explain it, only tell you that this afternoon I'm a young man in winter and someone's handed me a baby at a funeral—but also that I'm fifty, and the man I love is here and the sun is going down—and also that I'm older than I am now, and Grace is knocking at my door! Everything still happens within me—how else can I make sense of time? How else can I explain that I am lonely, and never lonely—that I despise my friend and I miss her—that James Bower causes me the worst pain I ever knew, and no pain at all?"

Come here would you, Thomas, lend me a hand. We've lost the sun.

DISORDERED TIME

THOMAS HART, *ESSEX CHRONICLE*,
21 JUNE 2017

I wonder if you've ever shared my feeling that things happen not one after the other, but all at once? I expect it's just the folly of old age, but lately I've had a habit of saying to myself: Everything that will ever happen has happened, and is happening.

Many years ago (or tomorrow, or yesterday) I happened to see a palimpsest in the British Library. A fifteenth-century liturgy had been overwritten on parchments including a ninth-century gospel and a twelfth-century study of Plato; and to look at it was to hear a chorus of voices singing together in one place, but not from one time.

Now this is how the whole world seems to me. I've lived in Aldleigh all my life, and imagine I'll die here—so as I walk past the market square and the war memorial, or go through Lowlands Park toward the river, I experience the town not with this present self, but with all the selves I have contained, and will ever contain. Sometimes I meet myself on the stairs, and sometimes I see friends who died

or left me in other ways—and my experience of them now consists of every experience of them I ever had. So you see, I've learned it's possible to despise and love a friend equally, in the same place and at the same time.

Since these days I look to physics just as I used to look to the scripture, and I find there a peculiar theory that appeals to me. This is the idea of the block universe, and is predicated on Einstein's theory of relativity: it conceives of the entirety of space and time existing together in a kind of three-dimensional cuboid. In this model there is no sequence of events unfurling on a timeline: it all occurs simultaneously, and our experience of it depends on how the block is sliced.

I doubt I've understood or explained it well, but all the same it does illuminate my life. If everything that will ever happen has happened, and is happening, at last I understand how it might be possible to fall in love at a glance, and know a stranger like a lover—perhaps already that love and all the events that followed were already unfolding elsewhere, and elsewhen. And I also understand how it might be possible to despise those who wronged us, and at the same time to feel at peace, which is perhaps the backward echo of forgiveness we haven't yet seen. Now: my father was a preacher, and already I hear him chastise me from beyond the grave (or before it)—what comes of moral responsibility, Thomas, if the exercise of our will makes no difference to events—what would men and women do if they could shrug and say: It has all already happened!

I'll let the physicists and theologians argue over that, and look instead to T. S. Eliot. "If all time is eternally present," he wrote, "all time is unredeemable." Perhaps no matter how we conceive of it, time is unredeemable, and as soon as we do a thing, it's done. There was a time this would have made me sad. Now it refines every minute in my possession into something so precious I can't bear to throw it away.

On midsummer evening Ronald Macaulay labored up the iron staircase at the Jackdaw and Crow, and Grace opened the attic door to let him in. "Mr. Hart gave me a lift," said Ronald, kissing his daughter with his old dry kiss, "but said he couldn't stay" (and down on Station Road Thomas Hart drove home, and wouldn't look up at the windows). Ronald vaguely understood that he saw little of Thomas these days, but out of confusion or self-preserving ignorance had failed to grasp that Thomas had departed Bethesda, and departed Grace. It was never clear what he'd understood as he sat wearily at his sister's funeral. Possibly he'd accepted Thomas's nature quite equably as a consequence of original sin, and no more shocking than a tendency to break the speed limit, for example, or to be rude when under strain. But it was equally possible that the idea a homosexual had occupied Bethesda's pews all those years had been so shocking he'd simply refused it, or that in the haze of grief it had all passed him by. Whatever the cause, he stood on the doorstep of heaven, a happy man prone to falling asleep in the day, and surprised when he woke to find he wasn't yet in glory.

"Come in," said Grace. The declining sun illuminated the small kitchen in which she stood wiping her hands on a linen apron. She surveyed her father, who now roused in her a maternal worry that reversed the natural order: "You look thin,"

she said. "Whatever you've been eating, it hasn't been enough."
She brought him carefully into a room in which two sofas,
broad and low as beds, regarded each other across a shipping
trunk. Here, too, the sun had made its entrance, but nonetheless a dozen lamps shone in a dozen places (tell her she acquired her profligate habits of light from Thomas Hart, and
she'd turn them off one by one). These had been retrieved from
skips or thieved from provincial theaters, since Grace had
never lost her magpie's habit, and thought whatever she found
beautiful was hers by right. Lozenges of light were cast down
on overlapping carpets, and up on walls hung (despite the
landlady's edicts) with framed prints, and ugly oils in gilded
frames, and various tapestries and garments that time had put
beyond use, but not beauty. Plastic boxes were stacked against
the far wall, interspersed with open baskets out of which
spilled antique bodices and overskirts and horsehair bustle-
pads awaiting Grace's needle; a corkboard in hopeless disorder
was covered with receipts, postcards, sketches, letters regarding unpaid council tax bills, and frail samples of fabric. A broken violin she had no idea how to play hung from a nail beside
the door, and everywhere rinsed jam jars were stuffed with
cow parsley from the verges, and carnations bought half-dying
from the market as it closed. There were few books, since
Grace had never liked to read; but her childhood Bible was
within reach of her sewing machine, as if she'd consulted Ruth
or Esther for how best to finish a seam. Her visitors, looking
about, often thought how like the woman herself it all was:
suspended between the modern age and unplaceable time
past, the laptop and mobile phone and television anachronis-
tic, and the fading tapestries and linens in their proper place. It
was so romantic, they said, so beautiful, admiring the fringed
shawl that made do for a bedroom door, and sighing over the
pearly shells she'd ranged on the kitchen windowsill; and

thank you, she said—but really it was difficult to make do with what little she had, and humiliating to think she wasn't far off forty and could lose her home on the landlady's whim. On certain mornings in certain weathers the place had the disconsolate look of a tired child trying to be happy; but at these times Grace would see her own bare scalp lit by strip lights in a Hackney room blackened at the skirting boards with damp, and persuade herself to be content.

Ronald sat with difficulty on a sofa that was draped in a quilt from which patched pieces were coming loose. Noises from the street sifted up, becoming indistinct under the eaves, and someone out there was singing Leonard Cohen. Grace put a white cloth on the trunk, and it was pressed with such care its creases produced a grid of shadows: "My ship has come in, Dad," she said. "Last month I couldn't pay the council tax, and now I'm in the money! We're having crab, and prawns, and smoked salmon—so stay awake a bit longer, if you can."

"Very good," said Ronald vaguely, "yes: very good. The Lord provides."

"I have a new job," said Grace, "a good one"—she was bringing out a chipped porcelain dish, on which shellfish grappled with slices of lemon—"it'll keep me gainfully employed for weeks." She put the tray on the packing trunk beside a basket of her own white rolls and gestured to a corner: "Look at those boxes. They've been knocking down houses for flats in West London, and I suppose one of the houses must have been a tailor and cleaner once (here: take a napkin. Take this plate). Look what they found—all these furs and gowns and a man's coat with a box of matches in the pocket. Everything left behind and forgotten, sealed in paper with the old camphor balls rolling out, and bits of moth wing and dust, and the tickets still sewn on (shall I butter you some bread?). I've been given the best of them to restore, then off they'll go to film studios

and theater companies and thin eccentric women—it isn't difficult work," she said, asserting professional pride, "but I will
do my best, and that's the rent until Christmas."

"I'm sure you will," said her father, with a sweet vagueness
that exasperated Grace: Thomas, she thought, would have
asked which garments in particular needed what work in particular, and asked to be shown them, and approved her answer
in his reserved fashion. Well: it was his fault he'd no idea how
she kept herself busy these days, and more fool him—"Shall
we say grace?" said Ronald, and closed his eyes. *For these and
all thy mercies, Lord, we give thee thanks*"; and Grace looked
out over Aldleigh, and ate buttered bread.

When all remaining was a bowl of cherrystones with scraps
of red flesh attached, Ronald folded his hands over his stomach and said, "Yes: very nice," and slipped into sleep. The singer
was still out there busking for tuition fees, and now Bob Dylan
had arrived on the departing train—*let us pause in life's pleas-
ures,* went the song, *and count its many tears*; but the passengers were heedless, and the evening swifts were screaming out
to Lowlands Park. Now and then Ronald choked for breath,
then returned to his childish sleep, and a skittish sound behind the skirting board was perhaps a rat inured to the poison
Grace sometimes put down. The song went interminably
on—*a pale drooping maiden toils her life away, with a worn
heart whose better days are over*—and how good of him it was,
thought Grace, to sing for me. Hard times, come again no
more! Sweat formed between her shoulder blades and ran to
her waist and settled there, and later, when the sun went down,
the damp place on her clothing would make her cold.

There was nobody to speak to, and nothing she wanted to
do—I am in my life, she thought, surprised by despair: this is
my life, and I am in it! She had a vision then of her old room

in her father's house, with the shadow of the silver birch swaying on the carpet, and the mottled mirror in which she'd examined her own body each night with troubled awe—saw
again the narrow bed that had once tilted up at the foot and
sent her falling forever upward, but never coming to an end.
That's how it has always been for me, she thought, falling
toward nothing—she pressed at a sore place on a pricked finger where infection had set in—soon enough I won't be a
woman who doesn't have children, but a woman who didn't
have children—soon nobody will see me, and there'll be no
more surprises. But her self-pity these days was as sudden and
brief as her temper always was, and there again was the rat going about its business, and distantly a train coming in from
Colchester or London—she crossed to the cardboard boxes in
the corner, and saw a frilled black cuff coming out between
strips of packing tape with an imploring gesture: "Yes," she
said, "yes, I know: me too."

She opened the box, and there was the smell she loved, because it marked out her own territory: camphor and cedar to
repel moths, certain fungi that thrived in damp cloth, and
what remained of the sweat and fragrance of dead women and
men. Over on the sofa her father shifted and snorted, and the
lamps were brightening against the dusk. Carefully she lifted
out the dress. The black silk rasped against itself, and spoke.
She listened. The narrow sleeves terminated in long cuffs fastened with mother-of-pearl buttons fixed with silver thread,
and were set in stiff pleats at the shoulder. Grace marveled
at the craftsmanship, skilled and arduous as that of a
stonemason—hours by daylight and gaslight, she thought,
eyes and back perpetually sore—reverently she examined the
high neck trimmed with rotting Belgian lace, and the immense
skirt with a deep embellished hem. She took it to her

workbench, and turned on a lamp that set the clock to noon. Again, that rasp of silk, which was as telling and particular as a voice—Grace bent to examine the needlework, and saw heavy silver thread couched down in whorls, here and there coming loose and recoiling against itself. Stitched among the whorls were so many seed pearls, in such a massed weight, the dress could only have been worn by a strong woman whose love for extravagance and style exceeded the desire for comfort. She passed a loving hand over the hem, and the dress complained: hair-fine silk threads disintegrated, and dozens of pearls dropped to the floor. "I'm sorry," said Grace, "I didn't mean to hurt you." She laid the dress down, and surveyed it from a distance with an expert's eye. Sewn between 1880 and 1890, she thought, judging by the set of those sleeves: the lace would need removing entirely, and she'd seek out another piece—this part just here (affectionately she passed a finger through a hole) could be patched and made good—the pearls and couched silver thread could be returned to their pattern, and that would be time-consuming, but it was all billable hours. And what after all was the pattern (a sleeve shifted; the silk spoke)? From that vantage it was possible to make out a sequence of ugly stiff-petaled flowers on absurd curved and leafless stems, and against such extraordinary workmanship this failure of skill and beauty was aggravating.

"Tomorrow," said her father in his sleep, "God willing"—and yes, thought Grace, I'll look again tomorrow. She moved away, and this caused her shadow to pass over the beaded hem and alter the look of the flowers—"Oh!" she said, with a curious tightening sensation on her scalp: not flowers, nothing like that—the stiff silk of the dress softened and spread, until it took over the room in a canopy, and the stitched whorls of silver began to turn with the look of water going down the sink; the pearls after all were not individual pricks of light forming lifeless flowers, but composed themselves into shining objects drifting down the hem, trailing curves of shining dust: "Comets!" said Grace, laughing, almost convinced her bare feet were rising above the carpet, and her own body was in motion. "It's comets," she said again, seeing them clearly, drawn down their orbits by the sun, and interspersed with galaxies.

Her inertia dissipated. She was alert, as if responding to a high summoning note. Time collapsed—surely she stood ankle-deep in Lowlands mist; surely it was possible to put out her hand, and pluck the sleeve of a good tweed coat and say, "Thomas, the strangest thing—do you remember Maria Văduva, do you remember I found her in the lake?"

"*Why art thou cast down, oh my soul?*" said Ronald, reciting psalms in his sleep, "*and why art thou disquieted in me?*" But Grace—disquieted but not cast down—was attending devoutly to the dress, and to a paper ticket fastened with a rough stitch to a bodice seam. She opened it. The looped pencil scrawl, preserved from light, was easily legible—the words spoke frankly down time: *C. S. / Foulis Street / for collection.* "I see," said Grace. "Yes, I see." The ticket dissipated, and in its place she saw a sheet of notepaper grown brittle at the fold: *to the only beloved inhabitant of Foolish Street . . .* "Maria," said Grace. "There you are." Thomas had hoped and hoped, she thought, and it occurred to her that she could phone him now as the sun went down, and begin again that schoolboy hunt for a vanished woman and her comet—"Foulis Street, Thomas!" she said aloud, briefly inhabiting another possible world in which she was comfortable at his table. "Don't you see? Maria's friend C. lived at Foulis Street, and she called it Foolish to tease her"—she felt an instinctive flare of pleasure and pride, and quickly suppressed it. No: he didn't deserve it. Let him limp back and forth to the *Essex Chronicle*, to wherever he went these days, and have no idea Maria Văduva was in motion—

"Should I be going home soon?" said Ronald, coming to his feet and smoothing what remained of his hair. "Won't Anne be waiting for me?"

"Yes," said Grace, "she'll be waiting. But I don't think it'll be too long now."

A LITTLE NIGHT MUSIC

THOMAS HART, *ESSEX CHRONICLE*,
23 JUNE 2017

It's common knowledge, isn't it, that in space, no one can hear you scream? But I'm afraid the difficulty with knowledge (even the common sort!) is that it tends to open doors, not close them. And if you opened the right door and listened, you'd hear the earth singing.

I'll try and explain. Sound requires substance—you can hear nothing at all unless the air and its molecules are made to oscillate, creating sound waves like ripples in a cloth. When these ripples reach your eardrums, that membrane also begins to vibrate, and so you hear someone calling you, or music playing in another room.

Since space is more or less a vacuum, there's no cloth to shake. But you should never think that nobody is screaming just because you can't hear it. In fact, the planets can never keep their peace—they are constantly radiating electromagnetic waves, and some of these are radio waves that fall outside the range of human hearing. It is possible to process these emissions, and show how they might sound if the matter of space could vibrate with the music, and make the music audible to us.

If you're curious—and really I think you ought to be!—you can find these melodies online, and listen to a little night music. I've taken to listening as I examine the planets with my telescope, and the effect is eerie and beautiful. When I hear Jupiter, I think of a Buddhist's singing bowl; when I hear Neptune I think of waves crashing on a pebble shore, while the wind blows through some abandoned structure yards away. Io, Jupiter's devoted little moon, sounds like an orchestra down in the pit, tuning its instruments before the curtain rises—and Earth, of course, is singing, too: with chirps and whistles like the calls of unfamiliar birds startled by the passage of a train.

Meanwhile, the human body—constantly occupied in respiration and digestion—vibrates at very low frequencies. Your heart, for example, resonates at less than a single hertz, far below the beginning of the range of human hearing. I wonder if somewhere there is an animal capable of hearing all the quiet business undertaken in the chambers of my heart? *You are the music*, said T. S. Eliot, *while the music lasts.*

There was a change of weather. No rain yet, but clouds coming from Gwent and Gloucestershire on the western wind, and nights drawing imperceptibly in. A woman recently struck by a train was cremated two miles north of the station (it was said she'd wanted her ashes disposed of in Lowlands Park, but the authorities wouldn't have it). A white cat was missing on Lower Bridge Road. Since the seeing was bad for stars, insomniac Thomas took to looking for it in the small hours, walking off the ache in his hip and reciting the Foolish Street letter: *you cannot ask this of me.*

Late on a Friday afternoon, Grace Macaulay walked down to Lowlands House. An inky bank of clouds was drawing over Essex, and in the dimming air the bindweed and buddleia in Potter's Field were luminous against the wall. She stood there for a time. Its neglect by now had become something noble, and not despondent—moss had taken hold on the piles of bricks, and all night it was noisy in the nettles and bracken. This is where I found Nathan, she thought, this is where I found Dimitru, and both of them have gone. Meanwhile there was Bethesda, implacable, unchanged, its gray roof seeping into gray clouds. She waited to encounter the operatic tides of sorrow and loss she once might have summoned up, and could only locate a placid fondness for the smooth clear pane of glass that replaced the window a careless boy had broken. Inevitably she thought of Thomas Hart, and there was her old temper after all, in a vivifying flare—all week she'd removed and restitched pearls from the hem of the black gown, and the pad of her thumb was calloused with pricks: now she rubbed the callous with a vengeful smirk she might have thought unpleasant if she could have seen it.

Then she went through the screen of silver birches behind Bethesda and struck out for Lowlands Park. Summer had thickened the hedges at the boundary, and these resisted her entry and tore her skirt—she came through to the clearing, and saw lawns rising faintly to the house that stood unpleasantly white against the sky. A wind was getting up and the oaks shivered. She walked on. The lawns had not been cut: it was like wading. The lake was on her left, altered beyond her recognition: it had been dug out deep and square, and was bordered by pale slabs of York stone and four black iron benches with sea serpents forming curved arms. A high yew hedge bounded it on three sides and enclosed the sky with mathematical exactitude. Maria Văduva, clean and empty-handed, stood at the eastern end in the breach in the yews, looking forever at the house.

Vaguely Grace thought of a story she heard once about a girl who bruised her shaved scalp on a statue as they pulled her from dirty water—but that has nothing to do with me, she thought, despising that girl with her shorn head and her temper. She came near the house, and made out careless people on the terrace watching the weather come in, and lights on in the new glass wing where Maria's telescope went unused. Now the air all around her was peculiar, and uniform darkness was coming overhead like an early dusk. She went on walking, conscious of a nervous pricking sensation, and had no idea whether it came from her, or was imposed on her by the unsettled weather. Rain began. It struck the nape of her neck with a volley of blows, and soon the soaking air caused the house and the copper beeches to blur and dissipate—everything was composed of water, and so was she; it was all a gathering wave that at any minute would break, and her own matter would be forever indistinguishable from that of the lawns, the oaks, the Lowlands brick and plaster—wind pleated the rain, and her unaccountable nerves gave way to hysteric pleasure in the wind and water. So she went through it reveling, watching men and women go running from the terrace, laughing and shaking out their clothes. Her own dress was soaked, as if she'd just come out of the baptistery, and she stumbled once in tangled cloth and paused to right herself.

It was because of this she failed to see an old man until he was close by. He was stooped, hesitant, reliant on a walking stick; he'd never outrun that bad weather. He tracked across the lawns from the margins of the park, and Grace—whose own body had never much betrayed her—found pity and irritation moved her equally. It was inconvenient, this trespasser on her solitude, and probably he'd be all right on his own. That cautious walk called Thomas Hart to mind; but in fact this man was not as tall as Thomas, and nothing like as old, nor were his clothes so fine. Now the long grass and irregular ground were giving him trouble, and it occurred to her that she ought to be good; so she went toward him with her hand held out.

The Potter's Field jays, aggrieved by rain, flew over with their horrible cries, and this startled the man. He looked up. The jays were gone. He saw Grace. He stopped abruptly, which appeared to cause him pain; he made a sound as if choking on his own discomfort. He was looking at her with a furtive downward tilt of his head, and this was curiously intimate, and not quite a stranger's look—then he set his stick hard in the wet lawn and turned his back.

How shocking it was, to have offered her hand out of

kindness, and to have been rejected—a bleak sensation settled on her that was not proportionate to a stranger's departure, or even to the cooling rain now causing her to shiver. Grace felt she might cry, and this too was an irritation and a shock: was she really so prone to loneliness and sorrow, after all these years, with a gray streak in her hair? Two children, thin and uncannily alike, were darting about aimless and quick as insects, going into the rain and out of it with delight; they came near the man and laughed at him and mimicked his pained walk—I hope they fall and hurt themselves, she thought, I hope nobody comes when they cry.

There was an interruption in the rain. Briefly the air was clear, and in this pause Grace heard children shrieking, and jackdaws squabbling in the oaks; distantly a train drawing out of the station, and a man's shocked cry, more familiar than it ought to have been. Her body returned shock for shock. A pulse set up in her ears. Now the man was supine in the grass, his stick was out of reach. His jacket, black with water, was spread out: he was on his back. Twice he raised himself then fell. The rain set in again. Grace moved toward him. She tripped in mud and righted herself: she was a quick, strong animal. She reached the man, who turned away from her. His hair was fair and rather long: it obscured his face. Grace went down on her haunches in the mud. She took his wrist; he took it back. "You're being stupid!" she said. She felt she'd like to hit him. She also felt she'd like to sink down with him. He made the choked noises of a man who has been taught not to cry. Jackdaws flew over: What's all this? they said. What's going on, and why? Lowlands House looked out of the copper beeches, untroubled and unsurprised.

"You can't just lie here," said Grace. "If you do, I'll lie here, too. Why won't you look at me?" His hair could do with a cut, she thought.

He turned his head a little. He wore glasses to which the rain adhered in shining blots that blinded him. He took them off. There was a kind of splitting sensation, as if her conscious-ness had run ahead and reached an understanding, while her body lagged behind in the mud—"Just fucking get up!" she said. I'll hit him, she thought, I really will.

He said, "I can't." He raised himself on his elbows. "You can see that I can't." He fell back and gestured to his left leg. "It doesn't work properly," he said, "and my back is bad." He looked at her. The rain came down. He went on looking, not blinking away the water. He let out his breath, and resigned himself to the mud.

Grace took account of his face. It was thin. Possibly it would be fair to say that it was gaunt; that the cheeks had sunk more than they ought to have done, that he was too pale, with a waxen poreless look. Still she found him beautiful. She raised her hands. His eyes were very blue, and more thickly lashed than hers. "No," she said.

"I tried to get away," he said. "I did try."

"Nathan." It was not a query. "I've been looking for you," she said, "I've been looking for you all my life." She wanted to touch him and didn't know how. Her hands were in her lap. But they wanted him and were compelled: she thumped him twice on the shoulder. "All my life!" she said.

"Get me up," he said, blinking rapidly. He's angry with me, she thought, and was grateful, because that was a kind of inti-macy, and all she had for now. "Get my stick," he said. She reached for the ugly metal tube in the grass. It was wet, and slipped. She dropped it. He swore. She gave it to him: she wanted to hit him again. "You'll have to help me," he said. "Left side." It struck her that this was all ordinary to him—the fall, the humiliation, and the need. His pallor reached his lips. He sat up, braced against his stick; then he raised his left arm and she burrowed under it and took his weight. With a hard sharp cry, he was standing.

His hand shook on the stick. He said, "One minute." Sixty obedient seconds counted silently. Idiot thoughts: were there streaks of makeup on her face? Was her hair dank and unlovely, would he like the look of her? "Come on then," he said. He maneuvered his body as if it were a vehicle he didn't trust and had never been taught to drive. The rain was receding, but not the clouds. She was alert to him in all the particulars: the soaked jeans, the dragging foot, the shirt tucked in at the beltless waist, the smell of soap and mud, the marvelous implausible fact of his weight. "All my life!" she said.

"Yes," he said. "Yes, I know."

"Nathan," she said.

"Yes," he said. "Grace."

They'd come to the terrace. Windows once blinded by boards now looked placidly out over the lawns. The children, done with play, stood watchful by the door.

"You're heavy," Grace said. They came to a table, and Nathan put his body in a chair. His hands shook on his cane; he let out a cry, and was white. He asked for something to drink, and Grace went to fetch it. She had the giddy sensation of a woman on a high ledge. It was all unbelievable—it was all inevitable. She brought tea and water on a tray, and found him occupied in pressing pills out of their packets; he took them with the look of a man underwater waiting to come up for breath. His eyes were closed. Privately she examined his face, and found the boy she'd loved.

The sun was out. It hardened against the glass. Nathan opened his eyes, and examined the tea in his cup. The waxen pallor was receding. "What a coincidence. There you are."

"Here I am," she said, "gone round my orbit again. I looked

for you everywhere, and never found you. Where have you been, Nathan, where did you go?"

"Kent." There was the easy untroubled smile she remembered.

"As far as that! Those children are watching us. Look."

"At that age everything is interesting." His shallow quick breaths were gone. "My daughter," he said, softening still further, "is just the same."

Grace looked at her tea. Dust had settled on it, and the hair of a stranger. I had him to myself for half an hour, she thought, for only half an hour. "Nathan," she said, "tell me what happened to you" (and she was in love with the jacket drying on the back of his chair, the empty pill packet on the table, the hairs on his wrist, the glasses he wiped with a napkin).

"When I was twenty-five," he said, "I crashed the car. It wasn't so bad. Nothing broken, just always a threat of being hurt, like living with a dog that sometimes bites. Then two years ago I fell while walking, and two disks here, just here"—he patted himself, was rueful, offered her a smile—"ruptured. I was thirty-six and that was the last day I was young."

Grace, whose own body had spared her suffering, whose head never ached, was bewildered. "That's all?" she said. "You fell?"

"That's all. I lay on a mattress on the floor and counted the minutes until I could be drugged again. I would have killed myself," he said, "only the drugs were kept out of reach. Then they operated on me, and something went wrong. Quite a common thing, and not so bad, but the nerve was damaged, and now my foot won't work. You don't need to cry."

"I do." Horribly it occurred to her that perhaps she wept because in fact she did not want this real Nathan, in his compromised flesh. Was this what she'd waited for? Had she bartered her soul for a gaunt man with a wife and child and a dragging foot?

"This has been a bad day," he said, "you've seen me at my worst"; and this was so evidently said to reassure her, and so like his old easy kindness, that yes, yes: it was all she'd waited for. There was a moment when he took her in. His eyes are on me, she thought, I can feel them moving on my arms and neck, and I wonder how I'll have disappointed him.

"Tell me why you're here," she said. "Why come so far from Kent?"

"A death in the family," he said. He was not done looking at her. This look was new: intent, assessing, seeming almost amused. "My grandfather. Funerals and paperwork and probate."

"I am sorry. We should never have grown up!"

"I'm not sure we have. I'm not sure we can." Then he said, "And you? Are you still—" With a gesture he indicated the Bibles and baptistery, the prayers before eating, the drooping chapel hats.

Instinctively she looked out across the lawns to the silver birches, and Bethesda behind them with its iron gates unlocked. "Sometimes I think I am, because I can't help it. But I don't believe what I believed when I was a child"—though even as she said it, she was uncertain if it was true.

"And what did you believe?"

He has acquired authority, she thought, I can't resist that. "I believed I was elect—that I belonged to God. That I'd be forgiven everything I ever did."

"Then what do you believe now?"

She laughed, and saw his responding gleam, and was grateful. "If I wake up convinced there's no God," she said, "I'll find him by lunchtime. But if I go to bed and pray for the salvation of my soul, I'll know I've got no soul to save by breakfast." The children had come in from the garden and dripped between the tables, looking at Grace. A plaintive woman rapped on the glass. They ignored her. "I did come, you know," said Nathan, with sudden force. "I came to the church. You were standing at the front in strange white clothes; then something happened and you were down on your knees."

"I know."

"Thomas saw me and sent me away."

"Yes: I know he did."

"And I was glad he sent me away. I'd always been afraid of you, your father, the things you said and how you said them—there wasn't anyone like you then, there hasn't been anything like you since. I didn't understand what you were doing. I didn't know why you wanted to do it. I thought you wanted to be normal—I thought you wanted to be like me."

It occurred to her then that she could say: I bargained with God, I gave him my soul, and thought you would be my reward. But she was ashamed of her childish theology, and ashamed to have lost her bargain; and how diminishing, she thought, how absolutely debased I would be, if this man with a whole life elsewhere knew I'd set such a high price on his love! So she was silent, and perhaps a little sullen, and the silence seemed to cause his withdrawal. The intimacy of his attention was gone, as if it were an object he'd removed from the table and put in his pocket; he put his glasses on, and with polite interest asked what she did with herself these days, and what had become of her family. Her aunt was dead, she said, but her father was not; and desperately she wanted to give an account of the hospital bed in the dining room, the thin blue blanket on the floor.

"And what about your friend, Thomas?"

"Oh," said Grace, with elaborate vagueness she doubted he believed, "I think he's about. But I don't see him. It was so strange, wasn't it, it was so unnatural that he wanted to spend time with children." There briefly was that acute assessing look—whatever happened, Grace Macaulay? What did you do?—and Grace flushed at her slander.

Then again there was his withdrawal behind ease: "You know," he said, looking at the telescope in the vitrine, the wiped-clean tables on the swept-clean floor, "I haven't been here since the fire. Twenty years—I thought it might be difficult, but the truth is I hardly remember it—or if I do remember, it's as if it was all something somebody told me about another boy. Tell me, did you ever find out what happened to that woman? Maria, that was her name—remember how we came in here before the fire, when the windows were boarded up and there were no lights, and dead insects everywhere, and old bits of paper falling off the table and getting lost"—he looked about the bright clean room as if hoping to find dust settling on furniture and a rat crossing the floor.

"Strange you should ask—she comes back again and again, like a kind of ghost: sometimes I almost wish she'd leave us alone. They say she discovered a comet. They say it's coming back this winter—can you believe that?" And there's more, she wanted to say: I think I have something of hers at home, I think my hands must smell of her clothes. But she was afraid he'd tire of her.

"Yes," he said, "I can believe it. I could believe anything of you"—but his smile was charming, easy, costing him nothing; there again was the suspicion he spoke to her as he might have spoken to friends of his daughter, with a fondness that was instinctive and not particular.

Still: for lack of nourishment she feasted her spirit on crumbs. "Now I live over the Jackdaw and Crow," she said, smiling and lifting her hair from her neck, "and sometimes do shifts at the bar. So I spend my life in the den of iniquity my father would never go in!"

But Nathan was looking at his watch. "I'm very sorry," he said, "I can't miss my train, I must go. Forgive me?"

No I won't forgive you, she thought, I will not. Her temper arrived, quick and ungovernable: how dare he dismiss her? "Nathan," she said, "there are no offices here, no solicitors—there's no reason for you to come to Lowlands at all. So what were you doing here—were you just passing the time?"

He stood without apparent pain. "Whenever I'm in Aldleigh," he said, "I come here, and I look for you." He was buttoning himself up, he was moving away. The mud was dry on their clothes. An absurd gap was opening up between what they ought to have been, and what they were. He was holding his stick: "I'll walk to the station," he said, "but slowly. Will you go that way?"

Ten minutes of small talk! She'd rather have nothing at all. "I'll stay here," she said, "I haven't finished my tea." Together they looked at the mug, and the pale skin forming in it.

"Give me your number," he said, "and I'll give you mine."

Grace was obedient. The balances of power were in his favor. "We would never have had any trouble," she said, taking out her phone, "if we'd had these in our day." There was a polite exchange of laughter. Nobody watching, thought Grace, would have any idea where his mouth had been.

"Well then," he said. He put down his stick, and raised his arms.

"Well then," she said. He embraced her, and this was unmannered and ungentle: Christ, she thought, he'll break a rib. She returned to her seat. "Go on, then," she said, "go home." Her tea was thick and cold: she drank it. He stood aimless, looking at the blinded telescope as if it might afford a view of wisdom; then with a kind of resigned and hopeless shrug he left.

Later that same evening, half-drunk on the sofa with her bare feet on the packing trunk, Grace tended to a galaxy coming unstitched on the black silk dress, and discovered that her fingers were trembling and unequal to the task. This is like fear, she thought, it's as if I'm afraid for my life—and in fact she was afraid for her life, which she had created out of whatever leftovers she had to hand, and which she sometimes loved. It was small, strange, curtailed, and poor, but every day made new by the beauty she detected in torn table linen, dying stems of forecourt carnations, silk ribbons sold for a pound in charity-shop baskets: she was free to think as she liked, to say what she liked, to do as she pleased—sometimes on the Lord's Day she would attend Bethesda's morning service and cry in the last verse of the last hymn, briefly feeling the presence of the Son of God, then all night pour double measures at the Jackdaw and Crow, where nobody implored her to consider the condition of her soul. But Nathan had sat with her an hour, that was all, and already she was dissatisfied with her own life, and jealously constructing his out of the scraps she had to hand—who was it opened the door for him when he went home? Who took his coat, and asked after his back—whose face did he see in his child's face? Bitterly she pictured a happy woman, clever and competent and kind—she pricked her finger, and was glad she did it.

Thomas would understand, she thought, with horrible loyalty, Thomas would know—she finished her glass of bad wine. Briefly it occurred to her that she could call him—that if ever a man left his number unchanged in years it would certainly be Thomas Hart.

She pierced a comet with her needle, and for a time scrolled aimlessly through her phone. She arrived in time at the *Essex*

Chronicle: a fatal crash on the A12, a woman shot dead in Billericay, never any good news. And Thomas Hart would no doubt have written something recently—his little sermons, she thought, his godless parables—she saw the title "Disordered Time," and rolled her eyes. How like him, to think he had the authority! *I wonder if you've ever shared my feeling*, she read, *that things happen not one after the other, but all at once?* Yes, Thomas, she thought, I have, I do. So she read on, and experienced an instinctive softening against the determination of her dislike: his voice was in the room, accentless and precise and kind—"So you see," he said, explaining himself, "I've learned it's possible to despise and love a friend equally, in the same place and at the same time."

Grace put down her phone, put down the dress: there was an extraordinary pain behind her left breast, and her hands shook as if she suffered a disorder of the nerves. She doubled over and embraced herself, because there was nobody else to do it. "It's such a shame," she said childishly over and over, "it's just such an awful shame."

Comet 1899 III (du Lac), not truthfully named, is five months from perihelion. It is crossing the orbit of Jupiter. Obedient to Kepler's stern and perfect laws, the semimajor axis of its orbit sweeps out equal areas in equal time, which is to say: it's only going to get faster. It is excited. Already its hard cold carapace is thrilling to the sun and sublimating into gas; it has acquired a little atmosphere, and particles of dust are drawn out from the comet's faint gravitational field. It's seen by certain diligent observers in the southern hemisphere, whose twelve-inch telescopes pick out something blurry in the constellation of the wolf; but no naked eye has any hope until the earth has drifted a little farther down its orbit.

Meanwhile in Aldleigh: summer contains autumn, which

contains winter. There's the suggestion of burning in the beeches on London Road, and the verges of the A12 are blacker than they ever were. Ronald Macaulay recedes through the years and has not yet reached childhood, but often mistakes his daughter for his wife, though in fact Grace resembles Rachel no more than a changeling might.

The cat is still missing on Lower Bridge Road. Thomas goes up and down the lanes at night, looking for a fleet-footed scrap of white coming out from under a car. As he walks he composes phrases for his book on the motion of bodies in orbit, commits them to memory, and goes home to type them up—and everything that will ever happen has happened (he thinks), and is happening. Still he cannot bring the book to its conclusion—it is all question, and no answer. What can he say to his readers but "I wonder?"

Grace Macaulay is late for her shifts at the Jackdaw and Crow: she's rude to the landlady, who's rude in return. She cannot concentrate. She pricks herself and bleeds into the hem of the Foulis Street skirt, eats sometimes too little and sometimes too much. She's up on a high ledge and nobody can bring her down. "Give me your number," he'd said, "and I'll give you mine"; and after the tormenting decency of two days' silence he'd illuminated the phone on her pillow: *How are you?* Now they communicate most days and never plan to meet. Her phone runs out of charge by noon. She watches the screen for a sign. It illuminates: let it be him, let it be him! It is often him (it is more often her). How are things? Is it raining where you are? Saw this and thought of you. This wasted leaf. This sunlit gull when nothing else was lit at all. These bits of broken glass. That song. This one. And this one. Did you read this article? Did you know Maria Văduva's diary has been published in a book? In text he is not civil and kindly, but has a means of speech as easeful and merry as he always was. He is

ready with a printed kiss. He rarely mentions home. She conceives of him as solitary, speechless, on a hard-backed chair in
an empty room, waiting for her to come glittering in through
the window. Then he does mention home—he mentions his
daughter, he implies a wife, and never names either—and this
brings a grieving splitting sensation: there's a whole life there
she cannot see and will never occupy—a series of loves and
languages all incomprehensible to her, she is absolutely peripheral, bolted-on, and the bolts are coming loose.

She stands in the pound-shop aisles and bursts into tears: if
he died nobody would tell her, why would they, she wouldn't
know for days. And why does he never name the mother of his
child, who presumably nursed him when things were bad,
pressed pills out of their packets when he needed them most,
washed him, held his body when it was pliant with sleep, saw
the stitches dissolving in his spine? Sometimes at midnight
when her collarbone is slick with sweat she'll send an idle message and watch for a reply and meanwhile touch herself and
think: would he touch me like this? And will he? Time (said
Thomas Hart) is not what we take it to be, and everything that
will ever happen has happened, and is happening. All my life,
she thinks. And here we are. Thomas grows larger in her consciousness: he felt what I feel, he knows what I know. Occasionally it occurs to her that now forgiveness might be possible.
After all (her phone ignites again with Nathan's name) her life
was perhaps not destroyed in the baptistery, only altered—

On the second evening in August, Thomas abandoned his manuscript with a cry of disgust—at his imagination, vocabulary, wisdom, phrases, capacity for characterisation, and in fact the whole absurd enterprise of literature—and went through to the galley kitchen. There was bad news on the radio, and nothing worth his attention in the fridge and cupboards; he could neither read nor write, and the lens of his telescope had acquired a film of dust. The pain in his hip set in with the insistent spite it generally reserved for winter, and this was the effect of boredom: there was nothing else to occupy his mind. So it was a relief to hear someone knocking at the door, with the impolite demanding knock of a man in trouble, or instigating it—something to do with the lost cat, he thought, going quickly down the hall, or Nick Carleton needs me for a story—he opened the door, and the humid air of the evening entered the house like a breath.

"No," said Thomas to the diligent sparrow on the garden wall, "no, this can't be right"—it was all just collapsing time, he said to himself, some kind of echo: certainly that could not be Grace Macaulay standing on the garden path. But the image didn't dissipate into memory as it ought to have done, only insisted on being seen: Grace, changed and unchanged, dressed in loose white clothes that left her arms bare and carrying a woman dressed in black. This other woman was so thin and

frail her body had more or less disintegrated within the sleeves
and bodice, and there was an unpleasant moment when her
right arm disarticulated and swung impossibly loose from the
shoulder.

"Hello," said Grace, and this caused an abrupt alteration in
perspective: Thomas saw with relief that the dress was empty.

"What are you doing here?" he said, surprise and unease
sharpening his words to needless points. How difficult it was
not to say: That looks heavy, you wretched child—come in, sit
down. But then there was the vision of her hard eyes evading
his, and her fond hand on Lorna's wrist: You don't belong with
us at all.

"I don't need to come in. I just wanted to show you something. You ought to see it. Look"—she spread out the
skirt—"do you see this? What do you see?" Something detached from the hem, and rattled on to the path.

Thomas, shrugging, said he saw nothing but an old dress
that needed mending; but this was untrue, and behind him in
the hall there was a movement, and a remonstrating voice:
Look again, Thomas Hart.

"Look again," said Grace, with a stern authority acquired in
their years of estrangement. He looked. The loop of the skirt
resolved itself into an orbit down which a shining series of
comets moved, and moved so insistently and with such brilliance that night fell, and Thomas saw in a celestial parade the
comets Halley, Hale-Bopp, Hyakutake, McNaught. It was impossible to suppress a cry of surprise and pleasure, or ignore
the quick responding gleam in his visitor's eyes. "There," she
said. "You do see it."

"Where did you get that—what have you been doing?"

"Never mind that"—this was a deliberate closing of her
door—"but I have it. No it's best you don't touch it, the silk is
very old—but I wanted you to see this." Cautiously, as if

approaching an old unreliable dog, she came forward and handed him a folded square of rough paper. "That's the dry-cleaner's ticket. Open it."

Thomas did as he was told: "*C. S.*," he read. "*Foulis Street / for collection.*"

"Not Foolish Street," said Grace, with deliberate patience, as if she saw before her an old man grasping vaguely at fact. "That was only their joke: it was Foulis Street, which is a road in Kensington—and this was her friend C., and I suppose Maria gave her this dress." She folded the skirt, she extinguished the comets. "That was all I came to say. Keep the ticket." Now she was going, and there was the familiar headlong gait, the black hair glossy at the roots and tied with frayed ribbon— there, too, he thought, her temper, her thieving, her ungovernable joy.

Let her go, Thomas, he said to himself, bending to pick up seed pearls from the path. Have you learned nothing, all these years? Let these forces move her as they must, and bring her back in good order.

My dear James (that's what you are now, no less than you
ever were: dear, and mine),

It's been nine years since I saw you last, and ten since I
last wrote. And three years, two months and fifteen days
have gone since you were found (so they tell me) on the
bedroom floor, and I had no idea—saw no unfamiliar
shadow on the moon, felt no rupture in the air: only went
about my ordinary day, while the heart that had no room
for me gave up its various ghosts. But this evening I think
you're no more distant from me in death than you ever
were—closer, even, since there's nobody now to say: he is
not yours. He is not dear.

James, do you miss Aldleigh? It's autumn here. Mists are
coming up the banks of the Alder and nearly reach the
high street. No swifts now. Blackberries on the verges are
dropping sugar on the bones of deer. Orion has come back
as he always does, and the children have gone back to
their schools. There were storms on the sun, and they've
blown themselves out. Now when my bad hip aches, I feel
an echo of the pain in my good hip, in the joints of my
knees—my heart sometimes feels like it's failing, and
every month my hair is thinner. I don't need much sleep
these days. Sometimes I go out and think I hear the whole
world ticking.

James, won't you help me? I'm in a bad way. I understand
now what they mean by writer's block: I have on my hands
the book that I think will be my last, but if I go to it my
hands shake and I find all language and courage and
beauty and truth have deserted me. This book is too much
myself—it asks too much of me. I cannot even write my

columns. I have nothing to say. And it is not only a block to
writing—it is a block to living—I feel a kind of lifelessness
take over my body as if I have a disease of the nerves. I
don't like to cook, and when I cook I don't like to eat—
books bore or confuse me—I can't even see the cities on
the moon. I count loss after loss and mourn what I still
have, because I'll lose that soon enough. Even Maria
Văduva is fading from me—she thins out, she doesn't
speak to me, I see a shimmer by the window or a shadow
in the hall but nothing ever comes of it. You made me so
unhappy, but it never brought me to a standstill—it sent
me to the page. This is a kind of nothing. All I've done
lately that was worth doing was find a lost cat on Lower
Bridge Road and take her to her owner—but she was lost
again the following week, and so it all begins again.

And how I miss my old friend, my wretched child. I
thought I got on very well without that responsibility I
never asked for, but she came to my door the other day
and time folded in and knocked me over like a wave—
there she was, with Maria Văduva in her arms—and love
moved my body three steps down the path. Am I never to
be free of those troublesome women—am I never to be
free of my hope for freedom? And do you think I should
forgive, and ask forgiveness?

I have with me now a paper ticket. I've unfolded it and
folded it once too often, and it's cracked like a plate
across the seam. But still the words are so clear I think if
I listen well enough I'd hear the writer put their pencil
down—*C. S. / Foulis Street / for collection*. I wish you were
with me now—I wish I could explain it to you, and see
your face illuminate with pleasure and be the face of the

boy I never knew and would certainly have loved if I
had . . .

What should I do now, James? I've seen Foulis Street on
the London map, I know the look of the houses—I could
go there now and look through each letter box, and see if
comet-light comes out. But after all this time I have no
name and no house number, and what would I be but an
old fool limping back to Liverpool Street empty-handed
and alone, on streets paved with all the men and boys I
was once, and loved once?

It's absurd, this chase of mine—it's always been absurd—
it's three months to perihelion and Comet du Lac is
headed for the sun. Perhaps it's better I lay down my arms
and leave the field of battle where I only ever lost—
perhaps it's better to live with hope than disappointment:
to greet the comet and think with melancholy of what
might have been, and not endure the pain of failure?

So here I sit, and can do none other: Thomas Hart, an idle
man, for whom life has exhausted all surprises—

Thomas Hart, preparing to sign his name, was disturbed by
motion at his elbow—by the scent of fragrance and flesh in a
black silk gown too heavy to be worn with comfort; by the rattle of seed pearls dropping from the hem. *But Thomas*, said
Maria Văduva, summoned out of the privation of his spirit,
frowning and insubstantial at his elbow, *but Thomas: you forget the principles of proper motion! Don't you understand you
cannot help but move? Besides*—retrieved from the folds of her
skirt: a volume of Tennyson, cracked at the spine, the pages
folded disgracefully down—*that which we are, we are! Made*

weak by time and fate, I'll allow you that—doesn't your bad hip ache? Don't you wake too early, and sleep too late? But it's only a Tuesday in September, it's hardly half past ten—aren't we strong in will, Thomas Hart, don't the valves of our hearts open and close in good order—don't we keep the lenses of our telescopes preserved at all times from fingerprints and dust? Come now, Thomas. What is there to do but to strive, and seek, and find, and not to yield?

ON THE PROPER MOTION OF THE STARS

THOMAS HART, *ESSEX CHRONICLE*,
13 SEPTEMBER 2017

I want you to imagine you're standing by the River Alder, looking at an oak tree on the far bank. Behind this oak are other trees: three willows to the left of it, and three willows to the right. Now imagine you walk a little while along the riverbank, and look again at the oak. It has moved, or seems to have moved—now there are only two willows to the left, but four willows to the right. They call this effect parallax, and better astronomers than I'll ever be use this principle to judge the proper motion of the stars.

Proper motion is nothing like the movement we think we see as the stars turn west over Essex. This is all just the illusion of perspective, as the earth spins inside the celestial sphere. We like to reassure ourselves that although the stars appear to move, they're fixed in place—so we have something to pin ourselves on. But I'm afraid this is not at all the case. Nothing in all the universe is fixed, and everything is changing: stars have their own proper motion, and even the Pole Star is adrift.

Generally speaking, stars are so distant that their travel through space appears to us agonizingly slow, detected only over the course of tens of thousands of years. But some stars are quite nearby, and we can live long enough to see them move just a little: Barnard's Star, for example, has drifted some distance in the seventy years of my lifetime.

Now come back to the Alder with me. It's a cold clear night, and we're standing together on the bank. Overhead there's the whole black dome of the sky, and every star is out. Imagine also that time is racing by: that for us each hour is ten thousand years. So as we stand there watching, the oaks and willows quickly become immense, die back, reseed, and grow again—and overhead the stars are dancing in their proper motion: Orion throwing his spear, Delphinus leaping out of an infinite sea.

I have found the proper motion of the stars a comfort. It reminds me that we are all in motion, and we're never unchanged. Often it seems we stand still and lonely, absolutely solitary on the turning world. But all the same: we move.

Grace Macaulay
Carriage D
6:30 from Liverpool Street
27 September 2017

Thomas, don't think I forgive you. I don't and can't and
never will. I only write now like this because if I call or
email you'll reply, and I won't have you asking how I am or
telling me how to be good. But I've got something to tell
you, and then we don't ever have to speak again. That will
be that.

I'm coming home from London where I took back the
clothes they gave me to mend. I didn't want to give away
the comet dress, so I stole pearls from the hem and I'll
wear them until they fall off (there, you see: a sinner). But
Maria followed me. Did you see her leave? She was
wearing the dress and I heard pearls rolling under the
trains on the Tube where the mice were running. And
because of this I thought of Foolish Street. I thought of the
ticket on the dress, and C., and the comet. I thought of
you. I'm angry with you but I was never angry with Maria,
and I thought I felt her hand in mine. So we went to Foulis
Street.

It is a wide street and there are thirty-two houses behind
iron railings with bay trees by the doors. I walked up and
down and Maria was walking with me, but told me
nothing. The houses are big and white as wedding cakes,
and since nobody could be so rich and not be wicked, I
knew they wouldn't be kind to a stranger in a homemade
dress. It was all a waste of time, and my feet hurt, and I
wanted to go home, but Maria wouldn't let me. She

reminded me of a man I knew once who told me that
every census they ever took was kept in the archives at
Kew, and that if C. had lived at Foulis Street I'd find her
name in the books. That must have been Maria, mustn't
it? You know I've never been clever enough to think of
something like that. So there was Maria dragging me back
to the Tube and suddenly I was at the National Archives,
thinking how much it looks like a prison, as if they're afraid
all the dead names will break out and take over London.

Well, this is what I found out. On 5 April 1891 there was a
census, and a man took down the names of every person
who lived in Foulis Street that day. They let me see the
copies, and I took them to a table by the window and read
carefully because the handwriting was worse than mine,
worse even than Maria's. And I am angry with you and I
don't want to talk to you but it was like you were there,
too. I had Maria reading over my left shoulder and you
reading over my right, and I have the phrases memorized
like I used to memorize scripture—look, I can write it out
for you now: *The Undermentioned Houses are Situated
within the Boundaries* . . .

Three women whose names might be C. S. lived at
Foulis Street in 1891. Of course this is two years after
Maria disappeared and it may mean nothing at all. But I
wrote it all down, and I'm going to put this through
your door when I get off the train. You can do what you
like with it. It isn't my comet, it isn't my mystery. It
never was.

GRACE

Signing her name with a plastic pen that leaked, Grace had a vision of Thomas at home in the house she'd loved. This was so vivid it overlaid the outskirts of London as they scudded past—she saw the Persian carpet, and the precious Moser glass; smelled lilacs stuffed into translucent jugs, and those curious Romanian pastries thickly dusted with sugar. This did not diminish her anger, only amplified it: he took this from me too, she thought, returning gratefully to vengeance, he took my other home.

The train was not quite full. Shenfield arrived and receded: the sun was declining over Essex. She folded away the letter and the census copies—yes, she thought, I won't have Thomas tell me to be good—besides how can I be good, where Nathan is concerned? She summoned up the man she loved, composing him of the ardent boy under the Lowlands oaks, the man in the mud, the civil stranger drinking tea—he'd always contained it all, she thought, it had all been in the hand that broke Bethesda's window. At Chelmsford she read over and over their correspondence, which had neither the easy fondness of childhood, nor the compressed diffidence of when they'd last met, but a new way of speaking possible because it was disembodied—*I think I need you to keep me alive*, he'd said one Tuesday afternoon as she ironed the cuffs of a dead woman's nightdress; *yours sincerely*, she'd sometimes say, and *yes*, he'd say, *yours*.

Now the train was entering the evening. Waning moon rising, impetuous stars out first—quickly she wrote: *Clear night there? Look for the Great Bear later. Binary star in his tail. Two stars locked together because they can't help it.*

Nothing came. No light, no evidence of the filament that joined this hard seat in this rattling carriage and wherever Nathan sat with his good, kind wife seeing to dinner nearby, his daughter bent over her homework. How fragile it all was, how almost nonexistent: whatever was between them was un-latched from life, insubstantial as bored thought—abruptly she was weary of the train, of Nathan, of her self: she leaned against the window and dozed.

She was woken by a change of air. It came like spring. She couldn't account for it, only discovered that she was upright in her seat, untired and frowning, casting about for the cause. In front of her, a drab thin girl in gray, occupied with a drab thin book, looked up from the pages with a rabbit's dumb vigi-lance. The train was departing a station. The striplights over-head were replicated in the windows and cast unkind light on the upturned faces of the passengers. The thin girl put down her book. A compartment door was opened and slammed. A man came down the aisle. Those facing him looked up, and went on looking. Grace turned and saw him, and was inclined to laugh: this man was young, and immense. Thick reddish hair at the crown of his head almost brushed the strip lights; his shoulders would have cast shade for two men. He wore a white shirt unable to contain the span of his chest and the bulk of his upper arms; the sleeves were rolled to the elbow and showed burnished skin. The world bent to accommodate him: he insisted on being admired. His face, impassive, was that of a lesser god. The thin girl flushed and returned to her book. Grace felt her body respond, and this was a delight— she was only an animal, she could hardly be blamed.

The young man sat beside the blushing girl, and opposite Grace. His curved thighs were spread on the seat. His hair blazed. The girl shifted away from him with nervous care. Grace laughed, and covered her laugh; the young man, survey-ing the carriage, caught her in the field of his view, and flicked a bright black gaze over her body. Well: let him. It was a plea-sure to see and be seen. Restlessly she looked at her phone. No light, no sign. Her mood, dependent now on the whims of Nathan's affection, began to sour.

"Tickets, please"—and the inspector was coming down the aisle, expertly riding the carriage, looking from side to side. "Any tickets from Ingatestone, please." Tickets were retrieved, shown. The ticket inspector—whose belly strained his belt, whose clipped moustache was gray—arrived at the young man's seat and stood behind him. "Ticket, please," he said. He surveyed the young man's back, the hard curved thigh splayed out across the aisle. "Any new tickets?" he said, and wiped his moustache. The indifferent back did not move; the young man was looking at his phone. Now the atmosphere was charged, as if before a lightning strike. A woman in a purple coat leaned forward in her seat, avid for another look. "Sir," said the inspector, sharpening his voice, hooking his thumbs in his belt. "Your ticket." Still: nothing. The beautiful passenger examined his nails. The thin girl, astounded by such marvelous disobedience, put down her book. The inspector, seeming diminished in size, looked at his watch as if time's mechanism might take pity and hurry him on. He went a little farther down the aisle, turned to face the passenger and blinked rapidly, as he might have blinked at the beam of a torch. "Don't ignore me, young man," he said, reaching for the tone of an exasperated teacher whose fondness for his pupils had been tested, and not getting there. "A penalty fare will apply." He put his hand on the shoulder of the offender, who looked up, and with a shrugging smiling gesture brushed back a lock of hair and revealed a hearing aid. On that superb body, it had the look of augmentation, not correction; but nonetheless the inspector colored, softened, became helpless. "I'm sorry, sir," he said, "I didn't realize." He repeated himself, with overloud and careful diction: "I am sorry."

"It's OK," said the lesser god, "that's OK." He was untroubled;

he signed as he spoke. He reached in his pocket, and came up emptyhanded, then rolled his eyes at the inspector, who'd taken on a fatherly watchful look: all right, son, you've got all the time in the world. The young man took out his wallet and hooked a finger in each compartment. Nothing. The passengers looked on, their early worship amplified and made tender by their sympathy: nobody wished him ill. Now the young man was searching under his seat, and compelling the passengers to watch the articulation of muscles not concealed by his shirt—with a furious movement he raised himself, and spread his hands in hopeless apology. "Sorry!" he said. "I just don't know what's happened."

All eyes on the inspector, all bodies awaiting the spark—let him be, let him get home, give him anything he wants! The inspector was jovial. He clasped his hands. Where was sir getting off? Colchester. Oh that was all right. The barriers would be up this time of day, on account of sheer weight of passengers. Speed things up, you know? The lesser god nodded down from his great height. He knew: of course he knew. "Just go through"—with tentative reverence the ticket inspector put his hand on the sloping shoulder, and left it there a moment—"you'll be all right."

"Good, that's good. Thanks." A thumbs-up, done with shy majesty. All well: justice in carriage B, and mercy on the tracks. The inspector, sensing his passengers' approval, basked his way down to the buffet car. The woman in the purple coat was licking her lips; the drab girl smiled into her drab book. The young man seemed oddly to dwindle down, as if releasing the other passengers from his thrall. Interest receded from him. Grace looked at her phone: still no Nathan, still no light. Then she saw the young man lean toward the girl beside him. She flushed, and raised her book as a barrier. But he wanted to speak: he put his finger in the spine of her book, and lowered it. The girl gasped at the enormity of this transgression, and the radiant face. The young man whispered, "Never had a ticket, did I?" He grinned immensely; his teeth were white and small. "Didn't even have a ticket!"

Then, having handed her the burden of his guilt, he rolled his shoulders and looked out at the small town coming down the line—park, lake, floodlit cricket pitch, bus station, shoe shops, Essex bringing down its shutters for the night. The train slowed and halted. The young man stood, and after all was not so immense, nor so beautiful: possibly that had all been a trick of the light. He grinned down at the girl. He grinned down at Grace, who smiled complicitly—her desire was occupied elsewhere, but she was willing to concede her body had wanted his. She watched him leave the train, and quickly cross the platform as mortal passengers parted at his speed and power; saw him come up short against the ticket barriers, which were after all not open. He paused. The train was ticking on the tracks; the lights of the station struck radiant off his shoulders, the crown of his head. With no apparent effort and no backward look, he vaulted over the barrier and was gone down the narrow stairs.

Grace Macaulay, who all her life had tried to be good—who tried even when she had no idea what constituted goodness, or where to find it—felt a peculiar kind of exhilarated distress. Such a small transgression, she thought, such an infinitesimal sin, I ought not to have noticed—but imagine it, only imagine it: knowing what is good, and simply choosing not to do it! Again she felt the sensation of standing on a high ledge from which she could see the world—again that dizzied feeling of capacity, that fear her feet would slip. She looked for Nathan, she looked at her phone. Nothing. No light.

The following day—early morning; good clear weather—Nick Carleton left his miserable office and went as he often did to speak to Thomas Hart. The offices now were half what they were, and the desks bafflingly more or less paperless. Worst of all was the penetrating quiet, when once there'd been the invigorating clamor of ringing phones ignored or snatched exultantly off the hook, of keyboards pecked at long into night, and occasionally (he fondly thought) of something thrown against a wall. His staff these days were young, diligent, poorly dressed, and kind; they lived with their parents, they filed copy from their phones, they didn't drink, they couldn't spell nor did they need to. So Carleton made his way to Thomas with a grateful sensation, as if they were the last of a lonely species of which only a single pair remained.

At the far end of the corridor, where the high windows overlooked Aldleigh and were occasionally blotted with the imprint of birds, the door was ajar, and the departing light was as diffuse as that of a gas lamp. Music also departed with the light, and it was the melancholy kind Thomas favored these days. Troubled at the sound, Carleton reflected that in fact all had not been well with Thomas lately—he stayed too late at his desk, and wrote too little for the terms of his employment; it was no longer possible to rouse his elegant irritation by insisting for example that he stop using the world *whilst*, or confine himself to one biblical quotation a year. Even the fineness of his clothes had faltered these last few weeks (once there'd been the suggestion of a coffee stain on his cuff, which Carleton had ignored as he would have ignored nakedness), and it evidently had been some time since he'd seen his barber—in fact there'd sometimes been the sense that the strange machine that constituted Thomas Hart was winding down.

Then Carleton heard the music pause, and begin again in a kind of wild dance that stirred him without his consent. "What now," he said to himself, "what now?"—he went in, and discovered the Thomas of time past: upright, fastidious, self-contained, a silk handkerchief in pale green folded in the breast pocket of a sports coat in charcoal linen, the overlong hair not yet cut, but at any rate glossed and ordered by a comb. "Hello," said the editor, coming warily toward the desk: this abrupt reversion was as troubling as the slow decline.

"Young Nick," said Thomas, reverting to old endearments and adjusting a silver cufflink, "I was thinking of coming to see you. I have news. Sit."

Carleton sat. "Turn that off, would you? It makes my head ache."

Gravely and with good humor Thomas turned the music off. Silence in the office and the corridor; silence on the river, the railway, the market square: "You'd think," said Thomas, "that nothing is happening. But it is all happening, Carleton— it has always been happening: look at this." Spread on the desk, beside the cheap green notebooks that had accrued in a drift against the window, were three pages torn from a lined notepad and untidily written over in a leaking pen. Thomas moved these aside with what looked very like contempt, and instead passed Carleton a sheet of paper on which an old document of some kind had been photocopied.

"*The Undermentioned Houses*," read Carleton, turning the paper over as if hoping to find something more interesting on the reverse. "What is this?"

"That is a record of every human soul that lived at Foulis Street in London on a certain night in April 1891. That is the echo of a footstep that has followed me for twenty years, Carleton—that is the sound of hope!"

"Thomas. I am tired—talk sense: is this about that wretched woman?"

"If you mean Maria Văduva Bell, late of Lowlands House—astronomer, Romanian, unquiet spirit and friend—then yes: it is about that wretched woman, and that wretched child. Grace Macaulay—oh, never mind her—give me that. Look: you see these names underlined?"

Carleton, if tired, nonetheless drew from Thomas Hart a little of the energy that struck sparks from the finger that traced the page. "All right," he said, native instinct for a story surfacing, "let me look." He looked. The document showed a page from what he slowly understood to be the last census of the nineteenth century, taken at Foulis Street in London in 1891. Three names were underlined, and a note had been written on a blank part of the page:

THREE POSSIBILITIES AT FOULIS STREET??
(Women / names with C. S. / married.)
At no. 3: Christina Susannah Lord, 78. Too old?
At no. 17: Cora Seaborne, 24. Michael Seaborne (father?), 51
At no. 29: Clementine Louisa Stanton Yates, 23 (a husband,
    Eric Stanton Yates, 41)

"I see," said Carleton, who did begin to see (in fact: was there possibly the suggestion of moving cloth in the corner of the office, where lately Thomas had installed a coffee machine?). "You are looking for her friend."

"I'm looking for her comet!" said Thomas. "It is shut up in one of these houses, waiting to be let out! We know Maria gave her papers to her friend. We know her friend lived at Foulis Street. We know she was young, and married. Now she must be one of these women."

"But the census was taken two years after Maria disappeared—"

"Never mind that. Luck must eventually be on my side, for God's sake. She must be one of these. Not Miss Lord, I think, she was too old. Cora Seaborne I suspect was some clever spinster who lived with her father. Clementine on the other hand lived to see a hundred and two, and her son was elected Fellow of the Royal Astronomical Society shortly after the war, and that has promise."

"Cora Seaborne," said Carleton (and out of the corner— displacing the silk skirt, the coffee machine—there came the scent of a receding tide, and perhaps of oyster shells). "That's a good name."

"I've waited twenty years," said Thomas, "for this story to come to an end. Now at last we're getting there, and just as time is running out—Comet du Lac is coming and already visible to better telescopes than mine."

"I have every faith. But meanwhile: you owe me three columns." Carleton summoned his authority with effort. "You may be a grand old man of letters, you may be the jewel in our crown, but if you will take your salary—"

Thomas put his documents away. "Yes," he said, "yes—only I don't have a single thought in my head but Maria."

"You will think of something. Five hundred words, and six if they come to mind. And less quantum, Thomas, more Essex. Our readers are ordinary men."

"There are no ordinary men," said Thomas.

"Get out of Aldleigh. Head out Maldon way. Take a Thames barge up the estuary, eat an oyster. Do something about Aldwinter. See what they're digging up in Colchester these days."

Thomas surveyed his superior. "If you like," he said, with an immense and deliberate grace, "I could do the Aldwinter Knots."

"The Aldwinter Knots? They say it's a strange business, that." Carleton considered the strange business, and liked it. "Go on, then. Make it a feature. And careful you don't get in trouble: they're a right lawless lot, out there on the Blackwater."

Toward the end of September, the sun crossed the celestial equator, and briefly the opposed forces of night and day were more or less equal in Essex. A waxing crescent moon rose early in this lovers' truce, and it was a low tide in Aldwinter, where a quick brown fox came running out of the bracken on hind legs. It stopped and turned its avid face from side to side, then gulped and screamed and bolted. Other foxes followed—also hares, deer, a wretched badger with a torn pelt; a flightless blind owl and a slot-eyed goat. They were all singing. Pause: nothing for a time, no lame or headlong beast, then a rabbit came running with its white tail hanging by a thread, and screaming as it sang. Thomas Hart watched from his vantage near the tomb tree, where chapel pews and plastic chairs had been put out in ordered ranks, and sank each half hour a little deeper in the grass: Aldwinter was briefly inhabited again. Women and men had come down from Maldon and Colchester and Billericay, and from such far places such as Suffolk and Norfolk and Kent; and since it was the day of the Aldwinter Knots, all those attending had tied on their wrist or around their neck a bit of string, or ribbon, or whatever had come to hand.

Sheaves of wheat kept back from harvest had been stacked between the headstones that lapped the tomb tree, and twisted corn dollies tied with red ribbon were put here and there, and fell off, and were quickly put back. The split oak had not yet disposed of its leaves, which blazed and rattled in occasional wind; two dead branches white as stag horns rose from the crown. Summer seemed loath to leave the green, which still had its share of clover and loosethrift in the grass, and in the hedges the dogroses bloomed a little later than was decent. Thomas opened his notebook: *Two hundred in attendance*, he wrote, *and a fine day. Autumn hardly dares come in. The air is full of salt.*

The singing came nearer, sometimes unlovely and sometimes harmonious, punctuated often by a wordless screech from a panicked fox or hare. A great fish of some kind, slim as a serpent, came up behind a pair of deer and deliberately made them stumble; then it went on, shedding aluminium scales. *Whilst it is said*, wrote Thomas (having Carleton in mind), *that this is an ancient Essex rite marking the autumn equinox, I have my doubts, since it was never mentioned when I was young.* The fish slipped nearer. Thomas wrote *KNOTS?*, and underlined it three times. He considered the length of garden twine tied tight round the wrist of the man seated at his left. *Knots*, he wrote, *were of great interest to the Saxons, whose bones are perhaps stacked three deep under Aldwinter—*

"I heard it was all made up," the man next to him said, surveying a deer that danced itself frenzied and left rags of its own pelt on the looping bramble. "I heard it's only been going twenty years."

"I'm sure it is," said Thomas, "this ritual and every other—

made up, elaborated, misheard, remembered, amplified—
does it matter? Everything begins somewhere."

"I knew you'd say that," the man said, with shy unwarranted
sweetness. "I knew you'd say something like that." Thomas, receiving the sweetness with confusion and pleasure, turned to
look at this stranger. A walking stick was propped against
his right knee, and Thomas felt his own hip ache in
companionship.

Briefly the singers paused, then up from the Blackwater Estuary a split skein of geese headed elsewhere for winter, and
Thomas looked at the man again. He encountered a curious
clicking sensation behind his ribs, as if a key had been turned
in a lock. He knew that fair hair, left to grow too long, that astounding blue gaze. "Oh!" said Thomas. "Nathan," he said,
"there you are!"—as if all morning he'd been looking for the
boy who'd leaped easily among the headstones and never been
able to keep still. There he was—and with a kind of grief
Thomas saw the man's left foot turned faintly in; saw his thinness, and how the clean-shaven cheek had sunk under the
broad high bones of his face, and knew pain when he saw it.

"Here I am," said Nathan, holding out his hand; "Mr. Hart.
Thomas. I'd have known you anywhere. I think you and Grace
must be the only people in the world who never change."

It was not quite noon. High in the earth's atmosphere the
light refracted through ice crystals in obedience to certain
laws, and described a perfect geometric circle round the sun,
solid and unbroken as a city wall. "Do you see that?" said
Thomas, dismissing Grace and the echo of her name in the ves-
tibules of his heart. "They call it a sundog, or a parhelion, if
you prefer the proper term." I wonder if Grace can see it, he
thought, I wonder if there's a sundog over Aldleigh. So he
could not dismiss her after all, and the past few days had required an effort of will not to mount the iron staircase at the

Jackdaw and Crow, and summon his wretched child and say: look here, the comet is coming—twelve weeks until I see it with my own two eyes. But the vision of her hand on Lorna's wrist revisited him, and brought with it the completion of a lifetime's shame—and there, too, was the other shame, of his cruelty as she knelt by the baptistery. Now he was conscious of a bright assessing look from the man at his side: compelled as if in a confessional, Thomas said, "I haven't seen her lately. I'm not one for the chapel pew these days. Tell me, is she well?"

The other man was quiet. The sundog brightened. Then, "I've only seen her once in twenty years," he said, "and she was just the same, and it made me think I was, too. She's coming here," he said, with a curious secretive look, as if admitting a sin without guilt. "She told me she'd never been, and would meet me by the oak"—he took his phone out of his pocket and passed a thumb over the screen as if caressing a living thing—"she's on her way. Do you have to go"—instinctively and with a sound of refusal Thomas was rising from his chair—"do you really have to go? Wasn't she your friend?"

This was the frank simplicity Thomas had known, and it was charming to see the boy retained in the man. But how could he explain, given the appeal of that blue gaze now turned on him, that he and Grace had disgraced each other, and disgraced themselves? "You see," said Thomas, patting the pocket where his notebook was folded in two, "I must go and take a look at what's going on over there, or I'll have nothing to write."

"But look: there she is," said Nathan, with more wonder than he'd summoned for the tomb tree, the animals dismantling themselves, the shining loop around the sun. "There she is," he said again, and there she was, no better than she ought to be and coming through the crowd. She glittered. The equinoctial light was wonderful on her white dress, her bent brown neck. The dress was plain as a shift, though she'd done some elaborate beaded pleating on the sleeves, and the bodice was cut to show the bonework of her clavicle and shoulder blades, and the deep scoop of her lower back. Her skin retained summer; she'd picked at a horsefly bite and lifted the scab. Already her dress was dirty: coffee on the skirt, mud on the sleeve. The horsefly bite was bleeding. She had more than ever the look of a woman who belonged nowhere, and in no time. Immense irregular pearls drew down the lobes of her ears, and a few seed pearls were threaded on a length of silk around her wrist. Her mouth was blotted red, as if she'd painted her lips, regretted her sin, and rubbed her shame on the back of her hand.

Nathan stood. The walking stick dropped to the grass. Grace, blinded to Thomas by desire or vengeance or both, held out her arms. Nathan entered them, bending to do it, and it struck Thomas that the motions of their bodies had little to do with thought. "Do you remember," said Grace, drawing away, "do you remember my birthday, and the oak coming out of the fog?"

"I remember," said Nathan. This was kindly and politely done; he'd stepped carefully back and put distance between them. "It was a good day," he said, and sat down with a helpless noise that seemed to signal not the body's weakness, but rather its terrible capacity.

"Then we went home," said Grace, "and there was Dimi on the road to Aldleigh in his velvet coat. He died," she said, lightly touching Nathan's shoulder as she sat, oblivious to Thomas near at hand. "He died, and we didn't find out for months."

Now the animals had gathered around the tomb tree, and

looked out at the crowd with identical vacant eyes. At a signal their tuneless hectic singing resolved itself into a sweet and repetitious melody: "*Western wind,*" they sang, "*when wilt thou blow? The small rain down can rain.*" Thomas saw Nathan shift in his seat and put an inch of further distance between himself and Grace; saw, too, her look of bewildered hurt that arrived and was quickly concealed. There again was the echo, ringing against partitions raised against her, of his old instinct to protect and console: "But he isn't dead," he said, "not really—whenever anyone reads Maria Văduva's diaries they hear Dimi, too."

If he'd hoped for some kind of softening, none came—"What are you even doing here anyway," said Grace, turning her hurt on Thomas. Overhead the parhelion brightened and hardened. At opposite sides of the circle, where three and nine might be marked on the face of a clock, two vivid lights appeared and faintly showed the colors of the spectrum.

"Thomas says that's a sundog," said Nathan, and Grace's anger faltered against the gentle admonition in his voice—"Just sit down, Thomas," she said. "Where are you going? Can't you just sit down?"

"Maria Văduva," said Nathan. "Every now and then I'd remember that name—when I was late for work, or waiting for a prescription—and wonder about you."

"Yes," said Grace, glittering, eager—she leaned briefly against him—"yes, me too."

Nathan, upright in his chair, cultivated stillness that was uneasy because it was against his nature. And what will happen, thought Thomas, if he doesn't keep himself in check? Pain, I suppose. The green was full of women and men in morris costumes carrying wooden batons; others had put on party clothes. Someone nearby had set up a stall of Pyefleet oysters

and shucked them without doing herself damage. Everywhere
on the oak, bits of string or lengths of rope had been tied on
branches, and anyone might think the grass was full of infant
snakes. The animals were huddled beside the tree. A drum
struck up. The vacant eyes of the deer and foxes were intent on
something out of sight. From somewhere there came a high
plaintive note that dislodged the jackdaws from the oak; then
again there was the drum, and the animals put up their limbs
and plucked away their faces. Masks of papers were thrown on
the grass; the heads of anxious children now appeared, seeking
families out.

"Isn't it strange," said Grace, speaking to Nathan or to
Thomas or to nobody, her right hand on her left breast, "I feel
the drum more than I hear it."

Yes, thought Thomas, receiving her old look of thunder-
struck joy with a responding joy of his own, yes: it's like all Essex has a pulse—it is life, life, eternal life!

The beat quickened. The children clapped with a clever er-
ratic beat, and sang words so ancient as to be nonsensical. It
was noon. Men on the margins were setting up tables with
kegs of beer, and the morris men tied ribbons to their knees.
One by one the crowd joined in the song as if they knew it,
and in due course it seemed to Thomas that he knew it, too—
had always known it, had heard it at his mother's breast. He
began to sing, and so did Grace, because Bethesda had given
them the habit of song—but Nathan sat upright, politely smiling, interested and untroubled, his stick sinking into the grass.

A creature shook its torn white tail and moved between the
lapping headstones to tie a ribbon to the tree, and wept when
the ribbon unwound and dropped. Then more children came,
knotting their scarves and bits of string: it looked as if the oak
had been taken over by some parasitic vegetation that would

strip its leaves by dusk. The crowd swayed and clapped, and there was the scent of beer spilled by the trestle tables, and of the tide on the Blackwater turning. The parhelion crowned the oak with silver. Three suns shone.

Now there was only wordless music, piped and drummed, and men and women going up with bits of thread and ribbon, careful of the headstones and the sheaves of wheat. A young man carrying rope came close by where they sat: he was immense, with curling reddish hair; he'd taken off his shirt, and the hair on his body was also reddish and grew thick toward the navel, so that he had the look of an upright animal. Thomas was inclined to laugh in delight and derision at how monstrously handsome he was; then "You!" said Grace, with an inflection of satisfaction and chastisement that affected Nathan, who flinched in his chair as if struck. "It's you," said Grace, laughing, and seeming for a moment to forget the man at her side; "It's you," she said again, and caught his eye with an imperious gesture. He paused, and shifted the rope on his shoulder, and gave her such a long assessing look that Thomas flushed as if he'd been caught out spying. "I know him," said Grace, smiling now at Nathan, and watching with open pleasure as the young man moved on, hurled his rope over a high branch, and laughed as a nearby girl wound the rope three times around her waist. The exchange had caused Grace's eyes to bloom, as if something had entered her bloodstream; meanwhile Nathan inhabited his own body as if afraid he'd break it. Anything might happen, thought Thomas, there's no doctrine or government here—and what is there for an old man to do, but cause mischief? "Let's drink," he said, "let's get something to drink."

"I can't," said Nathan, "not really, not with the painkillers they give me—and I have to drive home."

"Go on," said Grace, putting her hand on his thigh and

quickly removing it, "go on"; and very briefly there passed between her and Thomas a complicit look that stirred him unbearably. From a nearby trestle table he bought dark beer in
plastic cups that spilled easily as he handed them out; and
there was a moment when all three drank to slake their various
thirsts.

"But what does it all mean?" said Nathan. "Why do they do
it?" Wool and ribbon were streaming from the oak like Spanish moss, and musicians in absurd clothes were bringing instruments out of black cases left open in the grass. The drums
pulsed on.

"What do you want it to mean?" said Grace. "What do you
want?" Her bloomed eyes took him in; and it was possible to
see the boy Thomas had known looking down at her, amused
and puzzled by his strange companion, and restless with life. "I
don't know," he said, smiling, shaking his head, "how should I
know?"

The wind changed. Low pale clouds blew up from the estuary and put the sundog out. The Aldwinter sky took on the
pearly look of an upturned oyster shell.

"I want to do it," said Grace, done with her drink. "I want to
tie something—I want to tie myself up and leave myself behind."
She'd left her seat and was drifting nearer the tree. "How can we
go until we've done it? We'll bring ourselves bad luck."

Slowly Nathan followed her, leaving his stick in the grass.
His weak foot dragged and lifted. The crowd at the foot of the
oak was thinning out, and here and there children stood between headstones, reaching for the lower branches.

"I don't have anything," said Grace, lamenting, "I have nothing to tie. I could tear my dress, I could do that. Oh—there
you are again," she said, laughing and glittering at the immense
red-haired young man whose rope now hung like a pole from
a branch. Nathan halted nearby; he watched. He surveyed the

man with a baffled expression of envy, awe, contempt. The red-haired man took the end of the rope in his fist and shook it wordlessly at Grace. "Come on, then," he said, "come here, you," and Grace went forward with her skirt in her hands: "But I know I can't trust you," she said, "I know you can't be trusted." He offered her the rope and she took it. The crowd nearby was dancing, and their movements were deliberate and slow because they'd tied themselves together about the wrists or waist or sometimes, foolishly, the knees. The young man pressed his wrists together, and offered them to Grace, who—with a child's diligent, obedient frown—tied them with the rope. Then dancers came by, and for a time obscured the view: old men and young ones, half-drunk or drunk entirely; girls clasped together and turning in stately circles; old lovers quick-stepping in practiced concourse. Dazed by beer and music, Thomas saw all the threads that bound them in varieties of human bondage—knots made of habit, blood, resentment, desire offered and withdrawn, love met and not met, all tying and untying as he watched. Bleakly it struck him that in all Aldwinter only he and Nathan were alone. With pity amplified by the remembrance of desire, he came near the younger man, and put his hand in his pocket, hoping to find a bit of string to join their ruined bodies. Then the dancers parted, and Thomas saw Grace standing small and dark beside the man, whose shoulders covered half the span of the oak's trunk. She leaned indolent against a marble headstone and idly tugged at the rope fastened round the young man's hands, as she might have tugged at a dog's lead: "Come here, then," she said, as if she had some particular sin and punishment in mind.

"What's happening?" said Nathan. He gripped his right hand with his left. "What are they doing?"

"They're just playing," said Thomas. The drums beat on. Rooks began to gather on the green. Grace under the oak was immense, glittering, her white dress showing plainly in the diminishing light. The man seemed to have dwindled, become humble; now and then Grace threw a black look out at Nathan, assessing his distance, his manner, the composition of the air between them. Nathan had become rigid, and the long line of his throat was hard and beating with the drums; he doesn't like this, thought Thomas, he can't bear it, the power has shifted, after all this time. Laughing, Grace gave a sudden pull on the rope and the man stumbled forward with a grunt, and his body covered hers against the headstone, which rocked between the roots of the oak. "Look at them," said two women going slowly past with white ribbon round their necks. "Would you look at those two. Anything goes!" Grace was concealed by the man's immense body, but there was the impression of intent unseen movements made out of sight—"Stop it," said Nathan, quietly seeming to implore himself. "Stop it!" he said again, now taking in the crowd, the drums, the aimless children, the declining sun—"Get off her!" he said, going as quickly as he could, which was not quick. He reached the man, and wrenched at his shoulder. "What are you doing?" he said. "Get off her!" How pitiful, thought Thomas in a daze, how absurd: you can't impose your manners out here, with everything tending to the mutinous sea.

The man turned and looked with surprise, and no rancor. He smiled, shrugged, drifted away; was claimed elsewhere by acquisitive women. Grace leaned smiling against the headstone. Her breasts and neck were wrapped with rope: she gave the impression of a hangman's having done a poor job and gone off to seek another profession. "Look what you've done!" said Nathan. He was cruel as a father. "Look what you've done to yourself!" But Grace would not shrug off the rope as she decently should, and Nathan, chastising her with words not audible to Thomas, fumbled with the rope; then Grace shook herself free like a dog, and leaned against the headstone as if exhausted.

The rooks on the green rose in a dense black mass and settled in the oak to roost. "Get up," said Nathan, and she did. Her sleeve was torn. She bowed her head in mute humility; then surveyed the headstone, and saw how it shifted now in the roots of the oak.

"What have I done this time?" she said. She rocked it. "Look what I've done. I didn't mean to."

"It's all right," said Nathan. "It isn't that bad. Anyway, she's dead." Thoughtlessly he took her hand. Grace accepted it. Thomas saw against the coming dusk two careless creatures, suspended forever between childhood and maturity and as innocent and sinful as the day they were born: I did love you, he thought. I have loved you.

Softly Grace began to pet the headstone like a living thing. It was a slab of marble, thickly mossed; it listed away from the oak toward the estuary, as if it wanted the water. Grace traced the lettering. Not dark yet. Small fires on the green. She spoke to Nathan, who stooped with her to read. She burrowed against him with an impulse of affection and pleasure. It seemed to Thomas that even to watch them was a trespass, and nobody, he thought, a bit of old string in his hand, nobody on earth was ever as solitary as me. But Grace was beckoning him, and this was extraordinary, and Nathan was raising his arm: "Thomas!" they were saying. "Thomas Hart! Come here!"

Thomas walked forward through Aldwinter as it was, and had been, and would be—"There," said Grace. "There, you see?" She stood aside. Thomas was at the headstone. It was difficult to read by firelight. The face of a fox grinned out of the grass. Then it seemed to Thomas that letters formed themselves because he wanted them—that he summoned them up as he watched:

CORA SEABORNE FGS

1867—1921

FRIEND AND MOTHER

"Look closer," said Grace. High tide on the Blackwater, sea
frets on Aldwinter Green: "Look!" she said. Thomas stooped
to the work of the stonemason, and with his forefinger traced
in the marble an ammonite fossil, coiled like the horn of a ram.
Beside it, dim and unmistakable in the astronomical twilight,
he saw a comet with a curved and double tail: hankering after
light, but impounded in the stone.

"Take me to Bethesda," said Grace Macaulay after dark. Nathan, dazed by beer and pain relief, and persuaded to leave his
car until morning for the sake of the law, sat upright and civil
beside her in the back seat. Thomas placidly regarded them
both in the rearview mirror, and thought of Cora Seaborne.

"Take me to chapel," said Grace, glittering at him.

"I am taking you home," said Thomas.

"Isn't that what I said?"—another look: only you understand what I mean, Thomas Hart.

The Blackwater receded behind them; so too did the fires
set on Aldwinter Green, the morris men, the pulsing drum.
Ordinary Essex came quickly into view: rush hour on the outskirts of Colchester, cheap planes fleeing Stansted; oaks going
over, and cars dying on bricks outside freshly painted front
doors. "Don't you want to see it again?" said Grace. "Don't
you ever wonder who sits in your pew?"

"Cora Seaborne, friend and mother," said Thomas. "FGS.

So then she was a Fellow of the Geological Society. And dead at fifty-four, which seems to me now no age whatever. And a comet on the headstone," he said, with as much pleasure as if du Lac had just then crossed the ecliptic and come into view above the A12's dual carriageway, "which settles the matter, to my mind. What we must do is this: establish what happened when the Aldwinter graves were disinterred, and whether this Seaborne woman had descendants who kept her papers and correspondence. I doubt she was very important," he said, experiencing at that moment, and for no evident reason, a bolt of pain in his hip, "I doubt she'll have troubled the history books, even if she ought to have done."

"Please take us to chapel, Thomas," Grace said, "please"— not enough room in her heart these days for the dead—"that was all downright ungodly, back there, and I'd like to go and sit in a pew."

"I'm not sure it's godliness you have in mind," said Thomas; then the car struck a pothole, and Nathan cried out in his seat: "I'm sorry," said Grace, as if she herself had damaged both the tarmac and his spine, "I'm sorry, love"—the endearment passed without notice.

"It will be locked," said Thomas. He wanted only to be at home in the shadow of the railway bridge, with his cheap green notebooks to hand, drafting a letter to some council official: *I wonder if you might direct me to some documents*—"It will be locked," he said, "and I have a book to finish" (they were coming to Aldleigh now, and he heard above the engine the old harmonium playing, and the cadence of the prayers).

"Look," said Grace, "there it is, there's Bethesda, like it's sailing toward us down the road."

"There it is," said Thomas, and found himself nodding as if at an acquaintance: there was the austere chapel, huddled in

the car park beside Potter's Field, all as it had ever been. The
traffic lights on London Road were red; so they waited where
James Bower had waited, and saw what he had seen.

"What time's the last train?" said Nathan, with the civility
of a man who had duties at home—who had never, for example, unraveled rope from the breasts of a woman who toppled
a headstone; whose throat never beat with the drums. "I've
work tomorrow, I ought to get back, my phone is out of
charge."

"It was good for you," said Grace. "It was good to step out of
your life and into mine—go in, Thomas," she said. "Look, here
we are." Thomas saw Bethesda's gates standing open, and the
bay tree flourishing in its small black bed; and briefly a muddle
of resentment and affection left him speechless.

"Go in," said Grace, "please go in." Helpless against forces
he could hardly make out, Thomas turned through the iron
gates; and "Somebody's there," said Grace, "somebody's cleaning the pews." A dark and busy thing went by the mottled glass
of the window. There was no music.

"I used to play there all the time," said Nathan, looking at
the vacant plot beside the chapel. "I used to watch you all going in. Do you never go now, Thomas?" he said, with his old
frank interest. "Have you both abandoned it all?"

"It isn't that," said Grace, "you don't understand, that's like
asking if we've abandoned our bones."

"I'm not a man of that faith in particular," said Thomas,
"and haven't been in almost ten years. It was made clear to me
then that a man like me was not welcome, and never could be
welcome." (A brief glance at Grace; briefly, her shame.) Thomas
cut the engine, and released himself from his seat: "But I'm
still a man of faith, I think." An image in mind: small ships,
and the pilot light hazy on the dock. "Often when I wonder
what it is I believe, and how I can go on believing it, I always

come down to this: that wanting God is God himself. He exists in the stars not because he made them on the fourth day, but because we have the inclination to look up, and wonder."

"Yes," said Nathan, "I see, or hope I do"—he was leaning on the wall and looking over Potter's Field. A slow smile came. "I remember my red coat," he said, "and how I broke the window. Sometimes I think I have no memory from that year that doesn't have you in it." Grace came to lean beside him on the wall, and very slightly he moved his body away.

Thomas meanwhile was at the threshold, standing on that same bristled mat. How extraordinary it was that Anne Macaulay would never again come through the lobby with her hymn book in her hands; that Dimi would never again drink from his bottle in the last pew by the door. Who played the harmonium now? Who handed round the silver communion plates? He looked back to Potter's Field, and saw Grace put her head on Nathan's shoulder, not with her old hard nudge of love, but with a kind of acquiescent shame. Then she saw Thomas going in, and followed him. Nathan followed her. The green bay tree was flourishing. The lobby doors opened, and a woman came out, and greeted Grace—it had been a long time, hadn't it, yes, and they'd missed her: was her father well? Yes, said Grace, quite well, praise God; and might they stay a while, for old times' sake, and lock up after they were gone?

So Grace in triumph shook the iron chapel keys, and the obedient men followed her in. The loop of time enclosed them: here as ever the halted moons drifted under the pitched white roof, and the green walls were as ever cold to the touch; here the tulip of the pulpit still bloomed against the wall. Maria Văduva was standing by the communion table, this do in remembrance of me; there was broken glass in the aisle. The cleaning woman had raised dust that rose on drafts of air, and Thomas saw it depart through open windows and go streaming over Essex to the upper atmosphere, becoming blown in due course by solar winds into the tail of Comet du Lac.

Grace, not speaking, touched her old pew, which was stained with oil from her palms and the palms of generations of believers before her—she touched the closed harmonium, and stood for a time by the place where she'd been baptised. Tail lights were blotted in the narrow windows. Aldleigh passed them by. "You were standing there," said Nathan, "where you are now, and your dress was white that day, too." He had a curious dreamlike look. His competent fatherly manner was gone, and the old teasing levity came up like something unloosed from the bottom of a lake: "You looked ridiculous, in fact," he said, "but then you always did."

"The whole time," she said, "in every hymn and every verse I tried to think of my salvation, but was waiting for you to come in."

"I did," he said. Together the children turned to Thomas, and regarded him.

It was difficult for Thomas to see Grace's small white body pressed against Nathan, whose stick was on the communion table; to see his bewildered grateful look. So he turned to the harmonium and pressed without skill at the pedals and keys, and an old thread of an old hymn went up with the sea air in the pipes.

"It was here they taught me I ought to be good," said Grace. "But isn't love goodness, and wasn't I good for waiting all this time, and didn't I see you first?" She was laughing—it was all a game, having no significance at all.

It was hard for Nathan to stand so long without his stick. He stepped back, but stumbled; so he took hold of her dress at the hip, and held it. "I ought to go," he said. "Does anyone know when the last train leaves?"

"I should have brought string," Grace said. "I should have brought rope, I'd tie you to me. You see?" she said, and shook her skirt where he held it. "You don't want to let me go."

Thomas would have prayed for them both if he could. No use, he thought: I can't put my hand out and stop a body in orbit, not when my bad hip aches—"That was it," he said. He stood. "That was the last train. Didn't you hear it go?" Grace heard nothing. Two hands now at her hips, the stick dropped by the baptistery; again a helpless quick embrace, and a sound that might have been pain, and the small strong body burrowing hard against the man it wanted. Thomas Hart was not seen and not wanted. He left his pew again.

Grace Macaulay, no better than she ought to be, stood fastened against the man she loved and wouldn't let him go. Soon this also caused him pain, and Grace heard the little cry, and pitied him, and because of this desired him more. "We can't stay here," she said. "Why don't you come with me?"

"What else can I do?" he said. No answer. Lights out in Bethesda; fires dying on Aldwinter Green.

They walked slowly and without speaking past Potter's Field, and on down the high street with the Alder running on their right; and all the while Grace had the helpless sensation of an object dumbly submitting to the laws of motion. She said nothing, because anything that came to mind seemed to her ridiculous: did you know, Nathan, that you can know what it is to be good, and simply choose not to do it? Sometimes he spoke in the civil way of a colleague remarking on the weather—how warm it was, how Aldleigh was altered these days; and was it always so busy at the Jackdaw and Crow? Then she'd encounter an intent assessing look, bewildered and half-amused, and have no breath left in her.

It was difficult for him to climb the iron stairs. She gave no help. He would have refused it if she had. She unlocked the door, and locked it behind them; and after this there was a time of inconsequential conversation, embarrassed by themselves and by each other, feeling how inconvenient it was, how humiliating, to be tethered to bodies that insisted on all this: yes it was cold up here in the winter, yes sometimes she was woken by the trains. "So this is where you sleep," he said, as if it were all marvelous, "this is where you sit, when we speak at night." Stolen lamps lit, baskets of cloth spilling on the carpet; the white cloth on the shipping trunk, her unmade bed and the smell of her body in it. He looked angry and unhappy. He took his jacket off. He put his hand on the buckle of his belt and it was appalling to discover how the gesture unmade her. Carefully he sat on the bed and she undressed and knelt at his feet, and smiled as she did it: see how abject I am—see how I'm brought to my knees by pity and want? She took off his shoes and socks, and then the submission was his; but it struck her that another woman knew how best to help him, and she was overtaken by sorrow. Why don't you go away, she thought, why don't you just go away and leave me alone; but she had his weak foot in her lap and was touching the calluses there, and loving them, and loving the limp that made them.

"Stand up," he said. She did. She put her right hand on her stomach where it was soft, and he tugged it away quite harshly: "Let me look." When he'd done looking, he lay down. "Come up here," he said, "come over me, I have to look, I have to see everything," and now she was biddable again, and knelt above him, and this seemed to humiliate and elevate her equally. She pressed her palms to the wall, and sometimes her forehead, and occasionally the noises she made seemed to her those of a lunatic, and at these times she would raise herself from his mouth in a kind of ecstatic despair. But he always seemed to anticipate the withdrawal and bring her down, grasping her hips with extraordinary compensatory strength; and later, when he was able to speak, he said, "Does this hurt? Am I hurting you?"—because his movements after all weren't gentle, and caused her the curious cleaving pain that sometimes came when she'd gone a long time without; and "Yes it hurts," she said, "will you do it again?" So it went unbearably on. All those little deaths (her mouth was fastened to a mark on his shoulder; she was set on obtaining every part of the body she'd desired for so long), all those little deaths—but this is annihilation, it will kill me, there'll be nothing left. So after all that time—after the years of loss and envy and coincidence, and all those terrible negotiations of holiness and wanting—it all came down to this: mutually assured destruction, and streetlight hardening on the bedroom wall.

Subject: Aldwinter Tomb Tree
9 October 2017

Dear Dr. Syed,

I'm writing in my capacity as a journalist for the *Essex
Chronicle*. We're hoping to publish an article on the
headstones relocated from the Aldwinter church cemetery
to the oak on the village green. It's my understanding that
the bodies were reinterred in the municipal cemetery in
Colchester in 1952 following the North Sea flood, and I'm
looking for any documents relating to the removal, which
may possibly be kept by the Essex Museum Services. I am
particularly interested in the headstone of Cora Seaborne,
1867–1921.

I'd be so grateful if you could give me any information on
this matter.

Best—Thomas Hart

Re: Aldwinter Tomb Tree
14 November 2017

Dear Thomas,

Do forgive the delay. I hope you'll be pleased to hear that
we've uncovered some information regarding the
Seaborne grave which may be of use. A number of objects
were removed from Aldwinter during the 1952
disinterment, and where possible returned to the families
of the deceased. An item was discovered intact in the

Seaborne grave, and this was donated to the museum by her surviving relative in 1965.

The item in question was a small and quite elaborate lead box of Eastern European make, possibly designed to protect its contents from damp. A note made at the time of acquisition in 1965 lists the following:

A/1952.65.CS 1: A Book of Common Prayer, containing—

1(a). A letter dated 26 April 1915 (from a Rev. Ransome, chaplain of the Essex Yeomanry stationed at Ypres)

1(b). A blue square of fabric, possibly a handkerchief

A/1952.65.CS 2: A large trilobite fossil of exceptional quality

A/1952.65.CS 3: Four documents in a leather case

The box is on permanent display in Chelmsford, and the trilobite was acquired by the Natural History Museum in London. The fabric together with the prayer book and its letter have unfortunately been lost. However, it appears from administrative records that in March 1997 my predecessor James Bower requisitioned a number of documents relating to Aldwinter, including the remaining Seaborne papers. To my knowledge they have since been held in storage at the Aldleigh Museum. I've alerted my colleagues there that you'll be in touch, and I'm sure they'll be pleased to help you. Look forward to the article. Good luck!

S. S.

Dear James—will you let me write just one more letter, one more time? I can't have your last sight of me being that of a self-pitying old man stagnating in his little life.

I'm sitting at the table where once you and I would eat and talk and raise Maria from the dead. The moon comes under the railway bridge, bad music comes from next door. It's midnight. Grace Macaulay is sleeping in an armchair nearby, worn out by her own misery. Sometimes she talks in her sleep but I can't make it out.

She came to the house again this afternoon. I knew her knock. Who else ever hurled themselves at my door? I opened it and her anger came in like wind—"You did it again, didn't you?" she was saying. "You sent him away again." James, did you ever think yourself guilty, because somebody said you were? For a moment I thought: yes, yes, I must have done—I did, and I'm sorry! Then her anger dissipated and my wretched child arrived down time: small, dark, all love and fury, seeping into tears. "Come in," I said, and she did, and for a moment I was not a complicated man: my friend was in my house again.

She went through the hall and into this room as if she owned the lamps, the sideboard, the rug, the plates and forks in the kitchen, the lunar telescope on the windowsill, and sat where she is sleeping now—"Did you?" she said. "Did you send him away?"

"No," I said. "Not this time."

We were quiet for a long time, or so it seemed to me: I suppose we each considered what the other had betrayed.

I saw her hand on Lorna's wrist, and saw her diminish the battle of my nature against my soul into something small and furtive and cheap—but more clearly and with more pain I saw Nathan at Bethesda's door, and that look of bewildered relief when I turned him away. I had been responsible for her pain then, and I was responsible for her pain now; and it was like that first day in Bethesda, with the infant stranger in the wicker basket and a new obligation in my heart. "What happened, Grace?" I said. "What did you do?"

She asked for something to drink, and I gave it to her. Then she told me that briefly and after all those years Nathan had been her lover—one night, in her room over the Jackdaw and Crow, after the Aldwinter Knots. He was changed absolutely from the last time, she said, and he was absolutely the same—it had been an appalling surprise to find him at Lowlands, it had been inevitable. But he had a wife and a daughter—his life was sealed up, there was no way in. "And at first," she said, "I persuaded myself I could have him, and still be good. I said to myself: to love a body and the soul it contains, and never touch it, not once—that would be a crime against love, it would be a lie! But then I understood there was another way—that I could know how to be good, and choose not to do it. Only you will understand how frightening that was, how it was like being given a power I'd never asked for and didn't know how to use!"

Now, she suffers. He's gone away from her, she says, that kind of drifting a woman feels more than she sees. "It's like he was holding my hand," she said, "and let it go one finger at a time until I was clutching at air."

I knew that look she had. I knew how bewildering it is to love and know your love goes unmet and unmatched. It's the law of harmonies, I thought, it is all as Kepler said, and this is what we have in common: our bodies moved by forces not possible to resist. Then she said, "He is gone again, and now I'll be as sad as you."

I was angry with her then. What need did I ever have for her pity? What need have I ever had for anyone's pity? I'm a man who lived, as all men must live: that is all.

So I told her this: that it's true that I've only rarely been happy, and perhaps more often been sad. But I have been content. I have lived. I have felt everything available to me: I've been faithless, devout, indifferent, ardent, diligent, and careless; full of hope and disappointment, bewildered by time and fate or comforted by providence— and all of it ticking through me while the pendulum of my life loses amplitude by the hour.

All the while she sat crying in her childish way. And I wanted to console the child I'd loved, and so I told her this: that in the ordinary way we love because we're loved, and give more or less what we're given. But to love without return is more strange and more wonderful, and not the humiliating thing I'd once taken it to be. To give love without receiving it is to understand we are made in the image of God—because the love of God is immense and indiscriminate and can never be returned to the same degree. Go on loving when your love is unreturned, I said, and you are just a little lower than the angels.

She cried harder then. "You ruined my life," she said. "I don't forgive you, and I never will."

"Well," I said, "you ruined mine. I would have left Bethesda when I was young, I would have been free—then there you were, and because of you I took my shame to the pulpit every week, and because of you I left the comfort the pulpit sometimes gave me. And I don't forgive you," I said, "nobody was ever as cruel to me as you."

I wish I could say: James, we forgave each other in the end. I wish I could say: she put her head on my shoulder and I welcomed it and we laughed and said all was well. But in fact we were quiet for a long time, and we heard a television laughing over the road and the train leaving for Liverpool Street, and then she said, "Do you think we can love each other and never ever forgive?"

I didn't know, I said. But I thought we ought to try.

THOMAS HART

As Thomas walked through the town the following afternoon, he found his attention turning not to Grace, or Maria, but to Nathan. Poor man, he thought, poor boy, picturing again the walking stick in the grass, the dragging foot, the remarkable eyes uncompromised by time and pain. Poor man, never forgetting that strange girl in her strange clothes, while the world turned and brought him before he knew it into employment, and mortgages obtained and renewed; a child who doubtless loved her father, and whose mother was doubtless sensible and kind (there, again and as ever on London Road in autumn, James Bower was carelessly kissing his wife). Then in due course pain, and the clock ticking, and Bethesda best remembered as a dream—but the trouble was that while you cannot re-enter a dream, the trains went from Kent to Essex via London Bridge on the hour every hour—poor Nathan! Poor boy!

He passed the war memorial and came to the old town hall. Here Aldleigh Museum, defunded and dispirited, occupied dingy quarters accessible only two afternoons a week, and Boudicca had been disarticulated by careless men. Nonetheless Thomas felt a movement in his heart like that of a compass needle seeking north, as if James Bower might still be at his desk, filling in those thin pink requisition forms, having in his hands the solution to a problem he'd not yet foreseen. Or possibly he was only now arriving, coming up behind him and reaching out his hand. Oh it is possible, thought Thomas, it is among the probabilities—perhaps James Bower lives on undiminished in some thread of time running parallel to mine. And in fact he heard footsteps, certainly he heard them, and certainly no stranger would come so close—everything was happening, and time was never what he'd taken it to be! His breath was quick and shallow with the folly of his hope: he turned, and (this was absurd; it was improbable) found a familiar man walking in his wake, and looking at him now with a long-lashed intimate gaze: "Hello," he said.

"Hello," said Thomas, and briefly he felt his scalp flense from his skull; then reason returned, and his breath slowed. "My God," he said, lapsing into laughter, "is Essex so small? Can none of us escape each other?"

"In one of your columns," said Nathan, untroubled and unsurprised, "you'd say this is all to do with gravitational fields and orbits." He was dressed in a dark suit of some cheap cloth that was cut too large, and the effect was diminishing: he seemed a schoolboy not yet grown into his uniform.

"I expect I would. But what are you doing here, Nathan?"

Nathan gestured to an anonymous building nearby, and explained it had been necessary to see a solicitor about a will, blinked rapidly behind his glasses as if ashamed to have been caught transgressing. "I'm sorry," he said, and there was the impression that if he listed his causes for apology they might very well be there all week. How young he is, thought Thomas, softening suddenly, how young they both will always be: standing outside Lowlands with their stolen cigarettes, peering in between the broken boards, as innocent as the day they were born and no better than they ought to be—"Tell me," he said, "are you busy?"

"No, not any more, and my train isn't for an hour"—he had a half-shamed, half-hopeful look, like that of a dog.

"No," said Thomas, as gently as he could. "No, it isn't Grace. But I want you to come with me—I've hunted Maria's comet all these years, and weren't you there at the beginning? Don't you think you should see the end?"

It seemed to Thomas that the other man was relieved and despairing in equal measure: "Yes please," he said, with his old merry willingness to take part in whatever was at hand. So the two men walked together favoring the parts of their bodies that ached, Thomas explaining that possibly—and after all this time!—what he'd wanted most to find had been in Aldleigh, but they'd never thought to look.

"It should seem strange," said Nathan, "it should be unbelievable. But these days I just think: of course." The museum entrance was relegated now to the side of the town hall, its door blotted with torn posters and bolted against curious passersby.

"Look," said Thomas, raising mischief in himself, "look, light coming under the door, dust on the doorstep—the comet's in there, waiting."

They knocked once. A woman came out; and really, thought Thomas, she was hardly more than a child. She surveyed the troubled weather, then brought them into the dim hall with courtesy he suspected owed more to his age than his reputation. Dr. Syed was on leave, she said, leading them down corridors in which artificial lights flickered in fly-clotted fittings, and most of the doors were locked, but everything was ready. They passed a larger room in which display cases were kept polished and in good order, but nobody looked at their contents. "Here we are," said the young woman, with an indulgent smile at Thomas, and a more speculative one at Nathan, "would you like tea?"

"Thank you," said Nathan, who'd taken off his glasses. "You are kind."

"Go in," she said, flushing against his blue gaze. "Do go in." Shyly she directed them to an open door. Faint light came over the threshold containing sifting particles of dust.

Thomas went in, and looked cautiously about as if anticipating pain. Weak lights overhead hardly brightened the air, and a scent like that of leaf mold in autumn came out of the carpet. The ceiling was soiled with mold. The Essex coat of arms had lost a seax, and furniture no longer in use had been draped in sheets that shifted in the drafts. Only a handsome desk with a gilded leather surface remained uncovered, and a pair of plastic chairs sat nearby. A desk lamp with a harsh white bulb illuminated a cardboard box from which a plastic label was coming unstuck. A bit of paper was taped to it: F.A.O. THOMAS HART.

"What is it," said Nathan, "what have you seen—are you all right?" He came quickly forward, and put his arm around the older man with such competent strength that Thomas realized with shame he'd been swaying where he stood, weakened to stupidity by the desk with its tea stains, the dust that sifted in the morning light, the broken coat of arms—"I'm all right," he said, and would have liked to shrug off the enclosing arm out of pride, but couldn't—in fact could not see Nathan at all, or the boxes stacked against the wall and the shifting sheets: the room contained nothing but James Bower.

Nathan said, "Sit down," and put the other man in a chair, then greeted the young woman arriving with tea on a tray: yes, they were fine, thank you—no, they needed nothing more. Thomas looked at the tray, and at the green teacups on green saucers, and all the valor with which he'd configured his loss into an act of grace dissipated, and he felt again that he knelt in the gutter on London Road, choked with confusion and shame. There was silence for a time, and the sensation, encountered as if from a great distance, of Nathan patting his back with a diffident uncertain affection that only amplified his loneliness. Then slowly Thomas became aware of movement in the margins of the room, among the disconsolate sheets and cheap stacked chairs, and looking up discovered his household ghost, pulling a pearl from her hem in a temper: *What are you doing here, Thomas Hart? Can you not let the matter rest at my feet, where my heart is?*

"You see, I have never been alone," said Thomas, "not really." Then "Thank you," he said, taking the green cup Nathan offered. He took a notebook from his pocket and put it beside the cardboard box. The blinds tapped the windows. Distantly down the corridor the young woman was speaking on the phone. "The difficulty is," said Thomas, "that if what I've been looking for is here, it is all at an end. What would be left for me then? What would I have to move me?"

Maria Văduva was coming to the desk, and there were seed pearls on the floor; and there was a woman with her whose fingernails were full of Essex clay: *Get on with it*, they said, *get on with it*, and rapped the table three times. So obedient Thomas moved the lamp to get a clearer view, and took out from the box a file containing documents. The first of these was a requisition slip, pink fading from the paper, requesting the transfer of a number of items from Chelmsford to Aldleigh, for cataloguing and possible display. *James Bower*, it was signed, *March 1997*; and with a kind of ecstatic misery Thomas saw the day of his arrival at the office, and the familiar stranger seated at his desk.

"Thomas," said Nathan, "are you sure you aren't ill?"

"I'm sure. Stand back. Let me have light." A letter then,

typed and corrected in a minute and fastidious hand, dated 1965:

> I am not certain of the full significance of this box and its contents, but it seems to me that my mother must have erred in her actions, as she was sometimes inclined to do. Therefore I give them to your care.
>
> FRANCIS SEABORNE

"But there's no box," said Nathan. "What box, Thomas, and where?"

"It would be a lead box," said Thomas, "of Romanian make. They keep it in the Chelmsford Museum, but there's nothing in it." Carefully he took out a leather document case, greased black by the hands that had held it, and marked with a gilded monogram: *C. S.* This is the end, he thought, it is finished: I'd rather burn it and throw the ashes in the river! But the women were watching from the corner of the room, and Nathan was holding his breath; and isn't the loop of your orbit closed, Thomas Hart? Doesn't your end encounter your beginning? Time's getting on, Thomas, the light is ticking on the wall—

Maria Văduva Bell
Lowlands, Essex
JUNE 1889

Beloved Cora—my child—this is the last you will have of
me—I shall never write to you again! It is not that I intend
my body to die—though perhaps it might, now that my
blood is become nothing but salt water—it is only that my
spirits have at last deserted me—

I have received news from Bucharest—and it has blighted
me, as one sometimes finds a solitary tree in the wood
struck dead as bones—the man I love is dead. He is already
in the ground—so my light is gone! I cannot see the stars—
or I will not—and what we will not see has no form or
being! I have blinded my telescope—what use do I have for
it now? I was to have a comet in my name—I was to outlast
myself—but all I ever saw, I saw for him—it was his comet,
and never mine—it was all done only that I might make
myself worthy of his admiration and his love. How very like
a dog I have been, rooting in the sky for a stick to bring her
master!

I struck a match. I put it to the paper containing my
observations. But I find I cannot burn it—I burned my
finger first—so I give them to you. You may take pleasure in
them, out of your fondness for knowledge—and I give you
my comet dress, which once I said I should be buried in—
but what use do I have now for the stars, even dead stars
made of pearls—

You have said you love me. Very well—I will test your love,
as a musician tests her instrument!—if you love me, you

will allow the manner of my grief! When this comet is falsely named for its false discoverer you will keep your silence—and when you die, you will inter the comet with you—so the depth of my love may be measured by the height of what I have lost: they will say what a love that was, that she loved him more than her comet and more than her own name!

And my Cora, let me tell you this before I go—you set too much store on loving and on being loved—this is a hopeless cause! Do you think the act of loving secures love's return? It does not! It cannot! You must learn to prize your mind above your heart—you must seek out your comet where you can, and wonder at it—whether it is above your head, or under your feet! For my sake, do some great thing that will told among men hereafter!

And forgive your friend—

MARIA

11:12 p.m. 17 June 1889

At Lowlands House, Aldleigh, in Essex

Right Ascension 0h42m30 / Declination 58° 45' 12

Object in Cassiopeia having bright nucleus and double tail
extending four degrees northeast, of bluish color

MARIA VĂDUVA BELL

"What will you do now?" said Nathan. They were coming out of the town hall arm in arm, neither man certain who wanted help or who gave it. "Cora Seaborne did what her friend asked—will you?" The pewter sky had acquired a polish in their absence, and Aldleigh was contemplating closing for the night. Here and there early Christmas decorations pricked the streets with implausible lights, and the wind had worn itself out; behind them the girl was locking the museum and singing out of tune.

"If Maria wanted her secrets kept," said Thomas, averting his gaze from the woman who walked beside him in forbidding silence, "she ought to have known better than to confide in a writer, for whom the whole world is nothing but a store of sentences. I'll write this evening to the International Astronomical Union in Paris and request an inquiry of some kind: less than a month to perihelion, and no hope of seeing the comet properly named by then—but it never leaves without beginning its return, and isn't there always time, after time? But look," he said, speaking now with the authority of his years, "I want a word with you."

Nathan, flushing, was again the boy who'd broken Bethesda's window: he had a look of equal guilt and mischief, knowing that he deserved to be chastised, and not much minding. "I know," he said. "She talks so easily about love, she always did! But how can she know what she means? If she ever loved me that was twenty years ago, and we were children. I am a different man—an ordinary man, I have a whole life! And I was never what she imagined. I can hardly myself remember the boy she knew. Thomas, I love my wife. I love my child. Do you think Grace alters that? It doesn't. It never could."

"I don't understand it all," said Thomas. "I've wondered all my life what I owe to love. There was a time I felt that because I loved a man, he was in my debt—that he'd made me love him, and so he owed me his love in return. And now he is dead, and I can never receive even a part of what I gave! But the world turned and I came to believe that all we owe to love is humility and gratitude that we were ever loved at all. You think it's humble to say it cannot be real—that she's mistaken, since you're not free. But that's a kind of pride. Real humility is submitting with wonder and gratitude to being loved—real wisdom is understanding how amazing it is, how improbable and really absurd, that she was summoned out of nothing as we all were, and happens to breathe this air when you breathe it, and see this world when you see it, and that out of all her billions of fellow travelers it is your word she waits for as she sits alone in her room! Well: that's a responsibility and probably a terrible one, and I can't help you with it. You must work out your own salvation with fear and trembling, and let me work out mine."

Overhead a canopy of clouds had split from east to west; and at the far end of Aldleigh—over the newsagent's and shoe shops and the man in old boots clearing dead leaves from the gutter—bands of shining coral deepened and hardened as they watched, and the effect was of walking toward seams of quartz that traversed a quarry wall. The sun was setting: for now.

N, Thomas told me how you met in the street. He said you were with him when he found Maria's comet. I can't believe it's been in Aldleigh all this time. But I can believe it. It seems right somehow. I am glad you were with him. I wish I'd been there too — G.

But won't you love me, Nathan? Won't you let me love you? Isn't this as terrible for you as it is terrible for me? Don't I love you and haven't I loved you all my life? Don't I need you to keep me alive, and don't you need me?

Come here, Nathan. Come here. Meet me at Lowlands when the comet comes. We'll watch it and I'll put my head on your shoulder and I won't speak. I won't say I love you, I promise, I won't say a word.

Just come.

Shortly before the perihelion of Comet du Lac, Thomas Hart sat surveying an image cut from a magazine with the attention of a pious man turning to his scripture. It had come that morning in the post marked with an almost imperceptibly small kiss from Grace, and a note that said yes, she'd come to Lowlands tomorrow, she'd take a look at his wretched comet; and that she'd seen this thing, and thought of him.

Thomas conceded to himself that he couldn't fully understand the image, only comprehend its beauty and trust in its significance. It was (said the accompanying text) a map of the galaxy Supercluster Laniakea, this meaning "immeasurable heaven": radio emissions from the near universe distilled into a gold cloud drifting against a ground of blue, speckled with white dots seeming to move as particles of water might move in mist. The shape of this cloud was the shape of a human heart, and it was marked all over with shining filaments that coursed out from the center with the look of capillaries carrying vital blood. These white dots were drifting galaxies, and these shining filaments their flow toward the center of mass; and on the edge—set like a city on the mouth of a river—there was the Milky Way, there was home. A red dot marked the place, labeled as a map might be in Aldleigh's municipal car park: YOU ARE HERE. Thomas rested his head on the table, and his hand on the image. The gold heart was beating against his palm: you are here, you are here, you are here.

Then roused by himself, or by his diligent ghost, or by the passage of the London train, Thomas poured cardamom coffee and attended to the remaining post. Charitable causes, admonitions from readers, dispatches from utility companies, all were set aside with noises of boredom or disgust; then last of all, in a thin blue envelope, a letter postmarked Paris. Thomas looked at it with the sensation of a man in the dock looking the jury in the eye: here it was, verdict of disinterested strangers on whose whim the outcome of twenty years' hope and despondency depended. Quickly there came the sensation of distracted grief he always encountered at the end of a task: the manuscript was nearly done, the comet was at his doorstep; all that mattered was coming to an end—what to do then, with the brief time remaining? The glass was falling hour by hour, but wouldn't fall forever—*Get on with it*, said Maria Văduva, settling herself on the windowsill, boots two inches deep in Essex mud.

"Get out of my light," said Thomas. Lifting the letter to the window, he encountered the baroque translated sentences first with frank amusement, then in due course with delight:

Dear Mr. Hart,

The International Astronomical Union places much emphasis on a felicitous collaboration between nations, institutions, and individuals of both the professional and amateur kind.

Thus we were pleased to hear from you regarding comet 330P/1889 (du Lac). Having surveyed the evidence, and examined the comet's orbit and position in the year of its

discovery, we consider it a probability that Maria Văduva
Bell, of Aldleigh in Essex, first identified the object on 17
June 1889 at 11:12 p.m. in the region of Cassiopeia. It is the
policy of the Union to name a comet after a maximum of
two primary observers, and it is therefore our proposition
that the comet should now take the designation
330P/1889 (Văduva–du Lac). We regret that this resolution
arrives too late for the present perihelion, but trust you
will be satisfied with this outcome.

Amitiés sincères,

PROFESSOR DAVID LANE

Thomas put the letter down, and looked for a time at the opposite wall. The glass was falling hour by hour, and now had
fallen further—he rested his head on the table, and with
confusion and shame felt the arrival of tears. He'd anticipated joy and satisfaction: what came was a sense of loss.
What now, Thomas Hart? What will you do with your remaining time?

Up you get, Thomas, said Maria Văduva, standing at the window, having knocked over his coffee in a temper: *past ten in the
morning, and work to be done.* Past ten in the morning, and
work to be done, and meanwhile Grace Macaulay mourned in
her cold room under the eaves. Thomas, thinking of her sorrow, felt the old movement in his heart, and what came to
mind was an infant in Bethesda, carried in a basket like a suit-
case to the door. He'd entered then into a contract from which
he'd never be set free, the terms of his employment set and cir-
cumscribed by love, and now it demanded he should act. Maria sought out his eye, and nodded once: *Do what you must,
Thomas Hart.*

Nathan—did Grace tell you the comet is coming? Perihelion tomorrow. Now: humor an old man. Come to Lowlands 8 p.m. They promise clear skies—and didn't you help me find it? Isn't it almost yours? T. H.

Shamefully swift, a response:

Thank you. Not sure if free, will check, hope to see you there—N.

You are not free, thought Thomas, and you never were. More coffee then, and toast with too much butter, and another note (Maria left him to his business):

Dear Nick,

I am writing to resign from my position at the *Essex Chronicle* with sadness, and with immediate effect. You will smile now, and you will say to yourself: Thomas, it is not before time.

Please see attached my last column. I hope it will give you pleasure.

God bless you and keep you!

THOMAS HART

He felt again the dreadful peace that threatened to leave him motionless at his table; but it occurred to him that nights these days were cold, and that Grace would expect him to bring something to eat. So he shook his own body as if freeing it of dust, and went out into the kitchen where he decanted milk into a blue-banded bowl, and crumbled in a cake of fresh yeast. There was the scent not of new loaves, but of champagne. Then Anne Macaulay was coming down the hall, arriving out of the shadow of the coat stand and sewing a plastic pearl button on her nightdress: "Give it a pinch of sugar," she said, "give it a helping hand." So a pinch of sugar for the yeast to fatten on, and Thomas, not surprised by her arrival, waited by the window. It was not yet dark, but already a canopy of cloud was drawing over from the west and putting out his hopes. "No clear skies yet, I see," said Anne, examining the yeast, "but possibly tomorrow: have faith."

"It is currently in the constellation of Perseus," said Thomas, "turning and turning as it comes. You remember Hale-Bopp, you remember the Great Comet of 1997, and the girl who set the fire? There was never another like it, not in all the years since, and I won't live to see Halley again—so I must pin all my hopes on this."

He cut cold butter into a bowl of sifted flour and Maldon salt; and "Yes," said Anne. "I remember. You'll be wanting to rub lightly, Mr. Hart: fingertips only, remembering at all times that heat is the enemy of good pastry." In with the foaming milk, with the yolk of four large eggs and a teaspoon of Madagascan vanilla—"Turning and turning through Perseus," said Thomas, "coming at a thousand miles an hour; and as I understand it space opening out around it—bending, if you like: a fine net being pulled aside." No answer: Anne Macaulay had begun to thin out, to drift toward the door—she never did approve of his fascination with the matter of the stars. Now Thomas formed the dough, and kneaded it; he rolled it to the thickness of an old pound coin, and folded it around fragments of Turkish delight, as he was taught by a man who was taught by his mother.

The oven was ready. Powdered sugar waited in a bowl. It was the time of astronomical twilight, and there was darkness on Lower Bridge Road. Thomas moved across his kitchen, and fancifully it occurred to him that the motion of his body displaced the universe—that it slipped aside to accommodate him; that it might be said that he was no less significant, and certainly no more, than a comet dispensing its days of ordinary grace. The gold heart was beating on the table. You are here, Thomas Hart. Here you are.

THE MOON ON THE WATER

THOMAS HART, *ESSEX CHRONICLE*,
12 DECEMBER 2017

In the twenty years since I began this column, I've written many pieces on the stars, and the few principles of physics that have fallen within my limited capacity, and which I hardly began to understand. I never wrote as an expert, but as an amateur; and since an amateur is one who loves his subject, that's what I remain—I only hope I've been forgiven where I've erred.

Since this is my last column, I'm returning to the moon because I loved it first and best. Some weeks ago, I happened to be walking late at night after a day of rain when there were puddles in the streets, and I found as I walked that at certain times, when the position of the puddle and the angle of the light were judicious, the moon would arrive at my feet.

I looked for a long time at these commonplace reflections, and found them wonderful. They were not the moon, and not the water, but a third and separate thing: the moon-on-the-water, born like a child of the relation between the two.

Now: I've heard it said that at the first sip from the glass of the natural sciences you will become an atheist—then at the bottom of the glass, God will be waiting for you.

Some claim these are the words of the physicist Werner Heisenberg, and some say he never said any such thing—but it charmed me enough to seek him out on the shelves, and find as ever that my wonder and my comprehension did battle, and left me reeling. It seems to me that Heisenberg proposes this: that although the electron is certainly real, nothing we can say of its location now can do any more than say where it might probably be in the future. It is a mysterious thing, not quite existing separate from any other thing, and coming most fully into being at the moment of connection.

I wonder in that case if the world and everything in it—you, me, the moon and the water—consists not of solitary beings, but rather out of how each thing relates to another, so that in the end it is only out of connection that the whole world is made.

Dear reader: I'm grateful that you've been my companion all these years—that we have existed together on this page. I must leave you now, but as it happens a comet is coming in as I am going out: Văduva–du Lac, discovered in 1889 by Maria Văduva Bell of Lowlands House in Aldleigh, on a clear Essex night. If ever I gave you a moment's interest or pleasure, will you do this for me? Go out. Look up. Experience with me this act of grace which is common to us all. You cannot earn or command it: it is a gift, and it will be wonderful because of your wonder. Look up, with me, won't you? Look up—and at the moment of our looking there'll be this one marvelous thing, shining in time, under common grace: the comet-in-us.

Perihelion

Now: perihelion. Comet 330P/1889 (Văduva–du Lac) has crossed the ecliptic plane; it will rise in the east in the region of Pisces, tumbling head over heels in its haste. In the observatories of Paris and Kielder and Pulkovo, its apparent magnitude is judged to be -1: give it a clear night and a day or two, and it will outdo the Great Comet of 1997 and all the attending marvels and disasters.

Aldleigh is waiting with the patience of the saints. It has no choice. Tinsel in the pound shop, blowsy in the narrow aisles; white lights strung on yews and privet hedges winking out when the battery goes. Choirs rehearsing in town halls and sitting rooms and small cathedral naves: glory to God in the highest, and on earth no great expectation of peace. Ronald Macaulay is sleeping in slippers embroidered *R. M.*, to remind him of his own name—to assert that yes, here he is, here he has been: a man for whom no natural love could match his love for heaven. Children are coming home to Aldleigh on the London train, watching their own vast lamplit faces scud over Stratford, Shenfield, Chelmsford: we are giants in the land, they think, we could occupy the towns—and meanwhile their parents, nursing lifelong headaches, total up the costs of the day. Frost is paling the banks of the Alder, where smashed plates and dented wedding rings wash up in shopping trolleys full of silt; and in the basement of the old town hall Boudicca's dismantled breasts are pricked sore by holly wreaths.

The tills are ringing in the Jackdaw and Crow, where school-girls and women and men are by turns angry or peaceable and never conscious of the cause; they make one body heaving over to the bar, drawing breath and singing they wish it could be Christmas every day. Prayers holy and idle and sometimes profane rise like sparrows from bungalows and offices where the tinsel is already coming loose: my God, look at that and Christ, you frightened me and Lord, make me good (but not yet)! Snowdrops are coming up on the grave containing all that could die of Anne Margaret Macaulay, and she communicates in the litter blowing back and forth between the headstones: oh I did live, Thomas Hart, and I do, but I rather think the harmonium never really was in tune. Lovers are lying down in Potter's Field and can't believe they found each other, can't believe their luck. It's quick and hard on account of the cold but never mind that, never mind the admonishing jays in the bare trees on the margin, it's done and dusted and the night can get on with its business: be swift my soul to answer him, be jubilant my feet! Southend United is two-nil down and the hero born of woman crushed the serpent with his heel; the barrels are empty at the Jackdaw and Crow, and Thomas almost thinks that his Redeemer lives. The Bible is open in Bethesda's pulpit and the broken pane of glass is coming loose; so the wind gets in and turns through Genesis and Exodus and the Song of Songs: *Bless the Lord oh my soul and forget not all His benefits*, and meanwhile half a mile away the *Essex Chronicle* is going to press.

Gone eight in the evening. Thomas Hart is seated on an iron bench beside the Lowlands lake, and he's cold in his good winter coat. The air's hardening to frost in shining particles that punish the cyclamen coming up round the roots of the Aldwinter oak. Stars appear and disappear in banks of clouds tethered like lost continents off the far horizon, but overhead it's clear. Thomas looks out east to the breach in the yews, but no sign yet.

Nathan is here. Nathan was early, and has cut himself while shaving. He sits mute beside Thomas with his hands on his cane, and his body trembles sometimes with pain, or December, or anticipation. "She'll come," says Thomas, "she'll come," but in fact moment by moment he grows uncertain—might it be better if she stays in her room by the three-bar fire with her dressing gown on, might it be better if she has her pride? He attends to the basket he put down between his feet; he brings out white cloth napkins, a tin of pastries wrapped in paper, white rolls that drop flour on his coat. The body of the man at his side is all alertness, all expectancy and poise: "Thomas, is that it?" he says. "Is it here?"

It is here. It is risen. It drifts above the pricking skyline and emerges in the darkening sky like something rising to the surface of deep water. Thomas stands. The tin drops from his lap and opens and lets loose the scent of roses. "Oh, look," says Thomas with joy indivisible from loss. "Look." His eyes are latched to it as if by hooks: he is in pain. By slow degrees the sky darkens, and the comet brightens against it, and however will I do it justice, thinks Thomas, coming up hard against his incapacity, and the hopeless falling-short of language—it's a searchlight beam, it's a pearl crushed to a smear, it's the night worn thin and the Shekhinah glory coming through—it isn't like any of these and no use trying for a phrase.

Nathan stands and he's steady and silent on his feet—he reaches for Thomas, and finds him: "I didn't know what to expect," he says, gripping Thomas hard enough to hurt, "I never did." The comet, ecstatic in the company of the sun after its time of solitude, begins to show its double tail: here's the gas-jet, blue as the moon once was, here's the sunlit dust stream blown by solar winds and curved like the blade of a seax on the

Essex coat of arms; it is indifferent to every kind of doctrine and legislation, and its universal light is neither sacred nor profane.

Movement now beyond the lake, in the breach between the high black yews, and Nathan makes a sound that's very like that of his pain: here's Grace Macaulay in a red velvet coat, coming quickly like an animal only wanting one thing, with a whole company in her wake. They come through the breach, they assemble by the lake—every soul Thomas has ever loved: here's Anne Macaulay in her cotton nightdress, marveling over the thin blue blanket in her arms: *It is well, it is well with my soul.* Here's James Bower meeting his eye with affection and shame: I did know, I did know, I did. Here's Richard Dimitru Dines half-cut on whisky with his satchel on his back and his arm round the senior deacon, whose beard is blacker than ever; here's Maria Văduva Bell and she's got Cora Seaborne with her: "Darling child," she is saying, "let them never dissuade you from your course," and all the pearls have gone from the hem of her gown. Here's Grace Macaulay in a scarlet coat, scent of rose oil rising from her arms, giving out her uncontainable joy, coming first to her enemy and friend; there's her butt of affection so like that of an animal; how immense love is, thinks Thomas, how surprising, to go on unforgiving and undiminished. Now she is gone, she is going to her lover, and her body is hard against his: they're matter dispersed by time and circumstance, assembled for this moment according to the natural laws.

"You are here," says Thomas, surveying the company, "you are here." It is uncontainable, he cannot stand it: the comet is only going to rise, and equally dispense its pearly light on love offered and met and refused and mistaken, the law of harmonies unfailingly in operation on the human heart. He hears the ticking of his watch, and music drifting down from Lowlands

House: everything that would ever happen had happened, and was happening, and the heavens were declaring the glory of God. He hears all the dogs of Essex barking, and all the trains departing all the towns—hears time's first speech, and last recorded syllable—sees the early constellations dancing, and the earth's near star put out: it is all one engine of perpetual motion, driven by God or fate or unmotivated time, turning over and over through gain and loss and gain, every part of it remarkable, essential to the whole. How absolutely improbable it is, he thinks, standing amazed between the comet and the water, what a miracle that I am here at all—that out of matter I was made, to stand here with a button missing on my coat, heart broken by nothing but illuminated dust!

What now then, Thomas Hart, at the light of perihelion? What creed and consolation can you rustle up for your friends, now all of your notebooks are filled?

Perhaps this is the wonder, Thomas, and this is the whole of the law: you are here. You are here. You are here.

Acknowledgments

Thank you to my parents, who raised me in the light of God and science together.

Thank you to Robert Perry, who has listened so long and so patiently.

Thank you to all my family and friends, whose patience and affection for me must have been sorely tested during the many years I have worked on this book. I can never repay their kindness.

Thank you to Jenny Hewson, Susan Golomb, Hannah Westland, Katherine Nintzel, Suzanne Dean, Sarah-Jane Forder, Graeme Hall, Eliza Rosenberry, and Tavia Kowalchuk. Rarely has a novelist had more cause to be grateful to their agent and editors for their wisdom and skill—without them this book would be less than half what it is, and its writer less than a quarter. Thank you to all at Mariner Books for their work to bring this story to its readers.

Thank you to Kate Devlin, Chris Gribble, Mark Haddon, Sarah Hall, Caoilinn Hughes, and Louisa Yates for reading early pages when I most needed readers. Thank you to Gladstone's Library for being again a place of refuge.

Thank you to Dorian Jessu for assistance with Romanian. Thank you to Marilyn Sher and Adam Sheppard for assistance with keeping me more or less in one piece.

Thank you to David Butler, Paul Behrens, and Nathan Yanasak for their help with matters of physics and the stars. David, my father, raised me with an eye to the telescope and taught me the laws of Kepler, and in doing so enlarged my mind and my life; Paul kindly made me think more clearly and with pleasure. I am especially grateful to Nathan, who gave of his time and expertise with extraordinary generosity: I have quoted directly from him where tidal lock is concerned. Carlo Rovelli's writing has been vital to this book and to me. Where the novel errs in the matter of physics, the errors are entirely Thomas Hart's, or mine.

Thank you to S. G., for the orbits. This is his book.

About Mariner Books

Mariner Books traces its beginnings to 1832 when William Ticknor cofounded the Old Corner Bookstore in Boston, from which he would run the legendary firm Ticknor and Fields, publisher of Ralph Waldo Emerson, Harriet Beecher Stowe, Nathaniel Hawthorne, and Henry David Thoreau. Following Ticknor's death, Henry Oscar Houghton acquired Ticknor and Fields and, in 1880, formed Houghton Mifflin, which later merged with venerable Harcourt Publishing to form Houghton Mifflin Harcourt. HarperCollins purchased HMH's trade publishing business in 2021 and reestablished their storied lists and editorial team under the name Mariner Books.

Uniting the legacies of Houghton Mifflin, Harcourt Brace, and Ticknor and Fields, Mariner Books continues one of the great traditions in American bookselling. Our imprints have introduced an incomparable roster of enduring classics, including Hawthorne's *The Scarlet Letter*, Thoreau's *Walden*, Willa Cather's *O, Pioneers!*, Virginia Woolf's *To the Lighthouse*, W.E.B. Du Bois's *Black Reconstruction*, J.R.R. Tolkien's *The Lord of the Rings*, Carson McCullers's *The Heart Is a Lonely Hunter*, Ann Petry's *The Narrows*, George Orwell's *Animal Farm* and *Nineteen Eighty-Four*, Rachel Carson's *Silent Spring*, Margaret Walker's *Jubilee*, Italo Calvino's *Invisible Cities*, Alice Walker's *The Color Purple*, Margaret Atwood's *The Handmaid's Tale*, Tim O'Brien's *The Things They Carried*, Philip Roth's *The Plot Against America*, Jhumpa Lahiri's *Interpreter of Maladies*, and many others. Today Mariner Books remains proudly committed to the craft of fine publishing established nearly two centuries ago at the Old Corner Bookstore.